Praise for *The Long Game:*

'Elena Armas never misses. Armas has given us an entire
cast of funny, exciting characters wrapped in the most perfect
small town, slow burn bow. *The Long Game* has everything
you could ever want in a rom-com, including goats'
Hannah Grace, *Sunday Times* bestselling author of *Icebreaker*

'*The Long Game* is pure fun with chemistry so palpable it
will set your pages on fire while melting your heart. It's
honestly what sports romance dreams are made of'
**Sarah Adams, *New York Times* bestselling
author of *Practice Makes Perfect***

'*The Long Game* is utterly charming and gloriously
sexy—I couldn't put it down! Elena Armas writes slow
burn like a finely tuned symphony, and I wanted nothing
more than to be Cameron's darling by the end'
Lana Ferguson, author of *The Nanny*

'Elena Armas is the queen of steamy, vulnerable,
addicting romance. A slow-burn that had me sinking into
each page, THE LONG GAME is a love letter to becoming the
best version of yourself. I couldn't get enough of Cameron
and Adalyn and the way they made each other shine
brighter. And the chemistry? Smoking hot'
B.K. Borison, author of *Lovelight Farms*

'Armas is an expert on what makes a romance reader's heart race'
Tessa Bailey, #1 *New York Times* bestselling author

ALSO BY ELENA ARMAS

The Spanish Love Deception
The American Roommate Experiment

THE
Long
GAME

ELENA ARMAS

SIMON &
SCHUSTER

London · New York · Sydney · Toronto · New Delhi

First published in Great Britain by Simon & Schuster UK Ltd, 2023

1 3 5 7 9 10 8 6 4 2

Simon & Schuster UK Ltd
1st Floor
222 Gray's Inn Road
London WC1X 8HB

Simon & Schuster Australia, Sydney
Simon & Schuster India, New Delhi

www.simonandschuster.co.uk
www.simonandschuster.com.au
www.simonandschuster.co.in

A CIP catalogue record for this book
is available from the British Library

Paperback ISBN: 978-1-3985-2221-3
eBook ISBN: 978-1-3985-2222-0
Audio ISBN: 978-1-3985-2223-7

Printed and Bound in the UK using 100% Renewable
Electricity at CPI Group (UK) Ltd

For all the girls who might have lost it once or twice,
so what?
Let those beautiful feelings rain on them, babe.

CHAPTER ONE

Adalyn

The head rolled off his shoulders and halted at my feet with a thump.

Goosebumps erupted at the top of my spine and spread down my body.

I should have been familiar with the scene. I should remember something I had lived and was watching on a screen. But I didn't. So when silence fell, plunging the Miami Flames' facilities into a sudden vacuum, my heart dropped to my stomach. And when the voice of one of the camera guys was caught by the mic asking in a whisper, "Dude, are you recording this?" I was pretty sure I stopped breathing.

Oh God. What—

The top of Paul's head popped out of the headless neckline of Sparkles, the mascot's costume, and a wave of panic washed over me.

Paul blinked, anger and shock meshing in his expression before spitting a "What the fuck is wrong with you?"

My lips parted, as if some instinctual part of my brain wanted to answer him. Now. Even when it wouldn't make a difference. "I—"

The image on the screen froze, forcing my gaze up to the face of the man holding the iPad that had reproduced the thirty seconds that had been missing from my memory.

"I think we've seen enough," Andrew Underwood, CEO and managing director of the Miami Flames FC and Miami-based business mogul, stated.

"I beg to differ," the man by his side said with a light chuckle. "This is a crisis meeting and we should make sure we have all the details." A crisis meeting? "In fact," David continued, "I think we should play it again from the beginning. I'm not sure what Adalyn was grunting while decapitating our dear Sparkles. Was it just angry growling or actual words she was—"

"David," Andrew interjected, dropping the device on the unnecessarily large desk separating them from me. "This is serious."

"It is," the younger man agreed, and I didn't need to look at him to know he was smirking. I knew that smirk. I'd kissed that smirk. Dated it for a complete year. Then, worked under it when he'd been handed the position I'd dreamed of my whole life. "It's not every day we get the head of communications of an MLS club gunning for the team's mascot in six-inch heels." I sensed—heard—that smile widening, and I felt my face turning to stone. "A shocking turn, surely. But also—"

"Unacceptable," Andrew finished for him. "Everyone in this room knows that." Those pale blue eyes met mine, sharp and unforgiving. Which wasn't a surprise. I also knew that glare. I'd endured The Glare for most of my life. He continued, "Adalyn's outburst was inexcusable, but you shouldn't forget yourself. This is my daughter you're talking about."

I lifted my chin, as if the reminder wasn't something I tried to ignore on a daily basis.

Adalyn Reyes, the overachieving daughter of the CEO of the soccer franchise she'd been working for all her life.

"I apologize for the tone, Andrew," David said, and even if his tone had sobered, I still didn't look at him. I couldn't. Not after everything that had gone down in the last twenty-four hours. Not after what I'd learned. "But as VP of operations of the Flames I'm concerned about the repercussions of the incident."

The incident.

My lips pressed into a tight line.

My father clicked his tongue, returning his eyes to the device and unlocking it again.

His finger swiped up and down, and left and right, until a document popped open. Even upside down, I immediately recognized what he was looking at. It was the template I'd designed for the press and media reports. The one that everyone used now. I'd created the color-coded system for priority items that was currently making the screen shine with bright red.

Red, as in top priority. Red, as in crisis.

We hadn't had one in months. Years.

"I haven't approved that," I muttered, hearing my voice for the first time since my father had hit play on the video. I cleared my throat. "Every report should go through me before reaching management."

But my father only exhaled, deep and long, ignoring me in favor of scrolling through the—I leaned forward—fifteen-page report.

My eyes widened. "Can I—"

"Media impact of the incident," he said over me. "Let's start with that."

My lips popped open again, but David moved closer, his mane of dirty blond hair distracting me. His smirk met my gaze, and I could immediately tell he knew something. Something I didn't.

"Virality rate," my father continued, tapping the screen with his index finger. My stomach dropped. Virality? Of what? My father's eyebrows crumpled. "How is an impression different from a view?"

"What platform are we talking about?" I rushed out, squaring my shoulders. "That's why I have to approve these. I usually add notes for you. If you let me have a look I can—"

David tsked, his gaze dropping to the iPad in my father's hands. Then he quipped, "I guess it doesn't really matter, Andrew." His eyes returned to mine. "The video has six million views across all platforms. I think we all understand that."

The video.

Six million views.

Across all platforms.

My knees wobbled. *I* wobbled. And I wasn't one to.

Often, I'd been told I was too clinical, my humor too dry, and my smiles too rare. My assistant, Kelly, the only one in the Flames' offices who has made the effort to befriend me, openly calls me an unbothered queen. But I know most people here refer to me as an ice queen, or snow queen, or whatever variation of the term that references being cold and female. I'd never let it bother me.

Because I never wavered. Or wobbled. Or let things affect me.

Not until yesterday, when I—

David let out a chuckle. "You're officially viral, Ads."

When I'd gunned for the team's mascot in six-inch heels, as David had put it.

My lunch crawled up my esophagus, partly because of that *Ads* I'd always hated so much and partly because I . . . God. I couldn't believe this. I was viral. Viral.

"Six million views," my father said with a shake of his head when I didn't—couldn't—speak. "Six million people have seen you bulldoze into the mascot, scratch at his face, and pluck his goddamn head off. Six million. That's the population of Miami metropolitan." The tips of his ears went red. "You even have your own hashtag: #sparklesgate. And people are using it next to the club's."

"I didn't know it was all recorded," I all but murmured, hating how my voice sounded. "I couldn't know there was a video circulating, but—"

"There's no *but* in this situation, Adalyn. You assaulted a colleague." The word *assault* hung in the air, and my jaw clamped shut. "Paul is an employee and Sparkles is an entity of this team. He is a phoenix that embodies the fire, immortality, and transformation of the Miami Flames. Your team. And you attacked him while the press was in the house for the club's anniversary. Journalists. Cameras. The team and their families. There were children watching, for Christ's sake."

I swallowed, making sure my shoulders remained squared. Strong. Image was everything in these situations. And I couldn't break. Not here. Not again. "I understand, I do. Sparkles is an important symbol and he is well loved by the fans. But the word *assault* seems an exaggeration. I didn't physically harm Paul, I . . ."

"You what?" my father pressed.

Apparently, I beheaded a six-foot-two bird made of foam, polyester, and acrylic feathers that goes by the name of Sparkles and represents immortality. According to the video evidence.

But saying that wouldn't help, so my mouth hung open for what felt like the longest five seconds in history, and . . . I didn't say a single thing.

My father's head tilted to the side. "Please, I'd love for you to explain."

My heart pounded. But there was nothing I could say, not without prompting a conversation I wasn't ready or equipped for. Not right now, and possibly not ever.

"It was . . ." I trailed off, once more hating the quality of my voice. "A forceful encounter. An accident."

David, who had been uncharacteristically quiet the last few minutes, snorted, and my face, so often called indifferent and cool, flamed.

My father placed the iPad on his desk with a sigh. "We're lucky David persuaded Paul not to press charges or sue us."

Charges. *A lawsuit.*

I felt sick to my stomach.

"I offered him a raise, which he obviously accepted," David added. "After all, this was such an out-of-character outburst for our very . . . composed Adalyn."

The way he said the word *composed*, as if it was something bad, a flaw, hit me square in the chest.

"We asked for the tape of the event," my father continued. "After you all but fled the . . . *scene*. But someone must have recorded the incident with their phone. David suspects it was one of the interns that came in with the camera crew."

David tsked. "Impossible to know for sure, though."

I couldn't believe this was happening. God, I couldn't believe what *I* had done.

A foreign and odd sensation pushed at the back of my eyes. It was like a prick of warmth that made my sight . . . misty. Was this— No. Were these— No. It couldn't be. I couldn't be about to cry.

"It's just a video," I said, but all I could think about was that I couldn't recall the last time I'd cried. "It will blow over." The sting in my eyes increased. "If there's something I know about the internet it is that everything is fleeting and short-lived." Why couldn't I remember the last time I'd cried? "No one will care about it tomorrow."

David's phone pinged, and he slipped it out of his pocket. "Oh," he said, looking at the screen. "I somehow doubt that. Seems like we're getting more than a few press inquiries. For you."

That was definitely concerning, but something else clicked. "Why . . ." I frowned, looked down at my phone. Nothing was there. "That email should come to me. Why am I not cc'd?" David shrugged and my father exhaled loudly from his post. Again. I glanced back at him, and his expression made something in me shift into action. "We can turn this around." My voice sounded desperate. "I can turn this around. I swear. I will find a way to benefit from the wave of extra attention. Even the hashtag. We all know the team is not making headlines as it is, and we have been stuck at the bottom of the Eastern Conference for so long that . . ."

My father's face hardened, his eyes turning an icy shade of blue.

Silence, heavy and thick, crystallized in the room.

And I knew then, in the way his eyelashes swept up and down, that whatever battle I'd been fighting was over. I'd said out loud the one thing that made his switch flip. The Miami Flames were in the mud. We hadn't gotten to the playoffs in more than a decade. We were far from filling up stadiums. This was the one investment Andrew Underwood had made that hadn't turned a profit. The one that had cost him more than just money. His pride.

"I just meant that—" I started.

But my battle was now lost. "'Mascot Slaughter in Miami Flames' Home,'" he read from the iPad. "How's that for some extra attention?"

I swallowed. "I think the use of the word *slaughter* is a stretch."

He gave me a curt nod before continuing, "'MLS Miami Flames' Anniversary Ends in Massacre.'"

"*Massacre* also seems like the wrong word."

My father's index finger rose in the air. "'Miami's Favorite Bird Was Plucked and Roasted. Whose Head Will Roll Next?'" That finger returned to the screen and swiped. "'Sparkles Deserved to Die.'" Another swipe. "'A Love Letter to Lady Birdinator.'"

Lady Birdinator. Jesus.

I scoffed, earning a glance from a smirking David. "Those media outlets are just cashing in for easy clicks. They're not making any serious assessments that should concern us or the franchise. My team will put together a strategy. We'll send out a press release. We—"

"'Daughter of Miami Flames Owner, Andrew Underwood, and Former Runway Model, Maricela Reyes, on the Spot After Horrible Incident with Team Mascot.'"

That clammy sensation that had covered my skin since I'd entered this office climbed up my spine. Arms. Back of my neck.

He continued, "'Adalyn Reyes Unhinged. Who Is the Heiress to the Underwood Empire?'" I closed my eyes. "'Miami Flames FC Under Review. Is the Club Finally Crumbling Down?'" A drop of cold sweat trailed down my back. "'Has Dull and Boring Flames' Head of Communications Finally Found Some Fire in Her? Female Rage Explained.'"

Dull and boring.

Finally found some fire in her.

Female rage.

It didn't matter how straight I held myself in that moment, it was impossible to ignore how small I felt. Inadequate. And when I shifted my weight, even my tailored pantsuit felt wrong. Loose and prickly against my skin. Like I didn't belong in it.

"Well." My father's voice brought me back. I refocused on him. His face. The hardness in his eyes. "I'm going to be honest, these are a little wordy to be headlines, but I guess it doesn't matter when they hit the nail on the head." A pause. "Do you still think this is attention we could benefit from, Adalyn?"

I shook my head.

The man I'd looked up to and tried to impress so exhaustingly hard throughout all the years I'd worked for the club sighed. "Would you at least tell us what in the world prompted this?" he asked, and the question caught me so off guard, so unprepared, that I could only stand there, gaping at him.

"I . . ." I couldn't. Wouldn't.

Not with David right there. Maybe if he'd asked me yesterday, intercepted me and demanded an answer right as I was *fleeing the scene*, as he'd put it. Maybe I would have told him then. I clearly hadn't been myself. But I couldn't now.

I'd only prove that those accusations were right. That I was unprofessional. Unqualified for my job, and the job I aspired to have one day. How could I be in charge of anything when I'd lost it like that?

"Sweetheart," David said, making me turn toward him. I couldn't believe I'd ever allowed him to call me anything but Adalyn. But at least now, I knew why he had the courage to still do so. "You look so pale. Are you feeling okay?"

"Yes," I croaked, even though I didn't. Not by a long shot. "It's just warm in here. And I . . . I hardly slept last night." I cleared my throat, met my father's gaze, words toppling out of my mouth. "You know how hard I've worked and how dedicated I am to the club. Couldn't you just . . ." Forget this? Take my side? No questions asked. Be my father.

Andrew Underwood leaned back on his chair, the leather creaking beneath him. "Are you asking me to treat you differently just because you're my daughter?"

Yes, I wanted to say. Just this once. But the pressure behind my eyes returned, distracting me.

"No." He sliced the air in front of him with his hand. "I have never done that and will not start now. You're still an Underwood and you're better than asking for special treatment after embarrassing me and the whole club."

Embarrassing. I had embarrassed myself, my father, and the club.

I had always prided myself on not letting my father's words or actions as my boss affect me. But the ugly truth was that they did. That this, this boss-employee relationship was the only relationship we had.

This was all I had.

"You breached the code of conduct," he continued. "This grants me grounds to fire you. And I might be doing you a favor, all things considered."

I flinched.

In response, Andrew Underwood narrowed his eyes as he looked at me. And only after what seemed like an eternity, he let both his hands drop on the desk. "I don't like the media requests David's been getting all day." He tilted his head. "You're a distraction, so I want you to leave Miami while we fix this."

David muttered something, but I couldn't be sure. My father's words echoed in my head.

Fix this. There was a solution then.

My father stood up from his chair. "Your assistant. What's her name?"

"Kelly," David answered for me.

"She'll take over all communications and media inquiries," my father continued with a nod. "Adalyn will bring her up to speed before leaving." He took a step to the right, opening a drawer and looking back at me. "Get a hold on whatever is going on with you and let us do damage control over here." He stuck the iPad inside. "And I'd rather you not mention this to your mother. If she learns I've exiled her only daughter until the end of the season I won't hear the end of it."

Exiled.

Until the end of the season.

That was . . . weeks from now. Months. Away from the Flames and Miami.

I gave him a nod.

"You'll leave tomorrow. On an assignment. We have a philanthropic initiative that will require your presence and all that newfound . . . passion of yours." He paused. "It's something I've actually been thinking about for a while. So I guess now is as good a time as any." He walked around his desk. "And, Adalyn? I expect you to take this as seriously as your job here. Don't disappoint me again."

CHAPTER TWO

Adalyn

"The Green Warriors?"

I sighed, eyeing my phone on the dashboard of my rental.

"Are you sure that's the name of the team?" Matthew's voice came through the speaker again. "I don't think I've ever heard of them." A pause. "Hold on, is it the Charlotte Warriors?"

"I think I would know if I was being sent to an MLS team like the Charlotte Warriors." My shoulders sank as I gripped the steering wheel, but I tried to keep my tone as cheery as possible, which right then amounted to drained. "It's supposed to be a philanthropic project, so think smaller."

"Smaller, okay," he murmured, the keys of his laptop sounding in the background. "Isn't it a little odd that you're already heading for this place and you don't even know what for? Shouldn't you be briefed for something like this?"

"Odd situations call for odd solutions," I countered. "But I was briefed. I was given a location, a contact, and the name of the team. The problem is that I didn't have time to research." Not when I was left with twenty-four hours to get Kelly up to speed before catching my flight. A wave of exhaustion hit me, making me suppress a yawn.

"I barely had time to pack." Or sleep. "Luckily, I know someone who's good at research and works well on a time crunch because journalism is his job and passion."

"Career perks," my best friend muttered, his voice dripping with something I didn't understand. I frowned, but he continued before I could ask. "And I'll help you, if you let me tell you what I really think first."

"I forgot about that career perk," I deadpanned.

"What I think," he announced, ignoring my comment, "is that banishing your own daughter over such an idiotic thing is overreacting."

"Please," I said with a breath. "Don't mince your words."

"I was mincing my words. What I actually believe is that your dad is being a little bitch."

The tension pulling at my shoulders doubled.

Matthew had never liked my father, just like my father had never liked him. I didn't blame either of them. They were as different as . . . chalk and cheese. Day and night. Water and oil. Just like Matthew and I were. The man was outspoken, rowdy, and charming, whereas I—and my father for that matter—was measured, critical, and way too pragmatic to go around life joking about everything like Matthew did. Laughs and giggles didn't bring in results. Not in my world, at least.

It had always been a wonder how we were even friends. To me, at least. Not to my best friend. He'd been very clear about his intentions since we first crossed paths years ago in the line at Doña Clarita's Sandwich Shop.

He'd tried to hit on me and I'd looked him up and down before genuinely asking him if he was high. His reaction was raucous laughter, then an *I like you. You'll keep me on my toes.*

We somehow became inseparable after that day.

"My father has a point," I told him. "There's a mortifying video of me grunting and growling while I rip the head off the mascot of the team I work for."

"It's funny. And the world is vicious right now. People are seeing themselves in you. They're relating to that show of female rage." Not the female rage again. "If anything, it's empowering. Definitely not embarrassing."

Embarrassing.

You're better than asking for special treatment after embarrassing me and the whole club.

I swallowed, ignoring the way my stomach dropped at the memory of my father's words. "I think you know better than to try to sugarcoat this for me."

"I've seen worse things online, Addy. So you had a brawl—"

"It wasn't a brawl," I interjected, eyeing the maps app on my phone with a frown. "And don't call me Addy, *Matty*. You know nicknames make me feel like a child." It didn't matter if they came from my ex or my best friend. I simply hated being called anything but Adalyn.

"Fine," he relented, ignoring my tone. "So it wasn't a brawl. You had an altercation—"

"A scuffle at most."

"So you had a scuffle—at most—with Sparkles, then some idiot posted the clip on some app and now Gen Z's is all over it, so what? Everyone wants to be liked by zoomers. It's where the money is. You're probably their favorite millennial."

"I'm technically on the boundary. So in any case, I'm a zillennial, not a millennial." I checked my phone again, wondering why the road was meandering and the greenery thickening on both sides. I hadn't expected to climb so high, either. "Regardless, the video had close to eight million views earlier today. And when I checked with my assistant, she told me that paps were at the Flames' facilities today. Paps. Like I'm some . . . I don't know, some celebrity whose sex tape leaked in the mid-2000s."

"And look at how that turned out for Kim Kardashian. Now she has a fortune, a brand, a questionable trail of exes, and soon a law degree."

"Matthew," I warned with an exhale. "I'm not going to discuss why you think the Kardashians are the best thing to happen to the twenty-first century—again. Not only have I no interest in becoming one of them, but you only are obsessed because they have . . ." I trailed off. "You know, big booties."

"I also value their entrepreneurial abilities," he countered with a theatrical gasp. "And being an ass man is not a crime. Anyway, listen. The paps were probably just trying to catch Williams or Perez walking into practice. I'm pretty sure your assistant was blowing it out of proportion because David told her to. He's been your father's minion ever since he was hired for a job you'd be a million times better at. But that's Andrew for you. A little b—"

"You've been in Chicago for too long," I interjected. And ironically, it turned out David had never been my father's minion. Instead—I stopped myself. "I can't remember the last time a Flames player got that kind of attention." I heard the squeak of leather and glanced down. My fingers were white, gripping the steering wheel a little too tight. I released a breath. "My father is doing me a favor by giving me a chance to fix this. A way to redeem myself."

We were in silence for a long moment, and when Matthew spoke, his voice was serious. Careful. I didn't like it. "I know you have no problem standing your ground, but . . . this whole thing with Sparkles is not you." My stomach dropped. "Did something happen? Something that pushed you to . . . this?"

This. That overwhelming pressure that had been on and off ever since those horrible moments before I launched myself at Sparkles returned to my chest. But once again, I didn't feel ready to talk about what had preceded my outburst. All kinds of emotions clogged my vocal cords.

Seconds ticked by slowly until I cleared my throat. "If I had known you were going to start checking on my feelings, I would have dedicated this time to something else. Like a podcast. You know how much I love to drive to a deep voice recounting a complex and gruesome murder."

"I'm being serious," he said softly. Too softly. So much that it made that weight in my chest shift.

"Honestly, Matthew," I told him, my tone coming out a little harsh out of pure survival. "I expected you to have shirts with #sparklesgate or #LadyBirdinator printed and in the mail by now. This touchy-feely display is disappointing."

It wasn't, but I couldn't sift through everything currently rioting inside me.

The sound of him letting out a long and deep exhale came through the speaker. "Fuck, Addy." He laughed, and this time I let that *Addy* slip. "Now, you've ruined my surprise."

I felt myself relax. Only slightly.

Because just in time, I noticed the road ahead starting to twist, jutting in and out of a copse of trees. Where the heck was I?

"Can we get back to the reason why I called you?" I asked. "I should be close enough to my destination now, and I'd like to know what's waiting for me when I get there."

"All right," he agreed, the sound of the keys on his laptop coming through the line again. "So we're looking for the Green Warriors."

"Correct. In North Carolina."

A few seconds went by, then he said, "Nothing. Not a single thing. Are you sure that's the right name?"

Old Adalyn would say that I was. But I wasn't. The last twenty-four hours had been proof of how much I no longer was *old Adalyn*. "Try Green Oak. Try . . ." This was supposed to be a philanthropic venture, so perhaps I shouldn't expect the team to be making headlines. "Try recreational."

My last word seemed to hang in the reduced space inside the car, quiet except for the sound of the tires against the uneven pavement underneath.

When had I entered a dirt road? And why was Matthew not speaking? Was I out of reception?

I eyed the screen of my phone. The bars were there. "Matthew?"

A groan.

Oh no. "What did you find?"

"You're not going to be happy about this."

"Can you be more specific?"

"Have you packed sensible footwear?"

"Sensible? You mean house slippers?" I frowned. "I will be here for weeks, so yes."

"Not slippers. More like boots."

"Boots?" I repeated.

"The outdoorsy kind. You know, comfortable and sturdy and not attached to a five-inch heel."

"I know what boots are." I rolled my eyes, even though I hadn't been thinking of that kind. "I'm going to work, though. I'm not here for a day trip to . . ." I eyed the maps app again. "A very large ridge of mountains." Where in the world was this town? God. I should have really done my research before jumping on that plane. "I plan to dedicate as much time to the Green Warriors as I did to my job for the Flames. Plus, on the off chance that I have some free time, which I won't, you know that I don't engage in activities that include the use of Gore-Tex and the risk of falling off a cliff."

"Oh, but you will."

I frowned, taking a right on yet another dirt road. "What does that mean?"

The click of keys. Another groan.

My ears popped. God, how high was I? "Matthew, I'm about three seconds away from hanging up on you."

"All right. What do you want first? The bad news? Or the worse news?"

"There's no good news?" I asked, squinting my eyes and spotting the intersection I was headed for. I took the turn, the road changing to a mountain trail of sorts. Pebbles started jumping under the tires, hitting the bottom of the rental. I held on to the steering wheel. Tight. This couldn't be right. I was pretty sure I shouldn't be driving on a road like this one. The whole car was shaking—vibrating—with the bumps on the road that wasn't really a road. "I think I've made a mistake."

"That's what I'm trying to tell you," Matthew said. And if I had really been listening, I would have heard the urgency in his voice. But I was too busy wondering why this wasn't a town. I was entering a property tucked into the thick of the woods. *The woods.*

Matthew continued talking, his words getting lost in my head as I rounded a cabin. A cabin. An honest-to-God cabin with wooden beams and windows looking out at the mass of trees I'd left behind.

This couldn't be right.

For some unfathomable reason, on my way here, I'd built up this idea in my head. On the plane, I'd convinced myself that I was heading to a North Carolina city—maybe a suburb, which would explain why I hadn't heard of it. This was an assignment, after all. A philanthropic venture led by an MLS team. It was a serious project in a real town. But I found that hard to believe now.

Whatever place this property was attached to couldn't be a city. Or a suburb. It didn't look like there was a large enough town anywhere close, either.

I was surrounded by . . . nature. Woodland. Slopes covered in emerald greens and coppery browns. I'd driven down dirt roads that had led me to the kind of property I saw advertised as a rustic alpine retreat. There were birds chirping. Leaves rustling. Wind gusting. Silence.

I hated it.

I'd been too careless. Too hasty. I should have checked the location Kelly had sent me before programming it into the maps app. I should have researched. I should have—

"You've arrived at your destination," the female voice of my maps app chanted.

I ignored the clogging sensation at the bottom of my throat and rounded the cabin again, looking for a place to park. There had to be an explanation. A reason. Probably a major town I'd missed coming up a shortcut in the mountains. And, hey, at least the cabin was . . . tasteful. Most people would be glad to be given the opportunity to escape to such a peaceful place. Mountain-fresh air. Cozy sunsets under a blanket. A porch facing the greenery.

But I wasn't most people.

I hated the cold. And I didn't have that strange need to travel across the country in search of fresh air. I liked Miami's air. The city.

The coast. Even the overwhelming heat. My job with the Flames.
My life.

My stomach twisted, a ball of nausea climbing up.

Images of Sparkles's head dropping to the grass flashed behind
my eyes.

Breach of contract.

Female rage.

Embarrassing.

You're a distraction, so I want you to leave Miami.

My palms turned clammy again, the steering wheel feeling slip-
pery. Was the car still moving or had I put it in park?

"Adalyn?" Matthew asked, reminding me he was still there. Had
he been talking? "Talk to me."

But I was too busy trying to focus on whatever was going on
in my body. Was this exhaustion? Dehydration? When was the last
time I'd had water? Was I PMS-ing? I shook my head. Oh God, was
I losing it again? I—

Something hit the bumper with a thump.

I slammed on the brakes, the action so sudden, so rough, that
my whole body shot forward.

My forehead bounced against the steering wheel.

"Ouch." I heard myself groan through the ringing in my ears.

"ADALYN?" came from somewhere to my right. Matthew's
voice. It sounded muffled now. "Jesus Christ, what just happened?"

"I hit something," I announced, a stinging sensation burning the
right side of my forehead. With a ragged breath, I gave myself three
seconds, letting my head rest on the leathery surface of the wheel,
before I straightened up and turned my head, looking for my phone,
which had fallen from the dashboard.

Matthew's voice returned.

"Tell me you're okay or I swear I'll call your mother right fucking
now—"

"No," I croaked. "Please, don't. Not Maricela. She can't know."
I blinked, trying to clear the tiny spots popping around the edges
of my field of vision. "I'm good," I murmured, spotting something

moving outside the car. Something . . . that was running. And . . . Clucking? "I think I just hit a chicken."

Unintelligible swearing came from the speaker while I released the seatbelt and picked the phone up from the floor. I returned to the upright position and—

My head swirled. "That was a mistake," I murmured.

"That's what I'm trying to tell you, Adalyn. The Green Warriors—"

"I feel like I need to throw up."

"Get out of that car," he said. "Now."

With a nod Matthew couldn't see, I put the car in reverse. "The car is in the middle of the driveway so I'm going to park and then—"

"No."

"I can't just leave the car here." Pebbles jumped from under the tires as the vehicle started to move. "Maybe I should check on the chicken, too." A thought formed in the haziness that was my head. "Oh God. What if I killed it?" My eyes drifted to the direction the chicken had run off. I couldn't believe this. "Another stupid bird."

My eyelids fluttered shut. Just for a moment. It couldn't have been more than a nanosecond, a short-lived reprieve, but—

A thump jolted me.

A thump. I had hit something. Again. Something larger than a chicken. Something like a—God, don't let it be a bear.

My eyes blinked open, panic surging.

In the same breath, a growl—a bear-like growl to my utter dismay—came from the rear of the car. My foot shot forward. But my head was fuzzy and my basic reflexes clearly amiss, because instead of the brakes, I must have hit the accelerator.

And hurled the rental against a tree.

CHAPTER THREE

Cameron

$\mathcal{T}$ he woman inside the car was unconscious.

"Hello?" I called, squinting my eyes. I was trying to get a look at her face, but her head was against the window and the only thing I could see was a tangle of . . . brown hair. I knocked on the window and repeated, a little louder, "Hello?"

No reaction.

Christ. This wasn't good.

Pushing aside the pang of lingering annoyance and anger, I wiggled the door handle, hoping the car was unlocked and feeling immediate relief when it opened with a swift *click*.

Relief that vanished the moment the woman toppled to the side like a dead weight.

"Fuck," I muttered under my breath, catching her midair.

This had just escalated from inconvenient to concerning.

Without losing more time, I secured her against my chest and plucked her completely out of the vehicle so I could place her on the ground.

I kneeled next to her, that mass of hair still obscuring her face and pushing me to brush it aside with my hand. A set of parted lips, a button nose, and pale cheeks were revealed. Too pale, I noticed, my gaze inspecting her for obvious injuries. My eyes stopped at a bump on her forehead. It was an ugly shade of red and didn't alleviate any of my concern.

"Hello?" I called a third time, not obtaining any reaction from her. I patted her cheek softly. Still nothing. "Christ."

I tilted my head back for a second, dragging my hand down my face and dreading the reasonable course of action. I couldn't wrap my head around the fact she'd almost run me over. Missing the fucking bird that had been roaming the property for weeks was fair enough, but me? I had been standing right behind the car. And I wasn't a small bloke. She'd overlooked a six-foot-two man in broad daylight, then hurled the goddamn car against a tree.

"And now you're going to make me call a bloody ambulance, aren't you?" I whispered, shaking my head and pulling my phone out of my pocket. "Of course you are."

Just as I was unlocking it, though, she finally stirred, recapturing my attention.

A groan left her.

"Come on," I murmured, eagerly waiting for her to fully regain consciousness.

Her head moved to the side, her eyeballs flickering under the soft-looking skin of her eyelids.

I expelled a breath, growing restless. Once more, I reached out with my hand. I needed her to wake up and be fine. I was concerned about the likelihood of her having a concussion, sure, but I was also concerned about myself. And the last thing I wanted was having to report this and call in the emergency services or, God forbid, the authorities. I'd—

Her eyes popped open, bringing my motion to a sudden halt.

Brown eyes met mine.

"Who are you?" she rushed out in a strangled voice. Her gaze dipped toward my hand, just as it was about to make contact with her shoulder. "Don't touch me." She glanced up again. "I know self-defense."

I frowned.

"I could take you." Her voice turned into a whisper. "I think."

"You think? That's not very threatening," I muttered. She scowled at me for an instant, and then shifted, wincing with the motion. "What's hurting?" I asked, and when she didn't move or speak, I stretched my hand in her direction again. I'd assess her injuries myself if I had to, make sure she was okay, then drop her off at the closest hospital for a checkup. She wasn't my problem but I—

She swatted at me.

At my hand. One sharp and quick swat.

I blinked.

"I told you not to touch me." The woman all but spat. Outrage twisted her expression. Or perhaps it was fear. I frankly couldn't tell. I was also too baffled to give a single fuck. "So?" she insisted. "Who are you and why am I lying on the ground?"

I continued to stare at her, speechless. And when I could finally talk past my disbelief, what left me was, "You hit me with your car."

The woman frowned. "I did not hit—" She stopped herself, her jaw slowly falling open. "Oh." Realization washed over her face. "*Oh.*"

"Yeah. Oh," I deadpanned.

"The growl," she murmured. "It was you."

"Of course it was me, what did you think you'd hit?"

"I don't know. A . . . bear?"

My brows arched. "And you still didn't brake?"

"I tried to brake."

"You tried to brake," I repeated, my eyes flickering to the upscale and definitely not-suitable-for-the-terrain car as it rested against the trunk of an oak tree. She'd been lucky she'd been moving relatively slowly and barely managed to scratch the bumper of the car. I'd been lucky, too.

The woman remained silent, seemingly lost in thought and leaving me no choice but to watch her as she probably recalled everything—at snail's pace, too. My gaze trailed down, taking in her button-down shirt, pencil skirt, and heels. Everything about this woman, from her clothes—designer, no doubt—to her very impractical vehicle, reeked of entitled big-city life and overpriced beverages she snapped photos of on her way to the office. All of the things I'd intentionally left behind.

My eyes darted back to her face. To the spot on her head that was just as ugly as a few minutes before. "You should get your head checked. I'll drive you to the closest hosp—"

She jerked upward, bringing my words to a stop when she only managed to fall back.

"Absolutely not." I placed my palm on her chest to stop her from any other reckless attempt. She pushed upward and it barely took any effort on my side to keep her there. *You can take me, my arse.* "You're not jumbling your way into another stupid accident."

Her chin dipped, her eyes finding my hand. Right above her breasts. She scowled. "I told you not to—"

"Are you lost?" I interrupted her, undeterred by the menacing glance. My touch was purely clinical. Practical. "Is that why you're here?"

Her eyes narrowed. "Why would I be lost? I was parking my car when you got in the way—"

"You're either lost," I interjected again, "or trespassing. Have your pick."

That seemed to catch her off guard because she blinked a few times. I could see the wheels turning behind her eyes. "Oh God. Are you some crazy wilderness dweller who lives off scamming bypassers by jumping in front of their cars?" My brows furrowed and she shook her head. "I bet the beard and the accent are fake."

I tilted my head. Okay, she was either a lunatic or had the biggest concussion I'd ever encountered.

"I can pay you," she offered with a serious face. "I will if you go away. I can't afford the distraction of a scammer right now."

I took in a calming breath. "That cabin over there?" I pointed behind me with my head, hearing my voice harden. "I live there.

I'm not a dweller, I'm spending a small fortune renting it. Including the driveway where I was almost run over by you, and the oak you crashed against." The rooster unfortunately came with it.

"What?" she mumbled, her eyebrows knotting. She winced again.

My eyes shifted upward. To the spot on her forehead that was now swelling. "That needs ice," I declared, pushing through my exasperation. I released her chest and offered her my hand. "You likely need a doctor, too. Come on, I'll drive you. Do you think you can stand up without—"

"But I'm renting that cabin, the one right over there. And I did not almost run you over with my car."

I assessed her for a long moment, trying to discern how delusional—or concussed—she was. And then, without any warning, I moved. "All right, I'm done wasting time now," I said, my arms going around her back and legs. "I'm driving you to an ER, hospital, or anywhere that's not here."

A shrilling sound left her, piercing my ears.

"Jesus Christ—" I complained, and she twisted and turned in my arms. "Would you—" I lifted her up, her elbow hitting me square in the middle of the chest. "Oi—" I started moving in the direction of her car. Something pointy swung at my jaw. "Was that your knee?" It swung again. It was her knee. "Oh for Christ's sake," I mumbled, giving up and setting the tangle of arms and legs on the ground.

"I told you I know self-defense." She bristled, passing her palms down the fabric of her skirt. Even in heels, she barely reached my chin. "And you're not taking me anywhere. I feel okay, I don't need a doctor, and I'm not lost." Her shoulders squared, the image of sheer composure if not for the emotion swirling behind her brown eyes. "I've rented this place and I'd like to unpack. I have places to be and things to do, so you and your fake beard and silly accent can hit the road."

My jaw clenched. I inhaled deep and long through my nose. I counted down from ten. Very slowly. *Ten, nine, eight . . .*

"Well?" she continued, her tone insisting, infuriating. *Five, four, three* . . . "Being manhandled and then scammed is really the last thing I needed today."

I closed my eyes, something between a huff and a chuckle leaving me.

The absolute nuttery.

"What are you smirking at?"

I zeroed back on her. "Closest hospital is about thirty miles east," I said, not giving her a chance to butt into the conversation. "Now take Daddy's car and get off my property without killing anything or anyone on your way out, yeah?" The woman's mouth fell open with what I was sure was outrage. I turned around. "And put some goddamn ice on that before it turns blue and you spend a fortune on makeup covering it up," I added, walking off.

I was being a certified twat, but I couldn't care less about some woman's bruised feelings. I had tried to help her. She had refused.

So now I was done here. And hopefully, she was, too.

CHAPTER FOUR

Adalyn

$\mathcal{U}$nbelievable.

I couldn't believe he'd just said that and walked away.

Right back to *my* cabin.

With a huff, I stomped back to the car and fished out my phone.

The screen flashed with dozens of messages and missed calls. All from Matthew. I—

Shoot. I'd completely forgotten about him.

I scanned the notifications, finding everything from extremely concerned texts to threats about calling the fire brigade or worse, my mother, if I didn't give any sign of being alive. I fired him a quick text.

ADALYN: I'm okay. Call was dropped and I was out of reception.

The only truth in that statement was about the call being dropped. And Matthew must have been genuinely concerned because in matter of seconds I had an answer from him.

MATTHEW: WTF ADALYN. YOU HAVE ANY IDEA HOW
WORRIED I WAS?

I sighed. He was probably right to be a little upset but . . .

ADALYN: Stop worrying about me like I'm some helpless
child and trust me. I'm fine.

I stared at the screen, feeling like a jerk for snapping at my best
friend, but I was still rattled from the encounter with that . . . man.
The three dots started jumping, but I didn't wait around to see what
he was typing.

ADALYN: I'll call you later—and please, do not call Maricela.

I locked my screen and released a long breath, allowing myself
a full minute to regroup. My head was pounding but it wasn't anything a few painkillers couldn't fix. I didn't need a hospital. Or ice.
And I surely did not need a complete stranger telling me what I did
or did not need.

With a newfound surge of energy, I gave myself a shake and
made my way to the cabin—my cabin, which he was currently, and
possibly illegally, occupying—as I pulled out the booking confirmation from my email. After scrolling down a few times I found the
message. I clicked on it, scanning the contents.

There. There it was. Booking confirmation number. Adalyn
Elisa Reyes. Address. Lazy Elk Lodge, Green Oak, North Carolina.

Lazy Elk Lodge. God, that name painted a pretty obvious
picture—if one would actually check such things before arriving at
their destination, that was.

I climbed the steps of the porch and made the effort to push
that thought aside. Beating myself up over it wouldn't fix anything
now. My gaze roamed around and now that I was actually looking
at it, I understood why someone might come here. The cabin was

beautiful—if you were into that kind of thing. It was tall enough to accommodate two stories and floor-to-ceiling glass windows on each side of the entrance door, providing an elegant yet rustic look that perfectly complemented the landscape.

I reached the front door, allowing myself one single inhale of air before I rose my hand to knock.

The door swung open, as if he'd been on the other side waiting for me.

That face that was all hard and sharp lines beneath a short but unkempt beard was revealed. Green eyes I hadn't noticed being that green met mine. They were still angry.

I opened my mouth, but now that I could take a good look at him from an upright, standing position, a strange feeling struck me. There was something about this man, about his face or perhaps that head full of dark hair or maybe even the breadth of his shoulders, that was . . . familiar? But *how*? My eyes roamed some more, stopping at his mouth. His lips were pressed in a tight pout that almost rang a bell somewhere in my head. Maybe if they weren't obscured by all that facial hair . . .

"This was a mistake." I saw—rather than heard—his mouth move around the words.

I met his gaze. "What do you mean?"

But instead of answering, he started closing the door.

I thrust my hand and foot forward, placing them between door and frame. "Wait."

To his credit, he waited. He could have easily overpowered me and shut it. I wasn't what one would consider a small woman, and I was wearing heels, but he still managed to tower over me. He also looked lean. Strong. My eyes bounced to the shoulder and arm that were visible through the slit of the door. A single word came to mind: athlete. I recognized a high-performance athlete when I saw one. It wasn't the right moment, but I continued my inspection, returning to his face. My hazy brain was about to make the connection. I knew.

Yes. I'd seen those eyes before. That stubborn set of dark eyebrows that dipped low. That long and straight nose, too.

He muttered something under his breath, and I sensed his grip on the door changing. That's when my eyes dipped down, landing on his fingers. Strong, long. His middle one slightly crooked. His pinky wore a signet ring with a C.

A C. But it couldn't be. It—

He cleared his throat, making me snap out of it.

I lifted my phone. "Here's my booking. Have a look and see for yourself. I rented this cabin." I pushed the device into his face. "Lazy Elk Lodge."

He grunted something unintelligible and finally threw the door open again.

"Listen," I told him, using the voice I always employed in press conferences. Polite but firm. Straight to the point. "Worst-case scenario, this is an unfortunate case of double-booking, which would be none of our fault. But if that's what happened, we need to clarify this." I checked on his expression as he reluctantly scanned the screen of my phone. "Best-case scenario, you're simply wrong. In which case I'll leave you a few hours to vacate and be back later. I have things to do in town. No harm, no foul."

A snort toppled out of his lips. "That's an awfully bad apology."

"I'm not apologizing, I'm trying to be civil."

"You're also not the tenant of Lazy Elk," he countered, making my eyes narrow. "It says there that you booked the Sweet Heaven Cottage in the Lazy Elk Lodge." He arched that pair of angry brows, daring to look bored. "Wherever that is. Now, if you don't mind, I have stuff to do back in *my* cabin."

I retrieved my phone, zooming in on the details of the email. "That can't be right." I scrolled down. Two large fingers popped into my field of vision, bringing my attention to a line: Sweet Heaven Cottage, 423 Lazy Elk Street, Lazy Elk Lodge. "But that can't be right," I repeated. "I circled the property with the car when I got here and there was nothing." My eyes scanned every single foot of property around, searching almost desperately at this point. "There's no street. And there's no other cabin."

And there wasn't. Not really. But I did notice something else.

To the right of the porch we were standing on was a shed.

Not a cabin. Definitely not the cabin I was staying in, right?

Only, the more I looked the more impossible it was to miss the number hanging off a . . . timber pole that bent sideways under the September sun.

The number read: 423 LAZY ELK STREET.

My stomach dropped with dread and . . . something else.

I hadn't seen the interior, but I didn't need to. I wasn't equipped to stay there. That strange sensation intensified and for the first time in my life, I wanted to throw in the towel and run back home with my tail between my legs. I'd be a disappointment on top of being an embarrassment, but this? A *shed* in some rural area I was clearly unequipped for? It was too much. I—

A chuckle came from behind me, low and deep and dripping with such condescension that it snagged me right away from the edge of the hole I'd been ready to jump in.

This wasn't me. I promised myself this morning I wouldn't be wobbly Adalyn any longer.

"It'll be perfect," I announced, turning around and meeting his gaze. His green eyes widened slightly, but he didn't cower. It was right then when it finally clicked. I knew without a doubt who this man was. It was in the way he'd been so . . . conceited. So self-assured. This was a man used to winning. And he'd just won. I'd been in the wrong. I squared my shoulders with the last ounce of dignity I had left. "And rest assured, *neighbor*, now that I've found it, I'll get out of your hair and let you get to that very important stuff you have to do."

"I'm not your neighbor."

"Looks to me like we are sharing the property, though." I spread my arms. "The beautiful and cozy Lazy Elk Lodge, in lovely Green Oak."

"You're not staying," he said in a strange tone. "You can't possibly live"—a nod in the direction of the shed—"there."

The corners of my lips inched higher at the way he was telling me and not asking. "Of course I can. I've booked it and have very important business to do in town."

He let out a bitter, humorless chuckle. "Darling—"

"Please." My expression turned to stone. "Don't call me that."

He frowned, probably because I'd accidentally said please. "Adalyn," he said in that English accent I'd been wrong to assume was fake, making my name sound a way I wasn't used to. "Adalyn Elisa Reyes."

I didn't understand why he'd done that—said my full name like that. I narrowed my eyes. "So you know how to read, congrats."

Rather than annoyed, he seemed amused by my jab. "That's not a cabin," he continued. "It's hardly a cottage. It's a goddamn shack."

"Your point?"

His eyes gave me an incredulous once-over. "You can't possibly think that you'll make it in there. Not short- and certainly not long-term." He tilted his head. "In fact, I don't think you'll make it a single night there."

He wasn't wrong, I probably couldn't. But I'd spent half a lifetime surrounded by men just like him. Competitive, judgmental; I didn't like to be underestimated. And I'd already lost one battle to him.

"I guess we'll have to see about that." I turned around and climbed down the steps. When I was at the bottom, I looked at him over my shoulder and added, "Neighbor."

"What do you mean it's all booked?"

"There are no hotels, motels, or Airbnbs in Green Oak. There's no other available property to rent short- or long-term. Just the Lazy Elk Lodge. I could look in the towns close by, but that means you'll have to drive back and forth. It's also the end of the high season. There're lots of trekking routes, waterfalls, lakes, beautiful—"

"Kelly," I said, unconsciously using my boss's voice. "I'm not interested in what the area offers. I'm interested in finding some other accommodation. Any other. I can't stay here."

She hesitated, then said, "Define 'can't.'"

I appreciated Kelly, I really did. She always worked hard, had initiative, and never allowed anyone to walk over her, which was why I had snagged her from the ticketing division, where her raw potential would have been wasted. But sometimes she tested my patience.

"Picture a hunter's hut." I humored her, going for a clear enough picture of where I was. "Rotten and creaky wood that bends under your weight, one single window, the biggest set of antlers you've ever seen hanging off one wall." I zeroed in on the thing, goosebumps running down my spine. "And before you ask, no. They're not even the cool kind of antlers. They are the kind that make you think of death and flesh and bones."

She clicked her tongue. "But the pictures looked so cozy. Isn't there a little fireplace?"

My gaze jumped to the so-called fireplace. It was some sort of iron furnace that made clanking sounds. "In theory, yes. In reality, it's a black hole that probably hosts something I don't want to stir awake."

"You mean, like a spirit? Or—"

"Kelly," I said, shaking my head. "A living something, possibly with teeth and claws."

She hummed. "What about the bed?" I glanced at the horrible piece of furniture. She continued, "It was so . . . rustic and low-key sexy? Like the kind of bed a lumberjack would do nasty—"

"It's a very dated four-poster bed," I rushed out, my eyelids fluttering shut to spare me the sight of that monstrosity. "And I am— was—your boss. I don't want to hear about your sexual fantasies. Particularly not if they involve lumberjacks, and especially not if they involve the four-poster bed I'll have to sleep in tonight."

"I guess you're more of a bodice-ripper girl, boss. And I don't blame you. I'm just a little darker than that." I blinked, at a loss for words. "Maybe it's not so bad?" she offered. "Maybe all you need to do is yassify the cabin. Make it yours."

I looked around, wondering if I could take advice from this woman who claimed to have a migraine at every minimal inconvenience and once signed off an email with "apologies for existing. :)"

No. I wasn't Kelly. We weren't that far apart in age but we were universes away, and in my universe, yassifying wasn't something I could or knew how to do.

"Hey, boss?" Her voice brought me back. She hesitated, then said, "I need to go."

I thought I could hear someone in the background. "Is David there?" I rushed out. "With you?"

"Er . . ."

I couldn't believe what I was going to say, but I needed to escalate this. And unfortunately, that meant talking to my ex. "Pass him the phone. I want to speak to him."

There was some rustling. Then Kelly said, "Sorry, but we already have an office paper supplier." What? "We also are against deforestation. In fact, you should be ashamed of yourself. Paperless offices are the future, sir."

"I know David is there."

"I'll be right with you, David, yes!" she exclaimed, her voice piercing my ear. Then she added in a hushed voice, "I need to run, boss. Remember to stay strong."

Stay strong? "What do you—"

"Bye!"

And the call ended.

Stay strong. What did that even mean? And why had Kelly pretended to talk to somebody else? Something was amiss. And usually, that kicked me into action.

With a renewed sense of purpose, I unlocked my phone and started snapping pictures of this horrible, tiny, grisly shed-turned-cabin that had been decorated by a psychopath. I needed proof that this place wasn't . . . habitable.

Once done with that, I rolled my suitcase to the narrow and slightly crooked coffee table that sat between the alleged fireplace and a one-person settee I had no intention of ever gracing with any of my body parts.

I started working the zipper, side-eyeing the settee, the four-poster bed, and . . . everything, when his words smacked right back into me.

I don't think you'll make it a single night there.

With a huff, I pulled my suitcase open and located my makeup bag. I couldn't forget that I was on assignment here. I still needed to drive into town and find the Green Warriors. Who knew, maybe I'd misjudged the whole situation. Maybe this was just how rentals worked in the area. No hotels or motels, just . . . this. Cabin fever was a thing. In fact—

A noise outside caught my attention.

I stiffened, turned around slowly, walked to the window on my tiptoes, and shoved the flimsy curtain aside with a finger.

A tall figure was crossing the space between the cabins with long, determined strides.

I narrowed my eyes at him.

"Look at you," I murmured under my breath. "Strutting out of your fancy lodging like you own the place."

Which, technically, he kind of did. He rented the place. Or half of it, at least. The good, fancy half.

Now that I'd had a few minutes to myself, I couldn't ignore how bothered I was. It irked me that he'd been right and I'd been in the wrong. I wasn't used to being put in that position and when he'd pointed at Sweet Heaven Cottage, I'd felt . . . stupid. Dumb. And his quick judgment of my character, even if probably deserved, had made me feel even worse. He had hurt my pride, my intelligence, my sense of direction, and my ability to read. Perhaps, if this had happened at another time, I wouldn't have cared. But it had happened today, and I wasn't used to repeatedly embarrassing myself.

I could still see past my pride to know I should have apologized, though. At least for accidentally hitting him with the car. I felt horrible about that. And yet . . . as he walked the gravel path crisscrossing the property, I couldn't shake the way he'd looked me up and down, skeptical and knowing, as if he could see how everything about me was inappropriate and unsuitable. Out of place.

I was out of place.

But so was he.

What was Cameron Caldani—two-time winner of IFFHS World's Best Goalkeeper, former Premier League starter and, as of the last five years, MLS star—doing in Green Oak, North Carolina? The news about his retirement from the L.A. Stars had been sudden and relatively recent. I didn't keep tabs on every player in the country, especially if they played in the Western Conference, but it was my job to stay informed. I couldn't recall any particulars about his retirement being said. Just that he'd surprised everyone by announcing he'd hung up the gloves.

Cameron stopped at the curve closest to the edge of trees surrounding the property. I moved a little closer to the glass. The man was tall, which wasn't uncommon for a goalkeeper, but he seemed larger and wider in person. Our paths had never crossed, which wasn't strange, considering the L.A. Stars usually made it to the playoffs while the Flames never did. But I knew what he looked like. Cameron Caldani was a man hard to miss or overlook. It was the beard that had thrown me off. Probably the hit to the head. The setting, too.

One simply didn't expect to find Cameron Caldani in the middle of the woods.

Matthew—who was the biggest soccer nerd I'd ever met—was going to lose his mind when he learned that Cameron Caldani was in Green Oak. He'd probably make a shrine to the bumper of my car because it had grazed Cameron's body.

Which was exactly why Matthew could never know.

The man on the other side of the window knelt and picked something off the ground with those strong and slightly crooked fingers I'd seen up close and inspected. After a moment, I watched him search the vegetation in front of him.

His baritone voice rang out. Something that sounded like Cruiser or Booster. A pet's name? I waited with him, expecting something to dash out of the woods. A dog? What kind of pet did someone like Cameron Caldani have? I was so immersed, so intrigued, that when he turned around to face the window I was standing in, it caught me unprepared.

Green eyes landed right on me.

And I . . . I dove.

Straight onto the not exactly smooth or clean floor of Sweet Heaven Cottage. I didn't even know why I did that. It wasn't like I was doing anything wrong. I was being absurd considering I had faced meeting rooms and press conferences more intimidating than that man's gaze.

With a shake of my head, I counted to three, lifted my chin, got up with as much class as I could possibly muster, and peeked out the window again.

There wasn't a trace of Cameron Caldani.

He was gone, and in his wake he'd left behind what had to be . . . feathers.

"Oh God." I groaned, a new rush of guilt washing over me.

Cameron's pet. The one he'd been calling for just now. Cruiser or . . . Booster.

Could it be the chicken I'd hit with my car?

My eyelids fluttered shut. No wonder he'd been enraged.

CHAPTER FIVE

Cameron

Close to a dozen sets of eyes blinked slowly at me, as if I was speaking a language they didn't understand.

I frowned, wondering how in the bloody hell had I gotten myself into yet another bizarre situation today. Only this time, I knew the answer. I'd agreed to be here. Even if reluctantly.

The intensity of the fluttering increased, reminding me of one of those silly cartoons I used to watch on the telly when I was a boy.

"What is all that eyelash flapping about?"

"Pretty pleaaaaaaaase?" eight out of the nine girls in front of me chanted in unison.

"I said no," I told them, crossing my arms in front of my chest. "Now, whose turn is it to fetch the cones and balls? I'll get the practice goals later on."

The one with the asymmetrical pigtails stepped closer. "It will be just the one video, Mr. Coach," María—one of the oldest girls in the group at the age of nine—said. "You don't need to do anything but stand in front of the camera with us, and we won't even post it anywhere. I promise." She clasped her hands beneath her chin.

"Pretty pleaaaase?" she repeated, stretching the word again. "Mr. Coach?"

Not the Mr. Coach bullshit again. "Just Cam."

"Does that mean you'll do it, Mr. Cam?"

I stopped myself from rolling my eyes. "No. Now—"

"But your name is literally cam." She stepped forward, the whole group moving with her. "And what's a camera for? Videos!"

I stared blankly at the kid. Jesus, I really needed that extra shot of caffeine I'd missed today. "That's not where Cam comes from."

"Where does it come from then?"

"Cameron," I answered without thinking and immediately regretted it. "But you can call me Cam. Not Camera, not Mr. Coach, and not Mr. Cam. Just Cam."

María's head tilted, all that barely contained dark hair shifting with the motion. Out of the lot, she was the sassiest, most outspoken kid. Probably too smart for her own good. So when her lips popped open, I braced myself. Luckily, before she could speak someone shouted in the distance.

We all turned toward the voice, spotting a kid running toward us.

Chelsea.

I knew because out of the ten-player roster, not only was she one of the youngest kids at age seven, but also because she was the one that insisted on showing up to practice in a goddamn tutu. She had them in multiple colors. This one was blue, and it clung to her waist over her shorts.

Christ. That was why I insisted on them not calling me anything but Cam. Expressly, not coach. I was coaching them, but I wasn't their coach. I couldn't be.

"Sorry," Chelsea said when she reached us, breathlessly doubling down. "My ballet class ran a little late, and my mom thought my dad was picking me up. But my dad thought my mom was. So my mom had to call my dad to drive me all the way from Fairhill." Her chest heaved. "What did I miss?"

"Mr. Camera doesn't want to record a video with us," María said. "And he doesn't even need to dance."

Chelsea popped a piece of chewing gum into her mouth. "Why?"

"No gum during practice," I reminded her. "And can the tutu go?"

"She's channeling her inner Black Swan," María answered for Chelsea. "Right, Chels?"

Chelsea reluctantly took the gum out with her fingers, tucked it in the pocket of her shorts and gave a nod. "That's right, Mr. Cam."

I blinked at them. I was sure that movie had come out before any of them were born. "Aren't you too young to watch that movie?"

María shrugged. "My brother was watching it last week. I only had a peek, Mr. Cam."

I eyed the blue thing. "Wouldn't the tutu need to be black, too?"

Another shrug. I suppressed a sigh. "And for the last time, just Cam is fine."

"You are grumpy today, Mr. C," María muttered, bracing her hands on her hips. "So . . . Is Cameron your first name or your last name? Do you have a middle name, too?"

"No middle name. No last name. And now"—I pointed at the girls closest to the supply shed—"can you please fetch cones and balls from the supply room? We're losing precious time."

Four of the kids trotted away and when I returned my eyes to María, her expression was skeptical. "So you're like Zendaya?"

"No," I answered. "I'm not a *zendoya*, whatever that is. I'm Cam. Now let's all—"

"Oh. My. God," María said very theatrically. "He doesn't know who Zendaya is."

"How old are you, Coach Cam?" Chelsea asked, walking around me very slowly, as if she was inspecting me in a new light. Only when she made it back to the front, she said, "You look younger than my granddaddy. He wears suspenders under his shirt. Mom says it's weird, but I think it's funny. Do you have grandchildren?"

"Yeah, when's your birthday, Mr. Cam?" María quipped. "Oh, if you tell me, I could look for your astral chart!" She produced a phone from some cord she had been hiding under her shirt and started tapping at the screen. "I need date, time, and exact place of birth."

I brought my hand to the bridge of my nose, the start of a headache pounding at my temples.

"How old do you think Coach is?" I heard María pose to the group. "Eighteen fifty? Or, like, older?"

"María," a new voice huffed—Juniper, short hair, quiet, always listened when I barked out instructions. "Don't be ridiculous, he can't be over a hundred years old. He'd have to be . . . like, a vampire. Or at least someone who's been injected with a superpower *syrup* and then frozen for decades before being brought back to life to save humanity."

And much to my utter and complete dismay, that comment ignited a very passionate debate about sparkly paranormal creatures and . . . superheroes I didn't know shite about.

So I stood there, wondering how advanced kids were these days while the headache settled in. Jesus. I was—had been—a bloody footballer. A small-town kiddie team wasn't my place. I could barely get them to run a proper drill. I was here only because I had promised Josephine, and she'd caught me at a low moment. I'd had plenty of those lately. I just wished I'd had a goddamn coffee before practice. With that maniac who claimed to be moving in next door disrupting my routine, I hadn't had time to grab one on my way out.

I closed my eyes, unsuccessfully trying to drown the growing chatter, and counted down from ten for the second time today. Then, I brought my fingers to my mouth and whistled.

The prattling came to an abrupt stop.

They all turned toward me.

"Juniper," I said, pointing at the short-haired girl.

Her eyes grew wide. "I haven't said anything. I can't get in trouble for not saying anything."

I clenched my jaw, wondering if I'd been too harsh. I tried to soften my expression and tone. "Come here, please. At the front of the group."

Juniper looked as skeptical as she was flustered at my request.

María braved a question. "Does this mean you're going to tell us your zodiac sign?"

"How could this—" I stopped myself. "No. It means that I'm going to fetch Josephine. And until I'm back, nobody will leave this field and Juniper will be in charge."

Juniper immediately complained, "But I'm nine years old. I can't be in charge."

"Neither can I, kid," I muttered. And I apparently looked old enough to belong to a different century.

But I couldn't do this today, not without caffeine. It was my one indulgence in life. My one vice after a life of discipline and strict regime. Josephine was the sole provider in town, and I knew she was around the practice facilities because she'd mentioned something about some visitor coming in. I'd beg her for a coffee if I had to.

"But we should be at practice," Juniper countered. "And I've never led a practice before."

I turned around, broke into a jog, and shouted over my shoulder, "Then try to improvise. I'll be right back."

Out of the corner of my eye, I saw Juniper throw her hands up in the air, her gesture of despair turning into a . . . jumping jack.

"Jesus," I muttered, watching half of the girls imitating her. "That—"

The words died at the end of my tongue as I collided against something.

Someone. Someone soft and warm. My arms reached around whoever was plastered against my front and my gaze dipped down. A mass of light brown strands was lodged on my right pec.

We stepped back from each other at the same time, recognition hitting me the moment a pair of big brown eyes met mine.

"You," Adalyn seethed.

"You," I grunted back.

"Well, if that's not the most adorable meet-cute," Josephine said. Her hand fell on my arm in a friendly pat. "Cam, this right here is my newest friend and Green Oak resident, Adalyn. She's—"

"I know who she is," I deadpanned.

Adalyn's eyes narrowed.

Josephine let out a chuckle. "Oh, well. I didn't realize you two had met." Out of the corner of my eye, I saw her moving closer to Adalyn. "So where are you staying, Ada? Can I call you Ada? You were about to tell me before Cam all but plowed into you."

"I . . ." Adalyn's throat worked, a strange emotion flashing through her face. "I'd rather you called me Adalyn. And I'm staying at the Sweet Heaven Cottage." She recovered from whatever that had been, pinning me with a glance. "For however long I want. Because that's something I can absolutely do."

I gave her an unimpressed look.

"So that's why you know each other!" Josephine squealed. "You two are neighbors. How wonderful is that, huh?"

"It's just marvelous," I muttered.

Josephine nodded. "Oh, it really is. You get to share the lodge and work together with the team. Yay!"

Both Adalyn's and my head whirled in Josephine's direction.

The woman held her hands in the air. "Oh Lord, why are you two looking at me like I just kicked a puppy?" No one spoke. Josie clicked her tongue. "All right, I see there's some unattended . . . tension here. So let's take turns." An easy smile parted her face. "Adalyn, you go first."

"Miss Moore," Adalyn started.

But Josie let out a laugh. "Oh dear, please, there's no need for such formalities. I know I introduced myself as the mayor, but it's a volunteer role in a place this small." She lowered her voice, "Plus, I'm not even thirty and formalities make me feel ancient." I watched Adalyn blink at the other woman, before she pressed with another bright smile. "So? You were saying."

"Yes, um," Adalyn hesitated before shoving me aside with one arm and stepping closer to Josephine. I scowled at her profile. "There has to be a mistake of some kind. We are not working together with the team. He can't be involved with the Green Warriors, because if he was, I would know about it."

Now that caught my attention.

Josephine tilted her head in confusion. "But he is. Cam . . ." Josephine trailed off for an instant. "Cam is the Green Warriors' coach."

My mouth opened to correct her—I was only doing her a favor by temporarily filling in as coach—but Adalyn's reaction sidetracked me.

Her cheeks flamed a deep shade of pink, and her lips parted.

Wide and panicked brown eyes turned to me, and then she said, "He's fired then. Effective immediately."

CHAPTER SIX

Adalyn

Cameron Caldani, goalkeeping prodigy and Premier League legend, stared at me.

"That's right," I mumbled, but it wasn't right. I didn't know what was coming out of my mouth. "This is my first decision as . . . general manager of the Green Warriors." Oh God. Did I even have a title? "And as the new person in charge of supervising the team's activities and making sure they live up to their full potential, I'm deciding that we don't need him. Therefore, he is fired." My voice cracked, and for some reason I added, "Good day."

Josie fell silent.

Cameron blinked unbelievably slowly, his lips twitching in a way I couldn't interpret.

And as he watched me, I knew that if he mocked me right now, if he said something about my *daddy*, or whether I was lost, or how I didn't belong here and couldn't make it a single night, chances were I'd crumble down and cry. Or worse. God knew that I was unpredictable these days.

So when his lips came to a stop, giving shape to a pout I didn't understand, I held my breath. "You're going to do what now?" he said.

Okay.

I could work with that. With hostility. Cynicism. Even condescension. I was used to those.

"I'm not going to do anything," I told him, my voice gaining strength. "Because I already did. You are dismissed from your coaching duties."

Josie seemed to partially recover because she let out an awkward snicker. "I think the . . . fun and friendly banter is unnecessarily escalating. How about we let Cam return to practice and discuss this later over a slice of red velvet cake? It's Josie's Joint's special today, and cake is on the house for newcomers."

"There's no need to discuss anything," I answered, my eyes on Cameron, who had tilted his head to one side and was inspecting me in a strange way. "Who hired him?" Something occurred to me. "Did my father send him here, too?"

Cameron Caldani's eyes narrowed, the green darkening with a new emotion I didn't recognize. Why was this man a walking riddle I couldn't decipher? I didn't like that.

"I . . . did." Josie hesitated. "Well, I wouldn't use the word *hire*, as he's not being paid a dime. A better word is . . . recruited. Yes, I recruited Cam."

"You volunteered me," he countered in a bitter tone.

Josie laughed, a little more naturally this time. "I know, I know. But the girls needed a coach, and you needed, well, you know. Peace and quiet. So it was perfect, because you were already here and coaching a team like this is a walk in the park."

"What I need is coffee."

I ignored that because . . . Peace and quiet? The girls? A team like this? Working with a female team was a change that excited me, I decided, but I was still missing something. "I . . . I don't understand. Can we backtrack for an instant? Forget he's here and interrupted us?"

Cameron grunted.

"I guess this is as good a time as any to give you the proper introduction to the team," Josie told me. "The Warriors of Green Oak is—or maybe was—an institution around here," she explained with a playful wink. "Back when my mom was young, we happened to have the only female soccer team in the area. At least, until most young people started fleeing to larger cities and it all kind of went . . . downhill. The team eventually died out and turned into a good memory. Mom is no longer with us, but Grandpa Moe has the best stories." She patted my shoulder with a sad smile. "I'll introduce you to him. He runs Cheap Moe's and Outdoor Moe's. And he used to own my café, too, formerly known as Moe's Joint. He'll love you. Anyway, I brought the team back to life last year. I decided to rename it the Green Warriors so it'd be easier to remember."

This explained why Matthew had been reticent to tell me what he'd found about the team over the phone. It . . . It was a lot of information to chew on. The mayor of the town, a woman my own age in green dungarees with tiny daisies on them, had volunteered a lot of personal details in under a minute. And apparently the Green Warriors, formerly known as the Warriors of Green Oak, had been brought back to life only last year. "I . . . I think I have a few questions. Topics I'd like to clarify and discuss, ASAP if that's okay."

"I'll show you the pictures," she offered. "My mom kept all of them. And let me tell you, it's a blast from the past." She seemed to remember something. "Oh! I almost forgot the most exciting part: we'll be representing our county in the Six Hills Little League!"

That made me pause. "*Little league*?"

An enthusiastic nod. "The Green Warriors were the best U10 team in the county last season, so we qualified for the Six Hills. Yay!"

All the blood seemed to leave my face. "U10?" I thought I whispered, but my ears were ringing, and I suddenly felt faint. Josie's smile fell. "What do you . . ."

And before the question fully left me, we were being swarmed by kids. Children. Little girls. In colorful shorts and sneakers and ponytails that pointed in all directions and a tutu, shockingly enough. One of them held a soccer ball under her arm. And all of them looked, roughly, under the age of ten.

"Adalyn," Josie's voice made it through the haze of confusion and disbelief that was my head. "It is my pleasure to introduce you to the Green Warriors."

I blinked at the team. The kids. As they blinked at me in return. "But my father . . ." I started, but all I could come up with was a jumbled mess of questions. "My father never— This is not— Why— They're kids?"

Somehow, my eyes ended up on Cameron, who was looking at me like I was some puzzle he couldn't figure out. Or as if I was about to sprout a second head. I wasn't sure. It didn't make sense. Nothing did. I—

"Juniper," he called for one of the kids. "Can you please bring an ice pack for Adalyn?"

"I'll do it!" someone exclaimed, and a blur of pigtails and messy black hair passed right by me.

"Thanks, María," he grumbled under his breath, eyes still on me.

I should have probably complained. But I didn't think I had the energy. As I stood in that spotty field of grass, I really was feeling at my lowest. I'd thought that assaulting my team's mascot in a clear lapse of judgment had been rock bottom. Then, when I found out there was footage of it and the clip had gone viral, I was sure that had been the rock bottom under the rock bottom. But then, I'd been banished and sent away, only to realize I was stuck in some tiny and tacky hunting cottage in the middle of the mountains. And I'd thought, this is it. This is the real bottom.

I'd been wrong.

This was.

The Green Warriors were. This children's team that held the key to my redemption was my real rock bottom.

The girls moved around us, and I was vaguely aware of Josie interacting with them. My eyes blinked back to reality, and I found myself gaping at Cameron. At all that dark hair, the unkempt beard, the green eyes flashing with something between curiosity and . . . concern. He was even wearing workout clothes. A long-sleeved thermal that clung to his chest and made his shoulders look even broader, and shorts. Nylon shorts that reached the middle of his thighs.

"What . . ." I heard myself mumble. "What are you doing here? Why are you here? It doesn't make sense." I also didn't make sense. But I was so confused and blindsided, and my brain seemed set on fixating on the fact. "You're Cameron C—"

Josie's panicked face materialized beside Cameron, who was now looking at me with a hostility that hadn't been there before. "Oh no. No, no." She chuckled, but there was tension in her voice, now lowering to a loud whisper. "He's just Cam around here."

My still dumbfounded gaze flickered in Cameron's direction, and before I could prepare, he was turning around and walking away.

Josie sighed.

And I . . . What had just happened? Why was Cameron leaving so suddenly? And why was Josie concealing Cameron's identity?

But instead of asking any of those very valid questions, I watched him stride along the sidelines of the unkept facilities and asked, "Does he always storm out of places?"

"Don't think too much about it," Josie said with a conviction that made me glance at her in surprise. "Cam's a bit . . . standoffish, but I'm pretty sure he'll be back."

"I genuinely hope you're wrong," I blurted out, obtaining a curious glance from Josie. "I fired him for a reason." I simply needed to decide exactly what that reason was.

She laughed, as if that'd been a joke. Although perhaps it was just the way Josie operated. Maybe she was one of those always glass-half-full people. Always laughing. Smiling. Positive.

"It's for the best," I told her. "The dislike for each other is mutual. We didn't exactly start off on the right foot and he . . . has a good reason to hate me. I—" I shook my head. "I might have almost run over his pet this morning." Josie's eyes widened. "I know. I feel horrible, but it's not that easy to spot a chicken crossing a driveway."

Neither was spotting a six-something pro soccer player, apparently.

Josie muffled a cackle with a hand, the corners of her eyes wrinkling with humor. "Oh, don't worry about the poor thing, they are resilient creatures. I'm sure it's still alive and clucking. Did you see it running?" I nodded and she smiled before pointing at my forehead. "Is that how you hurt yourself? I didn't want to be rude and ask, but it looks recent, and Cam asked one of the kids for the ice pack." Concern entered her expression. "You should get it checked out."

"So I've been told," I whispered, defeat entering my voice.

"I'll take you to Grandpa Moe when we're done here. He used to be a paramedic and still volunteers around town sometimes."

"It's nothing," I assured her, wondering what else the man did. "It barely hurts."

"I insist."

"Okay," I relented, returning my gaze to the group of girls, now sitting in the grass and chattering between themselves. The one with the tutu shot me an accusing glance, as if I'd just ruined all the fun, causing an unexpected pang of guilt to surge in my stomach. I turned to Josie. "I know you must have been very excited about the perspective of having someone like . . . Cameron coaching the team, but I can assure you: you'll be fine without him now that I'm here."

Josie smiled, but it was short-lived. "I'd appreciate if you'd keep under wraps who Cam is." Her expression turned serious. "Nobody in town knows."

"But . . ." I trailed off, the wheels in my head turning. Was Cameron Caldani . . . hiding? Was that the reason for him staying in a place like Green Oak? I shook my head. "How is it possible that no one has recognized him?"

"The beard?" Josie offered. "The fact that he doesn't play football or baseball or isn't an influencer giving away cars?" Another shrug. "You're the first. And we should keep it that way. It's important to him, and I want to respect that." Her megawatt grin returned. "And you know how small towns are, the moment someone finds out, everyone in Green Oak will know, then the whole county, and before we can blink, there'll be journalists trying to snap a photo of a"—she lifted her hands—"retired soccer star, feeding the chickens."

I could see how that would make good news. Cameron Caldani had never gained celebrity status in the States, but I knew well how something like this could be turned around.

"Also," Josie continued, "besides the Vasquezes, I really am the only one who cares about soccer around here." A puff of air left her lips, falling quiet for a moment until she sent me a secretive glance. "I was engaged to someone in the MLS once. That's how Cam and I met." Her lips pursed with a flash of emotion I didn't catch. "He witnessed the whole thing go up in flames."

I turned away slightly, my eyes drifting toward the group again. I wasn't exactly uncomfortable, but that was a lot of personal information Josie kept volunteering. And I was a complete stranger.

"Oh, don't worry, honey," Josie said, misinterpreting my silence. "I'm okay now. It wasn't my only failed shot at love, either. But that's a story for another day."

"I'm glad you're okay," I ventured, racking my brain for something sensitive or friendly to say. "I . . ." God, I was so bad at these types of interactions. "I don't date in the MLS, either?" I offered, causing Josie's brows arch. "Most players are more work than they're worth and, well, last time I got involved with someone remotely related to the world, he— This is TMI. I—"

A blue-and-white ice pack was thrust in front of me, saving me from babbling something I'd regret.

I looked down at the small hands offering it. "Thanks," I said, snatching the pad from the kid's grasp and placing it against my forehead. It immediately stung.

"You're welcome," a brown-eyed kid said with a toothy smile. "I'm María Vasquez. When is your birthday? I need date, time, and exact place."

I heard Josie's snicker. "María, what have we talked about going around asking people's ages?" She patted the kid on the shoulder. "This is Adalyn, she's coming from . . . Miami, right?" I gave her a nod. "And she will be helping with the team."

"Helping is a simplification," I countered. "I will—"

"Are you the one who booted Mr. Cam's ass?"

"María," Josie warned again.

She rolled her eyes. "Sorry, I meant Mr. Cam's butt. He called it a bum the other day. He doesn't speak much but he uses funny words sometimes. I think he's a Taurus. And I don't trust Taurus men. What zodiac sign are you, Miss Adalyn?"

"Hmm, Virgo? But—"

"Exciting! Are you our new coach?" She shot a look at me, giving me a once-over. Her eyes found my feet. "Are you going to coach us in those?"

I glanced down at my heels. "I'm not—"

"Oh my God!" she squealed, the ponytails atop her head moving with the three words. "You look like Vanessa Hudgens in *The Princess Switch*. Are you doing a makeover of the team?" She turned around. "Guys, come here! We have a new coach!"

"I . . ." My lips bobbed. "What?"

The rest of the kids looked over at us, but none of them seemed anywhere near as excited as María. In fact, even in the distance, a couple of them looked . . . a little scared of me. One of them even grumbled, "She doesn't look like a princess."

"Can't Coach Cam continue to coach us?" someone else said.

"I'd rather have Grandpa Moe, honestly. He lets us play games most of practice."

"I also want Coach Cam. Why did she scare him away?"

My jaw fell to the floor at that last comment.

Josie linked her arm with mine.

"Welcome to the Green Warriors, Adalyn," she said in a cheery voice that didn't match the tone of the girls' debate. "I'll show you around town when we wrap up practice. There's not much to see besides a few shops on Main Street and the Vasquez farm, which is a few miles south, but you've made an important acquaintance: me." She grinned. "And that piece of red velvet is up for grabs if you want it."

The confirmation that Green Oak was that small of a town wasn't exactly uplifting, but Josie was nice. And I wasn't used to people welcoming me with open arms. As much as I'd led a privileged life with hundreds of opportunities that had allowed me to peek into all kinds of social circles, I'd always kept to myself. It wasn't easy for me to click with people, or perhaps it was me making it hard. Either way, the truth was that, besides Matthew, I didn't have many people I considered friends.

So I wouldn't turn away her offer. Or the cake. Being friends with the mayor would come in handy—and I definitely had more curves than Vanessa Hudgens, which had a lot to do with my sweet tooth.

Unfortunately, before I could even open my mouth to accept, one of the kids playing with her phone gasped loudly, drawing our attention.

"Isn't this Miss Adalyn!?" she all but yelled, pointing at the device. All the girls drew closer. My heart tripped and my eyes widened in alarm. Josie frowned in confusion. "Holy cow." The kid's jaw dropped in shock. "Why is she beating the crap out of a giant bird?"

Well, so much for that respite.

I was on my way to bed when my phone pinged with Matthew's message ringtone.

Before the silly five-second tune he'd set for himself last time we'd seen each other was up, my phone was in my hand.

MATTHEW: Have you checked socials since we talked? Or at all?

I sat on the edge of the horrendous, and I feared infested, mattress, staring at the screen for a few seconds. We'd talked on the phone a couple of hours earlier, while I was driving back to Lazy Elk from Josie's Joint. It'd been a short call where I'd brought Matthew up to date—I had cake, possibly made a friend, Grandpa Moe is a charming old man, Green Oak is unbelievably small, there're lots of outdoorsy things, my philanthropic venture is a children's team, they already know about Sparkles, one of them wears a tutu. And to that Matthew had said, *I told you so*. Or an extended version of those four words that encouraged me to pack my things and go back to Miami. I'd hung up on him.

> **ADALYN:** I haven't been online since the airport. Much to do and reception is spotty.

The three dots jumped on the screen for the longest of moments, making me shift in place and rubbing the worn fabric of the comforter against my bare legs. Unfortunately, I'd only packed a matching set of silk sleeping shorts and a tank top—which was what I always slept in and yet another way in which I'd been uncharacteristically careless. Had I done the proper research and known my rental was going to be covered in things like antlers, dust, and coarse flannel comforters, I would have ordered the thickest, longest pajamas I could find.

> **MATTHEW:** Just keep in mind that I am sending you this because I know you would hate not knowing about it.

That made my stomach drop. He was a shoot-first-and-think-later texter.

> **ADALYN:** Why are you warning me? Just send me the link.

> **MATTHEW:** Before I send it to you I want you to promise me that you will call me the moment you start spiraling.

> **ADALYN:** I don't spiral.

> **MATTHEW:** Call it what you want.

ADALYN: LINK.

A strange, scratchy noise made me look up from my phone. I inspected the barely lit cabin, wondering if on top of everything else, I also had to deal with some . . . wild animal sneaking in.

A link popped on the screen.

I clicked and was immediately redirected to TikTok. The clip that started was familiar. I was wearing my burgundy pantsuit now packed in the suitcase under the horribly large antlers hanging on the wall, and my Louboutin heels. The memory might have been blocked or buried somewhere in my head, but I recognized the clip that had flipped my life upside down. I knew what came next. I was about to—

A techno beat started playing. Although it wasn't a beat. Not really. It was the rip of the polyester of Sparkles's costume that was being repeated—looped—to create a beat. With horror, I heard more sounds being added to the mix. My grunts. Growls. Squawky sounds that had left me and I couldn't recall. Paul's "What the fuck." All of it. And it was . . .

"Horrible," I heard myself whisper.

Appalling. Really.

Because I was a remix now. A song.

My eyes closed as I remained there, the thirty-second techno mix echoing around the cabin in a loop. I felt a burst of pressure climbing up my sternum, and a noise that sounded a lot like a sob left my mouth. But I knew it wasn't one because I didn't cry. I wouldn't. Or couldn't. So my eyes remained dry.

I reminded myself I was an unbothered queen. A queen of ice.

Then, I swallowed it all up, shook my head, pushed that pressure down, as deep and far as it would go, and returned to my messaging app.

ADALYN: Impressive.

Matthew sent one of those gifs I didn't understand. But I didn't ask this time. I was on a mission. This wasn't important, and I was brushing it off.

ADALYN: So people are in need of more productive things to do with their free time. What's new?

MATTHEW: . . .

MATTHEW: You okay?

ADALYN: I'm not spiraling, if that's what you're asking.

MATTHEW: You sure? This is a lot. It would be okay if you were . . . I don't know. Running naked into the woods screaming bloody murder just out of pure frustration or something.

I rolled my eyes.

ADALYN: That's very specific.

ADALYN: Is that how you picture someone spiraling? In the nude?

MATTHEW: I picture everyone naked. Even you. I'm a simple man with a simple enough imagination. It's Occam's razor theory.

ADALYN: That's not what Occam's razor means.

MATTHEW: You know what I mean.

I actually did.

ADALYN: Well, I'm not spiraling. Or naked.

MATTHEW: Okay. I believe you. But . . . call me if you need me, yeah?

ADALYN: Sure. Good night.

MATTHEW: . . . You're such a bad liar. Night, Addy.

Yes. I was lying about both things.

With a sigh, I locked my phone and plugged it into my charger. I rolled on the bed, incapable of shaking that strange pressure off. As much as I tried my hardest not to give it any importance, learning of the remix had affected me. The clip was still getting attention. I was still viral. I was #LadyBirdinator, for crying out loud. And the girls—the kids of the team I was supposed to manage and use to create a success story that would redeem me and buy me a ticket back to Miami—had already found out about it. Josie had laughed it off, even bought my explanation about it being an accident. But it was a matter of time before the whole town knew and saw that video.

A very specific set of green eyes popped into my mind. *I don't think you'll make it a single night there.*

I shook myself, as if that would help shove that man's face out of my head. I needed to relax if I ever wanted to get any sleep, and Cameron Caldani had the opposite effect. So I focused on loosening up my limbs and tried to keep my mind blank.

The tune of the techno remix slammed right back into me.

"God," I muttered, reaching out for my AirPods.

I put them in, grabbed my phone, and hit play on a podcast.

"Hello, my true crime lovers," the voice of my favorite podcaster started. The guy's voice wasn't as deep as Cameron's, but he had a very similar accent. Which was ironic. And unimportant. I closed my eyes and let out a breath. "In today's episode I will be taking you along with me to the wildest tundra of Alaska. So lock your doors, sit back in your comfiest chair, and let's travel back in time, to the case of the Alaska's slaughterer of . . ."

Head burrowed in the pillow, I focused on the soothing tone and rich images painted in my mind. This was an episode I'd been saving for a rainy day, but as I ventured into the story, I wasn't so soothed by that voice anymore. And the images were no longer rich and in my mind. They were spooky and disturbingly familiar. Specifically the antlers that—

Something cackled in the cabin. Or cracked. Or creaked.

I paused the episode.

I sat up very slowly and searched the shadows filling up the cabin, praying that I was imagining things. But the truth is that I'd never had a great imagination. And I was sure I'd heard something on the other side of the cabin.

Another creak echoed. This one closer.

I held my breath, the beating of my heart quickly reaching my temples. I tore my AirPods out and searched every corner and shadow again, not finding anything.

A shiver crawled down my spine at the mere of thought of an animal or—Jesus—some crazy Alaskan butcher sneaking into the cabin and watching me. So out of some stupid instinct, I closed my hands around the comforter and brought it to my chin. The fabric was so itchy that it felt like something was crawling on my skin. But it had to be paranoia speaking. I grabbed my phone and turned the flashlight on. There couldn't be—

A set of small feline-like eyes blinked from the darkness.

And at the exact same time, something moved under my ass. Underneath me.

I screamed. I jolted straight out of that bed, snatched everything on my bedside table, and ran.

"No, no, no, no, no. *No.*" I went for the first pair of shoes I found. The stilettos I'd worn today. "This wasn't part of the deal." I raced across the cabin. I was terrified and furious at the audacity of the universe to throw this on my already full plate. "I was supposed to be on the bottom," I continued, making it to the antlers and grabbing my purse from where I'd hung it. "All the things that came before were supposed to be my rock bottom. There shouldn't be more."

But there was, apparently.

And what was worse, Cameron Caldani had been right. I was not going to make it. Not even for the night.

CHAPTER SEVEN

Cameron

"*R*eckless, stubborn woman," I said, glancing out the window.

I made the effort to blink a few times, even took another sip of my coffee—French press, a terrible watery joke considering I was an espresso drinker—but I'd left my machine behind and clearly, my eyes had to be betraying me. Either that, or I'd been right all along.

I turned on my heels with one clear objective in mind—the door—but I heard Willow calling for me from the kitchen. Before coming to Green Oak, I would have assumed she was wondering why we weren't having breakfast, but the incessant mewling and calling had nothing to do with food now. Unlike Pierogi, Willow had been bitching since the first box was packed back in L.A. Ever since arriving here, she'd been very clear about who was to blame for all the discomfort she was suffering. Me. So when I crossed the living room and found her poised on the kitchen counter, right next to the French press, I knew exactly what was coming next.

"Can you please give it a rest?" I asked one of my two cats. "I can only deal with one complicated, frustrating female at a time."

She held my gaze in silence, then moved closer to the pot. Challenging me.

"Willow," I warned. But her paw came out in response. "I swear to God, Willow. That coffee is no good, but if you make me—"

She mewled, interrupting me. As if telling me, *I don't care what you do or do not think.* And sweet Jesus, a humorless laugh burst out of my mouth, because how was it possible that the cat I'd adopted years ago could remind me of a woman I'd known for less than a day?

That tiny but sneaky paw inched closer, sobering me right up. "Willow," I said. Softly, this time, pleadingly. "I know you're not happy here, but we all need to—"

Willow jumped off the counter and dashed into the hallway.

"Adapt," I finished, my eyes focusing on the trail of mud she'd just left behind. I raised my voice. "And please, stop sneaking out of the house."

Pierogi lifted his head from the arm of the couch, giving me a charitable look.

"Thanks, P," I told her.

My phone pinged from the kitchen island. I grabbed it, a glance telling me who it was—Liam, my former agent—and what he wanted—something I didn't have the energy to deal with.

So I locked the screen, slipped it into my pocket, and gave myself five seconds to regroup. Then, I stomped my way out of the house and onto the porch. I wasn't going to fool myself, a large—and loud—part of me knew that I shouldn't be involving myself in anything concerning that woman. I shouldn't even be entertaining going to her. She knew who I was, and she'd almost blurted it out to the girls.

I'd gone through almost a month of anonymity. I went on my hikes, grabbed coffee from Josie's Joint, reluctantly ran practice three times a week since the season had kicked off, and kept to myself. Coaching was already a stretch on what I had been looking for here. Peace and quiet. Silence. Nature. Nothing football—*or soccer,* I thought with an eyeroll—related. Yes, even after five years playing in L.A. I still felt a prickle when I had to call the sport I loved something other than football.

The arrival of that woman had muddled everything up. Adalyn

Elisa Reyes was a major inconvenience and I should not be walking toward her car.

I should have been going in the opposite direction. Probably move away. To a different town.

I knew she'd bring only trouble with her suits and her heels and her plans to drive the team to its full potential or some bullshit I suspected would only bring attention I didn't need or want.

And yet, I found myself crossing my yard and banging my fist on the window of her car.

Ignoring the sense of déjà vu, I waited for the woman curled up in the driver's seat to react. Her head was once again against the window, and her lips were parted, but her expression was lax with sleep. My eyes betrayed me, dipping down her body and noticing how her arms hugged her bare legs. I cursed under my breath. She was wearing next to nothing. Just some flimsy silky sleep set that left very little to the imagination.

Something deep in my gut flared.

Was she mad? September was on the mild side in this area, but at night, temperatures could decrease at least twenty degrees. She could—

Ah, for fuck's sake. I didn't care whether this woman was cold or not.

I ripped my gaze from all that skin on display and banged on the window again. Much, much harder.

She awoke with a jolt.

Her whole body jumped as she clutched her meager top, looking so disoriented and frightened that for an instant I felt bad. Me. Feeling remorseful when she was being so recklessly irresponsible.

Her eyes found me. "You again," she scoffed, her words muffled by the glass. "You scared me! What in the world do you think you're doing?"

"What am I doing?" I repeated, flabbergasted. "Better question is, what in the world do you think you are doing sleeping in your car like this? Are you mad?"

"What I do is none of your business." She turned her head, giving me her profile.

With a slow exhale, I placed my hand on the roof of the car and leaned closer. "You are camped in my yard, that makes you my business. Can you roll down the window so we don't have to yell at each other?"

"Our yard," she said, gaze on the windshield. "And you're always yelling. Glass or not."

My exasperation sparked. "Adalyn," I said, and that word alone was somehow enough for her to shake her head and grudgingly press the button.

Once the window was down, she pinned me with an unimpressed glance. "So? What can I help you with?"

My brows shot to the top of my head. "Pardon me?"

"Oh, where are my manners." Sarcasm dripped from her voice. "Good morning, neighbor. May I help you with something on this crisp and beautiful morning?" Her lips curled up in what was the phoniest smile I'd ever seen. "That better?"

I blinked at the woman. Stared, really. I was at a loss. Again. Never—not even once—in my life had anyone managed to unarm me like this woman did. And I'd met some sneaky bastards throughout my career.

In my silence, she pointed at my hand. "Is that coffee for me? If so, no thanks. Not only do I not accept things from strangers but I don't trust you."

I looked down, noticing for the first time that I had brought my mug with me. Christ. What was up with me? "I'm not a stranger." I returned my gaze to hers. "And believe me, I wouldn't care to spike your drink or whatever the fuck you're implying. I've seen you unconscious and you're just as much work as awake. If not more."

"I keep forgetting how annoying your kind are."

My kind. "English?"

"Pompous players who believe the sun rises and sets on them." A shrug of a shoulder. "And by the way? You are a stranger. The only thing I know about you is your name and that you enjoy shouting at people, specifically women, while they sit in cars." She lowered her voice. "Sounds like a lawsuit waiting to happen if you ask me."

I narrowed my eyes at her. She thought she could deflect by insulting me. "I asked you a question."

"I might have missed it with all the aggressive yelling and intrusive pounding." Her lips pursed. "Actually, you—"

"Cut the goddamn bullshit, darling."

Her shoulders hiked up. "I have a name—"

"Oh, I know that," I interjected before she sidetracked me again. "I goddamn told you, Adalyn. I told you that you wouldn't make it a night in that bloody shack. So tell me, huh? Why are you sleeping out here? In your car. I'm sure you have a good reason."

She looked at me then. Really looked, the features on her face gentling, as if my words had caught her so off guard that her walls had dropped down. In that instant, I could finally see her. The Adalyn behind that bravado, pride, and hostility I didn't understand and who managed to bring my own temper out. And even with her hair pointing in all directions and the dark circles under her eyes, it was impossible to miss two things: Adalyn Reyes was beautiful. And she was also a hot mess.

She was a beautiful hot mess of an inconvenience I wanted out of my hair.

"Sleeping out here is not safe," I pressed, hearing my voice soften. "Or smart. It's irresponsible. So if you don't want to use the cabin you booked, then leave. Pack your things and go." She paled at that, but I continued. I needed the message to be delivered loud and clear. "If you've been sent here to fill in some silly charity quota for your big-time club, lie. All right? It's easy and all the clubs do it. Make up some reports or a story and go home. Stop the pretense and—"

She threw the driver's door open, bringing my words to a stop and making me stumble back a step. She stuck half of her body out and pointed a finger at me. "Listen," she hissed, letting me know all guards were right back up. "And listen carefully, you stubborn, cocky, infuriating, and exasperating . . . curmudgeon of a man."

I frowned. "What—"

"If you think you can boss me around just because you think yourself more important than me, or because you have developed some strange superiority complex due to trauma or a small penis, then I suggest you think again."

My brows bounced up, meeting my hairline. "I don't—"

"I'm not here for you," she loud-whispered, her face growing red. "I'm here for my franchise. And I'm not a journalist who can just . . . concoct a story. I take my job seriously, and that silly charity quota is my one ticket out of here."

I opened my mouth again, but she pushed at the door, opening it even wider and smacking me in the stomach. "Jesus Christ, woman. What is with you and hitting me with that goddamn car?"

Adalyn didn't answer me, she was busy stomping out of the car—barefoot, I noticed—with a pair of shoes dangling from her fingers.

"Adalyn," I called, following her with my eyes as she walked past me. This had escalated in a way I hadn't been expecting and now I felt like a giant twat. "I'm—"

But Adalyn didn't care for what I had to say. She stopped her strut to turn and point at me with one sharp stiletto.

"Save it, because I don't care," she said, making my jaw clamp shut. "And let this get into your thick skull: this is the only place I plan to stay for the foreseeable future." She swallowed, and it was then that I noticed her chest heaving up and down. Fuck. Had I been that big of a prick? "Believe me," Adalyn continued, her voice cracking. "I wouldn't be in Green Oak if I had a say in it. I wouldn't be here if I hadn't been banished from my life like I'm disposable. So congrats, you were right. I didn't make it a night. But know that I wouldn't have slept in that car if I had any other reasonable, not-crawling-with-God-knows-what choice!" Her pitch rose, getting squeaky high. "So if my presence bothers you that much, then just act like I'm not here. Because I've got a news flash for you: I'm not going *bloody* anywhere, *mate*!"

Bloody. Mate. Was she taking the piss out of me? "Ada—"

She whirled around, making her way inside that decrepit cabin while I remained frozen in place, obtaining the answer to my two questions. Yes, she must have been mocking me and yes, I had definitely been a prick.

I closed my eyes, shaking my head briefly until I heard a thud and a yelp.

My eyelids lifted just in time to see a stiletto flying out of the cabin and landing at my feet.

A stiletto.

Walk away, I told myself again. She just gave you an easy out. Ignore her.

I squared my shoulders, downed the rest of my coffee, grabbed the flying shoe, and headed for her door.

The first thing I saw when I ventured into Sweet Heaven Cottage was Adalyn. She was still breathing heavily, her hair still very much a mess and her legs and arms on display. Once again, I couldn't stop myself from letting my gaze get a little lost in that last fact. And once again, I was honest enough to admit that I liked what I saw. I liked the curve of her hips and thighs, the sight of her bare feet, and even how her breasts moved with her breathing under that thin top. I was, after all, a living, breathing man. And she—

"I don't have anger management issues," she announced, making my gaze return to her face. "I wanted to clarify that before you ask or point it out. I really don't. I was dealing with a frustrating situation. With my shoe."

"Not to be a *bloody* ass, *mate*," I purposely said in a thick accent, throwing the words back at her to break some of the tension. "But that's what someone with anger management issues would say."

She let out a small huff, her shoulders coming down an inch. "Would you rather I take my frustration out on something else? Because I have another shoe."

"Oh, were you doing that with something in particular?"

A look was shot to her right, and it was only then when I spotted it. The massive and dated four-poster bed. I arched my brows, noticing one of the poles was hanging at a weird angle. I had to bite back a smile. A goddamn smile. "Were you perhaps using the shoe as a hammer of some sort?"

"I'm resourceful like that," she answered simply. "It was either that or taking my anger out on someone."

My eyes jumped back to her. And the mental image took shape in my head so wickedly fast that this time, I could do nothing to stop the corners of my lips from finally twitching.

Her expression turned horrified. "Oh God, no. No. I meant—"

"I know what you meant," I said with a shrug. "And I must decline. Being shanked by a little bird like you is not on my priority list." I placed the shoe I'd retrieved from outside on the floor. "Not today, at least."

She froze for an instant before rolling her eyes, but I didn't miss the way her throat and cheeks flushed. "I don't even know what that's supposed to mean. Shanked. Plus, I'm not little. Or a bird."

I took a few steps forward, dropping my mug on some eggshell-colored cabinet in what I supposed was a kitchenette. Christ. This place was in worse shape than I'd thought. "Listen, I've come in here to extend a temporary peace treaty, okay?"

She eyed me with a skeptical expression, her gaze traveling up and down my body. "Why would you do that? I didn't even apologize for yesterday."

"Are you actually sorry?"

A defeated puff of air left her. "I was having a particularly horrible day."

"Well, then. Consider your very poor and much too late apology accepted."

I ignored the sound leaving Adalyn and stepped further into the cabin. The wood creaked under my feet as I gave my surroundings a quick glance. Every surface was clean, and there were marks on the floors as if heavy furniture had been moved around. I wondered who in the world had decided to repurpose this shack into a holiday accommodation. Someone who hadn't been here, clearly.

I extended my arms. "I can see how this cabin is a problem. It would be for anyone who has minimal living standards. But I can't have you camping out in your car. It starts by sleeping in there one night, turns into two, and then by the end of the week you'll eventually be careless, leave food out and attract some wild animal."

That got her attention. "A wild animal? Like a bear . . . or something like that?"

"Black bears are not exactly rare in this area." She paled, and I took the chance to continue. "And I can't risk that. I have a family to look after, okay?" And I couldn't seem to keep Willow indoors.

"Oh," she breathed out, and to my complete surprise, her face . . . softened. Her lips parted, relaxed, and a light shade of pink filled up her whole face. "I didn't know, I never read or heard that you were married. Or had kids."

"I don't."

She looked at me like she wanted to ask about the specifics, but she only bit her lip.

I ripped my eyes off her mouth and busied myself with every tacky piece of furniture around her. "Do you think this is a scam?" I pointed with my head at the bed, although I meant the whole place. "Or just an honest-to-God crime against décor?"

"Maybe a mix of both?"

"Well, I hope whoever booked this for you is at the very least fired now."

"How do you know I didn't book this myself?"

I glanced back at her, finding her eyebrows knotted. She absently touched her forehead and flinched slightly. My voice turned hard. "Did you get that checked?"

"It's not my assistant's fault," she said, ignoring my last comment. "At least I don't think so. And it's not like I'm in a position to fire anyone right now anyway."

"The banishment?"

Instead of answering, she averted her eyes. "The cabin will be fine. This is all fine, really."

"You could have fooled me. You could have fooled that bed for that matter."

We stayed in silence for a long moment, and to my complete

surprise it wasn't charged or filled with that hasty and explosive tension that had accompanied every conversation before. I looked at Adalyn, who was quietly staring at the bed, seemingly lost in thought.

A soft hum left her, and when she spoke, I couldn't tell if she was actually realizing that. "I can't believe I used to dream about one of those when I was kid."

"You did?" I murmured, curious enough.

She seemed startled, maybe even a little bashful about her confession, but she didn't take it back. "Yes. It's too bad this one's infested."

"*Infested*?"

All of that softness vanished. "Why do you think I was sleeping in my car?"

This cabin was an atrocity, a sick joke, and I knew that, but now all that inexplicable exasperation I'd been experiencing flared back to life. Jesus. So much for that comfortable silence. "Because you're a spoiled daddy's girl who can't bear the thought of less than a five-star hotel?"

In truth, I hated saying that. But a part of me had pushed me to. A part that I didn't understand. The part that wanted nothing to do with her.

All that fire I'd seen earlier reignited behind her eyes. "You know nothing about me."

And you know too much about me, I wanted to say. But I extended my arm and held up my palm. "Give me your phone."

She blinked. "Do you even know any normal social cues? I thought I could be difficult but you're impossible."

"I surely am. Impossibly annoyed." I wiggled my fingers. "Phone. I'll text my number from yours."

"And why in the world would I want your number?"

I could think of about a hundred reasons, none of which I looked forward to, but I'd offered her a goddamn truce. And I wasn't a monster. "I'll forward you Lazy Elk Lodge's contact information when I'm back to my cabin. The one I was given. Ring them and say you're calling on my behalf if you want them to act faster. Ask them to refurbish the cottage."

Her lips popped right open, shaping a wide O.

"Say you're my assistant, if you will," I continued. "Complain about some crazy neighbor living in a toolshed and wreaking havoc. I'm sure that'll get their attention."

Her gaze jumped between my face and extended palm a couple of times.

"I don't have all day," I told her. "And I'm helping you."

"By calling me spoiled and being a smug, self-conceited p—" She stopped herself.

"Prick. You can say it out loud, darling." I stepped closer. "Now, phone."

She blew a gulp of air through her lips. "It's in my car."

"Christ," I whispered, producing mine from a pocket, unlocking it and offering it to her. "Save your number in mine then. I'll text you."

Her hand hesitated but then she snatched the phone from my grasp, her fingers grazing the back of my hand briefly but managing to make me notice the touch. Her cheeks flushed and she said, gaze cast down, "I still don't trust you. And if this is some way to play some tricks or pranks on me I . . ." She trailed off for a second, something crossing her expression. "Save yourself the trouble."

The blood in my veins froze.

"Look up at me, please," I told her, and my voice was low and deliberately hard. "Do I look like some dumb college boy to you?"

That blush turned into an intense shade of pink. She frowned but shook her head.

"Do I look like I have nothing better to do than play little pranks on you?" I stepped closer, making sure she met my gaze. She gave me another shake. "That's right. Because I might not like you, and you might not like me in return, but I promise you, Adalyn, I'm too old to waste my time in pointless things like tricking you for sport."

Her throat worked, dragging my eyes there for an instant.

I returned my gaze to hers. "I only play when there's something worth winning. So save your number in my contacts and hand over the phone. The sooner you realize this is all Green Oak has to offer, the sooner you'll be out of this town."

CHAPTER EIGHT

Adalyn

$\mathcal{M}$y Flames credentials had been suspended.

I hit the key again, balancing the laptop on my knees as I sat on the bleachers.

Your username or password do not match any user in our system.

I reentered everything again, refreshed the portal, disconnected and connected the laptop to the hotspot on my phone. Same message.

My stomach twisted.

This couldn't be happening. Not without a warning of some kind. This . . .

"Miss Adalyn?"

I looked up from that blue pop-up window that was sending waves of dread up and down my body, finding one of the kids. "María Camila Vasquez, right? You brought me the ice yesterday." Ice that hadn't stopped a section of skin from turning dark—just for a few days, Grandpa Moe had said—and had led me to cover my face in makeup this morning. Just like Cameron had predicted. Ugh.

María seemed a little confused for a second, so I pulled the roster out of the stack of files Josie had handed to me yesterday and that

I had spent all morning studying. There was information about the Six Hills Little League—named that way because the best teams of six adjacent counties took part—a game schedule, tentative dates for the teams that made it to playoffs, and the pièce de résistance: the reason why the Green Warriors had qualified. They were the only U10 soccer team in this county.

I scanned the printed list. "Yes," I said, checking the photo of the nine-year-old and glancing up at her. "María Camila Vasquez. You look a little younger in the roster, but it has to be you."

"Just María is okay," she declared, her cheeks turning pink. "Nobody calls me María Camila anymore. Except for my dad maybe. And that's only when he's really angry at me because I sneaked out to play with Brandy instead of doing my chores. He doesn't care that Brandy is lonely, and that's why I sneak out to see her." I opened my mouth but found I had nothing to say, which María took as an invitation to continue. "She kinda reminds me of Dad sometimes. I think they could be friends, but Dad is always so busy with the farm that he has no time to play with anyone. Not even me." Something seemed to occur to her. "I could bring her over if you want to meet her."

I blinked at her for a second. "Oh . . . Hmm. Is Brandy your friend?" I eyed the roster again. "I guess . . . I guess she could try out for the team if she wants, but I'd need to check the U10 guidelines to see how many players the team can have on the roster. How old is she?"

"About . . ." She stuck out her hands and counted on fingers. "Six . . . ?"

"She might be too young to try." I started shifting through the stack Josie had given me. "I must have the regulation somewhere. Hold on. Chelsea is seven, anyway. So maybe . . ."

"She's big for her age, though. When you compare her to any of the other goats."

My hands came to a halt. "Goats?"

"Brandy's a goat." María grinned. "She's also blind. And suffers from anxiety." A pause. "Hmm, maybe she's five months old and not six. I'm not sure now."

God. It took me a moment to gather myself because, how had I gotten here? To the point where I was telling a kid her anxious six- or five-month-old blind goat couldn't apply to the soccer team?

I set down the stack of papers. "I think there's no place for Brandy in the Green Warriors. Unfortunately."

María nodded, nothing but understanding behind her eyes and that smile pointed at me. In silence. For a very long time.

I cleared my throat. "So . . . Did you want something?"

"Ah, yes." Her expression brightened. "Everyone's scared of you, so they sent me here as representative of the team."

Shock and dread flashed through me.

Scared. The kids were scared of me. I pushed aside how that made me feel. "Well, that's understandable. Not everyone likes strangers and that video wasn't the best introduction."

"I like you, though," she countered. "I think you're pretty and I love your clothes. And I don't think you have a resting witch face, like the rest do."

I started to scoff but covered it with a cough. "That's very kind of you, thank you, María."

"You're welcome." María nodded, her smile splitting even wider. "I also think that we don't really need Mr. Camelback."

That time I couldn't muffle my reaction. I snorted. *Mr. Camelback.* "And why is that?"

"Because you should coach us. Just like I said yesterday. Have you thought about it?"

"Oh." My shoulders tensed. "No, no. I don't think that's a good idea. I'll look for a new coach, though." Josie had said nobody was particularly excited about soccer but there had to be someone in this town who could coach a group of children. I'd do the rest. I'd start with the parents coming to pick up the girls later today. Some had given me a few skeptical glances at drop-off, when they'd discovered Cameron wasn't around, but Josie had been here to appease them.

"I think it's the best idea ever," María insisted. "It won't be hard for you. Chelsea and I googled you and you work for, like, a real team. Our last coach was Grandpa Moe, and I'm sure you'll be much better at it than him. He's fun, but one time he called a corner kick a touchdown when Juniper sent the ball off the field."

I chewed on that information. No wonder Josie had been so keen on recruiting Cameron. "Is that what the team sent you to ask me?"

"Oh no, they sent me to talk to you about the plan to get Mr. Camomile back, but I think we should boycott the plan and do our own thing. We'll be . . . a two-person team. Like Wednesday and Thing. Oh, can I be Wednesday?"

I . . . "What?"

María's mouth opened but my phone rang.

"Hold on, this could be Miami." I fished the device out of my purse and saw my father's name on the screen. My father never called. Hope flickered in my chest. Maybe they'd realized I was needed in the office. Maybe I wasn't all that disposable. "María, how about you go back to the girls and do some warm-up drills while I get this? Maybe . . . make a line with some cones and try to jog the ball between them? I'll be watching from here."

She turned around with a cheery "Okay!" and dashed back to the group that had gathered in the middle of the field.

I looked back at the ringing phone for an instant, then picked up. "Dad—"

"*Ay mi*, Adalyn," was immediately bellowed.

"Mom?"

"Adalyn, *mi amor, dime que estás bien*," my mother all but screamed into the phone.

I stumbled back into the bleachers. "Mom, what are you doing in Dad's office?"

"Don't Mom me," she warned in that thick accent that she'd never lost. "You know how much I don't like that. Mom this, Mom that." A dramatic huff. "That's all I get after I find out that your father has kidnapped you."

"Maricela," I heard my father say in the back. "I haven't kidnapped her, Jesus. I merely—"

But Maricela Reyes was angry, and when she was, there was one thing you couldn't bring up.

"Do not bring Jesus into this!" she spat at my father. "Are you telling me you're not keeping my only daughter somewhere against her will?" she continued, and I swore, I could perfectly see her clutching her chest in outrage. "*Es mi única hija, Andrew. Mi sangre. Si mi santa abuela viera esto, nunca te lo perdonaría. Si . . .*"

And so my mother went on and on about how my father didn't know anything about the real values of blood and family. In Spanish, of course, which was my mother's default when she was upset.

"Maricela," my father pleaded on the other side of the line. "English, please. I don't understand you when you get like that."

I had to bite back the urge to defend my mother. But after years, I'd learned to stay quiet when they argued like this.

"And whose fault is that, huh?" she spat back. "Maybe if you'd ever made the effort, but no. *Nunca. Porque tú . . .*"

And so she went on again.

I exhaled long and deep, blocking out an argument I knew well. This was exactly what my father had wanted to avoid by keeping my mother in the dark. A conflict. One that always managed to find me in the middle, which was why I had agreed to his demand. It didn't matter that my parents had never been married; on occasions like this, I knew what having divorced parents was like.

"Mom," I said after a few moments. And when it went unacknowledged, I said, in Spanish, just like she always encouraged me, "*Mami, por favor.*"

As expected, that got me her attention. "I'm sorry. I just worry about you, Adalyn," she said, her voice softening and my father immediately forgotten. "Are you okay?"

"Of course I am," I lied. And because there was no point in burdening my mother with things she couldn't help with, I added, "I promise. I'm perfectly fine."

"*No mientas*, Adalyn."

Ugh. She knew me too well. "I'm not lying," I insisted, brightening my tone and feeling like a total fraud. "This is just a work trip." I had to swallow before continuing, and even that way, my voice wavered. "Everything's going great and there's nothing for you to worry about."

A thick silence followed my statement.

"See?" I heard my father tell her. "She's okay. She's also an adult, for crying out loud. You're smothering her."

I heard another of my mother's gasps, followed by rushed steps and a door closing.

"Hello?" I asked into the phone. *"Mami?"*

"Your father is being annoying," my mother announced. "Like always. That's why I never married him." She clicked her tongue. "I went into the bathroom of his office because I don't want you saying things you don't mean because he is listening."

That . . . stung. But I didn't think I had the heart to argue it. "It would mean a lot if you could trust me."

"Trust," she huffed, but it wasn't with malice. "Then why didn't you say anything? And why is your father not telling me where you are? Why did I have to come here to find out that you had left Miami?"

"What are you doing in the facilities?" I dodged. My mother never set foot in the stadium. She barely ever left Coral Gables.

"I came looking for you. After I saw that horrible, awful video. I was talking to Matthew, you know, during our weekly call and he—"

"I'm going to murder him, I—"

"Adalyn Elisa Reyes."

"Sorry," I said, even though Matthew was still going to hear about this. A gulp of air left my lips forcefully. "I'm also sorry about not telling you I was leaving. And about the video." My eyelids flickered closed for an instant. "What I did is inexcusable."

"Inexcusable." A trail of curses in Spanish I didn't catch left her mouth. "You're my daughter. There's nothing you can do that I will not excuse. And that Paul? He always had a mouth on him. What did he say to you, huh?" Something in my stomach twisted. Paul hadn't said anything. The worst he'd done was be in my way when I'd . . . lost it. "You know what? I don't even want to know. I'm going to go down to wherever he is and tell him that he's old enough to look for a real job. You know, one that doesn't involve costumes with feathers."

"Please don't," I said, biting back a groan. "And he's a performer, you know that. We pay him well for what he does."

"Too much, probably. I would like to see him in a restaurant's kitchen. Now, that's hard work. Not swaying his ass for a crowd."

"Mom." I groaned. "You used to be in the entertainment industry. You modeled. That's not so different from what Paul does."

"And I was in many kitchens before that. Ugly, filthy kitchens at that. I bet that boy hasn't lifted a finger in his life."

"I . . . There's . . ." No point in discussing this. "There's something I need to talk to Dad about. Can you please pass him the phone?"

Maricela Reyes sighed the sigh that told me she wasn't done with me. "Work. It's always work. *¿Y qué hago con los pastelitos que te traje?* I thought they'd cheer you up. The internet is so mean. The comments under your video are—"

"Kelly will love them," I interjected. I did not want to hear about what the internet was saying. "Give the sweets to her."

"Fine, I will. And I love you, okay? Call me if you need me, *¿sí?*"

"I promise," I lied again. I wouldn't need anyone but myself to get out of this.

There was some noise on the line as she returned to my father, and then, his voice cut a curt, "Yes?"

"I . . ." I started, making the mistake to trail off for a second too long.

"Adalyn, I don't have all day."

I squared my shoulders, even if my father couldn't see me. "I thought you were calling to update me on the status of . . . things there. In Miami."

"It was your mother calling." A pause. "And I remember very clearly telling you to give all your focus to the assignment."

"If there's anything that I can do from here, I—"

"You're not needed over here, Adalyn. Your assistant is handling things. And I was very specific: no remote work."

That sliver of hope was snuffed right out, leaving me with a hollow spot in the middle of my gut. "Is that why my access to the system has been revoked?"

"Yes," he answered quickly. "You'll reach out to David if there's something urgent that needs my attention. You must still have his private number from when you two . . . were involved." *Involved* seemed to be a stretch now that I'd learned what I had. "Anything that's not urgent, you will account and detail and record to—" He stopped himself with an irritated sigh. "Have you not read the memo?"

The one-page memo about the Green Warriors where it was not specified that the team was a recreational U10? I had. Now. A little too late apparently. "Yes, I have."

"Then you know what to do. We're sponsoring the team now, so think of it as an extension of the Flames. I expect to get a good story out of this. You should arrange for a few journalists to write about how much good we are doing for a rural community. Create a success story out of it." Another sigh. "This is a waste of time. Everything should be obvious to you, Adalyn."

I felt myself sink into the bleachers. Maybe it should be. "Speaking of the team, though, the, um, Green Warriors. It's . . . not what I expected." I waited for him to say something, and when he didn't I felt the need to fill in the silence. "The accommodation is also less than ideal, unfortunately. The cabin is—"

"What exactly are you trying to tell me, Adalyn?"

"That . . ." I could have said a hundred possible things. I used to be someone who worked well under pressure, so I knew I could have come up with smart, well-reasoned arguments as to why this whole thing was . . . ridiculous. Way under my paycheck. But instead I blurted, "My accommodation is subpar and I'm supposed to work with a children's team."

A bitter burst of laughter echoed in the line. "Well. You lasted all of twenty-four hours before giving up."

The words felt like a blow to the middle of my chest. And for whatever reason, my head decided to throw a very similar statement back at my face. Cameron's. *I don't think you will make it a single night there.*

"I don't blame you," my father continued. "Leaving behind the comfort of the life I've provided for you is not easy. So fine, I'll send you somewhere else. Have a pick, Underwood Holdings has enough options to keep you busy until this blows over. I always believed you'd be better suited for real estate anyway."

All the blood left my face, dropping to my feet with a swoosh. "But that's not what I want. You know that."

"What do you want then?" he asked me even though he knew the answer to that: the Miami Flames. My job. My life. Respect from him and David. He pressed, "Run back home? You can. Contrary to what your mother said, I have no intention of keeping you there against your will. But I can't give you your job at the Flames back. Your face is still dangling around like we're a bad joke."

A bad joke.

My throat dried. My heart was pounding. Everything from that day came rushing back. I felt cold and warm, all at once. "I'm not running back home. I can do this. I will fix this."

"That's what I want to hear," he said, and I hated the relief that half-hearted comment made me feel. "Now, if you don't mind, I need to go search for your mother before she wreaks havoc in the office."

And before I could say another word, the call ended.

My hand fell to my side as I blinked, staring into empty space.

I remained like that for long time, I wasn't sure if it was a minute or five. I tried to find peace in the September crisp air, slowly bringing the pounding in my chest to a normal pace, searching for the comfort of the late afternoon sun on my face. It felt good. Or as good as something could feel when one was standing on the real—seven feet under bottom—rock bottom.

A bird chirped in the distance, the sound echoing through the absolute silence surrounding me.

I frowned from my post at the bleachers.

Why were we in absolute silence?

My eyes dashed to the spot where the team had been but found no one there. No kids in tutus doing cartwheels, no incessant chatter, no one lying on the grass.

Panic entered my system in one powerful and overwhelming wave. Phone in hand, I jerked up and climbed down the bleachers at supersonic speed.

"Hello?" I called, my growing desperation loud in my voice. "Girls?"

But no one answered.

I speed-walked along the sidelines, my gaze searching every corner and edge in the facilities. Where in the world were they? I couldn't believe I'd just lost a whole team's worth of children. God. This was a new low. This was also why I wasn't fit to be their coach. I didn't belong on the sidelines and I was useless with kids. If they'd wandered out into the nearby woods or the street, I'd never forgive myself. I—

A loud noise followed by a burst of giggles came from the opposite direction, and I immediately veered that way. The supply shed? More clattering sounds followed the first one, as if all sorts of things were crashing against the ground, making me speed up and wish I wasn't wearing a pair of heeled sandals that were digging into the grass.

"Please don't be hurt. Please don't be bruised or bleeding or . . ."

I came to a stop the moment I spotted a ball rolling out of the shed. The metallic doors were thrown wide open, one of them was hanging off its hinges, and hushed voices came from inside. Another ball rolled out. Then a third. And a fourth.

Chest heaving, I ventured inside. The space was larger than it seemed—it had a tall ceiling and it was at least half the size of my cottage—and . . . all kinds of things were scattered on the floor. Vests were spilling out of cabinets. Cones were scrambled on the ground, nets filled with balls that had seen better times were strewn all over the place. There were even cardboard boxes with other sports' equipment.

It was a mess. And in the middle of it all, there were the girls.

The giggling came to an abrupt stop.

Making an effort to settle my breathing, I asked as calmly as I could, "Is anyone hurt?"

They all shook their heads.

"No bruises? No bleeding? Nothing? Everyone's whole?"

They all nodded.

Only then, I let myself relax.

The girl with the short, auburn hair, Juniper Higgins, as per the roster I had memorized, stepped forward. She hugged her middle. "Miss Adalyn, I tried to stop them, but they wouldn't listen."

"Juni!" one of them complained. "Snitches get stitches."

Juniper flushed. "It's the truth. I told you we would get in trouble. And now Miss Adalyn is looking furious."

"I'm not furious," I said. Not at them. I was angry at myself.

Someone whispered, "But she always looks like that." That seemed to get a grumble of agreement, bringing a different kind of heat to my cheeks. "Didn't you see the video?"

Something in my stomach soured.

"She's not the monster she seems on that video!" a muffled voice countered, dragging my eyes to a corner and finding María with a yellow cone locked over her head.

"Oh God. How did that even happen?" I walked to her and tried to extricate the thing off her shoulders, but it wouldn't come off. Shoot. "It's not coming out." I groaned. "Are you okay?"

"I'm fine," María answered. "See? Would a monster try to help me?"

"Butt-kisser" was murmured.

"Okay," I said. "Rule number one: no name-calling in the team, okay?" I took the reluctant group grumble as a yes and continued my attempt to free María from the cone. "And I'm not angry. Or furious. I was . . ." I pulled at the thing but it remained stuck. "Worried."

Unlike they believed, I wasn't a monster. I might not be good with kids, but I'd never forgive myself if something happened to them because of my own irresponsibility.

The same kid whispered, "That's what all grown-ups say, but we get in trouble no matter what." She turned her head toward Juniper and said more loudly, "You're so getting stitches."

"Rule number two," I dictated with a hand in the air. "No one is getting stitches."

Except maybe me. This was all my fault.

In my haste to take control of things, I'd clearly miscalculated and misjudged the situation. The fact that these were kids wouldn't make my job here easier or my workload beneath what I was used to back in Miami.

It'd probably be the opposite.

And now I had a kid stuck in a cone and a supply-room pandemonium.

Giving up on María for an instant, I braced my hands on my hips. If I wanted to make a success story, like my father had put it, out of this I didn't just need someone to look after them during practice. I needed a coach. Someone who would make a difference. Someone—

A group gasp startled me back into reality.

Then, a deep voice that drawled words in an accent I was growing very familiar with said, "What in God's name happened here?"

I whirled my head, hoping to find Cameron's eyes wide and full of horror as he took in the state of the shed. But they weren't. He was looking straight at me.

And to both of our surprise, I answered, "Oh, hi, Coach."

CHAPTER NINE

Adalyn

"Coach," the man sputtered like the word was poisonous.

I didn't blame him.

Even I didn't like the idea. But that was life. Sometimes you needed to put your big girl panties on and suck it up. Or in this case, work with the exasperating retired pro soccer player you had mistakenly fired and who happened to live next door.

Cameron Caldani held my gaze as he clutched two take-out cups from Josie's Joint. I wondered if he really was that much of a coffee drinker or if he was carrying that second beverage for somebody else. Perhaps for someone in the family he looked after, as he'd said.

My eyes flickered down, noticing he'd changed since our encounter this morning. Now, a green fleece covered his chest, and instead of sweats, a pair of trekking pants with more pockets and zippers than any normal person could possibly ever use stretched over his powerful thighs. He was also wearing boots. Outdoorsy, Gore-Tex boots. Yikes.

"What's up with cone-girl?" Cameron asked, snatching my attention away from his attire.

"I'm María!" she complained. "And rule number one is no name-calling." A muffled huff left her before she added, "Mr. Camomile."

Cameron expelled a puff of air, and in three long strides, he was by my side, freeing María with one hand while the other held the two drinks.

I rolled my eyes at how easy he made it look.

"Thanks," María muttered.

Cameron dropped the cone to the ground and turned to me. "So. Are you going to explain what this mayhem is now?"

Nope. I really wasn't. "How was your day, Cameron?" Now that he was closer, I could notice the traces of dried sweat on his temples and the way his skin was a little red from the sun. "Do anything exciting today? A hike maybe?"

His eyes turned to two thin slits. "You mean besides finding you right in the middle of another grim yet somehow unsurprising situation?"

Some of the girls gasped.

"Do you always have to be so unpleasant?" I retorted.

The girls oooh-ed.

"I don't know." He shrugged. "Do you plan on bringing anything but trouble into town?"

The girls aaah-ed.

I bent my lips upward. Not only had I no interest in this man's passive-aggressive babbling, but I couldn't forget I was a woman on a mission. "So, Coach—"

He barked out a humorless laugh. "Absolutely not."

My mouth cracked open with a complaint but suddenly Josie's head was popping over one of the metallic doors.

"Oh my God." Josie panted, leaning on the frame and bringing a hand to her forehead. "Thank goodness I found you." She was as out of breath as I'd been a few minutes ago. She was also wearing an apron with JOSIE'S JOINT in big green bold letters. "There's a code yellow."

We all blinked at her. Even the girls.

"Code yellow?" I ventured.

"The parents," she explained, her eyes going wide and panicky. "They're pissed." She looked at Cameron. "Why are you still holding that? Please me tell you are not drinking it. I told you the second *Josephino* was for her!"

Cameron's lips pressed into a flat line. "Believe me, I heard you."

Had Josie made one for me? I shot Cameron a furtive glance, but he didn't hand me the drink so—

Josie shifted at the door. "What in the world happened here? Never mind, we don't have time for that." She whirled her head, checking something over her shoulder before facing us back. "Hey, girls, how about we move this back onto the field? You can play whatever you want until practice wraps up. Yay!"

The girls cheered and immediately obeyed, streaming out.

"We're right behind you!" Josie called, sending us an urgent glance and ushering us out of the shed.

She stopped us somewhere along the sidelines, and I made sure to face the field so I'd get a clear view of the team.

Voices—adult voices that had nothing to do with the ruckus the children were producing from the grass—reached my ears. I tried to look around Josie, but she snagged my face with both hands.

"Adalyn," she said, bringing my head right in front of hers. "I need you to focus, we don't have time. Or a game plan. And we seriously, seriously, need one. This is a code yellow, probably even black." Josie's eyes landed on Cameron, and she huffed. "Jesus, Cam, why are you still holding the Josephino?" She released me, snatching the cup from a still scowling Cameron and shoving it in my chest. "Here. You'll need this."

I accepted the cup, making myself ignore the weight of Cameron's eyes on my profile. "Okay," I told Josie with a nod. "What's wrong with the parents?"

"The parents are what's wrong," Josie rushed out. "We were all at the café and it was all fine until they started talking about coming back here and interrupting practice. They have a plan. They're sending two representatives. They were saying they didn't want to"—she gestured for air quotes—"make a scene. But that's impossible when Diane is involved."

Cameron let out a grunt I didn't understand.

I kept my focus on Josie. "Make a scene about what?"

The voices grew closer, and this time, I spotted two adults, a man and a woman, over Josie's shoulder.

Josie swallowed. "They know, Adalyn. They've seen it."

CHAPTER TEN

Cameron

$\mathcal{I}$ shouldn't be here.

I should have left around the time the word *coach* had left Adalyn's lips for the first time. Way before Josie and these two other people showed up and started babbling about rules and parent associations and the well-being of the kids and a dozen other things I didn't care about.

They'd been going at it for at least twenty minutes and I still didn't understand what they were really discussing. Something about Adalyn that I didn't understand and didn't concern me, clearly. That's why I'd used the time to keep an eye on the girls while half of them played around and the other half . . . recorded shit on their phones. Dances. I didn't even know what for. I hated smartphones, social media, and anything that was remotely related.

I looked down at my empty cup.

Bloody Josephino.

That's what had started all of this. All I'd wanted was to pop into the café for a quick cup after my hike. I should have refused to deliver the extra beverage Josephine had prepared—without thinking of telling me, naturally—for Adalyn. But Josephine had a way of . . .

sneaking up on people. She threw you a couple of questions and next thing you knew, you were coaching a kiddie team or delivering drinks.

She would have made a great sports agent.

". . . And that is why my good friend Cam"—the mayor of the town patted my arm—"is right here."

"Unfortunately," I muttered. I'd tuned out a while ago but being stuck here was definitely unfortunate.

Josie cackled, startling me and making me notice that every eye in the small group was on me. The two parents—a woman with quite the bright hair and a tall man in red rimmed glasses—were giving me a once-over. Adalyn was, too, and not for the first time. I needed a shower. I was sweaty, my clothes and boots covered in dust, and I was done with whatever this was.

"Well," the woman said, that head covered in a blinding shade of yellow still moving up and down my body. "He is tall." I blinked at the observation. "And athletic. Also European."

"He's the whole package, really!" Josephine clapped. Clapped. Christ. "And he was—and is—doing such a great job with the girls. You know that."

"Were you training the team dressed like that today?" Diane asked. "I can't recall seeing you in anything like this when I've dropped off Chelsea in the past."

I didn't even look down at myself. "I—"

Josie cut me off with a pitchy laugh. "Oh no. He just got here! Cam had to take today off to take care of . . ."

"His chicken," Adalyn offered quietly.

My what?

"Cam loves his animals," Josephine agreed. "The animals love him in return. And you know who else adores Cam? The girls."

I arched an eyebrow. "What in the world are you—"

Josephine cackled again, silencing me. "Ah! Kids. We love 'em. Anyway, you trust Cam, and that's why he will be the perfect complement to Adalyn." My brow climbed even higher. "He will take care of the technical side of things, like practice, games, all that stuff. While Adalyn focuses on the more practical things. Did I tell you Adalyn is a real-life boss-lady? She's an exec for a team in in the big leagues!" She set one hand on my shoulder and one on Adalyn's. "They already are the perfect team. Look at them!"

I wasn't exactly comfortable with them studying me up close after that statement, but if no one had recognized me in weeks, I wanted to believe I was safe. So I shook my head and shot Josie a bland look, catching Adalyn's face as she stood beside her. Her gaze was downcast. I frowned.

The woman in front of us huffed. "I don't know. I trust him but I still have reservations about her. I'm very concerned for Chelsea, and the rest of the girls, for that matter. They are third and fourth graders, and very impressionable at this age. Trust me, I'm the president of the PTA for a reason. I would know these things."

So she'd said. About a hundred times.

I didn't even know what they were so worked up about. Something about not really knowing Adalyn, something they had *seen* online and not trusting *someone like her* with the kids, whatever that meant. They were constantly talking around whatever the real issue was. Not that I wanted to know. My only concern now was Josephine's statement about Adalyn and I being a team. The woman had fired me. Several times in the span of a few minutes. Me, as if I wasn't a pro footballer who was doing the team a favor. Which she apparently knew. She'd dismissed me as if she had a problem with exactly that.

I had no interest in finding out what the specifics of that problem were.

"And as the vice president of the PTA," the man added, adjusting the glasses on the bridge of his nose. "I share that concern. My husband and I had a long talk with our Juniper after we found out about the whole . . . ordeal and while we support the free expression of, you know, emotions, we still think it's not setting a good example for the girls."

"My husband—" The woman stopped herself, her cheeks turning red. "Ex-husband, heard Chelsea saying something about wanting to switch from ballet to . . . kung fu or something outrageous like that. Do you know how unsettling that is? My daughter is a peaceful, delicate soul and now she wants to fight. Fight!"

I eyed Chelsea in the distance, with a black tutu over her clothes, furiously pirouetting while María clapped. That kid had no intention of dropping ballet.

"Diane. Gabriel." Josie's smile turned wider, tenser. "I understand everything you're saying, I do. But can we please make the effort to put ourselves in Adalyn's shoes? I think she's been chastened enough for today. Don't you think?"

I looked in the direction of the woman in question. The bags under her eyes seemed more noticeable than earlier today. My eyes flickered down her body, noticing how she was tapping her fingers around the cup. I didn't think she'd touched her Josephino.

"Give me a chance," Adalyn appealed to the group. "I understand where you're coming from, but I promise you, I will be fully dedicated to the girls." She hesitated. "I will take the team to new heights—"

"With Cam," Josephine added.

Adalyn's cheeks flushed. "With Cam," she agreed quietly. Too quietly. "There's also an MLS team backing me up. That means new kits, training supplies, sponsored gear . . . Anything you can think of. There is a budget allocated to spend—"

"Do you think you can buy us?" Diane sputtered. My eyes flashed to the woman, zooming in on her face.

Adalyn's voice didn't waver. "No. Of course not."

Diane bristled anyway. "I know your kind. You saunter into small places like ours, in your fancy clothes and cars, wanting to make big changes." She took a step in Adalyn's direction. "This has happened before. To the Vasquezes' farm. So, no. I don't trust you and your money, missy!"

"Diane!" Josephine exclaimed. She set a hand on Adalyn's arm. "Diane doesn't mean that. I promise you she's just passionate about the kids and the community. She unfortunately gets a little heated sometimes."

Gabriel murmured something that sounded a lot like, "Here we go again."

And as if on cue, the woman waved a hand in the air. "I am not heated." She walked around Josephine and pointed a finger at Adalyn. "And if anyone knows about getting heated it is this woman right here. Next thing we know, someone's hurt or . . . *decapitated*."

A strange sound left Adalyn in response.

Before the woman could say another word, I found myself between her and Adalyn, holding a crumpled empty coffee container in my fist. I willed my fingers to relax, then pushed it inside a pocket on my pants.

"I'm about done listening to this," I announced to the group. Diane's head tilted back, lips bobbing wordlessly at me. I sent a quick sideways glance at Josephine. "So, if we're finally through with this nonsense, I'd like to wrap things up and go home."

Josephine's eyes were slightly wide, but her lips were parted with a big grin that made her look deranged. She looked straight at me as I remained in the exact same spot.

"Christ. What now?" I asked.

She shrugged, that smile frozen in place. "Nothing. And yes, we're done here." She made a little pause I didn't miss before adding, "Coach Cam." Then, she was on the move, grabbing both Diane's and Gabriel's arms. "Okay, you two. How about I treat you to a delicious slice of raspberry tart? On the house, of course."

And before I could blink, I was watching them walk along the sidelines in the direction of the other parents that had gathered to pick up their kids and were all looking this way.

I sighed, forcing my shoulders to relax and bracing myself for whatever show of hostility was waiting for me.

But when I faced Adalyn, her gaze was cast down again. As if the toes that I'd already noticed peeking out the hem of her pants held all the answers in the universe.

"You didn't like the Josephino?" I heard myself ask.

Her fingers tapped on the container. "I don't drink coffee after noon."

"Well," I breathed out. "I thought it tasted like shite, if it makes you feel any better. You're not missing anything."

She huffed out a sound that I would have interpreted as a laugh if it hadn't been so bitter.

Oddly enough, Adalyn remained quiet. Inexplicably, I felt the need to test her, so I took the drink from her and had a sip despite my last words.

No smart remark came. Instead, she tugged at one of the sleeves of her blouse, lost in thought. I'd expected her to call me on my bullshit. There was something off with her. There had been since Diane and Gabriel had showed up.

"Have you googled me?" she blurted out. "You have my full name from the confirmation email I showed you, so you could have." A pause. "Have you, then?"

My brows knotted. "Why would I google you?"

"Right." Something wavered on her face but she soldiered on. "You didn't need to intervene back there, by the way. I could handle Diane on my own."

I bet she could. Any other day, maybe. Right now, Adalyn was a shadow of the woman who had been busting my balls since her arrival in town. "Odd way to say thanks," I told her, earning a slightly harsher look from her. "Not that I should explain myself, but it wasn't about you."

I had a low tolerance for bullies, which had gotten me in more than a few scuffles that had made the press rounds throughout my career, and that mother had been a step away from turning into one. I didn't care that she was just a concerned parent and not some cocky winger or forward running in my direction and spitting ugly words about my *nonna*.

Adalyn gave me a curt nod, leaving it at that. "I guess we should address the elephant in the room then."

"Those impractical shoes you're wearing?"

"I can pay you," she said, ignoring my jab and looking at her feet again. "For your time. The budget is smaller than what I'd like and

I'm not exactly on good terms with the . . . CEO of my club back home, but I have resources. I could—"

I watched my hand land on her forearm. The warmth of the skin beneath the fabric of the blouse seeped into my palm. Her head snapped up. "What in the world are you talking about now, Adalyn? You don't even want me here."

"What I want doesn't matter," she countered, and I retrieved my hand with a huff. "Apparently, there's no me without you. The parents won't trust me without you here to interact with the girls. That is, if Josie convinces Diane not to start a crusade against me or something."

My jaw clenched.

She continued, a new emotion fleeing in and out in record time, "The girls are terrified of me, Cameron. But they like you. They listen to you. Can you please forget I said that thing about firing you?" Her voice did an off thing. "You'll be doing them a favor, not me."

My teeth were pressed so tight, I could feel them gritting against each other. I let my gaze roam all over her, trying to get a goddamn read on this woman.

"This whole thing the parents were so worked up about," I finally said, piecing some of what I'd heard together. "Does it have anything to do with your banishment?"

She gave me a nod. And I was surprised, almost impressed by the fact it wasn't a shy one. There was nothing but determination in that nod.

What the fuck had she done to land herself here?

"I breached the conduct clause of my contract," Adalyn said, providing me with the answer. "I . . . got physical. With someone. I messed up."

I considered her words for an instant. "Were you provoked?"

Her brows knotted.

"Was there a good reason for you to do it?"

That determination wavered, but when she said yes, it was a firm, curt word. "There was."

"All right." I turned around, spotting a mostly empty field, and the few girls behind already with an adult. "Let's go, I have something in the boot of my car for you."

We started toward my parking spot.

"So does that mean you're in?" Adalyn pressed, catching up with my pace. "Also, you really need to work on your social skills, the line about the boot of your car was a little creepy."

I ignored the pang of relief I felt at seeing her snark was back. "Sure thing, darling."

"Still not your darling," she quipped.

"Still don't care."

I was speed-walking at this point, and she was almost breaking into a jog, but even in those silly shoes, she was still keeping my pace. I was impressed.

"So?" she insisted, as we crossed the lot outside the Warriors' facilities. "Cameron?"

I headed for my 4×4, throwing open the boot and extracting the box. "Where's your car?" I turned toward a wide-eyed, and a little out of breath, Adalyn. Her lips bobbed. "I would love to finish here and finally jump in the shower, so if you don't mind."

Adalyn blinked at me and when I started moving, deciding I didn't need her to find her car, she stopped me with a hand. Just like I'd done earlier, her palm settled on my forearm. Only this time I couldn't really feel the warmth of her skin through the fabric of the fleece I had on.

"Cameron," she said slowly, making me realize I'd been looking at her hand. I met her gaze. "What's this?"

"A box."

"What's in the box?"

"Not my patience, that's for sure." She shot me a glance. "I said I had something you could use."

"Can you please stop answering all my questions with cryptic messages I need to decipher?"

"Camping supplies," I explained, already regretting this. "Inflatable mattress, pump, sleeping bag. I think it'll be obvious when you take it home and open it. Now, where's your car?"

Adalyn's brown eyes widened. "Oh no." Here we go. "I'm not—I am—"

"You're not what? Sleeping on an inflatable mattress?" Her lips pursed in a tight pout. "Is the idea of sleeping on the floor not good enough for the princess? You know where the exit to the highway is, then."

"I'm perfectly okay with that," she remarked, voice turning to ice. "And don't call me a princess, you don't even know me." Her head shook. "One thing is admitting out loud that I"—she struggled with the word—"need you to make this work. And that I'm sorry for dismissing you so hastily, okay? Because I am. That's why I will go as far as unearthing funds for—"

"Christ. I don't want money."

That made her pause. "What do you want then?"

"For you to stop being so absolutely exasperating." She frowned, like she didn't understand. Jesus bloody Christ, she was going to drive me up the closest hill. "Take the goddamn box. The mattress in your cabin is infested, Adalyn."

Her chin lifted. "I'm not accepting charity from you. I can handle myself. Unlike everyone thinks, I'm not some pampered brat who can't survive in this place. I just need you to coach the team."

"Charity?" I couldn't help but hiss. Her expression wavered, but there was something in her face. Something that had to be motivating her to act so . . . proud. Distrustful of me. Thing was, I didn't care. "This is not goddamn charity, Adalyn. It's human decency."

Her face hardened, turning to smooth-looking marble if not for the pink flushing her skin.

Frustration, heavy and thick, solidified inside my chest. "I'm not giving you this out of the goodness of my heart, believe me. I would love nothing more than to see you pack your things, leave town, and never look back."

"That's honest," she deadpanned. "And a little repetitive."

I heard the sound that snuck up my throat. "You want more honesty?" My eyes roamed all over her face, finding nothing but more of that hardness. "You've brought me nothing but trouble since you arrived in this town. You've broken every one of my attempts at the peace and normalcy I came looking for. And you haven't even been here for a goddamn week." Her lips twisted, urging my next words. "I don't know you, you're right. But guess what? You don't know me either, darling."

I dropped the box at her feet and something in that façade broke.

I stepped back. "But you'll soon learn I'm not a very charitable man. I am selfish. Proud. And a little mean when I have to be." My voice dropped. "So do as you please with the fucking box, but don't think I'm helping you with shit."

Turning around, I headed for the driver's door. I was so done with that woman. I was—

"I'll tell everyone," she said from her spot at the rear of my truck. "If you don't coach the girls. I'll tell the whole town who you are."

CHAPTER ELEVEN

Adalyn

"You WHAT?"

I lowered my voice to a whisper. "I blackmailed him. I think."

"You think?" The pale blue in Josie's eyes flashed with confusion. "But . . . How? When? WHY?"

"Let's see." I held up a finger. "I threatened to expose him to the whole town." A second one. "Last night, right after you left with Diane and Gabriel." And a third. "Because I'm desperate and I . . ." A shiver crawled down my arms. "I need him, so I panicked. The words came out of my mouth before I could stop them."

Josie's eyes remained that full-moon size for a long moment. I was almost sure she'd stopped breathing. That is, until she threw her head back and laughed.

"I just confessed to a crime." I blinked at her. "The second one I've committed in the span of a few days. Maybe even the third, if you count me hitting Cameron with my car." My throat worked. "That's it. I'm going to jail."

"Wait, wait," she said breaking off the cackling. "You did what to Cam?"

"I . . . I bumped into Cameron," I confessed. "With my bumper.

Right after I almost murdered his chicken. I also kind of momentarily fainted and he— It doesn't matter. I didn't say anything because I thought you'd be horrified."

Another burst of laughter left the woman in front of me. People scattered around the café turned at the noise. All right, maybe Josie wasn't horrified.

"Oh God," she wheezed out, patting her chest like that had been the best joke she'd ever heard. "I wish there was a way I could get Lazy Elk's security footage of that exact moment."

I felt myself pale. Not another incriminating video. "There's a security camera?"

"Oh, I don't know, but wouldn't that be great?" She shook her head. "If there is, though, I wouldn't really have a way to get that tape. The property belongs to a hospitality company of some sort. They were the ones who renovated the big cabin last year." A shoulder was shrugged. "Ah, how I wish I had the money to make my place look like that."

"I've been trying to get a hold of the owner actually." I'd gone as far as doing as Cameron suggested—which I'd never admit out loud—and pretended to be his assistant when I called the managing agent. "With no success."

"Oh, is there something wrong with the cottage? I could try to help if you need me to."

Words that had been thrown at me by two different men in the last twenty-four hours rang in my ears.

Leaving behind the comfort of the life I've provided for you is not easy.

Is the idea of sleeping on the floor not good enough for the princess?

"The cottage is perfect," I said. "It was about something else. Invoices. I need them for my travel expenses."

"That makes sense," Josie said, pushing a tray in my direction. "Try a macaron. It'll erase that look from your face." She pointed at the green one. "Pistachio is my favorite. Plus, it might be the last one you ever get to eat. You know, if they lock you behind bars for all those nasty, gnarly crimes."

"It isn't funny," I deadpanned. But she chuckled and I snatched one either way. Before bringing it to my lips, though, I ventured a question I hadn't had the courage to ask. "How are you so okay with all of this? With what I just told you about Cameron but also with the video of me . . . being so uncivilized."

Josie's permanent smile wavered for what probably was the first time since I'd met her. "I've been engaged four times," she told me. "And never married. I know a hurt woman when I see one."

I studied the woman in front of me. Her kind and beautiful features were framed by waves of light brown hair. In the short time I'd known Josie, she'd been so relentlessly optimistic and happy that her confessing to being hurt—four times at that—shocked me. Not by the fact she'd been engaged numerous times before thirty, but by how her inner light had dimmed just now.

"My parents split before I was born," I offered. "He proposed when they found out my mom was pregnant, but they never married. I have the suspicion they still love each other, even when my mom is relentless in her reminders of how happy and blissful her life is—not despite, but because she never married." I felt my cheeks warm. I never talked about my parents' relationship. And just like that, I heard myself say, "I've only ever been in one relationship. At some point, I thought he'd propose, but he broke things off with me instead. It never hurt me, not like it should have. So I never resented him." That sensation right at the bottom of my stomach stirred. "Until I heard him saying some things about me a year later."

Josie nodded her head, only the remnants of that stern expression hanging around her features. "This is why I like you," she said, her smile returning full force. "Everyone else would have asked for the story. What caused those four engagements to end. But you didn't."

My chest warmed in a way I wasn't used to. Josie liking me was important. I needed an ally in Green Oak and I . . . liked this.

"So," she resumed, popping a macaron into her mouth. "I have questions." Her eyebrows arched. "First one is, did Cam show up at practice today?"

Something in the middle of my chest twisted at the reminder.

"He did. He stormed in and out, not even sparing a glance my way." I'd thought I would appreciate him ignoring me but I hadn't. I felt horrible over what I'd done. But I also needed him, so how was I supposed to take my words back and have him stay? "Diane was also there, by the way. She dropped off Chelsea and kept watch from her car."

"Expected. But I told you he'd be back," Josie pointed out with a tilt of her head.

I checked the nearby tables, confirming Josie's Joint was still mostly empty. "He believes I blackmailed him, Josie. Of course he was back."

She shrugged, grabbing another macaron and chewing on it slowly. "You forget he was coaching the team before. And I don't know Cam super well, but I know enough of him. He probably took the whole thing about you b-wording him as playful banter."

Not that again. "We don't banter, trust me." And also, "B-wording him?"

Josie chuckled. "That was cute, wasn't it? It's like we're back in high school and we're two girlfriends whispering about going behind the bleachers with a crush." She grimaced. "I don't think you should go behind the bleachers, though. The structure is really old and I should probably ask Robbie to have a look at it. He's María's dad and Green Oak's unofficial handyman."

"Sure, I'll try not to sneak behind the bleachers until Robbie checks them," I conceded in a dry tone.

"Unless the proposition comes from someone . . . interesting," she countered, lips curling in a way I didn't like. "Someone banter-y who has jokingly been b-worded like—"

"Nope," I cut her off. "Not even a possibility."

"Fine." Josie rolled her eyes. "But—"

"So, games start in a week?" I deflected by asking even though I already knew. I knew everything there was to know by now.

Her face scrunched up with thought. "Oh! You could approach him to talk about that. Make a little small talk to smooth things over. First team to beat is the Grovesville Bears and they'll be a tough cookie to crack." That got my attention. "You don't even need to wait until next practice on Monday. Just go to him and say—" Josie's words came to a stop. "Code yellow."

My brows furrowed. "Why would I—"

"Code yellow," Josie insisted through a toothy smile, her eyes jumping quickly behind me. "Code bright-Diane's-hair-yellow."

"You need to stop calling for codes I don't—"

The bell on the café's door rang.

The sound of heavy footsteps followed.

"Act cool," Josie whispered. But one of her eyes started twitching.

I opened my mouth to ask her if she was okay but before I could, a large hand was flying in front of my face.

A palm that ended in five long and strong fingers—some crooked, and a pinky wearing a signet with a C—placed something right beside the macaron tray.

I waited, but Cameron didn't speak.

"Odd way to say hello," I finally said, feeling the weight of Cameron's gaze on the top of my head. I nodded at the flyer in front of me, still not looking at him. "What's this?"

Nothing came from him.

"That's Green Oak's activity brochure," Josie whispered loudly, leaning in. "It has the full list of seasonal activities on offer. There's sports, our end of summer celebration by the lake, arts and crafts, our fall fest, the—"

I shot her a glance, and she answered me with a complicit glance. "Well, this is great. But I don't see why it's been thrust in my face."

Instead of talking, Cameron let out one of those throaty noises that made him sound like someone straight out of the Paleolithic era.

I felt my throat work. "I don't need this."

"Oh, you do," he finally said, and it was his tone—or maybe his voice—that brought my gaze up. Green eyes were pointed right at me and he looked so . . . cocky. Smug. "I signed you up," he announced. "For every single activity on the agenda from this weekend to the end of fall."

The chair I'd been sitting on scratched the floor of the café, the noise making me realize my body had just sprung up. "You did what?" I squeaked.

Cameron's lips twitched beneath that beard I was growing to resent so much. It made getting a read on him so hard. "Diane—you remember Diane, right?" he asked, and I blinked away my reaction to that name. "Besides being president of the parent association, she also happens to be council secretary. And guess what she's in charge of?"

"Some of the organizational tasks," Josie answered for me, making us both glance at her. She was holding the brochure. "Actually, I remember very vividly telling her not to use this font. God, the color scheme is also wrong. I . . ." She trailed off the moment she looked up. "Oops. Please, continue."

My attention returned to the man to my left, finding his eyes on me. Again. "She was so concerned about your involvement in the community," he said, shrugging those wide shoulders and daring to look . . . flippant. "I thought to help you tilt the balance in your favor."

"You thought to help," I repeated, and when his eyes dipped to my mouth, I realized I was pressing my lips so tight, I probably gritted the words. "How generous of you, Cameron."

"Some would say *charitable*," he shot back calmly, making my cheeks heat at the reminder of last night's conversation. "I wouldn't feel obligated to go to any of these, though."

Josie cleared her throat. "Diane is actually a little bit of a . . . stickler for rules? She kind of hates people signing up and then not showing up. Last year Grandpa Moe accidentally signed up for our fall fest worm race." I glanced at Josie with horror. "You should have seen Diane when Grandpa— Not helping? 'Kay. I'll tell you about it later, though. It's a fun story."

"I'd love to hear about it," Cameron piped up in a serious tone. "Adalyn, too, I'm sure. She's signed up for that, too, after all."

My head whirled in his direction. "I—" I was mad. Extremely frustrated. But I deserved this. I . . . "I'm a big fan of worms, actually."

Cameron tilted his head, studying me, and the motion made me notice a dark spot peeking out of the neckline of his thermal. Right above the right side of his collarbone. Ink. It had to be—

"Oh hey, Diane!" Josie blurted out suddenly. My whole body stiffened. Could I please catch a break? "We were just talking about you and the wonderful brochure you put together. Wow, this year looks better than ever."

I ripped my eyes off Cameron Caldani's collarbone and looked over at the mayor of Green Oak with an obvious question: *What are you doing?*

Josie shot me a quick glance: *Trust me.*

It was either that or storm out of here, so I braced myself for the worst and watched how Diane crossed the distance to our table.

"Thank you, Josie," Diane said, after a curt hello and a skeptical look in my direction. "I took some creative liberties with it this year. I'm particularly proud of the font."

"Which is stunning," Josie agreed. And boy, she was such a horrible liar. It was painful to watch. "You know what else we were talking about? The girls' soccer team."

Diane frowned. I did, too. And Cameron . . . Well, he was now scowling in the general vicinity of the conversation.

"All right," he grunted, taking a step back. "This is my cue to lea—"

"Love," Josie finished for him. "This is Cam's cue to finally acknowledge how much he's loving working with the team. And Adalyn. And—"

"And the activities," I blurted out. My eyes widened at my own words. "So much that he also wants to sign up. Right along with me."

Cameron's gaze fell so heavily on me that I could swear I felt my skin heating up under all that silent hostility.

Oh God, what was I doing?

"A team bonding exercise!" Josie squealed with a clap. "To build their camaraderie and trust. How FUN. Now that's what I call dedication. To the girls, of course."

As if some strange kind of vengeful self-destructive autopilot had been switched on, I asked, "What do you say, Coach?"

His lip started to twitch.

And I stared at him, feeling sick to my stomach over what I was doing. What I had done. God, ever since Sparkles I'd been unhinged. But this man . . . There was something about him that made me spring up on guard and attack before he could hit first, as if—

Cameron's mouth bent, one of the corners moving upward and giving way to a smirk.

Even with all that facial hair, it was obvious. Visible. Right there, on display. And he didn't even look amused. No, he looked . . .

It was in that moment that my memory decided to throw back at me something he'd said.

I only play when there's something worth winning.

Oh God. Oh no.

Had I . . . just given a highly competitive man like Cameron Caldani a reason to take me down?

CHAPTER TWELVE

Adalyn

*G*oat yoga.

With baby goats.

And Cameron Caldani. In workout pants and a skintight long-sleeved thermal.

This was the first activity on Green Oak's fall brochure—or how I imagined Cameron referred to it in the privacy of his mind: small-town activities that will guarantee Adalyn's demise. That was why I knew the brochure like the back of my hand. Just like with the Green Warriors, I was on the quest of never being blindsided again, so I could recite every detail of every activity scheduled from this weekend to the end of fall.

Number one being Green Oak's Goat Happy Hour, referred to as GOGHH, taking place the last Sunday of every month at noon in the barn located on the south entrance of the Vasquez farm.

My quest also included the man I was up against, so now, I also knew everything public there was to know about Cameron Caldani. Born in the outskirts of London, to an English mother and an Italian father. Signed his first contract at the age of seventeen with a small team and flourished as one of the best goalkeepers in the Premier League. He went on to play for clubs based in London, Manchester, and Glasgow and was called twice for England's national team early on in his career. Five years ago, when his prominence started fizzling out, he made the jump across the Atlantic and came to the US to play for the L.A. Stars. Until a couple of months ago, when he announced—in a rather out-of-the-blue manner—that he was hanging the gloves. For every team, he's worn the number thirteen kit.

The latter I'd already known. Number thirteen was a rare choice for a keeper, but who I was to judge?

I was prepared. I'd even run to Outdoor Moe's and gotten myself suitable clothes for yoga. Leggings and the only tank top he'd had in stock in a women's size. It had SOMEONE IN GREEN OAK LOVES ME printed on the front, which didn't ring exactly true, but I couldn't come to GOGHH in a suit. I had, however, come here in heels. But it was okay. This was meant to be done barefoot—I assumed. And I was equipped with data, knowledge, leggings, and a shirt with a dubious advertisement. I was ready to show Diane and everyone in Green Oak the civil, responsible, and absolutely not unhinged person I was.

One of the baby goats bleated, startling me into the present and making my eyes gravitate to my right.

Okay, perhaps I wasn't completely prepared. But I don't think anyone could have been for the sight of Cameron Caldani standing barefoot on a pink mat, with the sun shining down on his outlined pecs.

Not even the dozens of pictures I'd browsed.

Accidentally.

Sort of.

Turned out, Cameron was on the reserved side of the spectrum where players were concerned. No major ad campaigns, barely any interviews, and hardly a picture of him with anything that wasn't the full uniform, training gear, or a suit. There wasn't a single picture of Cameron shirtless—which I hadn't been looking for—that could have prepared me for that pec outline I was seeing right now.

With a shake of my head, I faced forward, spotting María in the distance as she walked in the direction of the group that had gathered for GOGHH. She was carrying a goat in her arms. One that wasn't as young as the ones currently bouncing and swirling around the mats and definitely too big for María's arms. Her eyes found me, and she tried to wave a hand at me, only managing to drop the goat to the ground.

I heard—and made the effort to ignore—Cameron's grunt from my side. Exactly where sneaky Josie, who happened to moonlight as yoga instructor in addition to café owner and mayor, had placed him. *This is what we always do at GOGHH,* she'd said with a twitching eye. *I personally assign all the spots.* She'd been full of it.

"Hi, Miss Adalyn!" María squealed, suddenly by my side. "Miss Josie doesn't let me participate in adult activities, not even when they're right here on my farm, but I wanted to introduce you to Brandy."

The goat at María's feet bleated.

Oh. "Brandy," I said. "The six-month-old goat who is blind and suffers from anxiety."

"That's her!" she confirmed. "I knew you'd remember her. Do you want to pet her?"

"I . . ." Really didn't. "Sure. Maybe in a little while. Yoga should be about to start."

"Oh wait, you know what? I can leave her here with you, you can do yoga together. And after you're done, I'll be back so we can hang out." I watched her eyes shift to a spot to my right. Her expression changed. "Hi, Coach Camelback, I'd also invite you to hang but you don't pass the vibe check. You could hang out with my brother, Tony, though, he's not cool."

I had to press my lips to suppress a snort.

"Thanks, María," Cam drawled.

"María?" Josie said from the front of the group. "I love you, honey, but you know the rules and GOGHH is about to start. So . . ."

"Sorry, Miss Josie!" María turned around, all that messy dark hair bouncing with the motion. "See you later, Miss Adalyn," she said over her shoulder. "Take care of Brandy for me! Oh, and don't make super sudden noises? They freak her out and she starts pooping all over the place!"

My eyes widened at that last piece of information.

The goat bleated in what I interpreted as confirmation.

I looked down, finding her slit-shaped eyes directed at me. "That's, um, okay. Brandy." She took a step my way, and I forced myself to smile at her in case she could sense my energy. I softened my voice. "We will be fine. No freaking out, okay?"

A snort came from my right. And when I glanced in the direction of the sound I found Cameron—and his stupid skintight thermal—with his eyebrows up. My smile fell.

"So that really is your smile," he said, shifting his gaze forward. He lifted his arms, stretching the length of his body and bringing my attention to new muscles that were being delineated by the fabric of his shirt. I swallowed. "Yeah, no wonder."

Making an effort to rip my eyes off his chest, I settled them on his . . . left ear. "No wonder what? There's nothing wrong with my smile." I returned my attention to Josie, who was leading the group through a stretch. "I was smiling for Brandy, not you. And she liked it just fine."

"Isn't Brandy blind?" he asked.

My cheeks flushed. But I lifted my arms in the air, drawing an arch in the air, just like Josie was doing. I was going to ignore Cameron and be my best-behaved self. Civil. Calm. A through-and-through GOGHH lover. I'd never done yoga, but how hard could it be?

"All right, guys," Josie's calming and commanding voice sneaked into my ears from her post at the front of the group. "I want you to inhale . . ." She trailed off, taking in a loud and noisy breath through her nose as she lifted her arms up in a graceful motion. "And now . . . exhale." She released both arms with her breath, letting them draw a perfect semicircle in the air as they fell. "And we fold forward."

I gaped as everyone followed along, heads and torsos disappearing from my sight. Diane and Gabriel and some of the team's other parents were here. They all had their hands on their mats. Including Cameron.

Yes. Cameron Caldani, who was a six-foot-two mountain of lean and firm-looking muscle.

I gave it a shot and . . . my fingers didn't even reach my ankles.

Okay. Maybe yoga was going to be a little hard.

Josie cleared her throat, catching my attention. She smiled, giving me an encouraging nod as she guided the group through a third repeat of the same exercise. I looked down at my legs, bending my knees a few times, as if doubting the flexibility of the leggings. I lowered myself, arching my back again. But . . . it didn't feel right. Muscles pulled in the wrong places. Like . . . my ears. Or my butt.

I craned my neck, my eyes unfortunately landing on Cameron, who was now upright. Just like everyone else. I sprung up.

Josie moved on to a new stretch, and one more time, I was incapable of following. I let out a loud sigh of frustration, and Brandy, who had camped at the foot of my mat, bleated. I gave her an apologetic look. "Just a little frustration. No need to get anxious, okay?"

Just as if I'd developed some new and useless sixth sense, I felt Cameron's eyes on my profile.

Mood plummeting, I turned my head, and just like I had known, those two deep green eyes were on me. Intently. Keenly appraising all the ways I was doing this wrong. It was impressive, really, the ability of this man to do that while his head hung so low between his legs.

Contrary to me, the man was flexible. And that position in particular was making every single muscle on his legs and arms stretch and flex and . . . pop. So much that it was impossible not to stare. Biceps, triceps, quadriceps, calves, even his ass as it stuck out in the air. It was a flexed-muscle-fest, and that stupid thermal he was wearing had no business being so tight.

My face shouldn't have been feeling so warm, either. I—

Cameron's eyes met mine again, and I cast my gaze away.

What in the world was I doing ogling him like that?

I refocused on Josie's voice as it transitioned from whatever pose that had been to something that sounded like some Slavic dessert. Parlova? Pablova? I didn't know, but I lifted an arm, flexed a knee, and looked down, trying my best to mimic Josie's stance. Just as I was on my way to do a very awkward version of the Parlovskana—which included a strange leg flex—something ran into my side.

The leg supporting my weight was kicked from under me and I was knocked over.

Almost. Because hands closed around the top of my arms, securing me upright.

And thanks to the grunt reaching my ears, I didn't need a sixth sense to know who those large and warm palms belonged to.

"Bloody goats," Cameron grumbled, his hold shifting up and engulfing my shoulders.

I glanced down, finding Brandy at my feet. "And here I thought you were on my side, Brandy."

The blind goat nudged my leg again, and I felt Cameron's grip tighten.

Curious about that reaction preceded by the *bloody goats*, I looked over my shoulder, finding his face right there. So close that I could see the slight wrinkles around his eyes. The specks of brown in the green of his eyes. The smooth-looking texture of his skin. An unsolicited wave of warmth climbed up my neck. Cameron's hands dropped.

"Listen to the goats," Josie said, suddenly in front of us. "They are here to help, and Brandy was trying to tell you something. Probably that you shouldn't give up." She placed her hand behind her ear. "What's that, Brandy? Oh yes. Brandy wants you to give this your best shot."

I blinked at Josie. "I'll try?"

"Don't act so shocked," the man slightly behind pointed out in a dry tone. "You were talking to the goat a minute ago."

Josie's gaze shifted to him. "She wants you to try your best, too, you know?" She tilted her head. "Hmm. You look tense, Cam. Would you feel better if I got a second goat to come over here?"

"No."

I frowned at the curt and direct answer. Was it . . . Was it possible that Cameron didn't like the goats? "Well, I think I would love another goat," I heard myself say. "Maybe even a few more."

Before I could get a reaction from Cameron, someone from the back of the group piped up. "Josie, honey? Can we switch positions?" Diane's voice was strained. "We've been holding Crescent Lunge for so long I think Gabriel is about to pull a muscle in his back."

Josie's eyes widened. "Sorry, Diane!" she called. And then, she snapped into action. "Okay, you two—or three," she said, pointing at Brandy, too, "are stalling the class." She walked around me, and next thing I knew Cameron's hands were on my shoulders again. The warmth returned to my face. "And you, my dear Adalyn, are struggling," Josie pointed out.

"I have it under control," I complained. "I don't need a private lesson. Or him. Or his hands on me."

Cameron grumbled something.

Josie's grin turned tight. "I'm not driving Gabriel to the ER again. GOGGH is going to go smoothly and without a hitch today. So, Cam"—she shifted her gaze behind me—"stop looking like you're sucking on a lemon and help her. You clearly know what you're doing."

"But—" I tried again.

"No buts." Josie's expression morphed, giving her a strangely threatening look for someone who was wearing a yoga set in neon pink. She turned around and said in that soothing voice from earlier, "Aaaaaaaaand, warrior position!"

Cameron released a deep, loud breath.

One that I felt right at the back of my neck.

I swallowed, suddenly hyperaware of how close he was standing. Of the weight of his hands. Of the warmth of his body. Of what we were about to do. Together.

"I hope you're happy," he muttered. And the palm that been limply resting on my shoulder flexed, wrapping around my shoulder blade with clear intention. He was guiding me through this.

"What do you mean?" I asked distractedly, feeling how his thumb swiped along a muscle that had been bunched up with tension.

I sensed him step closer. "Team bonding," he explained, the

words reaching me in a murmur. "You set me up, Adalyn. After you forced my hand." A pause. "You even recruited Josephine."

"I didn't recruit her," I let out in a shaky breath. "This is all Josie's doing."

His thumb swiped again, as if trying to loosen me up, and a rush of electricity raced down my spine. "So you're saying you didn't plan to volunteer me for this?" he asked, my whole body growing warm. Warmer. As if a furnace had been flipped on beneath my skin. "You just happened to take me down with you?"

I steadied myself. He was distracting me, baiting me, and I was not allowing that. I was not being knocked over by Cameron Caldani. Leaving this town without my success story of the Green Warriors wasn't an option. Mostly because I didn't think I'd ever be able to return to the Flames without it.

"Can we just . . . get through this?" I closed my eyes, focused on the pressure of his palm, and not his words. On his fingers, as they slid down one of my arms in what felt like an unnecessarily slow pace. They ended at my wrist, curling around it in a gentle but swift motion.

"Arm up and in a straight line," Cameron indicated, his voice now falling right against the shell of my ear. A shiver crawled down my spine, and I had to make a serious effort to follow his command. "That'll do," he said. And before I could complain about the backhanded compliment, his fingers were curling around my other wrist. Sidetracking my words. This time, it was him who lifted my limp limb.

I released a strange exhale.

"Keep them up for me." Cameron's voice came again, his tone focused, deliberate, not a trace of reluctance there. I swallowed. "Hold right there." I held. "Beautiful."

Beautiful.

"I . . ." Didn't like this. Or how that word had made me feel just now. How he was making me feel. "On second thought, I think I can do all of this on my own."

Cameron sighed forcefully, and the puff of air leaving his lips hit my skin. A shiver crawled down my spine. "You need me."

Outrage blossomed in my stomach. And I was glad for the change. This I could process. This—

His hands landed on my waist.

And if I'd thought his palms had engulfed my shoulders before, if I'd thought his touch had been overwhelming when it had been on my wrists, that's because I hadn't felt his hands where they were right now. Those fingers that had endured more blows and cracks than most reached the bottom part of my rib cage, the warmth of his skin making my top feel suddenly too thin.

Cameron maneuvered me, rotating my torso. And I felt myself go stiff. Tense. The fabric separating his hands from my skin sticking to me, as if melting under his touch. Or perhaps it was my own sweat. God, why was I sweating so much?

"I . . ." I blurted out. "I'm a little warm, sorry."

"You think a little sweat will scare me?" he drawled, making my stomach drop for some unfathomable reason. "Posture is wrong," he continued. "It's your hips." One palm moved along my hip bone. "Your torso needs to come down slightly."

"How?" I croaked. I didn't think I knew how to function on my own.

You need me.

Cameron's hands readjusted around my body, one climbing up my side and the other clasping firmly around my waist. He pushed down.

But I was so caught up in the way I could feel the tips of his fingers creating ten pressure points on my skin, making it tingle, flush, buzz.

"You're as stiff as a stick, darling," he grumbled. "Relax for me."

Stiff as a stick.

My throat worked, the memory of very similar words being said about me throwing me off. Unaware of my inner struggle, Cameron's body shifted behind me, allowing me to feel the entire length of his front on my back. Chest, torso, thighs. He was right there. Rock solid. Warm. Close.

"Spread your legs," he said.

And without a single coherent thought left in my head, I spread my legs.

I sensed his head coming down, and then I heard, against my ear, "Take a step to the side and plant your foot firmly on the mat." Something switched in me, releasing the control to him, and I moved. His palm fell on the back of my thigh and when he said, "Flex," I flexed.

His long fingers stretched, wrapping around the inside of my leg. I puffed out a breath.

"Lock it in," he ordered. And as much as my whole body seemed to burn, and as much as that spot on the inside of my thigh seemed to pulse under his touch, I did. Or tried.

Because Cameron hummed in what I interpreted as disapproval, and in a swift motion, one of his arms was around my waist, and his foot was shoving one of mine out, widening my stance. The motion brought me right against him. His lap. And he grunted, "Hold."

I held.

"Beautiful," he repeated, the word falling right between my ear and my neck. "Good job."

Beautiful. Good job.

My stomach flipped at the praise.

Something right in the middle of my belly swirled. All the blood in my face seemed to swoosh down before bouncing right back up.

What was happening? What was going on? Why were three very ordinary words making me feel this way?

A strange sound left Cameron, and I thought there was a chance I had passed out, right there and then, against Cameron's lap. Because I didn't think I could tune in Josie's voice anymore. Or listen to the baby goats bleating. Or Brandy. Or the sun, the barn, the vastness of the Vasquezes' farm, or the fact I was surrounded by hills and had left Miami for Green Oak. I was on sensory overload.

All I could feel was Cameron.

And I couldn't recall a single time, a single instance in my life, when I'd felt like this. Just like when I'd tried to remember the last time I'd cried, I couldn't pinpoint a specific moment in time when I'd been this overcome by a man's touch. When I'd been this . . . hot.

This singlehandedly aroused.

I'd never slept around, but I'd been with two men before David. Three, counting him. I'd thought I'd been touched enough to know what physical touch was.

I was apparently wrong.

Because nothing, not one touch or brush or caress or moment of intimacy, had felt like this. Like Cameron's hands felt on my body—even over my clothes. Like his chest and thighs pressing behind mine. Like his arms engulfing my sides. And this wasn't even sexual. This was yoga. With farm animals. The man wasn't trying to arouse me. He didn't even like me.

God.

Had I fooled myself into believing that what I'd experienced in the past was the norm? That the dispassion I'd felt when David touched me was okay? Or had I been alone for too long after him? Jesus. Had I neglected my body so much that now it was jumping at the chance to be touched? By a man I could hardly talk to without locking horns?

Cameron's hands guided me into the next position. I wasn't sure. I couldn't be, frankly. My head was chaos. Confusion. And when my chest started to feel tight, one thought solidified. I had to be the problem here. Cameron couldn't be feeling any of this. I was stiff as a poker.

Frigid, boring, and forgettable. Dodged a bullet.

"Take a deep breath, darling," Cameron said, making me realize I was gasping for air, and it had nothing to do with the workout. "Adalyn," his voice came again, more firmly. "Focus on your breathing." His body was still wrapped around me, his warmth somehow feeling like too much. But not enough. What was wrong with me? "In and out, darling." What had to be his palm fell on my collarbone, firm, heavy, providing a physical tie I could focus on. "That's it, just like that."

My rib cage expanded at his words, the air coming in and out more easily.

"Good job," he murmured, my breathing gradually returning to normal. My mind slowly slipped back into place. "Well done."

When I started feeling more like myself, I glanced around, searching the group and expecting to find every head turned. Even the goats. But no one was looking. Everyone was focused on their own practice, and Brandy was now resting on my mat. Close to our feet. Cameron's feet.

"The goat," I rushed out, feeling the need to issue the warning. He didn't like them.

Cameron's body tensed behind mine, just like it had every time one of the furry animals had come close to him. His fingers spread, grazing the base of my neck. And when he spoke, I could hear the strain in his voice. "It's just a goat."

I slipped out of his hold, pretending I was frustrated at his blatant denial. I wasn't. What I was was embarrassed. By Cameron, of all people, witnessing such a moment of weakness on my side. By him having to remind me how to breathe because I'd been too lost in my head over—nothing.

"You're scared of them," I told him, whirling around to face him. The green of his eyes was dark, his features hard, and his stance tense. I stepped back. "You're scared of the goats."

This wasn't important. I didn't even care whether he had some strange animal phobia. A part of me I was trying really hard to ignore even softened at the knowledge. I was deflecting, though.

And Cameron seemed to see right through me. "We're all afraid of something in this life, darling," he said. "The little freak-out you've just had is evidence of that." A muscle on his jaw ticked. "It's only a matter of time until I find out."

Find out about what? I wanted to ask.

But Cameron Caldani was leaving my mat and walking back to his.

Storming off in a way and leaving me with too much to think about.

One more time.

CHAPTER THIRTEEN

Cameron

Coaching the Green Warriors wasn't going to be the walk in the park it had been until now.

It had nothing to do with the girls. Practice had been what you would expect from a group of kids under the age of ten: chaos with the occasional moment of pure and sheer desperation and a pinch of madness.

The problem was the new general manager, as she loved to call herself.

I watched the last two girls walk off in the direction of their parents—and Diane, who had once again kept watch from her car all during practice—and whirled on my heels, immediately spotting the woman camping out on the bleachers. I'd assumed last Thursday had been a one-time occurrence. But there she was again.

With a resigned shake of my head, I started in her direction and watched Adalyn while I crossed the shoddy grass with long and quick strides. Her laptop was balanced on her knees, and she was leaning slightly forward, engrossed by whatever was on the screen. My eyes followed the line of her shoulders and arms, taking in the pressed button-down blouse. She'd taken off the blazer at some point between me giving up on teaching the girls the simplest way to dribble the ball and getting Juniper—our keeper—to learn how to dive for the ball so she wouldn't hurt herself. I'd managed neither.

My gaze tipped down as I got closer, irritation rising at the sight of those bloody heels again. It boggled my mind that she consistently moved in those things in a town where, besides Main Street, most roads weren't even paved. She'd even come to that goat yoga happy hour nonsense in them. In a heartbeat, I was thrusted back to Sunday. To Adalyn, in those leggings. The tank top. To the warmth of her body beneath my fingertips. To how—

Something rippled in my gut at the unfinished thought, and when I finally reached her I couldn't stop the words from taking shape in the way they did. "Why are you here?"

Here. In Green Oak. My head.

She seemed more surprised by my being there than by my question when that little frown formed. "Where else should I be? The facilities don't have an office where I can set up. So the bleachers seemed like the best place." Her fingers slid across the mouse pad a few times. "My hotspot isn't working today, do you get good reception here?" She looked around, as if searching for something. "Maybe tomorrow I can try the other side of the field."

"So you really mean to sit here through every single practice?"

"Of course," she confirmed. As if that was the obvious thing to do. And before I could say how I felt about it, she was switching topics. "How do you feel practice went today? I was thinking we should have a weekly meeting to evaluate how things progress. I'll print a few copies of the roster so we can make notes on every player to develop their strengths and assess their weaknesses." She pulled a blue binder out of her bag. "Here, take this home, in case you want to get ahead. Josie gave me some printouts on my first day. I went ahead and filed them. What do you think of Wednesdays? There's practice on Mondays, Wednesdays, and Thursdays, so middle of the week makes the most sense."

I blinked slowly. "We don't need meetings. They're just kids."

"They are." She nodded, still holding the binder in the air. "And they also are qualified for a regional little league that will be starting in less than a week." Her lips pursed. "Did you know the only reason the Green Warriors made it through is because they're the only U10 team in the whole county?"

No. I hadn't known. "They still are just kids."

"Wednesdays it is," she said. "First game is on Saturday. I think we can use the chance to see how they do and take it from here. A copy of the game schedule is in the binder, too." I opened my mouth, but she went on. "They will be playing five other towns in the up-coming weeks. Grovesville, Rockstone, Fairhill, Yellow Springs, and New Mount. The organization of the league is funny, actually. It's point-based but the teams only play each other once. The two that end at the top will get to the final."

I glanced down at her hand. "Are you really explaining to me how a league works?"

"I said it was a strange structure." She pushed the binder in my direction and when I didn't take it from her, she dropped her arm and let it rest on her lap. "You're going to make this harder than it should be, aren't you?"

"Me?" My brows wrinkled. "You think I am the one complicating this."

"I guess I deserve that," Adalyn murmured, reaching for her bag. Something stirred in my gut at the slight tone of defeat in her voice. She pulled out a second binder. This one was red. "Saturday's game is against the Grovesville Bears."

Once more, I was more than a little impressed by the way she pushed through what I threw at her. I didn't think she deserved it, but I still didn't like that she was here, in Green Oak, sucking me into her vortex. She moved to her bag again and pulled out a Post-it stack. I tilted my head. "What do you have in there, a print shop?"

"Close," she said dryly. "I went ahead and researched every team and town playing the Six Hills," she added, scribbling something on a sticky note and plastering it to one of the pages inside the binder. "There wasn't much but everything I found is here." She looked up and met my gaze. "It would be great if you could go through what's in here about the Grovesville Bears before our meeting on Wednesday. You have about a day and a half. I've just marked it for you."

I stared at her, that set of brown eyes waiting, expecting a confirmation or a promise that I would, if I had to guess. But with her hair up in a tight bun, it was hard not to get distracted by all that weary tiredness clinging to her features.

The question toppled off my lips, "Are you getting any sleep on the air mattress?"

Her eyelids swept up and down a couple of times. Slowly. She shook her head. "This Saturday is a home game for the Green Warriors," she said. "Depending on the outcome, I'll pitch you my press angles. But first I need to see how well the Green Warriors can do."

My whole body went alert at the mention of press.

Adalyn must have seen that, because she explained, "My focus is on the girls and the success story I'm here to make happen." She made a careful pause. "Your focus should be on getting them the points that land them in the final." Another moment of hesitation. "You win the games and I'll keep you out of my angle. That's all I ask."

That was all she asked? As if she hadn't asked enough already.

And yet . . . There was that moment of hesitation. It told me she was more bark than bite.

The red binder was pushed against my chest. I didn't take it.

"Okay," she murmured, standing up suddenly. Thanks to the difference in height of the stand she was on, her chest lined up with my gaze. "Don't take the binder, then," she continued, her breasts rising and falling with a deep breath. My jaw clamped down at the trail of memories triggered by that sight. Sunday. Yoga. My hands on her. Softness and warmth under my fingers. My palm on that exact spot on her chest as she'd struggled for air. Her hand flew to one of the tiny buttons of her blouse, returning me to the present. "I guess we should wrap up here."

"Please," I breathed out, my gaze locked on the button as she fumbled with it.

Neither of us made the attempt to leave.

"Oh," Adalyn started, her voice distracted and the pad of her thumb toggling with the tiny thing, twisting it side to side. "Have you seen the uniforms, by the way? Taking care of the new ones is up on my priority list, but I don't think they'll be ready for the game this week." A pause. Her thumb stopped. I felt my Adam's apple bob. "Josie said we were covered for now, whatever that means, but something tells me we should check them before Saturday."

Adalyn's hand dropped to her side, leaving that one button crooked to one side. She inhaled deeply and her chest swayed again, testing the resistance of the slit. An unwarranted thought popped up in my head. What kind of underwear did a woman like Adalyn Reyes hide under such an adept and prim façade? Did she wear lingerie or was her underwear just as proper and decorous as the outer shell?

My gaze dipped down, as if trying to discern the lines through all that thin and soft-looking fabric and getting a little lost on the dip of her curves. Breasts. Waist. I'd had my hands there, on that exact spot on her waist. I knew how soft—

"Cameron?"

I glanced up, returning my eyes to her face.

Jesus fuck.

What in God's name?

"I haven't seen the uniforms," I told her. "We can ask Josie about them tomorrow."

"But I just said—"

"I'd like to head home. Rest." It was obvious I needed a fucking night of sleep to clear my head.

"If we must," she said, starting to gather her things together. "Let's continue this tomorrow. There's so much on my to-do list that we haven't even broached."

Of course there was. "No wonder they shipped you off here," I heard myself mutter under my breath.

Adalyn's expression morphed at my words. There was a new emotion there now. One that made my goddamn stomach shift. She pressed everything she'd been holding in her arms against her chest with a jerky frustrated motion and turned her body to the side. Out of some strange and unexpected urge to explain myself I moved, too, pushing her to walk around me to climb down the stand.

I huffed at her, and she huffed at me right back.

"Adalyn—"

But Adalyn was intent on avoiding me and getting away from me as soon as possible. Thing was, those goddamn shoes of hers didn't seem to aid in her quest, because one second, she was upright and the next, she was plummeting down.

Cursing under my breath, I lunged for her. Arms outstretched, I placed my body so I could intercept her now free fall. She crashed against my chest with a little yelp, and all I could do was secure her against me and say, "I got you." I shifted my arms, my palms clasping her sides. "You're okay."

Adalyn murmured something in response, but I was too distracted by the wave of relief coursing through me to know what. Her scent was also sneaking into my lungs, the simple—but definitely not plain—way she smelled overpowering me. I'd only caught hints of it during yoga. But now it was all I could smell. It was clean, fresh, and so fucking sweet it felt like a blow to my face. Like cotton left in the sun in a lavender field.

Fuck. I was really losing it.

"I'm fine," I heard her say more clearly. "I think you can let go of me."

My throat worked, swallowing hard before I could release her. I stepped back, feeling my hands prickling when they fell to my sides. I flexed them. Then I met her gaze, finding the brown in her eyes dazed. Her cheeks flushed.

"Those fucking heels," I said, hearing the harshness in my voice. Her brows wrinkled. "You're going to break your bloody neck one of these goddamn days."

Adalyn blinked a few times, then shook her head. The dazed look disappeared from her face. "Do you really need to talk like such a walking stereotype?" She lowered her voice in what had to be an attempt at imitating my tone. "*Those bloody heels, mate. Bollocks, innit? I'm chuffed to bits! Fancy a cuppa?"* A huff left her. "If you tell me you stop your day at five to have tea, and keep a tweed flat cap in a drawer somewhere, I swear I'm going to lose my ever-loving mind."

I stared at her.

For a long time. Then, I barked out a laugh.

It was loud and boisterous, and I was pretty sure I hadn't laughed like that in a long goddamn time.

Adalyn rolled her eyes. "You have that flat cap, don't you?"

"I do," I confirmed with a nod. "But I was raised with an Italian *nonna*, darling. So I'll take a good espresso over a cup of tea any day of the week."

"Not your darling." Adalyn released a breath. "And I guess I shouldn't be surprised. You really have a caffeine addiction from what I've seen," she added in a serious tone, but I could see the corners of her lips bending slightly upward.

I wondered how her smile looked. Her real one.

I made myself look somewhere else, my eyes landing on her chest. The button I'd been so preoccupied with moments earlier had come undone. And it allowed me a glimpse at the fabric of her bra.

It looked like satin. Lavender.

Christ.

My eyelids fluttered shut, out of pure survival. I even turned my body to face away. Searching for something else to look at and focusing on the first thing I found. The shed. Which still was in a state of complete disarray.

Exactly how I felt.

CHAPTER FOURTEEN

Adalyn

This was it. I was done. I really was.

I let the screwdriver I'd bought at Cheap Moe's fall to the floor and absently wiped my hands on my legs, leaving twin trails of dirt on the fabric of my leggings. I looked at my tank top. Also filthy.

"Great," I whispered. "This is just great."

Not only did the parts of this monstrosity of a bed seem to be held together by some kind of super powerful dark magic, but now I was covered in dirt and sweat and I'd ruined the only casual items of clothing I had.

Grabbing my sandwich and fruit salad from the kitchenette's counter, I tucked my phone under an arm, walked out to the sad and grisly porch that consisted of a single step, and plopped down. Something sharp pricked my ass, but I felt so helpless in that moment, so done, that I didn't even bother moving. The leggings were dirty anyway. And it wasn't like I could drop them in the washer because, turned out, there wasn't one in the cottage, so whatever.

So whatever. I didn't recognize myself.

With a sigh, I unwrapped my dinner and looked ahead as I chewed on the sandwich. I contemplated what was supposed to be the peaceful and beautiful expanse of nature before me, and saw this place for what it was. A few hills. A bunch of trees. An ugly cabin. A chip of rotten wood under my ass.

A gust of wind picked up, making me curl my legs closer to my chest. I took a new bite, recounting the winter clothes I'd packed: zero. I didn't even own more than the one winter jacket that I hadn't used in . . . years. Which was one of the things I loved about Miami.

I shook my head, deciding not to think about that. I'd make do with what I had. The nights and early mornings were growing cold the closer we got to October but it'd be fine. I'd have to be fine.

My phone pinged with a message, providing a welcome distraction, so I shifted my sandwich to my left hand and held the device up.

MATTHEW: Bad news.

Alarm surged in my belly as I typed my answer. I'd talked to Matthew on Sunday night, but besides providing him with a good laugh at the image of me, doing yoga—with goats, and without Cameron, who I still hadn't mentioned to Matthew—there hadn't been any developments on the #sparklesgate front.

ADALYN: It must be really bad if I'm not getting a goat gif.

MATTHEW: It kind of is.

A link followed that. I tapped on it with my thumb, and I was redirected to the site of an energy drink. I didn't recognize the brand, so I scrolled down, wondering if he'd sent me the right thing.

That's when the animation kicked in.

A colorful can rolled in, a slogan flashing underneath it in bold letters: CHOOSE ENTERTAINMENT OVER DIGNITY. The can shook then, trembled, as if about to burst, and poof, something materialized at the front.

With a disbelieving blink, I stared at the logo that had just been stamped on the container.

It was a simple illustration, but even that way it was impossible to miss the similarities. I knew what I was seeing. I recognized it. By now, I had watched the clip so many times that I could probably summon my face, jaw unlocked and expression unhinged, if I closed my eyes.

It was my Lady Birdinator face.

And turned out, I was on a can.

Dread and shock swirled inside me, making the few bites of turkey I'd taken turn sour.

MATTHEW: I've done some research. It's a new energy drink company. Pretty small. Vegan. Miami based. Targeting Gen Z for the most part. They have been very smart about it. You wouldn't make the connection if you haven't watched the video. But . . .

ADALYN: But millions of people have seen it.

MATTHEW: I'm sorry.

A wave of nausea hit me straight in the gut at that *I'm sorry*. I didn't want anybody's pity. Not even Matthew's. Because that . . . That made it all worse. I swallowed, trying to push down everything that was bubbling up in my throat.

MATTHEW: You think you can sue?

ADALYN: I'll talk to my father. I'm sure he's already seen it and is taking legal action to protect the franchise.

MATTHEW: I'm more concerned about you.

ADALYN: I'm part of the franchise.

I stared at my own words, that sensation in my chest intensifying. But I was still part of it, wasn't I? I was his daughter, and employee, as much as I'd been temporarily suspended from access to my account and banished. My father would protect me. I knew he'd done that in the past, I now knew that he'd—

One of the bushes across from me moved, capturing my attention.

It moved again, making me narrow my eyes, and then, before I could prepare, something charged out of the bushes.

My phone and sandwich were startled straight out of my hands, and I even heard myself yelp as I shut my eyes, bracing myself for whatever that thing was. A bear? A ravenous rabbit? I'd read about several species of rattlesnakes in the area that were deadly. Whatever it was, it wouldn't be worse than being claimed as the image of an energy drink whose marketing campaign was based on my demise and lack of dignity.

When seconds ticked by and I wasn't attacked, I opened one eye.

The chicken in front of me clucked.

"It's you. You're Cameron's pet." The bird batted her wings and stomped on my sandwich. "Hey. That was my dinner, you know?"

Her head bopped forward, in the direction of the food, as if telling me, *Now it's mine.*

"Have at it, then," I relented, carefully leaning down to pick up my phone and sitting back on the porch step. "I guess it's only fair after the other day."

The thing clucked, scratching at the floor.

"Yeah, yeah. I'm sorry, okay?" I said with a sigh. "I was having an odd day. Or fine, maybe it was more of a bad week. Actually, I don't think the streak of bad luck is over. I seem to be going through a long string of bad."

Cameron's pet chicken bobbed her head before pecking at the bread.

"I'm not sure if a chicken should be eating turkey," I murmured with a frown. "It must be some sort of animal cannibalism." The thing continued. "Your eggs will come out . . . strange. Probably."

"It's a rooster," a deep voice said in the distance. "Not a hen."

And naturally, just like always, my spine straightened in response to that voice. My cheeks also flushed—a relatively new development.

Cameron's boots moved the gravel around as he walked closer to me, making me wonder if he, too, had come out of the bushes. He stopped in front of me, and when I looked up from his feet, the first thing I saw was the humor dancing in eyes.

That was also new. Cameron apparently did something besides grumbling and storming off places. He also laughed.

"Looks like a chicken to me," I said from my post on my not really a porch.

My gaze dipped, trailing down his body. Another of those outdoorsy fleeces hung off his wide shoulders, zipped up to his throat. And he was also wearing a pair of those pants with zippers and pockets he favored so much. They were dark gray and the fabric clung to his legs. His wide and strong thighs. Which I seemed to be fixated with.

"It's a cock."

I nearly choked. "Sorry, what?"

The tiniest of smirks hid beneath his beard. "A cock," he repeated, and I still blinked, feeling my whole face heat. "Not a hen. The shape of the comb is a dead giveaway." He pointed at the top of his head with one of those large fingers. "But when in doubt, roosters also have sickle and hackle feathers." He paused, pushing his hands inside the pockets of his jeans. "Hens don't."

Oh. Oh? I cleared my throat. "Thanks for the poultry anatomy lesson, Attenborough."

Cameron's lips twitched. "He's also not my pet."

I narrowed my eyes. "Were you spying on me? How long were you standing there?"

He shrugged. "Josie came to me with some ideas for a coop. Apparently, someone told her I had a pet chicken and she has decided I should have a brood."

The thing clucked and batted his wings, as if acknowledging Cameron's words.

I flinched back. "I don't know how I feel about having more of these around."

Cameron closed the distance to where the rooster and I were, then kneeled down and started picking up the mangled remains of my sandwich.

I remembered his warning from the morning he'd found me sleeping in my car and felt like I needed to explain myself. "I wasn't feeding it my dinner, by the way. I'm not stupid. I dropped it when—"

"I know," he said, confirming he'd been there enough time. "You might be a lot of things, but I don't think you're stupid."

I knew a backhanded compliment when I heard one. "Thanks."

Cameron put the food leftovers he'd collected inside one of the pockets of his pants and then checked his watch. "A bit early for dinner, isn't it?"

Yes. But I'd been exhausted from unsuccessfully disassembling that bed in order to *yassify* the stupid cottage. And I'd had nothing else to do. Today was a Tuesday, and without practice to occupy myself . . . "I was hungry."

"Are you also a toddler?"

I shot him a bland look. "Don't you have anything else to do?"

Cameron shifted closer, and before I knew what was happening that large body of his was plopping down beside me, providing the answer to my question.

My breath caught at the sudden closeness, just like it did last night, when he'd caught me in the air after that miserable trip. Or Sunday, when his hands had been all over my body. Because there it was, his scent again. There was a hint of perspiration in there, as if he'd just come from a walk or maybe a run, but he still managed to smell so . . . good. Like outdoors and musk and—

I shook my head.

Sweaty men were something that I usually had to make myself tolerate. Live with and try to avoid. That was why I never set foot inside the changing rooms after games or practice unless extremely necessary.

"How's the renovation coming along?"

Glad for the distraction, I thought back to the mess I left behind. "It's going great," I lied. I caught Cameron giving me an inquisitive look over his shoulder and I looked away. Was I flushed? My face felt warm. "How do you know I'm renovating?"

"The constant screeching coming from your *cottage*," he explained, and I didn't miss the way he said the word *cottage*. "Then there's the dust you're completely covered in."

I fought the urge to touch my hair. Brush my hands over my top. I swallowed. "You really love to continuously complain about me, huh?"

I glanced at him in time to see him shrug. "It's hard to focus on anything else."

The warmth covering my cheeks intensified.

"You seem to be everywhere I turn."

Right. "Well," I said, willing my expression to remain as indifferent as possible. "Luckily for you and your very delicate eardrums, I'm done with the renovation until further notice."

Cameron's eyes roamed around my face, making me . . . self-conscious, exposed, for a lot of reasons I wasn't ready to pick apart at that moment. I brought my knees up, hugging them to my chest.

"What are you doing in Green Oak, Adalyn?"

I clasped my hands over my knees. "We've already discussed that."

"Besides that," he said, and his voice sounded so . . . earnest, so unlike any of the other times he'd huffed something at me, that I shifted on the step. Away from him. As if I needed the physical distance to properly think. "What are you trying to prove?"

I stared at the man sitting nothing but a handful of inches away from me, surprised by his choice of words. That was . . . a loaded question. One that I didn't know how to answer without giving myself completely away. Because for some bizarre reason, Cameron didn't know what had brought me to Green Oak. He hadn't seen the video half the country was mocking. I remembered him asking if I'd had a reason for whatever I'd done and being content with my answer. He didn't want the whole story. And perhaps I was fine with that.

"I have a life, if that's what you're asking," I told him.

Cameron shook his head, as if that wasn't the answer he was expecting.

"I have a job and hobbies," I insisted, even though I was quickly realizing I didn't have either. "I do home renovation."

"Darling," he drawled, a chuckle following that word. The sound made me think of his laughter. My stomach tumbled. I didn't like it. "You can't renovate shit clad in a pantsuit and armed with a hammer."

"I also have a screwdriver," I countered. "And I'm not wearing a suit."

"Believe me, I know. I have eyes."

I frowned. What did that even mean? "I'm not a lonely, sad workaholic," I felt the need to say. "I have a life," I repeated. "I listen to podcasts. True crime. I have an impressive memory, too. I can recite the complete roster of the Green Warriors to you right now. Or Green Oak's activity brochure, point by point. I could even enumerate every—"

Every single thing you've accomplished. Award and trophy you've won. Championship you've played. I can even recite the number of saves you made in the last World Cup you played. That was how good my memory was.

That was also how much I'd read about Cameron by now.

God. I really needed a hobby.

"So that's what you're listening to while brandishing that hammer," Cameron muttered. "Bloody murder." Another chuckle left him and I—I really hated how distracting that sound was. "Still not a hobby, though."

"I didn't know I was talking to the hobby police."

"Darling—"

"I'd rather you didn't call me that."

Amusement entered his expression. "Listening to podcasts is something you do while doing something else, like home renovation—if you were really into that." He glanced at my hair and gave me an unimpressed look. "And having good memory is a skill, not a hobby."

"Fine." I clicked my tongue. "What about you, then? What is a retired pro soccer player doing with all this free time on his hands?"

His eyes roamed around my face slowly, and for a moment I thought he wasn't going to answer. That he would stand up and leave. It wouldn't be the first time he got skittish after I brought his career up.

But to my surprise, he said, "I hike. Camp. I love the outdoors. And I do yoga, too. Not the kind we did on Sunday."

And just like that, hundreds of mental images of Cameron were flashing behind my eyes. I'd never had much of an imagination, but it didn't take one to picture Cameron on any of those instances. All those outdoorsy clothes on him, skin dripping with sweat, lost somewhere on a trail. Or the muscles I'd seen firsthand flexing as he did a plank. I . . .

"Well," I breathed out. "It's hard to picture you doing anything besides grumbling."

Cameron barked out a laugh, the sound traveling all the way to the bottom of my belly. Ugh. "I meditate, too," he offered.

More images came, floating freely into my mind. "You meditate?"

"Among other things, yeah."

I swallowed, now suddenly frustrated by this man who apparently was full of surprises. "If you tell me you also knit, I will stand up, leave, and never believe a word you say."

"I don't knit." He tilted his head in thought. "Although I tried. I've tried many different things." Well, that was just fantastic and not making me feel like a hobby-less person at all. He continued,

"It's said to be good to keep your mind off things. To disconnect. To appease your mind when it gets too loud." He lifted one of those paw-hands in the air. "But my fingers are too big and battered for it, and I have little patience."

I could have said that I knew how little patience he had, but I was busy taking the chance to inspect that hand up close. In detail. Without needing an excuse to. Just like I'd glimpsed in the past, he did have long and strong-looking fingers. Rough-looking, too. And his middle one in particular was crooked, like I'd seen the day we'd met, as if he'd broken it and it hadn't healed right. The signet around his pinky sparkled under the last rays of sun.

"You should try," he said.

"Knitting?"

"Taking your mind off things. Stop overthinking and overanalyzing every single second of your and everybody else's life. Stop measuring each word that leaves anyone's mouth. Yours included."

I felt myself swallow. "I don't do that," I said, but my voice was pitchy. I was whining. I seemed to be constantly doing that and I hated it. "I'm perfectly able to take my mind off things and relax. I could try any hobby I wanted and be excellent at it, too. I could beat you at yoga if . . ." *Your hands hadn't been all over me.* "I practiced enough."

Cameron's lips twitched again. "You really are a fiery, competitive thing, aren't you?"

I scoffed. "Don't call me a thing."

"I guess I shouldn't be surprised," Cameron admitted, his gaze so intently on me that for a moment I thought he was peeking right into my brain.

I opened my mouth to ask what he could possibly mean.

But his hand reached out for my face. His outstretched palm brushed my cheek, making my breath catch, and then, the pad of his thumb grazed my skin. It skimmed softly along the line of my jaw, making my lips part and a wave of static blanket the skin of my face.

Quickly, like gunpowder lighting up, it spread down my neck. My arms. It tingled and traveled all the way down to my toes.

Cameron touched me, and I couldn't do anything but remain still, so very still, while the rough feel of his thumb brushed against my face.

Chest pounding, I watched his eyes dip down, inspecting that spot on my jaw that now was buzzing, burning, flaring under his touch. "You're going to hurt yourself if you keep this up," he said so softly that I couldn't make sense of his words. "You're in shambles, darling," he murmured, green eyes returning to mine. "I can hardly see you underneath the mess."

I should be moving away. But Cameron's touch—the physical tie I was feeling to him—was so powerful, so sudden and intense, that I was being sucked in. Like an energy field or a vacuum. I was trapped.

His hand cupped my jaw in a tender gesture I didn't understand or expect, and my eyelids fluttered closed. He shouldn't be doing this. He shouldn't be touching me like this, gently wiping dirt from my face like he cared it was there. And I—it shouldn't be feeling this good.

I jerked back.

Physically removing myself from his touch and whatever it was doing to me.

When I opened my eyes, Cameron didn't seem bothered by my reaction. Not at all. If anything, he looked curious. As if he'd seen something he wanted to examine up close.

Probably all the dust and dirt.

I couldn't do anything but furiously pat at my face with the hem of my shirt, outraged and confused, focused on showing him I didn't need anyone to do this. I only needed myself.

Cameron hummed deep in his throat before standing up, and only then he said, "Perhaps we're not so different." The green in his eyes darkened. "Maybe I'm also trying to prove a point."

CHAPTER FIFTEEN

Cameron

"Those are the uniforms?"

I nodded. "The very same."

Adalyn muttered something under her breath before mumbling, "But— But they—"

"Look like they're on their way to an eighties theme party?"

"Yes." A huff left her, and I couldn't say I didn't relate to that defeated puff of air. "When did—"

"Josie was here early. She came bearing gifts."

"But how—"

"Remember the story about her mother and the team back in the day?" Adalyn's eyes widened and I gave her a nod. "Yeah. Those are the uniforms they used. God knows why they kept them this long."

"Were they even—"

"Washed? Yes," I said. "It was the first thing Josie said."

Adalyn's eyes narrowed. "Do you read minds now?"

"No." But I was beginning to understand how hers worked. I turned toward the girls, who were scattering across the field. "Nothing we can do now."

"This is my fault," Adalyn said from my side. "I should have checked them beforehand. Just like I said I would. But Josie is so convincing when she wants to be." She huffed. "I'll need to see how fast I can order the new ones. But for that we need to get everything sorted. Jerseys, shorts, socks, shin guards, cleat boots, not sneakers. We need a color scheme and a style for the numbers. Everything. Maybe I—" A pause. "Oh my God. What is Chelsea doing with that tutu? What if they disqualify them? What if—"

"Darling—"

"Adalyn."

"Adalyn," I relented, just so she wouldn't get any more worked up. I really had no energy to deal with any extra sassiness right now. The crowd the Grovesville Bears had brought to town was larger than I'd expected, and it was starting to get to me. "This is just a game, yeah?" Her face scrunched up in disagreement, but I lifted a finger. "Chelsea refused to take the goddamn thing off, she's the bloody Black Swan or some age-inappropriate shit María convinced her of. But the ref said it's fine when I asked, and she's also just a kid. They all are. Forget about the tutu and the uniforms and try to get through the game without giving me a headache. This is just little league. It's child's play. Literally."

Adalyn frowned, and I thought for a foolish second that she'd leave it alone. I was obviously wrong. "But the team looks ridiculous."

I sighed.

She went on, "They're warriors, they should look fierce. Imposing. Serious. It's not even the fact that they're all in pink. We changed the Flames' third kit to a similar shade that was very popular among fans. But this?" Her hand stuck out. "They're ugly and dated and the team looks . . . unserious."

I didn't disagree. "Try to ignore it. Close your eyes. Look away. Maybe go away." She narrowed her eyes at me, and I faced the grass again. "There's nothing you can do now, so you either stop nagging or go home."

"You know I'm right."

"I also know I'm getting a headache."

"Just look at the other team," she pressed, but I didn't really need to. Adalyn continued, "They look like a miniature MLS team. Even their coach has a matching tracksuit." A pause. "I wonder if anyone is sponsoring them."

"I thought that binder of yours had all the answers of the universe," I said dryly, but I turned to the right and looked in the direction of the Bears' coach.

The lady in the tracksuit in question locked eyes with me across the field. I gave her a nod, even opened my mouth to extend a good luck, but then her eyes were narrowing and her arms were crossing over her chest. I frowned at her. And in response, she mouthed, *You're going down, bitch.*

"What the fuck," I muttered.

"Language," Adalyn whispered loudly. "You really need to stop swearing around the kids. It's unprofessional."

I glanced back at her, finding her engrossed in her phone. "But she just called me a bitch."

Adalyn's gaze lifted off the screen for an instant, looking in the direction of the woman, and then returned her attention to it with a sigh. Her fingers started flying across the device. Typing neurotically. She paused, lifted the phone, and started snapping pictures. Unconvinced, she took a few steps back, pointed her phone forward, and snapped a hundred more.

I blinked at her. "What in the world are you doing now? The game is about to start."

She returned to my side with a shrug and resumed the lightning typing. "What kind of question is that? I'm obviously working."

"You're going to burst a metacarpal at that speed."

"Is that a bone in my fingers? If so, I'm not. I'm used to typing fast when I'm brainstorming."

"Brainstorming," I repeated slowly. "For what? New ways to drive me up the wall?"

"Ha," she deadpanned. "For the new uniforms. I might also order a few banners with the new logo I can give away to people that come to the games." She bit her lip for a moment, dragging my eyes there. "I can forward you a copy of my notes. We can go over everything on Monday. After practice. Is that a good time?"

I remembered the last meeting we had. The button bursting open. Her scent in my lungs. The lavender satin. My jaw clenched.

Without lifting her head from the screen, she said, "Don't look at me like that, Coach."

I ignored that *Coach*. "How do you know how I'm looking at you?"

"Because you operate in two modes. Self-important and annoyed."

A snort escaped my mouth. She was probably right. "I thought we agreed on meetings on Wednesdays."

"Monday won't be a meeting." Her thumb swiped up and down, switching apps at an impressive speed. "It'll be a casual get-together to align ideas."

"Putting the word *casual* in front of get-together doesn't make it less of a meeting, darling."

Her index finger tapped one last time on the screen. She lifted her head, finally looking at me. "How about you call me boss?" Her eyebrows arched. "I'm not a huge fan of defined hierarchical systems, but I think I can make an exception here."

I stared back at her under the brim of my cap. Her hair was up in a tight bun again. Only this one was at the top of her head, making her features look sharper under the sun. The suit was back as well, this one a pale shade of beige that was paired with a blue glossy-looking top I wished that blazer wasn't covering.

It was possibly the dressiest she'd ever been. Even the heels she had on seemed higher than usual. Adalyn was dressed to impress today. Prim and ready to bulldoze over some poor soul. Me, most likely. And yet it was a welcome contrast to how she'd looked the other night on her porch. Covered in dust. In yoga pants. Strands of hair sticking out. I still hadn't figured out which version of Adalyn I found more disconcerting.

The skin in my palms tingled at the memory of the feel of her face under my fingertips.

I flexed my right hand.

"Where's the ring?" she asked, bringing my attention back.

I felt myself frown in surprise, but I patted my chest. "I'm used to taking it off for games. I have it on a chain."

Her cheeks flushed, but if she thought anything of it, she didn't say. "And what's with the hat?" She gave me a skeptical once-over. "Is this your game look? I could get you a hat when I order you a matching coach tracksuit. I could ask them to print COACH (RELUC-TANTLY HERE) on the front."

I narrowed my eyes at her. "Why are you here, again?"

"I'm the manager of the Green Warriors, where else should I be?"

"Not in the technical area. I'm the coach and this is *my* bench."

"Technical area is a stretch." She pointed at the humble space around us. "And you need me here. I'm pretty sure I heard the Bears' coach conspiring against you on my way in from the parking lot." A shrug. "I'd really hate to have to look for someone to fill in if you were to mysteriously disappear in . . . let's say the bushy area behind the bleachers nobody seems to venture into." A pause. "Not that I gave her any ideas."

If I hadn't been so caught up in the notion of Adalyn teasing me, I would have probably barked out a laugh. "Are you saying you'll protect me from her?"

"Don't look so smug," Adalyn huffed, not even looking at me. "You're my only employee, Coach."

With a snort I let her have this one and faced forward. Soon after, the referee finally whistled, indicating the start of the game.

I took a step forward, clapping my hands a few times at the girls. "All right. Soldier on, Green Warriors!"

Every Warrior on the grass turned her head toward me. The ball rolled. They all blinked at me.

"Oh God," Adalyn whispered from my side. "What did you do? Why aren't they moving?"

"Gaze forward," I instructed the girls, signaling the other side with my hand. "Don't look at me," I barked, pointing in the direction of the ball. But by the time the Green Warriors reacted, they were too late to stop the other team from stealing and making their way across the field with the ball.

María frowned from her position at the net. But— Why was María at the net? Juniper was our goalkeeper. Where the hell was Juniper? Shit. Fuck. I'd been so caught up with Adalyn that I—

The forward for the Bears jerked her leg back to kick. María turned, distractedly waving in my direction. No. In Adalyn's direction.

I started to warn her, "Watch out for the—"

But the ball hit the back of the net, passing effortlessly over a smiling María.

"Goal," I finished.

The stands erupted in cheers. The humble scoreboard changed. GREEN WARRIORS: 0 – GROVESVILLE BEARS: 1.

I looked over my shoulder quickly, shocked by the enthusiastic crowd from out of town. The Green Warriors were playing home and the only faces I recognized besides a few of the parents were Josie, Diane, and Gabriel. Granted, I wasn't exactly going around town making friends, but there was barely any green in the stands. It was all red and white.

A woman met my gaze, eyes flashing with something I hoped wasn't recognition. I whirled around, pulling my cap lower.

"Let's not worry," Adalyn said when the crowd quieted down and the game restarted. "This is just one goal. There's plenty of game ahead. There's more—"

Adalyn's words came to an abrupt stop when Chelsea stole the ball from one of the Bears and ran. We both gawked at the kid, who was moving as fast as I'd ever seen a kid in a tutu move.

Chelsea neared the Green Warriors' penalty area and Adalyn whispered, "What is she doing?"

But I couldn't answer. I could only watch as Juniper shouted something in the distance, and when Chelsea didn't stop, she raced after her. Undeterred, our tutu-wearing midfielder didn't seem to care.

Adalyn mumbled something, then she said more clearly, "Oh my God, do something, Cameron. She's going in the wrong direction."

"There's nothing to do, darling," I answered with a gulp of air just as Chelsea kicked the ball with a flourish. "Nothing would have stopped that kid from scoring that onside goal."

The crowd from Grovesville broke into a loud cheer again. Even if they hadn't technically scored, a goal was a goal. I kept my gaze forward and my cap low, that familiar buzz at the back of my neck getting louder with every clap from the stands. That hadn't been just an own goal, it had been complete and utter chaos.

I'd spent all week dismissing Adalyn's attempts to create a strategy, truly believing everything she suggested was overkill. I still believed it. But somehow, all I could think about, as the game restarted again and the girls shuffled across the grass, was the red binder. The other one, too.

I wondered if there had been anything in there that would have warned me of this. For better or worse, I was the team's coach, and I . . . well, I clearly hadn't done a good job when my keeper was in the middle of the field and my midfielder had just scored an OG.

Out of the corner of my eye, I spotted the Bears' coach. She was looking straight at me with a smug look I didn't like. Holding my gaze, she lifted her fists, bringing them under her eyes and pretending to wipe tears that weren't there.

I stared blankly at her. That woman couldn't know that during my career I'd put up with things that would probably make her pale. I—

Watched Adalyn shoot forward.

"Ref!" she hollered. *Hollered.* Getting more than a few heads to turn. "Unsportsmanlike conduct is not a nice look on a kids' coach."

"Ma'am," the ref—a woman with a no-bullshit attitude—warned from her spot on the grass. "Return immediately to the sideline."

Laughter rolled in from the opposite bench, and Adalyn spun. "Maybe she should be more concerned about her *little* team." The Bears' coach gave her a once-over that made something in my stomach turn. She lowered her voice, "Go home, *princess.*"

Princess.

The word was lost on those not paying attention, but not on Adalyn and me.

"*Excuse me,*" Adalyn squeaked, her voice hiking an octave. She veered in the coach's direction. "With all due respect, ma'am, I am not—"

My arm shot out and I dragged her back, toward me, until she was plastered against my side. A whiff of that lavender scent hitting me right in the nose. "Absolutely not, darling."

Adalyn seemed distracted for a moment because it took her a bit to answer. "She called me a princess," she finally said. My throat clogged for an instant. I had too. "And she's mocking you and the team. I won't allow that."

Something softened inside my rib cage, appeasing me. But while I was as shocked as I was flattered by that defensive strike, I was also protective of keeping my anonymity, and there was a rather large crowd around. "I don't know, boss. I say we be the bigger people and ignore her."

I *felt* the tension in her body fly away. My arm was still around her. "You just called me boss."

So I had. I searched our surroundings quickly, checking for curious eyes. Everyone but the other coach seemed distracted by the game. Ah, hell. "Remember how you said earlier we shouldn't worry?" She nodded. "I think we should."

"I could still get the ref to suspend that woman, you know?" she piped in. But her voice was softer. Calmer. "I'm convincing. And I also know very important people in the PRO."

A chuckle escaped. It wasn't the first and I was beginning to understand that it wouldn't be the last, either. "I don't think your contacts in the PRO are relevant here, darling. This is a little county league." She grumbled, and my arm shifted, my fingers helplessly reaching forward and brushing that top I'd been eyeing before letting go. It felt like satin. She didn't complain. "Let's meet on Monday."

Her chest expanded with a breath, and when she spoke it was only one word, "Why?"

Fuck if I knew, honestly. "Seems like we have work to do."

Adalyn hesitated for an instant, but then she stepped closer until the tips of those shoes I despised touched my boots. She lifted her chin, assessing me. There were tiny freckles on the bridge of her nose. "I see," she said slowly. "Maybe you have a third mode after all. Besides self-important and annoyed."

I knew I did.

And without me really knowing how, that switch had just been flipped.

CHAPTER SIXTEEN

Adalyn

"*My* dearest Green Oak volunteers," Josie said, opening her arms with a flourish. "Welcome to Green Oak's annual BBBBL, or as we all know it, Beer, Barbecue, and Boogie By the Lake."

Diane cleared her throat from the first row.

Josie's smile tightened. "Yes, Diane?"

"Why did we change the name again?" she asked, making Josie's lips stretch. "This was supposed to be our end of summer party by the lake. It should have been weeks ago, the last week of August, like every year." That head of bright yellow turned in the direction of the stands. "Where are the corn dogs or the mini glazed donuts? We're also serving more than just beer. And while you're at it, I still don't understand what you mean by *boogie*."

Josie let out a chuckle that didn't sound as lighthearted as she'd hoped, if I had to guess. "Well, Diane, if you would have paid a little attention during our spring council meeting, you'd remember that we were trying to spice things up for the upcoming seasons. You know, to bring in more people from all over the county with fun and catchy events that have fun and catchy names. Hence the boogie, hence the barbecue, hence the craft beer and hence"—her voice went high—"the change of name."

"But there's a coffee booth," Diane countered. "And our end of summer party was fine. It was the best one in the county, if I may say so myself. I don't get why we need to be attractive to folks from other towns."

Josie's whole expression bunched up as she launched herself into another discourse about why change was good.

The man standing next to me exhaled long and deep, catching my attention. His hand had risen to his hair and he was dragging it down the side of his head. By now, I knew a few of Cameron's tells. He wasn't happy to be here, and after watching him during yesterday's game, I could guess it was because of the people this could bring. He'd flinched every time the crowd had stirred.

"It's the boogie part, isn't it?" I asked him in a hushed voice.

My question seemed to surprise Cameron, because when he looked over at me, it was with a frown. "Yeah."

I wondered why he would put himself through this when he hated it so much. He really thought I would expose him. Guilt swirled in my stomach. "If Josie does so much as suggest we dance, I'm out of here."

"We?"

"The volunteers," I explained, feeling a wave of warmth climbing up my neck. The image of Cameron's arms around me took shape in my mind. "I'll hide in the woods if I have to. Even after Josie said some very disturbing things about them being possibly haunted. That is how bad I don't want to boogie tonight."

Cameron snorted.

"Out of everyone here, I'd thought you would believe that."

Amusement flashed across his expression. "And why is that, darling?"

"Because your kind believe in lucky rituals and things like juju," I pointed out with a shrug. I wanted to ask him if wearing the ring on a chain had been partly about that. "I've seen players do the most ridiculous things before games."

Cameron's eyes roamed around my face for a moment, as if

searching for something. That stupid flush returned. "Not all foot-ballers are the same." He turned away, facing forward. "If you're nice to me tonight I'll take you on a hike and show you there are no ghosts. But you can't come in those bloody shoes."

I huffed. "If I'm nice—"

"You two will be on beer duty," Josie said, suddenly in front of us. "Loving the look, Adalyn. But did you bring anything a little thicker than that blazer? Temps really drop at night by the lake. That's why we say on the brochure to come dressed in layers."

I looked down at myself. "This is tweed. I'll be fine."

"Alrighty then," she said, clapping her hands and turning around. "Follow me, please. I'll show you to your station." We trailed behind her. "People from town who signed up for the BBBBL will not be having fun just yet." She stopped at a stand with a sign that read JOSIE'S JOSTLER. I frowned. "This baby over here is my craft beer venture. I'm still working on the name."

Cameron muttered something I didn't catch under his breath.

"So . . ." I hesitated. "You've brewed the beer that will be served tonight?"

"Yes, ma'am." A bigger than usual grin parted her face. "It's a hazy IPA. I've been perfecting the recipe for months, and I think this is the one. You can tell me when you try it." She winked. "Okay, enough chitchat. People will be coming in soon and I want every volunteer set and ready to go." She pointed at a barrel with a device locked at the top. "Have you ever used one of these?"

"Yes," Cameron answered with a sigh before I could say a word. "And the spigot is not screwed in properly."

He rolled up the sleeves on that flannel jacket he was wearing tonight. My eyes dipped to his forearms and immediately spotted the ink spilling out of the rolled sleeve, covering his skin. Something lodged somewhere between my rib cage and stomach at the sight, something that wasn't just curiosity. I leaned forward so I could get a better look as Cameron's hands landed on the top of the barrel.

Forearms flexed as little pieces and bits were screwed off and on with determined motions.

I patted my cheeks. They were warm. And I—

Oh God. What was happening? I'd never been into manual labor. Or tattoos. Or forearms. Or flannel for that matter.

I was startled out of my trance by an elbow to the side.

Josie's pale blue gaze was pointed at me with a mischievous glance. *You're drooling*, she mouthed. My eyes widened in horror and my hand dashed to my mouth. She chuckled loudly, and when Cameron shot us a questioning look, she sobered up and said, "Thanks for taking care of it, Cam."

Cameron's answer was a shrug.

"Okay, now that I really know the Josie's Jostler is in good hands and that you, Cam, can show Ada how the tap system works, I'm going to cut straight to the chase." Josie's hand stuck in the air, in the direction of a black metallic box. "Everyone coming gets food and drink tokens at the entrance, so all you have to do is take a token and serve a beer. If you get any enthusiastic tippers, you tell them that there's a piggy bank in the shape of a goat by the hot beverages stand. That's where I will be. All tips will go to the budget of next year's BBBBL. Questions?" She waited for an instant, but when my mouth opened, she said, "No questions, perfect! Now I need to run to the grill station. Gabriel said something very disturbing about homemade vegan patties earlier. Have fun, and"—that mischievous look returned—"remember that you're here to pretend you're bonding. Diane is extra watchy today, so I suggest you be extra bondy."

And with a very suggestive wink in my direction that made my face turn beetroot red, Josie jogged away.

"You okay?" Cameron asked.

"Sure," I answered, walking around him and setting up somewhere where those extremely distracting forearms were not visible. "I was just thinking that I forgot to ask Josie what the boogie thing was about." I busied myself with the cashbox. "So how did you know about the spigot?"

Turned out Cameron had worked at a pub in his late teens. He'd also spent his summers juggling every possible job available before signing his first contract. It explained things. It also made a little spot on my chest expand.

But I wasn't going to pay any attention to that. Me having a sweet spot for hardworking people wasn't new.

It also turned out that the boogie part of the evening was a Green Oak band's renditions of seventies and eighties songs. A band in which Josie played the bass.

It was truly fascinating the number of things that woman could do.

Except for brewing beer, as it also turned out. I'd had a sip of the Josie's Jostler and let's say it was so hazy I could have chewed on it. I wasn't an expert on craft beer, and had always favored wine, but I didn't think a hazy IPA was supposed to work like that.

Not that the crowd in attendance seemed to care. The Josie's Jostler stand had been just as busy as the rest. I wouldn't use the word *packed*—by my or any standards—but busy enough for Cameron to do most of the work and relegate me to token duty. That, unfortunately, had involved more sleeve-rolling, forearm unveiling, and muscle flexing when lifting glasses and exchanging barrels. At some point, I realized I'd been staring at one of his forearms—at that one specific inked spot left of his wrist—so hard and long that I had forgotten to collect tokens. So I'd thrown in a few dollars from my pocket and continued my ogling.

That was when he'd produced a beanie from a secret pocket in his flannel jacket.

I despised flannel, beanies, and secret pockets now.

That was why the moment the first five notes to "Boogie Wonderland" from the improvised stage hit and most people shifted in the direction of the band, I ran away.

Yes. I was officially hiding. From Cameron, not the boogie.

I was at the far end of the BBBBL premises, near the lake, with the not one but two goats María had brought with her as my only company. And if a ghost was to come out and lure me and the goats into the woods, I'd go gladly.

Brandy bleated from her spot at my feet. And just like every time she'd done that in the fifteen minutes I'd been here, Tilly stirred in response.

"You two need to stop that," I whispered, obtaining another two baas. "*No*. Shush."

I glanced over my shoulder, checking the crowd for a specific set of green eyes, dark beard, and beanie. Not a trace of him. Good. I returned my gaze forward, just in time for a gust of chilly air to hit me in the face and make me curl into myself.

The tweed suit was the warmest outfit I had, but Josie had been right, now that the sun was setting, it hadn't been the smartest choice. Not that any in my wardrobe would have.

"But that's okay," I muttered under my breath, thinking back to Cameron's beanie. And boots. And jeans. And flannel jacket. And how warm he must be. Maybe I should go by Outdoor Moe's and get myself a beanie. Brandy nudged my leg with her head. "I know. I don't think I could pull off a beanie either." I could maybe do flannel. I sighed. "He could have at least left the jacket before leaving."

"Who left?"

I almost fell off the rock I'd been sitting on. "Jesus," I muttered, turning my head and finding that mountain of padded flannel a few feet to my left.

Cameron's brows knotted under his stupid, silly beanie. "Jesus left?"

I opened my mouth to answer, but another gust of air picked up, stopping my words and sending a shiver to crawl down my spine. I curled my arms around my middle and gave him a shrug.

If Cameron cared about the lack of confirmation from my side, he didn't say. Instead he crossed the distance separating us and planted himself right beside me. My eyes dipped low, to his forearms. His sleeves were down, thank God. His hands, however, were hanging between his legs. Relaxed. Rough. Large. That signet on his pinky. Ugh. What was wrong with me? I couldn't hyperfixate on every body part this man flung in front of me.

Tilly, who based on her size looked younger than Brandy, trotted to Cameron's side, providing a welcome distraction. He stiffened.

"You can go," I muttered. Offered, really. Because he'd be doing us both a favor. I couldn't hide from him if he was here.

"It's just a goat," he answered. Hadn't those been his exact words at yoga? "Two goats. And one is tiny."

Something else he said came to mind. *We're all afraid of something in this life.*

"I promised María I'd keep them company," I told him, just so I wouldn't think of that.

"Looked to me like you were avoiding me," Cameron said, making my heart drop. "And came to the place you knew I would stay away from."

My throat worked, a new shiver that had nothing to do with the cold sneaking down my back. "Looks to me like someone believes he's the center of the universe." The warmth returned to my face. "I was getting away from the music. It's not very good, in case you haven't noticed."

As if in cue, the music came to a stop and the crowd erupted in applause.

Brandy tensed at my feet, making me remember María's words about the goat suffering from anxiety and being triggered by loud noises. A warm shoulder came into contact with mine when Tilly bleated from Cameron's side.

He was inching away from the tiny goat.

I cleared my throat.

"I'm fine," he grunted. But he really wasn't. And as warm as his side was and as much as the chill in my body was somehow appeased, I still felt bad. Responsible, for a reason I didn't understand. I opened my mouth, but Cameron spoke. "I lived on a farm for a while. When I was a boy."

Oh. That information seemed to lodge itself somewhere inside my head, as if it was important. Worth remembering. "In England," I clarified. Which was redundant because we both knew that.

But Cameron nodded anyway. "My *nonna* hated it, though. So we moved back to the city."

I remembered his comment about being raised by his grandmother. I realized I remembered everything that left this man's mouth. "Are you two close?"

"Were," he answered, looking over at me. "She passed before I signed for the Islington West."

His first club.

I stared into Cameron's eyes, getting a little lost in how open, naked his expression was in this moment. There was yearning in his face. A little sadness, too.

"I never had the chance to meet any of my grandparents," I heard myself say. "My mother is originally from Cuba, and she came to the US a few years before I was born. She left everyone and everything behind. My father's parents . . . died when he was young." Cameron's brows furrowed. "I haven't experienced that kind of bond, but I genuinely believe your grandmother would be proud of you." I felt myself swallow. "Anyone would be."

His head tilted, his eyes leaving mine and roaming all over my face for a moment that seemed to stretch too long. There was something new there, in his expression. Something that had nothing to do with sadness. Something that made me shift in place.

"My *nonna* arrived in England with the change in her pocket and a handful of jewelry that wasn't worth much," Cameron offered, raising his hand and showing me his pinky. "This is the piece she treasured the most. It belonged to her father, and my own dad gave it to me when I turned eighteen." He exhaled through his nose, slowly. As if he needed the time. "This is all I have left from her, my roots. That, a head full of dark hair, and a ragù recipe she used to make for celebrations or bad days."

A tsunami of questions swept through me as we sat there, on that rock, in silence, with the boogie beats echoing across the lake. And, God, I'd never wanted to ask every single one of them so bad in my life. I wanted to forget I'd been hiding from Cameron and I didn't really like him. I wanted to pretend he didn't think I was some annoying spoiled woman he had to put up with and ask all about him.

"You do have great hair."

Cameron chuckled. And that chuckle didn't help. The way he was looking at me didn't, either.

I faced away, another shiver rocking me head to toe as much as the skin of my face was burning with . . . whatever I was feeling.

Something fell on my shoulders.

It was heavy and soft and warm. It was padded flannel.

"Cameron—"

"Don't," he said, shaking his head. "It's cold. And you've been shivering all night."

My lips popped open. I wanted to complain. But he was right, and for once, I didn't think I had the energy to fight. I inhaled deeply, tiredly, burrowing myself into his jacket. I filled my lungs with his scent.

"Thanks," I breathed out, ignoring how unbelievably good it— he—smelled. "I . . . appreciate this expression of human decency on your side. And accept it."

Cameron sighed, and I knew he remembered his own words. "I'll accept that you think I have great hair. I also believe I do."

I started smiling, and as my lips bent, Cameron's gaze dipped to my mouth. In the distance, the music came to an abrupt stop that was followed by one loud and boisterously clattering sound. As if an instrument had fallen to the ground and shattered. We both started to turn.

But a distressed baa stopped us. It was loud, and just as bois- terous.

And it was also Brandy.

Losing her ever-loving goat mind.

My arms reached out in her direction. "That's okay, Brandy," I said in what I hoped was a soothing tone. "You're fine. That was just a little scare. But you're okay, I promise."

But Brandy wasn't okay. And she wasn't soothed, either. Her head swayed side to side and her paws hit the ground back and forth. It didn't take a vet, a zoologist, or even a person who was mildly informed about goats to know that the poor animal was rattled to her core.

Helpless, I reached out again.

Brandy jumped to the side, almost hitting a log that had been resting against the rock we were sitting on. I lunged myself to stop the blind animal from hurting herself. But I missed. Again.

"Adalyn," Cameron warned, his voice right behind me. "Let me—"

"No," I interjected. Because he was scared of them. I couldn't possibly expect him to calm the goat.

So I resumed my quest, reaching for a panicked Brandy, but I—

Looked down, and found a trail of anxiety-induced poo.

"Oh God," I said as I veered for the opposite side. But Brandy was still distraught—and therefore, very much pooping all over the place. "Brandy," I tried again, seeing Cameron dash for me out of the corner of my eye. "Cameron, *no*," I warned him, thrusting one hand in his direction and the other one in the direction of Brandy. "The goat," I explained, watching how Brandy twirled and head-butted into my side with enough force to push me a step back. "The poo," I added, stepping on something soft and feeling my shoe slide forward. "The flannel!" I finished, miraculously managing to grasp the jacket with both hands and throw it up into the air.

I landed on my ass.

"Jesus Christ, Adalyn," Cameron barked. "Are you okay?"

"Tell me your jacket is safe," I answered from the ground, blinking at the now dark sky above me. Hmm, pretty. "And I'm fine. The goat poo softened the blow."

My suit on the other hand? Not so much.

A head popped into my field of vision. His lips were in an angry pout. Hands came around my arms. Sides. Head. Neck? I didn't know, because before I knew how, or where his hands had been, I was upright and the hands were gone.

"Hey," I complained. "I was fine down there. That was an intentional trip." His brows arched. "I was looking at the stars?" I tried.

Cameron's nostrils flared. "Fine. I fell. But you can't be mad, because I saved the flannel. And I really was looking at the stars."

"Fuck the jacket—" he started.

But something behind him distracted me. Brandy. Heading for the water.

"Oh no." I sprinted around Cameron. "Brandy!"

Cameron murmured something, or maybe he shouted it, I didn't know. And I didn't—couldn't—care. I was too busy jumping into knee-high freezing water to make sure a blind six-month-old goat named Brandy, whose poop I was covered in, didn't drown.

Cameron Caldani and his stupid flannel jacket would need to wait.

CHAPTER SEVENTEEN

Adalyn

*I*f I thought Cameron had been exasperating when he'd been indifferent toward working with me, that was because I had no idea how Cameron was when he was actually involved.

"You're being stubborn," he told me with that annoying arch of his brow.

"Me?" I scoffed. "You're the one who's been complaining about the color scheme for the new uniforms for a full hour. Honestly, for someone who dresses in technical wear that comes in colors like Smolder Blue, Northern Black, or Rocky Gray, you seem very keen on deciding what shade of green the socks should be."

He let out a grunt.

The fifth one in the last hour. As if he was some . . . bear-man.

"What's wrong now?" I asked. "Did I offend your fashion sense by saying the truth?"

"These bloody stands we're sitting on." Cameron shifted in his seat. "They are worse than I thought," he muttered, turning right and left as if the bleachers had anything else to offer but a hard surface and an iron structure that had seen better days. "How do you manage to sit here for two whole hours, three days a week?"

I rolled my eyes. "Oh, the audacity of men to doubt a woman's capacity to endure pain and discomfort."

Cameron scowled. "Pain?"

"Can you please focus? I need to close this today. We said we would discuss it on Monday after practice and got nowhere. Wednesday's meeting was fruitless too. Now it's Thursday, the second game is this coming Saturday, and the girls will play in the old uniforms again. Do you see the rush?"

"Not really," he had the nerve to answer.

Now that outright pissed me off. "I have reports to fill and a success story to create. For that I need a narrative I control, a social media presence to get eyes on the team, a strategy to win the Six Hills, and a team dressed in decent, up-to-date sponsored uniforms. So far I have none of that."

"You have me."

That stupid blush returned, and I made myself give him a bland look. "Yay."

But as ironic as I intended that, something heavy and unexpected settled deep in my belly. I really did have Cameron's help after that sudden change of heart during last Saturday's game. I'd seen the shift in how he ran practice this week. Cameron had been a lot less resignedly patient and more . . . assertive. Bossy. And to my surprise, instead of rebelling or complaining, the chaotic ragtag team that had been the Green Warriors had gone so far as to look disciplined.

For like ten percent of the time.

Cameron's large body shifted again, sidetracking me when the side of his knee collided against mine. An unexpected shiver crawled down my spine at the warm contact of his skin against the thin fabric of the chinos I was wearing in an attempt to look less scary and more approachable. My gaze fell on his bare knee, thanks to the workout shorts he religiously wore to practice. My eyes trailed upward, along his quad. The fabric had ridden up and his skin was on display, smooth-looking and—

Ugh. I was doing it again. Ogling this man's body.

"You're cold," he stated from my side. "Again. When are you going to finally understand that you're not in Miami and these flimsy clothes are not enough?"

"I'm not cold," I lied. I was simply affected by the brief contact of his leg. "I'm annoyed. And my clothes are not flimsy." I lifted up the forgotten binder from my lap. "If you want to participate in the decision process of the new uniforms"—and the matching tracksuit he didn't approve of but I was ordering anyway—"we settle on one now. Otherwise, I'll look for someone else's input."

"You don't have anybody else."

I didn't.

Besides Josie, and maybe Grandpa Moe, not a single soul in Green Oak was remotely interested in talking to me, much less working with me. Diane was still doubling as a PTA vigilante. But I wasn't complaining. I would also be hesitant to befriend the sicko who attacked a mascot and went by the name of Lady Birdinator online.

I pulled out my phone and opened my messages app.

Cameron craned his neck. "Who are you texting?"

I kept my eyes on the screen, ignoring how near he'd moved, and selected a few of the pictures I'd taken during Saturday's game. "Someone who might actually help."

"Matthew," Cameron murmured. "Is that your *daddy*?"

That stung more than I expected. Not because Cameron had implied more than once that I was spoiled, but because I didn't think my father would answer if I texted him. All I'd gotten from him in the last days was a message from his secretary to confirm the energy drink issue was being looked at. Not even a quick check-in. "He's my best friend."

It was stupid to ask Matthew, but I was trying to prove a point.

Cameron exhaled noisily, his whole body moving with the release of air. The side of his quad pressed against the side of mine. "Adalyn, I—"

My phone pinged.

"There you go," I said. "Quick. Efficient. Always willing."

Cameron grumbled something I ignored in favor of reading Matthew's texts out loud.

MATTHEW: WTF

MATTHEW: EXPLAIN.

I let out a quick celebratory *Ha*. "See? Now this is exactly the involvement I was looking for. Passion for discussion."

But then I scrolled down and I . . .

MATTHEW: Is that who I think it is?

MATTHEW: WHAT IS HE DOING THERE?

MATTHEW: Is this today????

MATTHEW: WTF ADALYN

MATTHEW: I CAN'T BELIEVE YOU ARE WITH Cameron Caldani (!!) and you wouldn't tell ME.

MATTHEW: What is he even doing in NC? What—

I immediately locked my phone.

For good measure, I brought it to my chest. Hid it. How had I— The pictures. Cameron must have been in them. God. My fingers clasped the device even tighter. I didn't want Cameron to believe I was going around giving away where he was.

I looked over at him, coming up with ways to explain myself, but Cameron was engrossed in my binder. The red one.

I blinked.

Take it as a win, Adalyn.

I shoved my phone into the depths of my bag and cleared my throat. "Yes." I scooted closer to him. Which I realized was a mistake, because all I could feel and smell was Cameron. I scooted back. "I think we can move on to strategy, good idea."

"Already on it," he said without looking at me.

A little passive-aggressive but I'd averted a crisis, so I'd give him that. "How's that looking?" I asked. "What do you have in mind in terms of game plan? We're playing against—"

"Rockstone," he finished for me. "It's here in your little binder." It wasn't little, but I let that go, too. "And my plan is for the kids to point at the right side this time."

"That's a good start," I admitted genuinely. "But we should probably start tracking something more specific. Like training plans for every player to cater to their individual needs." I stretched a hand over his lap and turned a few pages, getting to the individual cards I'd prepared. "Maybe if we—" I felt the weight of his stare on my profile. "Why are you looking at me like that?"

Cameron's head tilted, and when he spoke, thanks to my leaning in over him, his words fell on my temple. "You've got a section for me in your binder of hell?"

I did. But filed away in a box in my head. Something else in my head right now? How close his face was to mine. I jerked back. "Don't speak like that about my binder" was all I could say.

A deep chuckle rumbled off Cameron, as if I was this amusing thing he could poke.

"This is proving very unproductive," I told him. "Let's call it a day and go home."

All amusement vanished, and his shoulders went as far as sinking, even if almost imperceptibly. "Ada, darling," he said with an exhale.

Ada, darling.

That was new. I'd never been called something like that. It was . . . musical and beautiful and hearing Cameron say it made me feel strange. Not like being called Addy or Ads did, but different. I decided I wouldn't like it.

Cameron's expression shifted again, as if something was dawning, finally making sense. I panicked but then, what had to be his phone rang from his pocket, providing me with an easy out.

Relieved, I watched him reluctantly pull the device out of the front pocket of his jacket and check the screen. He straightened, his demeanor changing instantly. "I need to take this. Excuse me for a minute."

And just like that, he was swiftly climbing down the stands and I was left there, watching how the muscles in those sculpted calves danced with every stride.

"And I'm doing it again," I told myself. "Ogling him."

I exhaled, grabbing the binder from where Cameron had left it and hugging it to myself. I thought back to Matthew's trail of texts. If I was lucky, he wouldn't jump on a flight and plant himself on Cameron's doorstep to get his forehead signed. Or knowing Matthew, his ass cheek. Or—

"Hi!"

The binder was almost startled out of my grasp.

"Oops," María said. "Did I scare you, Miss Adalyn? I'm sorry. Sometimes I'm too loud."

I smoothed my expression into what I hoped was a nice smile. "You're never too loud, María," I told her, and for some reason, something my mother said came to mind. "And you should never apologize for being loud. Whoever makes you feel that way is the one with sensitive ears."

She made a face. "That makes a lot of sense." She nodded slowly. "Was that why you were staring at the back of his head? Were you staring at Coach Camouflage's ears?"

I sighed. "I was . . . wondering what conditioner he uses. His hair looks so shiny and bright all the time."

Her brows knit in the middle of her forehead. "I don't think I've ever used conditioner. Dad buys all the shower products for the house and Tony helps me out with my hair." I glanced up at the way her hair was in some lopsided ponytail today. "Maybe I can ask Dad to get me one."

I looked at the girl who had always treated me differently than everyone else, trying to remember if she had ever mentioned her mother. It wasn't any of my business, and it would be extremely inappropriate to ask a child about something like that, but there was something about this particular kid that made me want to know.

A teenager emerged around the corner of the stands carrying a plank of wood, distracting me from the thought.

"Oh yeah," María said, while I gawked at the unexpected sight behind her. "Tony and Dad are working on the supply shed. Remember how we accidentally broke the door and made a mess? Come, I'll introduce you, Miss Adalyn. They'll like you, I promise."

And before I knew what was happening, María was pulling me behind her all the way to where her brother and father were working.

When we reached them, María tugged at my hand and I blurted out a very loud "Hi."

Tony, a teenage boy that was all legs and arms who had been in the process of placing the plank of wood I'd seen on his shoulder against a workbench, dropped the thing to the ground.

His father cursed.

María chuckled.

"I'm so sorry," I rushed out.

"Tony has such sensitive ears," María quipped.

Tony turned around. "How about you clip it, you little monster—" He spotted me, his face turning cherry red. He seemed to choke. "Oh. Hello, ma'am."

"Ignore Tony," María chirped. "He gets like that when girls are around." The teenager's eyes widened. "Hey, Dad? This is Miss Adalyn, remember I told you about her?"

The man was already walking around the workbench and taking off a pair of security gloves. "It's hard to forget," he said with a smile that immediately reminded me of his daughter. "You're all she talks about." He stretched out a hand. "I'm Robbie Vasquez, pleased to finally meet you."

I took his hand and shook it. "It's great to meet you, too, Mr. Vasquez."

A lighthearted laughter rolled off his tongue. "Please, Robbie is all right." He released my hand and slipped his gloves back on. "It's nice to finally be able to put a face to the name everyone in town is chattering about. I would have loved to introduce myself during the goat happy hour but there was an emergency at the cow barn."

María tugged at my hand, and I looked down at her. "Carmen hasn't been eating. I think she's sad because Sebastian went missing weeks ago."

"Carmen the . . . cow?" I ventured. "And Sebastian the . . ."

"The rooster," María offered. "Sebastian Stan, Miss Josie named him. It was my birthday present."

"That would be them." Robbie chuckled. "María likes for all the animals we have to be named. But Carmen's stomach is all right now. Nothing to worry about."

Tony approached us shyly before I could ask any further questions. His face was still red, and his eyes were cast down. "All the planks are out of the truck. Can I run to Josie's for a minute?"

His dad clicked his tongue. "Fine," he relented. And the teen didn't waste time turning around. "But take your sister with you," Robbie added, bringing the teenager to a stop. "And be back in five. Tops. We've got work to do."

Tony shook his head, but he stretched an arm, sticking his hand out.

María shot running in her brother's direction, latching on to the outstretched limb. "I'll bring you a brownie, Miss Adalyn," she called over her shoulder. "You, too, Dad!"

Robbie laughed, but called back, *"Gracias, bichito."*

The Spanish words echoed in my mind. A part of me felt encouraged to exploit that connection. We had something in common, after all. A language. Maybe a culture, too. I'd know if I asked.

That was what my mother would do. But I . . . I didn't know how. My mind blanked in situations like these. What if the man talked to me in Spanish and discovered that mine wasn't very good? What if he expected me to be something I wasn't and then turned out to be disappointed? He seemed to like me just fine for now.

My gaze roamed around, desperately searching for something to say, and coming to a stop when I spotted a Miami Flames hoodie thrown over a toolbox.

"Are you a fan?" I asked, nodding at it.

"Tony is," he admitted, a slow smile parting his face. "The boy's crazy about soccer. Watches everything and anything he finds on TV, or his phone." A shake of his head. "I'm not one for sports, honestly, but their mother was. He, uh . . ." His smile fell. "He took after her in that way. María does, too, I guess."

Was. Their mother was.

I wracked my head again to say something appropriate and not bring this conversation to an awkward halt. "I work for the Miami Flames," I rushed out. "I know Miami is not exactly around the corner, but I could get you tickets to a game. You guys could make a trip out of it. Miami will be a good break from the cold by the time the Flames make it to playoffs. If they ever do, that is. We're not having the best season."

The cheery, kind man fell strangely silent.

"I'm the head of communications of the team," I felt the need to explain. "Well, I . . . was. I'm on a temporary leave—break. I'm on a break." Robbie frowned and I shifted my feet. "That sounds like I was fired, but I wasn't. I can get the three of you good tickets, I promise. My father is the owner. He, uh—" I swallowed, and God, I didn't even know why I was rambling to this man. "Andrew Underwood. I'm his daughter. So, even if I'm technically on a break I'm still able to get tickets for, er, people. Yes."

Robbie's expression closed off. He even took a step back. "But your name," he said. "It's Reyes. I didn't think—" He stopped himself.

I . . . I didn't understand what I'd said to possibly offend him.

Was he realizing that I was the crazy woman from the video the whole town was talking about? "I use my mother's last name." I clasped my hands so I wouldn't fidget. "And I promise, the kids are safe with me. That—"

"Thanks for the offer, miss," he interjected. "But I'm afraid I can't accept the tickets. We've already taken more charity than I'm comfortable with."

Charity.

The term seemed to hit me harder than it should have. Perhaps because I'd accused Cameron of the same thing. Robbie's and my reactions weren't that far off. So I shouldn't be all that hurt. Only I'd tried to be nice. This was María's dad, and I'd wanted to do something for him and his kids. It wouldn't hurt to have someone besides Josie on my side. I couldn't understand how it had backfired so miserably.

"Is there a problem?" a deep, accented voice said behind me.

Something happened in my body then, something that felt a lot like relief. Relief at Cameron Caldani being there. Here. It didn't make sense.

Robbie's eyes locked on a point over my head. He opened his mouth.

"Everything's fine," I interjected. "I was pestering Mr. Vasquez and not letting him do his work. Now that I think of it, I never arranged for the repairs of the shed. Did Josie call you? It was my mess to clean, and I'd like to take care of it. So who should I see about the cost?"

"It's all taken care of, miss," Robbie answered.

So we really were back to the *miss*. "But—"

"It doesn't matter," Cameron interrupted. He came to my side and took a good look at me. His expression changed. Something flashed behind his eyes. Concern? "Now, where's that binder with your detailed fifteen-step plan to make my life all the more complicated? I'd like to go home."

Mr. Vasquez's brows shot up.

Yeah, not concern. Whatever kind of relief I thought I'd felt had been a lapse in judgment. Clearly.

I said very, very calmly, and with that smile I knew he found so appalling, "Do you know what?"

"I don't know what." His lips mirrored mine, tilting. "But you're gonna tell me anyway, aren't you, darling?"

That stupid *darling* came back. It angered me.

"You." I planted a finger on his unshockingly hard chest. "Can really be an ass."

He looked down at my index finger as it impaled his left pec. An eyebrow rose. "I think you can do better than that." His gaze met mine again. There was a challenge in there. "I did insult your binder. Again. I deserve a little more."

He did. I narrowed my eyes, the words dancing on the tip of my tongue.

"Come on, darling," he said, lowering his voice. "Let it out for me."

Let it out for me? Who did he think he was?

"You." I stabbed his chest with my finger. Anger swirling up my throat. "You are so exasperating that I can't." Another jab. "I can't with you, you stubborn, know-it-all, curmudgeon of a man!"

My words hung in the air as Cameron looked at me with a face I didn't understand. A face that wasn't frustrated or angry or even remotely unhappy. In fact, it was the opposite.

"What's a curmudgeon?" María said. "Is it the thing that Grandpa Moe got on his butt?"

I turned my head slowly, confirming María and Tony had returned. The nine-year-old was holding a grease-stained brown box and the teen was looking down at his sister with an expression of pure horror.

"Shut up, María," Tony whispered loudly. But then he turned toward us. And his eyes landed on Cameron. They widened.

"Why?" she continued, glancing up at her brother. "They were talking about asses, and Coach Kisscam always looks like he's angry about something."

Tony remained silent, his face etched in a mix of shock and awe that I recognized well. He was starstruck. The kid had to know exactly who Cameron was and it looked a lot like he was finding out for the first time. "Don't call him that," he murmured, coming into himself. "He's Cameron—"

"He's just Cameron," I stepped forward. Meeting the teenager's eyes. My voice had been a little harsh. I cleared my throat. "Or Coach Cam." I stepped back. "And we should really head home."

There was a beat of silence.

María sighed. "Honestly, I would be angry, too, if I had a giant thing on my bu—"

Tony pinched her side. "Clip it, stinky monster."

"Hey!" María complained. "I'm not a monster! And one day I'm going to be a boss-lady like Miss Adalyn. And I'll kick your ass with my high heels like I know she does to anyone that calls her stinky."

My chest felt like it had been filled with concrete and I . . . God. All the fight escaped me.

I couldn't believe how or why someone would say that when I was nothing but a trainwreck who apparently called infuriating men names with minimal provocation, ripped mascot heads off costumes, was the face of an energy drink that praised entertainment over dignity, and fell into goat poo.

I'd never been liked or admired by anyone that fiercely. Like María seemed to do.

A hand fell on the small of my back, and when I was told, almost too softly, "Let's go get your things, darling. I'll walk you to your car," I went. Not even questioning when that very same hand dropped and brushed the back of mine as we walked away.

I was beginning to understand just how exhausted I was from questioning every single thing in life.

CHAPTER EIGHTEEN

Adalyn

$\mathcal{W}$e were at the Vasquez farm again.

Only this time, there weren't any yoga mats or fluffy farm animals jumping and bleating around. It was a Friday evening, the sun had already set, and I was holding my right limited-edition Manolo Blahnik in my hands.

Cameron killed the engine of his truck and got out of the vehicle. He wordlessly pointed at the shoe and shot me a questioning glance.

"The heel snapped," I explained in an unamused tone. Because how would I be amused? In one hand I lifted the beautiful, lavish stiletto I'd been stupid enough to wear, the heel in the other hand. "While I was waiting for you."

The truth was I'd been pacing. On pebbled and clearly dangerous terrain. But he was late and I . . . Well, I hadn't wanted to venture alone into the barn where tonight's activity was taking place. Cameron Caldani wasn't good company, but he was the lesser evil.

Cameron frowned. He frowned. Like he didn't understand. The last thing I needed was attitude. "Don't look at me like that," I deadpanned.

"Like what?" He finally crossed the distance between us and stopped in front of me. His gaze dipped and stopped at my naked foot. He sighed. "Maybe if you weren't parading around in those bloody things. But that's nothing I haven't told you before."

"'In those bloody things'?" I was outraged on behalf of my shoes. "These are Manolo Blahniks." His lips bent downward, as if the name didn't ring any bell. I pushed the loose heel into my pocket and returned the remainder of the shoe to my foot. "Don't pretend you don't know how much these are worth. You lived in L.A. for years," I told him, turning around. "And you even dated Jasmine Hill." I started marching forward. "No one dates a fashion brand ambassador and comes out of that relationship unchanged. Not even someone who dresses in moss-green or boulder-gray technical pants most of the time."

If Cameron thought anything about me knowing enough about his dating history to reference his only known relationship by name, he didn't say. Good. I'd purposefully outed myself in order to make a point and obtain what I wanted: silence.

"Let me help you to the barn," he said, suddenly there, right behind me. "You can't even walk in that broken *Banana Tonic*."

So much for that silence. "I don't need help. I'll continue to parade, as you put it, and risk the consequences."

A snicker left him.

I ignored it—and the way he hovered so close behind me—and limped the rest of the way to the barn. When we reached the entrance, his arm stuck out, that large palm pushing the wooden door open for me.

"Temper before age," he murmured against my temple.

I tried to ignore that, too, but the wave of tingles his breath created on my skin made my will waver.

Someone squealed and before I could set a foot inside, I was being wrapped in a hug, squeezed, released, and then pulled into the barn.

"You're finally here!" Josie exclaimed. "We were waiting for you two."

"We were held up," Cameron muttered. "By a ruined pair of Manolos."

I shot him a glance. So he knew. He more than knew. Only people who did called them Manolos.

"Now, that's just terrible," Josie crooned, making me return my attention to her. I gawked for a moment, distracted by the yellow dungarees she wore. "Oh, honey, no. You can't wear that for our pottery class. Tonight's Muddy and Mighty, and it's called that for a reason."

"But my clothes are fine," I countered, looking down at myself. "And I promise, the missing heel doesn't even bother me that much." It was the workout my calves didn't need, but I'd suck it up and be on my tiptoes all night if I had to.

Josie linked one of her arms with mine, moving us forward. "I'm sure you can do about anything at any given time, you're like our own Super-boss-lady." That seemed like a stretch. "But I won't let you ruin that beautiful blouse. Or pants. Not on top of the already fallen shoe. RIP." Her head turned to look over her shoulder. "Cam, sweetheart, go join the group. I'll be there in a minute."

Sweetheart? My heel-less limb wobbled. How familiar were Cameron and Josie? And how—I didn't care. They'd been friends before I got here. It wasn't important.

Or any of my business.

Josie dragged me all the way to the far end of the barn and pushed me into some kind of changing room that consisted of two foldable screens before disappearing for an instant. When she was back, she shoved something in my hands with a smile. "Come out when you're ready."

I looked down.

It was overalls. Pink. And sneakers. Also pink.

I thought back to my growing pile of laundry. My fallen shoe.

Overalls it is.

"You look so cute," Josie said when I rejoined the group. She gave me a once-over, her face brightening. "They look so much better on you than they do on me. You know what? You should keep them."

I doubted that was true. A glance at the borrowed clothes told me they looked as tight around my hips and chest as they felt. "That's . . . very kind of you. Thanks."

"Of course," she said with a wink. "Your workstation will be there. Right at the front." She pointed at the left. "I had to physically drag that man to the front of the class, by the way." I followed her finger with my eyes, stumbling upon a wide torso covered in a yellow apron with tiny daisies on it. "Can you do something to make him stop scowling?"

My eyes rose to Cameron's face. He didn't look happy. He was sulky and frowny and reminded me of a wet cat. It made me want to smile. "I don't think I can, actually. I think that's his face."

The corner of his mouth twitched.

"Cam?" Josie said in an overly sweet tone. "Will you be a doll and show Adalyn how to work the wheel? You said it wasn't your first time throwing a bowl. And today's really busy."

I looked around, taking in the ample space inside the barn and finding small groups of people gathered around waist-high tabletops. My eyes spotted Diane, who was pretending not to look this way.

I turned toward Josie. "I think this looks a little advanced for me. I'm a beginner."

Josie chuckled. "A pottery virgin." She smiled. I cringed. "Don't worry, you'll be in good hands." She gave my shoulders a push in the direction of my workstation. And the scowly man. "Come on, courage conquers all things. Even pottery!"

I reluctantly stumbled to Cameron's side.

His eyes dipped, his jaw clamping down. "Cute overalls."

"Cute apron," I answered while Josie started shouting instructions in the background. "The daisies really bring out your eyes."

He huffed out a chuckle.

I made a face at him, and his gaze dipped down again. Quickly. Wickedly fast. But I caught it. I resisted the urge to tug at the overalls.

"So, you know how this works?" I pointed at the wheel assembled on top of the high bench.

Cameron's hand entered my field of vision. He flipped a switch on its side, making the plate rotate slowly.

"Is there anything you don't know how to do?"

He made a show of thinking about his answer and had the audacity to look smug when he said, "No."

"Perfect!" Josie exclaimed, startling me with the sudden closeness of her voice. She clapped her hands. "You've turned on the wheel! Yay!" Then she scurried away again, praising how therapeutic pottery was in what I'd learned was her monitor voice.

"Jesus," I whispered, patting my chest. "How does she do that?"

Cameron didn't answer, instead he drawled, "Seems like we're throwing a bloody bowl, then."

"Yay," I murmured, watching him reach out for the block of mud. My gaze snapped at Cameron's hands, his long rough-looking fingers. He'd taken off his ring. I lowered my voice, "I could figure this out on my own. I've read about it and watched more than a few how-to videos. I've done my homework." His hands split the thing in two and started shaping one half into a ball. "I'm serious. You could just watch. Or leave."

Cameron stretched his arm in my direction, holding the clay ball in his hand. "Fix the ball to the wheel."

I hesitated.

That pair of forest-green eyes stared right into mine. "Stop overthinking and fix the ball to the wheel for me, yeah?"

He had that sulky look again, so I took the clay from him and let it drop on the plate with a heavy thump. I frowned at it. "Hold on, why aren't we sitting down?" I looked around. "Everything I watched and read was done sitting down. I'll get Josie—"

"Throwing while standing is better for your back," he said matter-of-factly, as if that explained anything. "Put your palms around it and try to seal the edges to the surface."

Lips pressed in a tight line, I tried to do as instructed, only managing to make the plate of the wheel turn when I pressed on the ball every time. I spared a glance at Cameron, expecting to find him reveling in my frustration. He was unbothered by my failed attempts. His expression was calm. Patient. It reminded me of how he treated the girls. He tilted his head to the side, still waiting. It hit me then, that he was either letting me figure it out on my own or waiting for me to ask him for help.

An unexpected thought materialized. He'd make such a great dad. Beneath that irate, hard façade, there was patience. Gentle command. Warmth spread down my— Oh God. Why did this thought have such an effect on me? Why was I . . . picturing things? I didn't even know if I wanted kids.

"You good?" Cameron asked.

"I . . ." I swallowed when I heard my voice wobble. What was wrong with me? "I can't do this. On my own. Could you, perhaps, maybe, hmm, help?"

Cameron's palms fell immediately on top of mine.

Once more, it was my whole body that felt the touch of his skin against the back of my hands. I lifted my head, meeting his eyes across the tabletop.

"Like this," he said in a low voice, the heels of his palms pressing on top of my knuckles. "You feel the pressure of my hands? Do like I'm doing. Feel the way the clay gives."

I looked down, shocked and strangely pleased at the sight of our hands as they fused together over the clay. I swallowed, less reluctant to allow him to take the lead, and more enthralled by the controlled motions before me.

With a silent nod, I started taking mental notes as best as I could, while he continued the motions.

"Let the wheel turn with the movement," he said, and I felt myself release all remnants of control. I'd let him guide me. My hands. Completely. "You need to press on the sides so it sticks to it." The plate turned with the motions of our hands, his voice turning into a focused murmur. "Just like that. Yeah. That's about right."

Once the ball was fixed, he grasped my wrists and lifted my hands in the air. He hummed deep in his throat, observing our work.

I opened my mouth to ask if there was something wrong, but all too soon, Cameron was releasing me and his hand was flying toward the clay.

He swatted at the ball.

Once, twice. Three times. And I—

Oh God. Was Cameron spanking the clay? My heart dropped to my stomach. Why couldn't I stop staring at his hand? Why was my face feeling like flames were licking at my cheeks?

I brought one of my hands to my forehead, checking how my skin felt to the touch. I must be coming down with something. This couldn't possibly make me so hot.

This wasn't erotic. This was just clay.

"Seems good to go," Cameron said next, grabbing a sponge I hadn't even seen there. He wetted it in a bowl. "We can get started with the centering."

"The centering," I repeated in a wobbly voice.

He nodded, and when the man squeezed the sponge gently, letting a few water drops fall onto the clay, I was certain. I had to be sick. Something was going on with me. Otherwise, I wouldn't be finding the way his wet fingers slid around the slick material so suggestive. My throat dried.

"Adalyn?" His voice made it through the insanity in my head.

I looked up at him. His eyebrow was arched. "Press the pedal, darling."

"The . . . what?"

"Make the wheel turn," he instructed, his tone gentle, so gentle it felt foreign. As if he was talking to somebody else. "With the pedal."

My lips bobbed, my understanding of basic things stifled by those unexpectedly suggestive visuals of the clay. "What do you mean?"

Cameron sighed softly, and suddenly he was on the move, walking around the table.

He placed himself behind me. "You're making this really hard, darling," he said, and before I could process his comment, his palm landed on my thigh. Strong fingers wrapped around my leg, slid down to my knee. He lifted my now numb limb, letting my foot fall on something. That warm, large hand pressed gently, his body coming slightly over mine with the motion. "Quit looking at me all soft and sweet and focus on pressing the pedal with your foot, yeah?"

I was shaken—so overwhelmed by the sudden closeness of Cameron's body and his words—that instead of pressing, I jerked my leg forward, hitting the pedal with uncontrolled force.

The wheel whirled, wickedly fast, splattering mud all over the place. Us.

"Christ," Cameron growled, his arms coming around my body, as if to protect me from the splashing mud, and his leg swiftly replacing mine. The thing slowed down. "You have to start at a gentle speed," he instructed, his mouth much, much closer than it had been a few seconds ago. Right beside my temple. His leg moved again, making me notice how it pressed right against mine. "See?" he asked, but I didn't see a single thing. Not with Cameron wrapped around me. "We have the control of the wheel. Us."

Us.

We.

I didn't think I was breathing but I nodded. So enthusiastically that the back of my head collided against his collarbone. "I'm sorry," I mumbled. "I . . . was distracted."

By you. Your touch. The way you're sandwiching me against the edge of the tabletop.

Cameron reached for the sponge again, and his jaw brushed my cheek.

My breath hitched.

His fell on my temple. "You shouldn't be disrupting my train of thought this easily, either."

Either. The fire in my face spread down my neck, sneaking into the neckline of the overalls. "Am I doing that?"

Cameron produced a sound that made his chest rumble. He grabbed my hands and placed them on the spinning clay. "If it's not well centered," he said, increasing the speed of the plate and keeping his palms over mine as the material slid beneath my skin. The inside of his thigh pressed on the outside of mine. He felt like a furnace. "The whole thing will be off balance."

I gave him a nod. But I was no longer listening.

"Press gently," he instructed, driving our hands upward and around the wet material. "This is the way we cone the clay up."

That *we* again. I . . . liked it.

I also liked the hypnotizing motion of the wheel and the blanketing sensation of Cameron's body around mine. I seemed to like one too many things about this. Things I shouldn't like.

"Just like that." His voice was now impossibly low, carrying the same quality I felt inside my chest. He moved even closer, his arms swallowing me up. "Good job, darling. Well done."

Something in me stirred at the simple praise. I was vaguely aware of this happening before, but my heart still pounded. It banged against my rib cage, just like Cameron's, and it felt good. So good that I leaned back, letting my head fall against his chest while we worked.

Cameron's exhale tickled the skin right beneath my ear. "Let's take it back down now," he said, interlacing our wet fingers and sending a rush of electricity up my arms at the sensation. He moved our hands and the clay changed shape. "That looks incredible."

That soft spot in my chest batted its wings. I hooked my thumbs with his.

A grumble climbed out of Cameron's mouth.

The flutter intensified, making me short of breath. I wanted to turn around and search his face. See if he was feeling like I did. But I didn't, I didn't want this to go away. Not yet. I was trapped by the moment. Captured by the solid presence of Cameron and the feel of his hands.

"It's been a long time since I've held hands with anyone," I heard myself admit out loud. "I can't remember something so simple ever feeling this way."

Cameron's hands froze momentarily over mine. It was just a second, maybe less, but I'd seen it. Felt it. He hesitated.

I was spat out of the vacuum.

Just like that, I was no longer calm. Or peacefully trapped in whatever this was. The reins I was so busy keeping a tight hold of snapped right back into my grasp. Here I was, telling this man who was reluctantly doing this with me that he was the first to hold my hands in a long time. That he made me somehow feel like I'd never felt before. What was next? To tell him that besides that one-liner Matthew had thrown at me almost a decade ago, I'd never been flirted with? That my only serious relationship had turned out to be a lie? That the man I'd thought had been ready to propose once upon a time had never seen me as more than a bridge to get to my father?

She's so frigid man. So . . . boring. I really dodged a bullet there. Too bad, because when the old man kicks the bucket she'll probably inherit most of his money. But nah. I can only endure so much.

Nah.

As if I'd been nothing more than an insipid and boring side dish you passed on.

I'll pass on the complimentary roasted veggies, thank you very much. But nah.

I hadn't been hurt. I didn't care that David had ended a relationship that brought little to my life. But as time had passed, I'd held on to the idea that I'd had at least that. That one relationship that proved that I wasn't . . . cold. Dry. That I could be loved. Desired.

So how was I supposed to not crack? How was I supposed to hear David laugh and say that he'd dated me just to sneak into my father's empire, that I was a bullet that was dodged, and not have something in me break? How was I supposed to not change when I heard everything he said right after that?

The image of Sparkles's head at my feet crystallized in—

"Adalyn." Cameron's voice cut through the loud disarray of thoughts in my head. Again. Just like it always managed to do. "Snap out of it, darling." It was angry. Rough sounding. "Come back to me."

I forced myself to make sense of my surroundings.

The blob of clay rested at a weird angle.

Strong hands held mine.

Beautiful, crooked hands that had been injured one too many times. Where was the signet ring he wore around his pinky?

The sound of my own breathing crystallized in my ears. The vacuum I'd been sucked in a moment ago, spitting me right out. This wasn't the first time. It wasn't the first time I found myself close to hyperventilating in this man's arms. I hated it.

"Where the hell did you go to?" Cameron asked. And when I didn't answer, his thumbs started tracing idle circles on the top of my hands. "How long have you been experiencing panic attacks?"

My spine stiffened. "I don't—I—" Panic attacks? "That wasn't a panic attack." It couldn't be.

Could it?

Cameron hummed deep in his throat, and I didn't know whether it was in agreement or complaint. He released one of my hands and snagged the flattened pile of material from the wheel.

"Is it ruined?" I asked him, hating how my voice sounded.

He discarded it on the side. "It is, yeah."

Of course it was.

After a long moment he said, his voice still gentle, his tone kind, his arms around me, "Darling?"

"Maybe you were right," I admitted, not even bothering to care I was not moving out of his embrace. "Maybe that was a panic attack."

"Okay," he said quickly. "But I was going to say something else."

"That this was as therapeutic as a kick on the shin?"

A low chuckle left him, and the sound felt different from every other time he'd chuckled before. "I was going to say that everyone in here is staring at us. And as much as I don't really mind, we either move, or we'll be everything everybody will be talking about tomorrow."

My head snapped up. I looked around.

Cameron was right.

A flat tire.

A freaking flat tire.

I braced my hands on my hips, noticing the splatters of clay on my borrowed dungarees. Great. Yet another thing I'd have to throw at the giant pile of laundry I already had.

Here I thought that having to wash my underwear by hand and hang it out to dry on the antlers had been the lowest point this week. Of course not. There was the stupid panic attack I just had. Me storming off out of the barn before the pottery class finished. And now this. I glanced back at the tire and I shook my head. Pressure clamped down in the mouth of my stomach. I wondered if I was going to cry.

I patted my eyes. Dry. The notion of me still not able to figure out when the last time I'd shed a tear came back. A bitter laugh escaped my mouth.

Another one followed, because God, I was a mess. Before I knew what was happening, I was cackling at the dark sky above my head. I let out my frustration. Although it quickly turned into anger. Disbelief. Desperation. "Shit," I heard myself breathe out with a humorless laugh. "Fuck." The cackling died out. My eyes fell on the tire. I kicked it. "Screw you, you stupid goddamn flat fucking tire!"

"That escalated quickly."

My whole body stilled. My back stiffened.

"Motherfucker," I murmured. Because I never swore but I was allowing myself to have this one moment.

"Oh wow," Cameron said, and I heard his steps coming closer. "Please don't stop on my behalf. I'm rather enjoying this."

I looked over my shoulder, finding him with the amused expression I expected from his tone. "Always happy to hear about how my misfortune amuses you."

He sobered up. "It doesn't," he countered, his gaze going up and down my body. Swiftly but thoroughly enough to make me pause. His throat worked. "It's you who amuses me, Adalyn. And I can't even figure out exactly why. Which bothers me. And fascinates me."

I shook my head. "Is that supposed to be a compliment?"

"Hell if I know, darling," he said, kneeling down. He checked the tire and straightened back up. "I'll drive you back to Lazy Elk, come on."

He pulled out his truck keys and unlocked the doors with an elegant *click*.

I opened my mouth, but he cut me off with a "Don't bother."

"How do you know I was going to speak? You were not even looking this way."

"Because I'm not the only one who operates in two single modes," he delivered in a sharp tone. "You do, too. You either over-think, or object. Both tirelessly, and usually directed at me." He threw the copilot door open and shot me a look over the hood of the car. "You didn't seem that bothered by me when I had my arms around you, so save the complaint and jump in the car."

My arms around you.

My face flamed. "That's different. Pottery and getting into an enclosed space with someone who could very well be planning to murder me and throw my body into some creek in the woods, hoping that putrefaction and scavenger creatures dismember it in a week so the bones sink straight to the bottom and all traces of the remains vanish are two very different things."

"Oddly specific." He tilted his head. "But creative." The corner of his lips twitched. "I think you'll survive this one drive, come on. I'll call Robbie on our way back and let him know your car will stay the night on the farm."

"That's . . . completely unrelated to what I was saying, but okay."

Cameron shifted on his feet, casually resting an elbow on the hood of the vehicle, looking like someone who had all the time in the world to pick my words apart. "Okay, you'll get in the car? Or okay, I'll continue bitching around out here, in the middle of the night, without a jacket on, just to spite me?"

I frowned. Spite him? I . . . All the fight left me. "I don't do things to spite you, Cameron."

"Jump in then," he said, and I swore his voice softened like never before. "I promise I won't feed you to the fish."

"Thanks," I clipped, closing the distance to his truck. "Just for the record, I want to state that I could know how to change a tire." I didn't. "You made an assumption."

A strangled sound left him when I reached him and slipped under his arm to get inside. I ignored it. I also ignored how horrible I felt for being purposefully difficult and how good his car smelled. Just like he did. And when Cameron pushed my door closed, walked around the car, folded his large body into the driver's seat, and did that thing where he placed his flexed arm behind my headrest and reversed the car, I ignored how squishy that made me feel inside, too.

Generally speaking, I did a whole lot of disregarding how he made me feel on the drive back to Lazy Elk. And Cameron must have been doing the same, because neither of us spoke a single word until he killed the engine in the driveway.

"I'll ring Robbie when I get inside," he said, his voice sounding so . . . deep and low and intimate inside the confinement of his truck. "We'll get the tire sorted tomorrow."

We. That we again, as if we were . . . an item. A team. My chest did some of that squishing at the thought.

"Thanks for doing that," I told him. I was so tired of antagonizing this man. "I'd insist on calling Robbie myself, but I don't think he likes me very much."

Cameron seemed to think about something. "His kids adore you."

I wasn't sure if he'd said that to make me feel better or because it was true. "I wouldn't go that far. María likes me, but a part of me believes she's trying to prove to the rest of the team that I'm not a witch." I shrugged. "And Tony is a teenage boy who calls me *ma'am* and barely talks to me."

Cameron's eyes roamed around my face. "Tony doesn't know how to act around a beautiful woman."

Beautiful.

I ripped my gaze off his face and let it settle on the dashboard. "What do you mean?"

"The kid fancies you, Adalyn." Right. "That's why he gets tongue-tied. That's probably why he calls you ma'am, too."

So Tony believed I was beautiful. Not Cameron. That was fine. I'd never been insecure about my looks or needed anybody's reassurance to feel good about my appearance. I definitely had other insecurities. But it didn't really matter, and it was foolish of me to think Cameron would ever look at me like that after how . . . our relationship had gone.

"I didn't say thanks," Cameron shocked me by adding. I looked over at him. His eyes were on me. "Tony recognized me back at the facilities, and you covered for me. I appreciate it."

I shook my head. I didn't deserve his gratitude. I . . . I fumbled with my seatbelt, overwhelmed by the sudden urge to exit this car. It released with a *click*, and I threw open the passenger door. "Thanks for the ride. I will, hmm, see you tomorrow. Game day. Big day ahead. Good night!"

And jumped out without wasting a minute. I shot in the direction of my cabin but quickly came to a halt.

"Oh no," I muttered, patting the pockets of my borrowed dungarees. Nothing. Empty. I groaned. "Oh God."

I turned around. But I—

Collapsed against a hard wall. One that smelled like a pine forest and felt boiling hot to the touch. I stumbled back. "Cameron."

"Why did you run?" wall-man asked, his chin tipping down to look at his chest. My gaze followed along, discovering my hands were planted on his pecs. I snagged them back. "What's wrong?" he pressed, flat-out ignoring I hadn't answered his first question.

"I forgot my things." I sighed. Yes, I'd focus on that. "Back at the barn. My clothes, my shoes, my phone, the keys, too. I think I left the door unlocked so I could get inside, but I need my phone."

"What?" he barked.

I frowned. "I was going to ask you to drive me back. There's strange noises in the cabin at night and I can't sleep without listening to—"

Cameron moved.

He bolted and walked around me. When the shock wore off, I whirled and went after him.

"I swear to God, Adalyn," I heard him grumble when I reached him. "There's no goddamn winning with you." His hand was clasped around the doorknob of the door. It opened without resistance. "Christ."

"I told you it would probably be unlocked," I scoffed. I stared at Cameron's back. He was . . . not moving. I'd expected him to be relieved, if anything. This gave him the perfect excuse not to drive me back. But I could . . . feel the anger leaving his body in waves. "You know what? That's fine. I'll make it without my phone. We'll just drive back tomorrow morning."

Cameron remained planted right where he was.

"It all worked out for the best so . . . good night," I insisted, popping my head over his shoulder. Cameron stepped inside. He flipped the lights on. "Hey, what do you think you're doing—"

"What in the bloody hell is this?" he asked. His words ricocheted in the confined and cramped space. Then he repeated himself, as if wanting to make sure I heard him right. "What is this, Adalyn?"

"My cottage?" I deadpanned, even though I was panicking inside. The place was a . . . mess. And I didn't want Cameron to see how much. My voice wobbled. "Can you please leave? I didn't invite you in."

He did the opposite and in two strides, Cameron was standing right in the center of the cabin, his shoulders so high and his back so stiff that I was shocked the seams of his jacket weren't ripping.

I swallowed hard and trailed behind him. I spotted the trail of panties currently hanging off the antlers I'd used as an improvised clothesline after washing them by hand. The inflatable mattress on the floor. The half-disassembled four-poster bed I'd given up on. The life I'd packed in a matter of hours scattered in one corner of one ugly cabin.

"Explain," Cameron demanded. "Please make it make sense."

"It's my home renovation project," I said, a bonfire cackling beneath my cheeks.

"Adalyn," he breathed out. Pleaded really. "You're still sleeping on the floor. Why?"

Green eyes blinked at me with . . . exhaustion. A hint of despair, too. I deflated. Gave up. "My plan was to disassemble the bed and get it out of here, but the thing seems to be welded together." I let out a shaky breath. "The cabin doesn't have a washer so . . ." I nodded toward my underwear. "The camping mattress is comfortable, though. So it's fine. I won't be here forever."

Cameron's jaw clenched. His whole face went tight. "Why didn't you ask for help?"

I closed my eyes. *Help.* How could I explain to him that Miami was flat-out ignoring me? That I'd been accused of being pampered and spoiled so many times that I wanted to prove that wrong. That besides Josie, I didn't have any friends here and didn't want to be a nuisance to the one I had. That all of this was my fault in the first place so I didn't think I had the right to complain. "I don't need help. I'm fine."

His Adam's apple bobbed. Once, twice, three times. All the air in his lungs was released. All at once.

"Fuck," he muttered. "Fuck me, Adalyn." He shook his head. "Jesus Christ, darling." He closed his eyes and let his head drop back. "Bloody hell."

I blinked at him. Confused. Shocked, too.

"I've gone a long life without this," he said, as if he was talking to himself. I opened my mouth but he turned around. "First the dungarees, now this. I'm unprepared."

"Cam—"

He stalked out of the cabin.

I stood there, looking down at my borrowed clothes, and wondering what had just happened. Wondering if I should close the door and call it a night, too.

Cameron reappeared.

He stormed right back into the cabin, still cursing like his life depended on it, but now, he was holding a metal box under an arm. I searched for his eyes, but he wouldn't look at me. He walked right past me, came to a stop in front of the mess of hardwood and dropped the box to the floor. Then, he kneeled down and threw it open with a jerk of his hand.

"Cameron?" I ventured, gaping at the scene in complete disbelief. "What are you doing?"

But Cameron Caldani was on autopilot.

He ignored my query, pulling a very large and serious-looking hammer out of the box, and straightened back up.

And then, without a word, he went full-on Hulk on the bed.

CHAPTER NINETEEN

Cameron

$\mathcal{I}$ couldn't catch a break.

With a shake of my head, I scanned the mess before me. Not only was Willow's food scattered all over the kitchen floor, but there were puddles of water and . . . Were those some of my coffee beans? I kneeled down to get a better look. Yes.

Joined by a few auburn feathers.

"Willow?" I called loudly, rising to my feet. I waited for the sound of her paws on the hardwood, or for one of her whiny responses, as I was sure she knew what she had done. But the cabin remained dead quiet. "Willow? You better not have chased down that goddamn rooster. *Again.*"

And although I hoped she hadn't, there was certain relief on the off chance that I wouldn't be startled awake by the insufferable crowing. The rooster, it seemed, had taken more of a liking to the Lazy Elk after pecking at Adalyn's sandwich. *Adalyn.*

I remembered last night, and a wave of hot frustration swept me head to toe. It had taken me a full hour to dismantle the goddamn bed and carry it outside to my truck. And fuck me, the past months spent in retirement had come at a price. My arms were sore, my back hurt from knocking the thing down, and I was almost sure I'd pulled a muscle somewhere on my neck when I'd driven us back to the farm to get her things. I—

I shook my head.

There was too much to do this morning, I couldn't allow myself to think of her. Of last night. It always started the same way. I'd recall something remotely related to her, and then I'd be summoning all sorts of other things.

Like those bloody overalls. They'd been so tight, making her look . . . Different. Homey. Inviting. Almost relaxed, for a change. Even with all those curves snug and confined. Ready to burst under the seams. Or my hands. They made me wish she would burn all her clothes and exclusively wear the goddamn things from now on.

My phone rang from the kitchen counter, snapping me out of that dangerous train of thought.

I stalked to the device and scanned the screen.

Liam.

I accepted the call. "What."

"Wow," he huffed. "Well, morning to you, too, sunshine."

I rolled my eyes. "I fired you. Why are you calling me again?"

"You didn't fire me," he countered in that smug tone I knew so well. "You encouraged me to resign. And most would appreciate the fact that our friendship is transcending a terminated business relationship."

I held the phone to my ear with a shoulder and served myself a second cup of coffee from the pot. "You were my agent, you were never my friend."

"God, I'd forgotten you're a prick," Liam said with a breath. "But I love you anyway, so I'm going to pretend you didn't disregard fifteen years of friendship."

"Don't pretend to miss me." I brought my mug to my lips and took a long sip. "We both know I was a nightmare to work with."

"Christ. You're in some mood today, mate."

I returned the device to my hand and crossed the living room area to the glass doors facing the front yard. "Maybe I am," I admitted, looking out and taking in the beautiful expanse of green before me. My gaze somehow ended on the shabby cabin to the right. I wondered if she was awake. What she would wear today. If her hair would be up or down on her shoulders. Lately she'd let it down and I— Fuck.

"What do you want, Liam?"

"Would you believe me if I said I called to check on you?"

"No."

"That's what I thought. It'd take a miracle for you to talk about your feelings anyway." A calculated pause. "How are my favorite girls doing, then? Ditched you yet?"

As if summoned by the man who'd been in my life for almost two decades, Pierogi climbed on the patio banister. She stretched her paws and laid on top of it, turning into an orange ball of fluff. "Pierogi's good. Napping half the time like she always does. And Willow . . ." I recalled the state of the kitchen floor. "Willow is still bitching at me every chance she gets. She hates it here."

Liam's chuckle came through the line. "That's my best gal."

"Far from it," I muttered.

A long pause followed. One that gave away the real purpose of the call. I knew my former agent like I knew the palm of my hand. I gave him shit because he gave me shit in return, but the truth is that we were like brothers. We'd risen together to the top, and he'd been loyal and honest to a fault. Letting go of him hadn't been easy. But I'd had no use for him after hanging up the gloves, and he'd known exactly why. That was why he insisted on checking up on me.

"Listen," Liam said, just like I knew he would. "I know you're still processing where you stand with this, but let me stress once more how great of an opportunity this is. The channel—"

I laughed, bringing his words to a stop. "I'm not processing. I know where I stand. That's why when you called the other day I asked you to kindly pass along my answer to RBC Sports."

"A 'fuck off' is not something you kindly pass along, Caldani. Specifically not to RBC Sports."

"Translate it into your language, then." I took another sip of my coffee, trying to focus on the smooth bitterness, and not on the way my stomach was tying up in knots. "Say it in some pretty way they'd like."

"Cameron," Liam warned, all lightness gone from his voice. "I know you're a giant twat." I snorted. "But I never had you for a fool."

And that's why I signed with him when we were nothing but nobodies with big dreams. Liam never tiptoed around anything or anyone, he said it like it is.

When I wasn't called up for the national team, he sat me down and told me to suck it up and move on. I was too old and there was younger and fresher meat. And when the smartest thing to do had been to pack up and sign for an MLS team, he'd never tried to sell me on the idea like it was some great plan to make me the legend I'd never be. He'd told me to move to L.A. and have one last hurrah. Make the contacts, take the cash, and get a break from the Premier League's politics I'd never had an interest in.

In every instance, I'd listened to him. Because I knew he wanted what was best for me. For us. I hadn't been a fool then. Was I being one now?

"This is a once-in-a-lifetime opportunity," he insisted. But I knew. I wasn't born yesterday. The RBC didn't call just anybody. Much less for a pundit gig on a prime-time show. "I haven't said no, not yet. I've told them you are thinking about it. Considering your options. They think the managing position in L.A. is still on the table, and I had one of my guys spread word around about a couple other MLS teams potentially sniffing around."

A ball of lead settled at the bottom of my stomach at the thought of how close I'd been to taking the L.A. Stars' offer to lead their academy coaching staff. How I'd be trapped in a gilded cage, with a life and a plan that no longer made sense, if I had.

"There's no thinking left to do," I told him. "I'm fine where I am."

"Are you, though?" Liam threw right back. "You might be fine now, man. But you don't know how you'll feel in three months. Or six. Or a year from now." The pause was long, and I knew it was intentionally so. "This is it, Cameron. It's a good deal. Just . . . consider it. Please."

I processed his words, I really did. As much as I'd been quick to say no, I didn't want to be the fool he'd accused me of being. The two boys who had shaken hands quickly after I'd signed my first contract in London were long gone, but I . . .

"I know you're hesitant to come back," Liam said, knowing exactly where my head had gone. "You'd have to be in London again, where the studios are." *And therefore lose all prospect of privacy*, he should have said next. But Liam was too good at his job to hand me an excuse like that. "You'd be easily recognized there. And I understand that after what happened in L.A., that's not exactly something you're looking forward to. I get it, mate. I do. I'd be traumatized, too."

Every muscle and bone in my body turned to stone. "I'm not traumatized."

"So you're not. Good. That's why you're hiding away in some town in the middle of nowhere. The question is, are you going to hide there forever?"

Sweat gathered at the back of my neck. "I'm not hiding."

He ignored my complaint with a tsk. "Enjoy your time there. Decompress. Relax. I know you're into the great outdoors and fresh air and all that mumbling nonsense. But we have that here, too. The proper countryside is a few hours' drive away from London." A pause. "Think of your future, man. You might not be on the grass anymore, but your career in football is far from being over."

Football. I missed hearing the word. I'd been in the US long enough but I . . . Fuck. I didn't even know. There had been no plan. I'd just come to Green Oak and decided to stay until I changed my mind. That had been the logic I'd applied to everything since that goddamn day.

Maybe I was traumatized.

I thought back to last night. To every day before that. I'd been so . . . busy with the hurricane Adalyn had brought to Green Oak that I hadn't had time to think about much else.

As if summoned by my mind, Adalyn materialized in the yard. She was walking toward my cabin and, fuck, thank Christ the pantsuit was back.

"You know what?" I heard myself say. "Relaxing might be over-rated."

Liam laughed, but there wasn't any humor in the sound. "So that's your answer. Out of all the things I said? Tell me at least that you'll think about it."

I watched Adalyn making her way up the steps of my porch, and I turned on my heels, heading for the front door.

"Caldani?" Liam insisted.

I reached the hallway, words slipping carelessly out of my mouth, "All right. Yeah."

"You've just made me a very happy man," Liam rushed out. I frowned, wondering why or how. "I'll ring you in a few days, then. When you've thought about it. Cheers, mate."

And he killed the call.

With a sigh, I slipped the phone in the pocket of my sweats and threw the door open.

A raised fist greeted me.

Her hand fell, revealing her face.

Adalyn's hair was down today, but not as straight as in the few instances she'd worn it like this. There were waves I'd missed when I'd spotted her through the window. It made her face look softer, her lips fuller. I cleared my throat. "What do you want?"

Adalyn didn't answer, so I looked away from her mouth. Her eyes were wide and focused somewhere down my throat. She blinked. Then, blinked again.

I frowned.

"You're . . ." she trailed off. Her cheeks were covered in a dark shade of pink. "Naked."

I dipped my chin. Right. With Willow acting up, and then Liam busting my balls, I hadn't had time to shower and put on a shirt.

"Half naked," she mumbled. "And tattooed. All over your . . ." A sigh. "Chest. And arm."

I had to fight the giant smirk from breaking out and parting my face. I really did. "I am," I told her, flexing my arms and chest like the cocky bastard I was. Her eyes widened. "If you ask nicely, I might consider removing my pants. I have more ink than just that."

Her lips popped open. The brown on her eyes glazed over. Then, her head snapped up. "Hold on, what?"

Deliberately slowly, I brought the mug to my mouth and took a sip of coffee, keeping my eyes on her. "I was saying that if you ask nicely—"

"Yeah, okay." She shook herself, but her face was still a bright shade of pink. Who would have thought, Adalyn Reyes getting flustered over an inked chest. If anything, I would have thought she wasn't a big fan of tattoos. What would she look like if she saw the design on my upper thigh? What would she say if I really dropped my sweats and—"I don't think that's something I, huh. . . need you to do. Keep your clothes on, thanks."

I tilted my head. I wasn't fooled by her words but I'd let her win this. "What do you want from me then, darling?"

It took her a moment to answer. "You promised you'd drive me back to the Vasquez farm. To sort out the flat tire."

"It's already sorted out." I leaned my shoulder on the doorframe. Crossed my ankles. Brought the mug to my lips again. "Anything else?"

Her brows furrowed. "What you mean it's sorted out?"

"It means that you don't have to worry about it. It's handled." I took a new swig of coffee and inspected the contents of my mug. Another good fucking coffee ruined after growing cold. I sighed. "Your car will be serviced on Monday." I glanced back at her. "Is that what you're wearing to the game? We leave for Rockstone in an hour. Remember to grab your magic binder, yeah? I want to add a few notes."

Adalyn's face wrinkled, as if she was having a hard time processing my words. "We . . . But you . . . You hate my binders. Leave in an hour for . . . where?"

"I don't hate them, I—" My eyes caught something behind her. Dashing across the front yard. A blur of fur I knew all too well. And it was moving quickly, chasing something. "Willow."

"I'm Adalyn."

"My cat," I muttered. "And she's after the goddamn cock again."

"Wh—"

I didn't wait around to hear. I moved around Adalyn and sprinted into the yard. So I had been right, Willow was out terrorizing the poor thing. And she was making me chase after her. Shirtless. Spilling whatever cold coffee remained in my mug.

I really couldn't catch a fucking break.

When I finally seized the ball of fur and fury, I had to one-arm clutch her to my chest so she wouldn't jump out again. "Are you happy?" I asked her, as I strode back to the porch. She mewed, but to her credit, she wasn't behaving like some wild predator now. She went as far as tucking her nose into the crook of my arm. "Yeah, give up that cute shit." I climbed up the steps with a roll of my eyes. "Daddy's not happy."

"*Daddy*?"

I looked up from the cat in my arms, finding an even more wide-eyed Adalyn blinking at me. And fuck, it was not the moment to think how that word raced straight to my gut.

"This is Willow." I dipped my chin. Willow's tiny paws curled around my forearm. "She's acting cute now, but she's taken a liking to prowling around the property and chasing the poor rooster down." Adalyn seemed too shocked to speak. "The other one is more well-mannered than this. Thankfully."

"The other one." Adalyn studied the ball in my arms. "You have two cats."

"Willow and Pierogi," I confirmed. "The rooster is not mine. But we already talked about that."

Something seemed to flash across her expression. "Oh my God," Adalyn whispered. "Sebastian Stan."

I frowned. "Who?"

"Robbie said something about a rooster they were missing," Adalyn explained. "His name is Sebastian Stan."

Oh. "Well, fuck." I gave Willow a quick glance. "That's going to be an awkward conversation."

Willow mewed and lifted her head, curious about Adalyn.

I stepped closer so the two complex and frustrating females that had been robbing me of sleep could survey each other a little better.

"She's beautiful," Adalyn whispered, while Willow sniffed her outstretched hand. "Her eyes are different, just like her face. I've never seen a cat like her."

"Willow's a chimera," I explained, my gaze fixated on Adalyn's face. Her smile was small as she inspected the cat in my arms. I liked that barely there tilt of her mouth. "They're born after two embryos fuse together. That's why she looks like that."

Willow purred, Adalyn hummed, and I felt myself relax for the first time this morning.

That was probably why I went on, "She was blind in one eye when I adopted her, I thought it might have been related to it so I researched."

"Oh," Adalyn whispered. "That's . . ." Her face turned serious. "Really sweet. You're full of surprises, Cameron." Her saying my name so softly did something to my stomach. "On top of having tried every single hobby that has ever existed, you have cats you call family and know about hackles and sickles and peeps. You're afraid of goats—"

"I'm not afraid of them," I interjected. "I find them untrustworthy."

She rolled her eyes but I could see it there, the way she was biting back a smile. A full one. A real one. "Still," she said. "I wonder what else you're hiding."

"Wildlife." The information toppled off my lips. "Not just farm stock. I find wildlife and nature fascinating. I've watched a lot of Animal Planet through the years. It helps me relax. Unwind." I re-adjusted Willow in my arms. "The hackles and sickles are nothing compared to what I've learned on there."

She tilted her head, and I knew to brace myself. "Tell me a random fact."

"You want me to prove it to you?"

"Only if you can," she said with a shrug. "Knock my socks off, Animal Planet man."

This woman. Issuing challenges like that at a man like me.

I looked at her straight into those chocolate-brown eyes. "Contrary to popular belief, the rightful king of the jungle is not the lion. Only a very small percentage of them live in the jungle. So small, they're endangered. A proper candidate for the title would actually be a Bengal tiger, leopard, or jaguar."

She nodded slowly, but I could tell she wasn't impressed.

I set the mug on the banister of the porch and held my free palm up. "Koala fingerprints are so similar to ours that they could be mistaken for a human's."

Her eyebrows rose in surprise.

I could do better than a brow arch. "The heart of a shrimp is in its head." I brought my hand to the side of her face and brushed her temple with the back of my hand. Her lips parted at the gentle touch. "And if a female ferret in heat doesn't mate for a prolonged time, the increasing levels of estrogen in her body can eventually lead to her death."

A shiver seemed to crawl down Adalyn's body. I let my fingers fall along hair that had fallen over her cheek. "She would die?" Her voice was soft again, gentle. Sad. "She would die just because she can't find a mate?"

I stepped closer and gave her a nod.

A small frown appeared. "That's . . . That's really unfair."

My eyes roamed all over her face, finding great pleasure in the vulnerability I saw in her expression. In how close we were standing.

I should have probably brushed this whole thing off, gone back inside and jumped into the shower so we wouldn't be late to the game, but something in me had shifted. Changed. "It's rather cruel," I said, letting the pad of my thumb flick across her cheek. "Don't you think?"

Adalyn's eyes fluttered shut, and when she answered, it was a whisper. "It is."

I moved my hand, reveling in the effect the gentle contact of my skin against hers had in me. Her. Both of us. "It doesn't seem like that's the ferret's fault."

Eyes still closed, her throat worked. "Maybe," she started. And this time, my thumb brushed her forehead, the spot that she'd hit that first day. The urge to place my mouth there was hard to tame. "Maybe, she doesn't have time to spare to search for a mate," she continued, a little breathlessly. "Or maybe there's nothing about her that's appealing to the male ferrets around her." She opened her eyes. The brown in her eyes had glazed over. "Perhaps she thought she was fine like that, alone. How is any of that her fault?"

"It's not," I told her, inching even closer. Gravitating toward her. Until there was barely any space separating us. I cupped her face in my palm. "Perhaps she's been neglected," I continued, craning my neck down. Now I could really smell her. Her shampoo. Soap. She smelled so fucking sweet. "Maybe she's being overlooked." I spread my fingers, my thumb brushing the corner of her lips. Adalyn's breath caught. "All of this sweetness, misjudged." I shifted my hand, digging the rest of my fingers in her hair. "What foolish males."

Adalyn exhaled, the puff of air hitting my chin.

And I— Fuck. I—

A sharp pang of pain cut straight through the moment, and I winced.

Willow mewed from my arms. And before I could stop her, she landed on the ground and flashed through the open door. I attempted to go after her, but Adalyn's hand was on my arm.

I looked down, finding her warm, gentle fingers against my skin as they probed, inspecting the scratch. "It doesn't look deep." Her tone was concerned and still so goddamn sweet it killed me. What was happening to me? "But I think you should disinfect it." The tip of her index finger traced the inked skin around the tiny cut. "Does it hurt?"

It did. But not in the way she meant. "No."

"Will it ruin the . . . design?" she asked, her thumb hanging over black lines I'd collectively sat down for many hours to get done.

There was barely a spot of skin that wasn't inked between my collarbone and the upper sleeve of my right arm. Same went for my right pec. And the top of my left thigh. None of them were tattoos I went around showcasing. They were not for anybody but myself and that's why I always wore long sleeves. Her hand moved, side-tracking me. I'd suffered through some of the most intricate ones yet somehow those delicate, light grazes of her fingers over my skin felt more powerful than all the needles I'd endured.

"This one is so pretty." Her palm had stopped at the side of my biceps, and I was so emboldened, encouraged by her touch that I turned my arm so she could properly see. "Who is she?"

Out of every possible tattoo she could have possibly chosen to ask about. It had to be that one. The one that held the most meaning. "I think you know, darling."

"Your grandmother?" she whispered. I gave her a nod and let her inspect it. I was thankful it wasn't one of the tacky or senseless ones I'd gotten when I was young and mindless. This one was an old-school rendition of a young woman with black hair. Simple. Thick lines. No shadowing or color except for two red flowers atop her head. "What about the rest? What do they represent?"

I had to swallow for the words to come out of my throat. "The beginning," I said, voice thick. "The end. Everything in between."

My eyes bounced back to her face. She was biting her lip. "Does Willow do this often?"

I shook my head, barely able to rasp out an answer with her attention on me like that. I liked it far too much. "She's never acted like that, but perhaps that's because I've never given her a chance to be jealous."

"Jealous?"

I nodded, my tongue still in twists. My head, too, when all of a sudden, I couldn't remember the last time a woman had tended to my wounds.

Had it ever happened? Had it ever felt like . . . this?

"Oh. *Oh.*" Adalyn jumped back, breaking the contact. My skin felt cold where her fingers had been. She huffed. "Well, she must be a very territorial cat if she's feeling that way over nothing." She looked everywhere but at me. "After all, you would love nothing more than seeing me pack my things, leave town, and never look back, right?" I winced, and she shook her head. "This is just temporary. I'll leave and we're . . . working together only because we must. I forced your hand."

I frowned. I had not expected her to say that. To bring up words I had seemed to make myself forget.

"Anyway." She walked around me, taking step after step down. "I'll see you in an hour. When we leave for the, uh, game." She made it all the way down. "Just horny— *Honk*! The horn. Or text. When you're ready and I'll come out. I guess that's the one perk of getting saddled with me here, right?"

She broke into a jog and I stood there, watching her get back to her cabin.

Only when her door had closed behind her did I say, "Right."

Because she was right about this being just temporary and me wanting to see her go.

Right?

CHAPTER TWENTY

Cameron

$\mathcal{T}$he girls left the middle of the Rockstone field and made their way toward the guest bench with red cheeks and ponies, pigtails, bunnies, and whatnot sticking in all directions.

I assessed them in silence, one by one, not surprised by the way they were dragging their feet or how they plopped on the ground around me and Adalyn.

"This sucks," Juniper muttered, taking her frustration out on the grass under her outstretched legs. "We suck. We suck monkey butt. We suck so bad, we probably suck worse than monkey butt."

Nodding heads created a wave of agreement, and I had to clap my hands to capture their attention before the conversation veered too deep into muddy terrain. "You don't suck," I assured the team in a firm tone. "You played a good game. You battled, hard. And left all you had on the grass."

"But we lost," Chelsea countered, tugging furiously at the remainder of her braid. Her tutu—which I now considered a lost battle—hung sideways. "We didn't even score. We've only scored once in two games. And it didn't even count."

I decided not to comment on the own goal. "You didn't lose. Nil-nil is not a loss."

Chelsea threw her hand up, resting it against her forehead as she sighed. "It's just as tragic as a loss, Coach Cam."

"We're losers," Juniper muttered.

"And we worked so hard this week," Chelsea added, encouraged by the other kid. "I haven't missed soccer practice, not even once. Not even for ballet class. I feel like I haven't danced in *aaaages*. I told my mom I could do both things, but I'm not so sure anymore. Maybe Dad was right. Maybe I should pick just the one thing and focus on it."

"I haven't been spending time with Brandy, either," María grumbled from her spot on the grass. "Or Tilly. Or Carmen. And Sebastian is still missing."

A somber mutter started picking up speed and volume. Every kid relating their own overdramatic version of their sacrifices for the game.

I brought my fingers to my mouth and whistled.

All mouths snapped closed.

"So you feel like you lost," I said stepping forward. "So you worked hard for a whole week, got here today, tried your hardest, and got beat." All heads were looking at me now, eyes wide and sparkly with a sentiment that, had I been smarter, I would have interpreted as my cue to shut up. But it bothered me seeing them like this. "Well, news flash, girlies. Life is not a walk in the park. Life is hard. Sometimes you win and oftentimes you lose. But this is only the outcome of one game. You fall and then you stand up and chase after the . . . little league cup."

I sensed Adalyn shuffle closer. "There's no cup," she whispered loudly. "The prize is a trip to the Jungle Rapids Family Fun Park."

"I love the Jungle Rapids," Juniper grumbled.

"So you fall and then stand up and chase after the . . . trip to the Jungle Rapids," I continued. "Tripping only toughens you. It's moments like these that harden you. And believe me, you have a minimum of three more games ahead of you, so toughen up."

María sniffed loudly. "But—" Another sniff. "I . . . I don't want to be hard. Or tough. I want to be soft." Her head turned toward Adalyn. "Miss Adalyn, tell Coach Carwash that girls can be both."

My gaze jumped from the girl to the woman by my side, who was now glaring at me.

"It's a figure of speech," I explained. But it didn't seem to make a difference with either of them, because María sniffed again, and Adalyn went from pissed to . . . sad. I shook my head. "Girls can be soft and hard, yes, all at the same time. I also wanted to win today, all right? I wanted you to beat those kids and wipe the floor with them. But you didn't." I heard a sob, and my eyes widened. "That's another figure of speech. Listen—"

"Coach." Adalyn's hand fell on my arm, and I could feel how cold it was through the fabric of my jacket. "I don't think this is helping."

"Adalyn." I stepped toward her, as if my body had a mind of its own. She was freezing. "Darling—"

"I'm fine," she said, but she had to be lying. She was shivering in that stupid trench coat she had insisted was enough. "But the girls are not. They're sad, and I know you mean well, but you're not making it better."

In confirmation, a few more sobs broke out in the group.

"I'm not good with motivational stuff," I muttered.

"I see that," Adalyn answered. She lowered her voice. "They are crying, though. And I don't know what to do with crying children, Cameron."

A throat was cleared behind us.

I turned to find Tony planted on my other side. He'd been hanging out in the stands after being asked by Adalyn to drive the girls to Rockstone in a minibus she'd arranged for.

"Can I . . ." He hesitated, scratching that mass of brown shaggy hair atop his head. "Can I suggest something? Hmm, sir?" His cheeks reddened. "Ma'am?"

"Please," we said at the same time.

"Sno-cones."

"Sno-cones?" I repeated.

"Yeah." He nodded. "It's like ice cream but . . . without the cream? Sorry, I'm sure you know what they are. I saw a coffee stand outside when I was parking the van. It's a little cold, but I know for a fact they will go crazy over them. The stand had a sign—"

"Yes," I rushed out. "Ice-lollies, of course. Ice cream." Some of the kids looked in our direction, still weeping but definitely interested. "How fast can you fetch them?"

"Huh, fast?"

I pulled out my wallet and slapped more than enough cash in his hand. "Grab me something hot, too, all right?" I checked the time. It was past noon. "Not coffee. Tea, cocoa, or whatever else they have. The largest size. And keep the change."

"Yes, sir," Tony said, looking down. His eyes widened. "Whoa. This is . . . thank you, sir."

"Just Cam," I told him. "Now go."

Tony shot off running, disappearing through the crowd of Rockstone parents and locals gathered around the field.

My wrist was squeezed.

With the commotion, I'd missed how Adalyn's hand had shifted to my sleeve and was holding on to it. "I hope the sno-cones work."

"I hope so, too," she said with a little tug at my jacket. Without thought or reason, I brought her hand between mine. Then, quickly snatched her other one and trapped both between my palms. Her words were wobbly when she spoke next, "You *really* suck at speeches."

I looked up at her, expecting to see a complaint in her face. But there wasn't any frown. Her nose was red, her eyes glassy, and her lips shaped in a pout that told me she was relieved by the way my hands were rubbing hers, warming them up.

"Maybe that's the one thing I don't know how to do," I admitted. I brought our hands to my chest. And when she gave me one of those tiny smiles, I had to stop myself from pulling her into me. "I can't believe I told them to toughen up."

"No wonder they cried," she said in a serious voice. "For a second, I thought even you were going to cry. It was terrible, really."

I stared at her. At her lips, now twitching. Bending upward. I couldn't believe she was teasing me. With a goddamn smile.

I pulled at her arms, gently but firmly enough to make her stumble toward me. Our hands were sandwiched by our chests.

"It was worth it."

Her breath caught. "What was?"

"The tears," I answered, my eyes fixated on her mouth. "Me making a fool of myself and bringing a team of kids to tears. It was worth it. Because it made you smile."

Her expression remained frozen for a second, and then it crumbled down. Her lips parted, her eyes glazed over, and her cheeks turned pink in a way that had nothing to do with the cold. "Cameron," she said. Just that. My name.

"I warned you," I told her, because I'd been serious. "I'm a selfish man."

A loud burst of giggles erupted behind her, making whatever bubble we'd just been in burst. Adalyn snagged her hands from my grasp. We both turned around.

Tony, who had returned with a tray filled with sno-cones, was passing along colorful cups, and the mood of the group was clearly lifting as they went around.

When the teenage boy reached Adalyn and me, I patted his shoulder. "Good man, Tony. That was fast, just like I asked." His eyes went wide, his whole face flushing a new wave of radioactive red. I lowered my voice. "Thanks for not making a fuss about who I am, as well. I appreciate it more than you know."

Tony's lips bobbed but his expression turned solemn. "I understand, sir. Hmm, Cam—Coach Cam? I understand how valuable privacy is. When my mom passed away—" He cut himself off. "Sometimes, people are nosy as hell." He shot a wide-eyed glance at Adalyn. "As heck. Sometimes people can be nosy as heck, ma'am."

Adalyn set her palm on his other shoulder, giving him a quick and gentle pat. The kid almost collapsed.

I took the tray with the leftover sno-cones from Tony. "You get something for yourself with the change?"

"I'd rather save it for something else, Coach. I'm supposed to go to college soon and I've been saving all I can to help my dad."

Adalyn's gaze bounced from me to the kid, and I could tell the gears in her head were working something out. "Tony," she ventured. "How would you feel about helping out with the team?"

The boy's face brightened. "I would love that. But the farm—" He frowned. "I don't know if I have the time. Personnel at the farm is tight and I'd hate to leave my dad hanging."

Adalyn's face fell.

"Let us talk to your dad," I said. "Now go sit down. We'll leave when the girls are done with the sno-cones."

The boy left with a nod.

"Are you okay with my idea to hire Tony?" Adalyn asked. "I probably should have run it by you first."

I snagged the takeaway cup of tea from the box and handed it to her. "No. I think it's a great idea, boss."

"He's a big fan of the game. So I thought . . ." She looked down at the container as it rested in my hand. "What's that?"

"Tea. It's for you. Take it," I told her, and her jaw clenched. It took her a moment but her hand wrapped around the cup. This time, it wasn't the touch of her fingers against my skin that caused something to tug against my gut. It was the way she was looking at me, as if I'd done this great thing for her by getting her a tea.

"Don't look at me like that, darling."

"It's just that you . . ." Remembered she doesn't drink coffee after noon. "You can be very nice, Cameron."

After how I treated her, it shouldn't surprise me that she'd think that way. I wasn't a complete asshole, but I didn't go around extending smiles and hugs. I hadn't lied when I said I was a little mean. I had been.

I threw an arm around her shoulders and ushered her toward her bench. We sat down. "Just keeping the manager warm, is all," I said, snagging a cone from the tray for myself. I moved closer to her, sheltering her from the wind that had picked up. "I'd hate to look for a new one. I'd probably end up saddled with Josie."

Adalyn gave me another of those small, beautiful smiles in response, and I could do nothing but watch her as she took a long pull of tea.

"Is the sno-cone good?" Adalyn asked, glancing sideways at me. "I don't think I've had one in ages."

I was ready to tell her that maybe sticking to the tea was a better idea, but her eyes dipped down at the thing with obvious curiosity. And who I was to tell her whether or not she could have a lick? Like I said, I was a selfish man.

"Have a go at it, darling."

I lifted the thing in obvious offering and watched her mouth near the small mound of ice, tongue out, gently grazing the top before really digging in.

My pulse sped up. And a voice inside my head said, *You horny bastard*. But yeah. There was no denying it. I was turned on. By Adalyn, not the ice.

"So, Coach Cornfield," María's voice cut through the haze. "How are the curmudgeons on your butt?"

My eyes, which had been on Adalyn's mouth, widened. And Adalyn, who had a mouthful of ice, snorted.

It was a shockingly loud sound, and it propelled some of the pink and blue mix out of her nose. Adalyn's hand flew to her face, covering the colorful mess dripping down her nose and chin.

A second of charged silence ensued.

Then, one of the kids said in what was, without mistake, awe, "WHOA. That is the coolest thing I've seen in my whole life."

Adalyn, who still had all my attention, seemed shocked by the kid's words.

But when Chelsea added, "Yeah, Miss Adalyn. That was super-cool. Do you think you can teach us?" The rest of the team agreed, and something else filled the face of this woman who seemed able to continuously catch me off guard like nobody else ever had.

Pride. It was pride.

And as my curmudgeons were quickly and luckily forgotten, the team's mood picked up, and the cones disappeared, my eyes remained on the woman sitting by my side. This usually exasperating and outwardly prim woman, who had just snorted ice out her nose and looked thoroughly pleased after getting the kids' approval. The tug in my gut intensified, pulling so tight that I had to catch my breath for a second. Something in my chest shifted. Warmed. Making me . . .

I froze.

"Fuck."

Her head turned, and she looked at me with that somewhat sheepish, somewhat happy look on her face. Jesus, she'd never looked more beautiful than right now. "What's wrong?"

"Huh." I cleared my throat. "What?"

"You said the f-word," she answered simply. Had I? "Did the ice get to your head?"

Definitely not the ice. "What do you mean?"

"The ice," she explained, taking a quick sip of tea from the cup. "It happens to me when I order iced lattes. It gets to my head if I drink too fast. But never mind. I guess manly men's brains don't freeze with sno-cones."

"That's what you think of me?" came out of my mouth. "That I'm some impressive manly man?"

"I didn't say impressive." She rolled her eyes, but fuck, the corners of her lips turned up again.

"What else do you think of me?" I asked, nudging her shoulder with mine. Something came over me. Something caused by the turmoil inside. I lowered my voice. "Anything that keeps you awake at night?"

Adalyn's mouth parted. Her tongue snuck out. And I thought, *Go on, love. Throw me a bone.* Because I wanted her to tease me. And I knew she wanted to, too. I could already taste the words coming out of her mouth, I could already feel them on my tongue.

But then, her gaze moved behind me. Her expression changed.

And just like that, all hell broke loose.

CHAPTER TWENTY-ONE

Adalyn

For a second, I'd thought I was wrong.

That I had to be wrong.

Because how unlucky did I have to be? How very unlucky was I that on the day I was somehow having a breakthrough, on the day I wasn't feeling like the failure I was—the embarrassment, the total and complete castaway—a reminder had to be flung back at my face?

One moment I was looking at Cameron, getting a little lost in the way his eyes were roaming around my face like he was seeing something, a little part of myself, perhaps even me, for the first time. Sitting there with the tea he'd asked Tony to get me because he remembered I didn't drink coffee after noon. A warmth that had nothing to do with the tea or the nearness of his body surging, breaking through me.

And the next, poof. Everything was gone.

At first it had been nothing more than a flash of color. A shape I'd told myself not to think anything of. But then, the guy moved, as if his intention was to approach us. His chest faced me, and I knew just how wrong I was. How foolish.

He wore a hoodie with the exact image I'd seen on the energy drink website. The can. The doodle of my face. The slogan: CHOOSE ENTERTAINMENT OVER DIGNITY.

It all came back to me then, the fact I'd never gotten an update from Miami. That I didn't know when or if they'd taken legal action. What I knew was that there was a guy with my enraged face on his clothes. In North Carolina. So I panicked. My heart dropped to my feet, I felt all my blood leave my face, and I did what I should have probably done that day I arrived in Green Oak, right after I pulled the pin and made my orderly, neat life implode.

I ran.

Or I tried. Because instead, I whirled on the bench I was sitting, tripped over the water keg, and plunged into the ground, managing to squeeze the take-out cup so hard, the lid flew off and the contents spilled all over me.

It wasn't pretty, and I was sure I'd gone down with a scream.

I should have been mortified, humiliated, really, because I'd been doing a lot of falling and tripping and I was, frankly, sick of it. And yet, even as I went through that hurdle, I kept thinking, *Well, at least Cameron will look at me. Not at the man in the hoodie. At least the one person in town who hasn't seen that horrible video won't find out this way.*

So I remained there, on the ground, like the dumbass I felt I was, catching my breath, and then, just as all the adrenaline started to come down and relief was quickly replaced by shame, Cameron was there.

His hands landed on me, and I didn't want to look at him, because I was really done with the world. But all I could see was him. Curse after curse left his mouth as he touched and poked and palmed every limb and part of my body in an almost frantic way. Some vaguely there part of me thought to complain, but I was too overwhelmed. By the trip and the reminder of what my life had become. By the fact that there was some guy wearing merch with my face and what that could imply. By the now real possibility that Cameron could never look at me the way he had minutes ago. By . . . everything.

Cameron moved even closer as he kneeled there, and real, understandable words finally started leaving his mouth. "What the fuck, Adalyn," he said those deep green eyes meeting mine with a gravity that shouldn't have been there. Had I tripped so miserably? "Tell me you're okay," he demanded. "Did you hit your head?" One shake of my head. "What the fuck happened?" Another bob of my lips. "Why are you not talking, love?" *Love.* Love? My breath got stuck in my throat. "I saw you looking behind me. Did anyone say something to you?" His expression changed, and he started moving away. "I'm going to—"

"No," I said, grabbing his arm.

He immediately halted, but that murderous expression was locked in place.

Why was he so mad?

There was movement in my peripheral vision, and when I looked, I saw merch-guy talking to Tony, then turning away. He was leaving, paying us no mind, and I should have been relieved, I really should have, but my heart was racing too fast and my head was all over the place.

I returned my attention to Cameron, noticing he hadn't moved an inch. I wetted my lips, cleared my throat until I could speak, and then, said, "Can we go?" He still didn't move. "Please. Can you take me home?"

That fierce and hostile emotion vanished from his face, and without a word, his hands moved, reminding me they were still on my body. They landed on my back and on my waist. He waited for me to take the first step, moving his shoulder closer so I could use it for support. I braced my hand there, pushed myself up, but the moment I placed weight on my left foot, I went down again.

"My ankle," I yelped. "I think I sprained it."

I was immediately lifted in the air.

My temple fell against a warm and solid chest. His scent surrounded me, making me feel things I didn't want to accept. I closed my eyes. "God, that was so embarrassing." A shaky breath left me. "I embarrassed myself and you guys. I'm so sorry."

Cameron's rib cage vibrated with something like a grunt or a scoff, I wasn't sure and I didn't want to know. I was scared he'd agree and tell me just how ridiculous I was. But those words never came.

He moved with those long and confident strides, holding me up in his arms, and the only thing he said was, "I've got you now, love."

By the time we reached Lazy Elk I was . . . an assortment of jumbled things.

For one, I was in pain. The drive back hadn't been long, and I'd been quickly checked by Grandpa Moe, but as my ankle cooled off, the pain had steadily grown into a sharp bite that kept a wince on my face.

I was also embarrassed. Still. It didn't matter that Cameron hadn't commented on the fall. It didn't matter that he'd limited himself to driving in silence, sending me quick glances to check if I was still there. I could hear the wheels in his head turning from the passenger's seat. He knew there was something wrong.

And last, but certainly not least, I was experiencing an array of emotions that went from confused to shocked to aghast to curious to giddy, only to return right back to confused.

Cameron had called me love.

He'd carried me to his car like the damsel in distress I'd never allowed myself to be, and called me love. He'd somehow produced an ice pack and placed it on my ankle after I had to endure those big warm hands prodding and touching and massaging my leg. His touch had been so clinical, such a medical, expert touch, that I'd scolded myself when those tingles had spread all over my body. I'd been mad at the electricity crackling under my skin, when all he'd been doing was checking on me.

I blamed the four-letter word that had come out of his mouth.

The *I've got you now*, too.

I didn't understand. I was perplexed, besides being in pain and embarrassed and mad and dazed and simply . . . tired. So tired I wanted to sleep all of this away. Close my eyes and forget about today, and last week, and the week prior to that. I wanted to hibernate until all the mess that was my life went away.

So when Cameron killed the engine, and parked in the exact same spot he always did, I jumped out of the car with all the dignity I had left and limped away.

And just like every time I'd indulged in a dramatic escape, Cameron was suddenly right there.

His hands came around my waist, and he said, "Let me—"

But I raised a finger, putting a stop to his unnecessary rescue mission with a simple, "No."

"No?" he repeated, but to his credit, his hands fell to his sides.

My voice wobbled when I said, "I don't need you to carry me inside like I'm . . ." Someone you care about. Someone you get hot drinks when they're cold. Someone you call love. "Something."

His expression tightened and somehow fell, all at the same time. Cameron looked . . . hurt, if I had to choose an emotion. And I felt like I'd just kicked a puppy. Or a baby goat.

With a shake of my head, I limped toward the porch, Cameron close behind, and found a small box on my doorstep. I craned my neck to inspect the label, recognizing Matthew's handwriting. I leaned down, flexing my supporting leg so I could pick it up, but everyone on this porch knew flexibility wasn't my thing and the task turned out to be, frankly, impossible.

In a swift motion, Cameron picked up the box with one hand and lifted me in the air with his other arm.

"I told you—" I started.

"Cut the bullshit, will you?" he interjected, and how infuriating was it that his scolding was delivered in the softest, most gentle tone? "Good. Now that you have stopped bitching for a minute, can you please unlock the door?"

I pulled out the key from the bag still hanging off my shoulder and did as I was asked.

Cameron kicked the unlocked door open with his foot and stomped inside the cabin, carrying me and the box in his arms.

"Box," he barked. "Where?"

"Beside the bed," I answered with a sigh. "Please."

He moved in that direction. "Not a bed."

"Yeah, I know," I admitted with barely any energy left. "Who knows, maybe Matthew somehow managed to fit a mattress in that tiny box."

My comment only seemed to spike Cameron's frustration, because instead of putting the box down, he let it drop to the wooden floor with a thump.

"Hey. What if it's something fragile?"

"I'll replace it." He shrugged, shifting my body and bringing me more securely into his chest. "Where?"

"Down on the bed, please."

With more gentleness than I was able to process in that moment, he set me down. His eyes roamed around my body. Down, and up, and down again. His jaw clamped down tightly.

"I'll be fine," I murmured. "It's just a sprained ankle."

His brow arched, his eyes still not meeting mine. More words were barked. "Shower, ice, painkillers, and sleep."

"Why are you enumerating things or barking out single words?" I fumbled with the buttons of my trench coat. "Why are you not talking or looking at me? I already apologized for earlier."

That muscle in his jaw jumped. "It's not an apology I want."

"What do you want then?" A pause. No answer. "Fine, don't talk to me then."

His gaze finally met mine. "I'm not talking because I don't trust myself," he said, the storm that I could tell had been gathering inside of him breaking free in the green of his eyes. "Because if I say more than a few words, you're going to find more reasons to hate me, Adalyn. You're going to throw a fucking fit, and you're going to make this extra hard for me. So, please," he said, his voice turning rocky and strangely low. "Shower, ice, painkillers, and sleep."

What, I wanted to ask. *What exactly am I going to make extra hard for you?*

But I knew the answer to that. Everything. Every single thing.

Because that was what I did best. Complicate things. So I managed a nod and told him, "You can go now. Thanks."

Cameron's eyelids fluttered shut, and he muttered a "Good fucking riddance" before turning away and walking off.

I waited for the door to close behind him and when the sound reached me, I did exactly the opposite of what I'd just agreed to do. First, I limped to the kitchenette, grabbed a pair of scissors, and returned straight to the box. Inside, there was a note stuck to something that had been rolled in tissue paper. It read:

MAKE IT UP TO ME.
YOUR (ONLY) BFF,
M.

Make what up to him? I wondered while I tore apart the paper. If I'd been a little more lucid and a lot less in pain, perhaps I would have immediately known, but it wasn't until I unwrapped it and turned it around that I understood.

I stared at the shirt—the black long-sleeved jersey with the number 13—and seven simple letters that spelled a name: CALDANI.

"This jerk," I said, dropping down my arms and setting aside what had been Cameron's L.A. Stars jersey for the last years of his career. "This jerk sent me this so I could get it signed for him."

Any other day, I would have called Matthew and told him that he could forget about it. Perhaps I would even ask how he'd managed to get this package here so fast. But today? I didn't care.

I grabbed my pajamas, limped to the tiny bathroom, set everything on the counter, and dragged myself into what passed for the shower. I let the hot spring water warm my body. Once done, I dragged the curtain back only to discover that both my discarded and sleeping clothes had fallen to the floor and were now drenched.

"Great."

I wrapped my towel around my chest and limped back to the bed. My gaze fell on the black jersey with the tiny white stars scattered around the shoulders and upper section of the sleeves. Hardly thinking, I snatched it up and slipped it over my head. Polyester and nylon weren't ideal fabrics to sleep in, but at least the thing covered my ass.

Clad in the very emblem of what had represented Cameron for the last years of his career, I let my body fall onto the mattress, wrapped my arms around my legs, closed my eyes, and cried myself to sleep.

It was fast, and the last thing that crossed my conscious mind was that at least now, I would remember the last time a tear had left my eyes.

By the time I woke up, it was dark outside.

All throughout the day, I was startled awake by violent gusts of wind hitting the cabin, slipping in a painkiller and going back to sleep. Except for this last time. Now the wind was too noisy, my mind was groggy after all that irresponsible self-medication, and my ankle was radiating waves of pain up my leg.

I rolled with a wince, hoping that it would help relieve the pain, and stumbled upon something. A source of . . . warmth. Wait. There was something on my bed. Something alive. Under normal circumstances, I would have immediately dashed out of the cabin, but I was so out of it that I found myself reaching out. I touched the object, probed it with my fingers.

It mewed.

I reached for my phone and lit the space before me, finding two eyes I'd seen before staring back at me.

"Willow?"

The cat made a noise I interpreted as a yes and climbed onto my lap, burrowing herself there. I saw myself petting her fur confidently, like this was something I did every night. Her small body started vibrating against my belly and chest. It was such an odd feeling, being purred on. But it felt so comforting. It almost made the waves of pain recede.

Was this why people had cats?

Was this why Cameron had adopted two?

"Do you curl up in his lap and purr?" I heard myself ask her in the darkness of the room.

A gust of wind hit one of the sides of the cabin, and Willow raised her head.

"S'kay," I drew out. "The wind's scary, but I'm here with you." A strange thought flashed through my groggy mind. "I've never been held through a storm, y'know. I never told anyone I'm scared of them. I grab my comforter tight and tell myself to be strong. But I'll hold you."

Willow settled again, as if convinced by my argument.

"I've been in Cameron's arms, y'know," I continued. "And you've been in his lap." Willow's head inched upward, resting against my breasts. "I think that makes us friends." I frowned. "Does he have a great lap?"

She prodded at me with her small bicolor snout.

"Yeah, that's what I thought." I closed my eyes, memories of a shirtless Cameron holding this very same cat. *Jealous*. He'd implied Willow was jealous. Of me. A thought took shape. "Oh no. He must be worried sick about you."

I opened my messages app and started typing, but my eyes felt weird and the letters danced. So I pressed on the tiny mic symbol on the corner, and started recording instead.

And when I was done, I hit send.

CHAPTER TWENTY-TWO

Cameron

$\mathcal{I}$ stole a glance at the silent phone on my lap.

It was driving me insane.

The whole day, I'd been at home, and as much as I tried to deny why, it wasn't because of the turn the weather had taken. It was because of her.

Was I a giant fool for listening to Adalyn and giving her space? Was I an idiot of epic proportions for storming out of there like that?

Yes. I was probably both things. And a man gone insane, too, soon enough.

Now, it was two a.m., and I was staring at the ceiling of my bedroom, blinking away the images that assaulted my mind. Adalyn at the game. Adalyn's smile. Her scrambling off the bench like she'd seen a ghost. The expression of pain when she'd tried to stand up. The shame that had been underlying all of that. Her apology for embarrassing us. Christ. Where the hell had that come from?

I didn't understand. I—

My phone pinged with a message, and in a flash, my hand was reaching out and flipping on the lights. I sat on the bed and unlocked the device.

A message from Adalyn popped up on the screen. A voice memo.

With a frown, I hit play.

"Hey, *wassup*," her voice drawled. Something was wrong. Adalyn didn't drawl. She also never spoke so . . . weakly, her voice so frail. I came to a stand and looked for my clothes, her voice filling the room. "She's here, with me. We're sitting in my bed that's not really a bed and getting through the storm together. I hope that's okay, because if you don't mind, I'd like to keep her. Just for tonight. Miami's storms are much scarier but she's keeping me warm and distracting me from the pain and the noise outside." A sigh left her lips.

But all I kept thinking was *Pain, pain, pain, she's in pain.*

My finger moved to stop the message, my body already in flight mode, but her words brought me to a halt. "I think I took one too many painkillers, I dunno. That was . . . very stupid. I didn't ice my ankle, either. Like Grandpa Moe and you said. But I remembered I don't have a freezer. Or ice. I . . . don't have many things here. I didn't complain about the cabin because I don't think I should, y'know? I was trying to be strong and independent. I . . . I don't think I have many friends." A brief pause. "I don't even know if I have friends back home in Miami. Does my assistant count? We went out for dinner once, but I don't think she had fun." A strange sound came through the line. "Maybe I'm not all that friendly. Or nice. I think you liked me today, but you don't like me all that much so, yeah. Anyways, Willow's with me. Do you think that's okay? I'm sure you have a great lap, but she looks comfy in mine."

I blinked at the screen, standing frozen at the side of my bed, the only thing moving was my heart, pounding furiously.

A new voice memo popped up, kicking me back into gear.

"I wanted to clarify," her voice explained when I hit play. "That I'm not thinking about your lap. Not too much. But if it's as hard as your chest, it'd explain why Willow likes it here. Because I'm soft. And you're hard."

A new message appeared.

"Your lap is hard."

Then another one.

"Not you." A pause. "Although you're hard, too. I guess? A hard-ass. Not your ass, but you. It's your personality that I don't like."

I shook my head, and looked up, finding myself at the foot of the bed now, with my sweats and a hoodie in my hand. I dressed quickly.

When I looked back at the screen, a new memo was in.

Jesus, she was sending them as I played them. Why wasn't she calling me instead?

I ran out the door.

And in record time, I was on her porch, the door, of course, irresponsibly unlocked. A trail of curses fell from my lips as I crossed the tiny cabin in three long strides.

The moment my eyes stumbled upon the sight of Adalyn, curled up with Willow, a strangled sound climbed up my throat. I rushed to the bed and I kneeled down. It slapped me in the face then. How impossible it was for me not to acknowledge the emotion stirring furiously against my rib cage. Christ, I wanted to shake her. To shake myself, too. To howl, for some fathomless reason that I knew had to do more with me than her. But I made myself push it all down, because she was passed out. Right where I'd left her. Vulnerable and alone.

Clamping my jaw down, I curled my arms around her, securing one at her back and one under her thighs. Jesus, she was so soft against me. And she felt so warm. Too warm. Stifling a grunt, I pulled her against my chest as tightly as I could and picked her up.

It was then, when I the blanket fell off, that I saw what she was wearing.

The charcoal black, the starred sleeves and shoulder pads, the team's emblem at the right side of her chest. It was my L.A. Stars jersey. Mine. I didn't need to see the back, because no one else on the team had worn black—only me at the goal.

I closed my eyes. All I needed was a moment. Just a few seconds before I did something reckless I'd regret.

Her head bobbed against my chest, and I reopened my eyes to

hers as they looked up. "Cameron?" she asked, blinking with confusion. Surprise. "You're here. Why are you here?"

"I shouldn't have left you here, alone." I swallowed hard. "I'm so sorry I did."

Adalyn blinked again, and then again, and Jesus fucking Christ, then she went and gave a smile. Big and sweet and beautiful. So much that the gorgeous brown in her eyes lit up.

Willow jumped off the mattress with a whimper, getting my attention. Walking lazily toward the door, as if marking a path. Encouraging me to take her home.

I returned my eyes to the woman in my arms and I followed behind.

I'd thought Adalyn would ask where I was taking her, or perhaps complain or put up a fight. But instead, she murmured, "But I didn't ask you to come for me."

My throat went tight with the words. "You never need to ask, love."

CHAPTER TWENTY-THREE

Adalyn

$\mathcal{I}$ woke up with a jolt.

The first thing I became aware of was how comfortable and warm I was. How good the linen around my body smelled and how plush the comforter was.

I rolled onto my side, eyelids blinking and trying to make sense of where I was. My legs bumped against something solid and warm.

"What . . ." I murmured, looking down and finding a ball of bicolored fur. "Willow? Why—"

Everything came back. Glimpse after glimpse of the last twenty-four hours, toppling right into my mind.

The guy with the hoodie. My panic. The pain emanating from my ankle and traveling up my calf. The irresponsible intake of pain-killers. Willow curling up on my lap. Cameron's arms. The feeling of his chest underneath my cheek. His palm against my hair. The soothing hum of his voice.

Cameron's arms.

He'd brought me to his cabin. With him. I couldn't exactly remember why. But if what I'd just recalled was right, he'd gone as far as . . . soothing me back to sleep. The image was too clear, too sharp, for me to think I'd imagined it. He'd sat by my side and stroked my hair until I'd fallen asleep.

A wave of heat climbed all the way up to my face. God, I must have been in really bad shape.

With more effort than I should have needed, I sat back on the bed, obtaining a skeptical glance from the cat as she stretched her paws by my side. "Sorry, friend," I told her, and she yawned at me. "Is that okay? That I called you friend?" She jumped over my legs and settled herself against my hip. I took her staying as a yes. "Thanks. I also think we are friends after last night."

Her head fell back on the comforter again, and I wasn't going to lie, the cat liking me back felt like a win I'd take. Especially considering the likely awkward conversation I had ahead of me today.

With a sigh, I rolled out of the bed, feeling the sharp bite of pain when I rested my right foot on the floor. I pushed through it. I had more pressing concerns to deal with. I limped my way out of the room and into a hallway, carefully stopping every few feet to make sure where I was going. The last thing I needed right now was to find Cameron in some inappropriate situation like, I don't know, changing or slipping out of the shower or getting undressed . . .

Or maybe you should simply stop thinking of Cameron naked, a voice screamed in my head.

I discarded all thoughts involving Cameron and continued my hopping. There was music coming from the far end of the hallway, so I veered that way and encountered the kitchen and living area.

Catching my breath, I braced myself on the white marble island and took a break to let my gaze roam. A cream-colored chaise longue laid right in the middle of the space, rustic and minimalistic décor scattered on shelves, timber beams crossed the ceiling, gorgeous windowpanes let the sunlight in, a half-naked man did a handstand, the table—

My eyes retraced their trajectory a step, snapping into focus.

Whoa.

There were very few instances in life that I'd been as shocked, as wholly and completely befuddled as I was in that instant. Was

I imagining this? No, there was no way my mind could summon such perfection. My imagination really sucked. So Cameron had to be there, at the very end of the living room. Gloriously shirtless.

And he hadn't lied.

Cameron Caldani wasn't just good at yoga. He excelled at it.

And I apparently excelled at getting hot and bothered watching him.

Because all of my blood was rushing to my face at the sight of him shirtless. With his elbows on the mat, legs up. In a pair of loose workout shorts that gravity was pulling down his beautiful quads. My eyes got lost in there for a second, in that muscled section of his thighs shining with sweat. I could make out the edge of a design there. A thigh tattoo? Oh God, I didn't think I could take that. It was bad enough that the arm he had covered in ink was now flexed. That his pecs—one of which was also covered in beautiful designs—were bunched up like I'd never seen muscles bunch in real life. It was . . .

"Ouch," I yelped, the moment the foot I'd kept up in the air unconsciously touched the ground.

Cameron's eyes blinked open. And before I could prepare to say anything, to do anything but gawk, his large, glistening, and ridiculously flexible body was toppling to the floor. Sideways. Landing on the mat with a loud *thud*.

I gasped, starting for him.

But he grunted from the floor, "Don't move." And I froze on the spot.

"Are you . . . okay?"

"Jesus fuck," he half growled, half sighed as a response. "I was unprepared."

I opened my mouth to ask *unprepared for what*, but a dash of orange shot past me, distracting me from my words.

"She's going to give me shit for that," Cameron said when I glanced back at him. He sat up with a groan. "That was Pierogi. She likes to lie down at the end of my mat when I work out."

Pierogi. His other cat. Yeah, I think I'd like to do the same thing, considering the views. "Are you sure you're okay?"

His jaw clenched and when he looked up, his eyes fell on my chest. Shoulders. Legs. His gaze was all over the place, as if he couldn't decide where to look next. He swallowed. "No point in denying that seeing you in my jersey sent me tumbling to the floor."

My eyes widened. His jersey. "I didn't mean to sleep in this. Matthew sent it so you would—" I stopped myself. "I didn't tell him about you. He found out accidentally. With a picture I took. He's such a huge soccer fan, he recognized you from your profile. I—"

"I'll give him a signed jersey," Cameron offered. Simply. Curtly.

"He will appreciate it. No, he will love you for that." And I had no idea why, but I remembered in that exact moment that I was wearing no underwear underneath. I tugged at the hem. "I . . . think we should probably talk? Last night was kind of a mess, and you must have questions."

"Will you?"

I frowned in question.

"Appreciate it," he said, standing up in a swift motion. He crossed the distance to where I stood in long determined strides and stopped right in front of me. Our eyes met. "Because I'm only offering for you."

I honestly didn't know what to do with that information. "Yes," I heard myself say. "I would appreciate it." I already did. More than he knew.

Cameron nodded. "What do you want to talk about, then?"

Everything, I should have said. But he was standing so close, with all that beautiful inked and glistening skin on display, looking at me so . . . intently, that I just babbled the first thing I could. "I owe you an apology. For last night."

Cameron's head tilted to the side. "You don't, not really." His arm rose and the back of his hand brushed my forehead. "How's the pain, darling?"

My lips parted at the touch. The question. "It's . . . I'm okay," I mumbled. "It's not that big of a deal."

A hum climbed up his throat. "I wonder who made you believe you don't deserve to be fussed over," he said so simply and honestly that I could only blink. "I was worried last night and I am worried now." His brows knotted. "In fact, I might be a little mad, too."

"You might?"

The pad of his thumb moved, grazing my jaw very briefly. I felt myself melt under that featherlight touch. "You should have called me."

The word left me in a whisper. "Why?"

"Because you needed me, and I wasn't there with you, and I hated that." His lips bent down, and my heart resumed at double pace from the weight of his words. "Then I get a trail of messages and I go to you and find you in my shirt. That some other guy sent you." He dropped his hand. "And I was never a jealous man."

A jealous man.

"I think I need to sit down," I said, hopping back a step.

Cameron's body followed behind mine. "Where do you think you're going?"

"To sit—" I was lifted up. "Oh my God." I snapped my legs closed, helpless to do anything else as Cameron whirled around with me in his arms. "You really need to stop picking me up like that."

"I'd rather not," he countered in a serious voice before planting me on a stool at the kitchen island. He turned around and produced a small pillow.

I narrowed my eyes at him. "What do you mean, you'd rather not?"

He wrapped a hand around my legs—one single hand—lifted them up and placed them on the pillow he had set on a second stool.

"Cameron," I hissed. "You really have to stop that."

"Go ahead and tell me why," he said, ignoring me and coming to my back. I sensed his head closing in, his chin touching my shoulder. "I'm sure there's some elaborate reason why I can't help you to a chair," his words fell on my cheek. Goosebumps erupted. "Feminism? A Taylor Swift song? Your twelve-step plan to drive me to insanity?"

"What—" The stool moved, with me in it, as I was pushed closer to the island. I felt the hem of the jersey ride up with the change. "Because I'm not wearing any underwear," I blurted out.

Cameron froze.

He did so for a very loud and boisterous instant, if a moment could ever feel like that. "Oh," he breathed out, the word falling on my neck. "How I wish you wouldn't have told me that."

"You asked the reason," I countered, because he had.

"I'll bring you a pair of shorts or sweats." A long exhale left him, moving away. "After."

"After what?"

"Breakfast." He went around the island, threw open the fridge, and looked at me over his shoulder. "Sweet or savory?"

I hesitated for just an instant.

An instant long enough for Cameron to start pulling all sorts of things out. An assortment of fruits, milk, juice, butter, eggs, a few jars of jam, something that looked a lot like overnight oats, cheese, and even ham. Prosciutto, if I wasn't wrong. And once everything was out, he moved along the cabinets and plucked a pack of sliced bread off a shelf and threw it on the now overflowing island.

I blinked at the display. "Are you like a human squirrel or some-thing?"

"I might also have frozen croissants," he said, nonchalantly, like he wasn't confirming that he, in fact, had squirrel tendencies. He went to the freezer, giving me a panoramic view of his almost naked backside in those rather tiny shorts as he leaned down, and pulled out what had to be the frozen croissants.

I gawked at everything before me, including him, brain still fuzzy from looking at his ass in those shorts. I shook my head. "Is this . . . what you usually have?"

I watched him toggle with the oven controls. "I already ate."

"Are you expecting anyone for breakfast?" The reminder I was in a soccer jersey and commando underneath slammed right back into me. "If someone is coming, I have to change." I tried to pull myself off the stool, but my legs were up and he'd pushed me too close. "I need to shower. Get dressed. I should probably go see a doctor to get— Oh God, my car. Is it still at the Vasquez farm? Maybe I could call someone to go pick it up. I don't know where my phone is. I—"

Cameron was suddenly there, by my side. "Ada, darling," he said with a smile. A big and soft smile. I was dazed silly. "What you need to do is stay where you are. In my kitchen. Hydrate. Eat breakfast. Then, couch or bed, your pick. The doctor will come see you here. I've already called."

I— What? "Don't—"

"Tell you what to do? Treat you like someone who had a horrible day yesterday and deserves a fucking break?" He gave me a shrug and placed a plate I hadn't seen him grab in front of me. "First, food. Then, shower. Then, doctor. Then, whatever else you want. Netflix and chill, or nap until lunchtime." A mug was produced and set in front of me, too. "I left you towels and a bathrobe in your room."

Towels. A bathrobe.

My room.

My chest felt funny. "Do you even know what 'Netflix and chill' means?"

"No." The smile returned. "But I don't really care," he said, returning to the other side of the island. "You didn't say if you preferred sweet or savory so here's all I have."

"Unless you're planning on feeding the whole town, I'd say that's a little too much."

Cameron glanced at everything he'd set on the island. His hand went to his chest, and he absently patted a spot right above a rose that spanned part of his tattooed pec. I decided it was my second-favorite tattoo. His fingers moved, and I wondered how the skin of his chest would feel to the touch with all that ink. Would it have texture? Would it be as soft and smooth as the arm I'd touched what felt like an eternity ago? I wanted to place my hands on him and—

"You need to stop looking at me like that, love."

My eyes snapped right back to his face.

Ada darling. Love. That smile on his face again.

I couldn't keep up.

"I was not looking," I whispered, cheeks flaming.

"You were, and my ego fucking loved it." He braced his hands on the island and leaned forward. "Other parts of me, too."

I thought I choked on my own breath. My gaze started to dip but I stopped myself. No more gawking. Specifically, not under his waist.

A chuckle left him, the sound as distracting as the rest of him. "I'll grab a quick shower while the oven preheats. Then I'll get breakfast ready for you before I leave."

And without so much as a nod from my side, he turned around and walked out of the kitchen, leaving me to my thoughts and a set of wildly inappropriate images of him under the water stream.

Sunday came and went in another blur of naps. And Monday wasn't all that different. So when Cameron returned he found me exactly in the place he'd moved me to before running out to do some errands: on his larger-than-life couch, clad in an indigo blue bathrobe, with my bad ankle up on a pillow and Willow curled by my side.

He appeared in front of me, his arms full of bags. "What did the doctor say?"

Leave it to him to cut straight to the chase. "You shouldn't have called and asked them to come. I can move just fine. A house call for a sprained ankle is a stretch."

Cameron carefully placed everything on the coffee table and ignored my complaint. His gaze returned to my face, his expression waiting, patient. Unbothered. He arched his brows.

I sighed. "It's a low-grade sprain. I should stay off it for a few days, and I'll be fine in a week."

He shot me a skeptical look.

I rolled my eyes. "From one to three weeks. It depends."

"That's what I thought." A slow nod. "Are you hungry?"

"I'm still stuffed from breakfast," I answered honestly. He'd pulled out so much food—again—that I'd had as much as I could just so he wouldn't have to throw anything away. And that included a new bag of mini croissants. I averted my eyes, summoning the will to say everything I'd thought about while he'd been away. "Listen, I appreciate you raiding your pantry, feeding me, and . . . helping me out, but I think I should go now."

"Why?"

This man and his questions. "Because."

"Because what?"

I glanced up. He was looking at me with a focused expression. "Because this is your home, Cameron. Because I don't have my clothes or my things or . . ." Any dignity left after this weekend, frankly. "You're an excellent host and even a better neighbor. If I were to leave you a Yelp review I'd call it high-quality grandmotherly care, but I can take care of myself and we can go back to normal now."

"Grandmotherly." He let out with a low chuckle. Ugh, those stupidly low chuckles he went throwing around. "Did not expect to be compared to a nan. What about me is grandmotherly?"

"Well, look at me." I waved my arms in the air. "You fed me, put me in the coziest bathrobe, and found me all the pillows in the house."

"Are you not comfortable?"

I shook my head. "I am. I don't think I've ever been this comfortable in my life."

The corners of his lips twitched, and I couldn't believe it, but he had the audacity to look smug. He pointed in the vicinity of my lap. "Willow doesn't like people. She hates everyone, and after dragging her here, that also included me." He tilted his head. "I don't think she's that bothered anymore."

I looked down at the cat, recalling that first time I'd seen her. She'd scratched Cameron's arm. "Maybe she senses something's off and feels bad for me."

"Maybe she can't stay away anymore."

Anymore? Our gazes met. And his was so intense, different, that

I flushed. Were we talking about Willow? "Maybe I . . . like that she likes me. It makes me feel special. Is that lame?"

"It's not," he said, Adam's apple bobbing. "But if you keep being that sweet, she'll stick to your side and never look back. And that . . ." Something crossed his face. "It would complicate things."

My heart pounded in my chest. "I'm not stealing your cat," I croaked, feeling my skin heat up under the bathrobe. "And I should really go."

Cameron's eyes were on me for one more instant and then, his focus shifted to the bags. He pulled out the contents. Sweaters, short- and long-sleeved shirts, wool-lined fleeces, pants, socks. Every item in shades of greens, burgundies, and grays. Every item just like the ones he owned, all very functional-looking and . . . small. Much smaller than what I expected his size to be.

"Cameron?" I asked, my voice coming out rocky, because he couldn't have, could he? "What's all of this?"

He grabbed a mustard beanie and inspected it up close. "These are clothes. You know, they're meant to keep your body warm and protected. And yes, they are appropriate for the area and season even if they're not up to *Vogue's* standards."

"You've lived in L.A., you should know that I'm the furthest thing from a fashionista or whatever you're implying. You've dated—"

"Your ankle begs to differ."

"My heels—"

"You don't need them now." He moved to a new bag and pulled out a pair of outdoor boots. "You'll look just as beautifully imposing in these." My lips bobbed silently. Beautifully imposing? "Once your ankle swelling comes down, of course. Until then," he paused, his eyes traveling down my robe and his face doing a strange thing. "You stay right where you are. I need to run back to town for practice, so Josie will come check on you. She insisted after she heard what shape you're in." A pause. "She also mentioned something about helping you move in to Lazy Elk, so be prepared."

My body sprung up. "I'm not moving in."

Cameron shrugged, but there was a smirk underneath the feigned indifference.

"Absolutely not," I croaked, pushing up. "I don't need—"

"We're going to hit pause on the independent routine, okay?" His voice lowered, all amusement gone. "You're staying here until you can walk. And I'm taking care of you, hear me? You're going to let me. And I hope to God you don't make me fight you over this, Adalyn, because I promise you, I will. I'll burn that goddamn shack down if I must."

Adalyn. It felt so odd to hear him say my name. So . . . ordinary after knowing what being called *Ada darling* or *love* felt like.

God. I was a mess.

"Okay," I said, and I must have been acting like a handful because Cameron looked shocked for a moment. I felt horrible. I settled down on the couch with a sigh. "Thank you for taking care of all these things." *Thanks for taking care of me.* "But please, don't burn down the cabin. I'd hate to have to bail you out after they charge you with arson."

He gave me one of those lopsided smirks.

I averted my eyes. The effect of him actively taking care of me was so loud and clear in my head that I feared Cameron saw it written all over my face. Saw how good it made me feel. Saw how sweet I thought him buying clothes for me was. Even if they were ugly.

The truth was that I didn't have much experience being in this position.

When I'd dated David, we'd spent most of our time busy with our own individual lives. He had never gone out of his way to do things for me, and I hadn't, either. Thinking back to it, we'd started seeing each other because it had been suggested by our respective fathers. Maybe even expected. It made sense for the son and daughter of business partners to date. So we . . . had. It hadn't been perfect or romantic, but I'd settled. I'd convinced myself I was content, that every relationship was different. I wasn't the loving, affectionate type so, naturally, I shouldn't expect the same from a man.

And now this one man who had been crystal clear about not

liking me was doing all these things for me. He was rescuing me and feeding me breakfast and getting me clothes and telling me he was going to take care of me. I didn't understand how we'd gotten here. And I didn't know what to do with all these emotions rioting in my chest, making it feel tight.

"Darling?" Cameron's voice brought me back to his living room, to the couch I had been carefully settled on by his arms, and all the plush pillows he'd placed around me. "What happened yesterday? What made you so frightened?"

Frightened. I had been scared, hadn't I?

I let out a shaky breath, and I was suddenly so tired of wondering why he even cared, or asked, that I didn't bother fighting him anymore. I answered with the truth.

"Someone reminded me why I am here. That I messed up back home. And I don't know how to fix it other than to do what I'm told. For a moment yesterday, I almost fooled myself into thinking that I'm fine and this is all okay and not a complete and utter mess." I shrugged, and perhaps it was the way Cameron was looking at me, not a trace of judgment in his eyes, or perhaps it was something else, but I added, "You were looking at me the way you are now. Just like that. I didn't want it to end."

His words were soft, barely a whisper. "Like what?"

"Like I'm something precious. Worth looking at."

His face fell. "Why would you think otherwise?"

"Because no one ever looks at me that way."

CHAPTER TWENTY-FOUR

Adalyn

*M*y pajamas weren't here.

Josie had come while Cameron was in practice with the team. He hadn't been joking, she'd shown up at Cameron's door with a box in her arms. It contained all my things.

"Move-in day!" she'd said with a cheer.

I didn't fight her. I didn't think I had any energy or willpower for that. My conversation with Cameron had left me . . . raw.

And as much as I thought I still hadn't done anything to earn Josie's kindness, I wanted it. So I let her fuss over me and be a little mad for not saying anything about the state I'd been living in. The horrible cottage.

Josie had called me silly and proud, and then she'd stuffed my mouth with cake and demanded I stop being so stubborn. I wondered if Cameron and Josie had ganged up on me or if I really had been so complicated to deal with.

Probably both.

With a sigh, I plucked the clean L.A. Stars jersey from the dryer, shed the robe, and put it on. I'd have to sleep in this, although at least now I'd be wearing underwear underneath. I slipped my arms back into the soft and cozy robe and brought the edges over my chest. I wondered if Cameron wore this around the house. Maybe right out of bed. Or maybe while he lounged around the place. What did he wear underneath? His sleeping clothes? Or was he one of those men who slept in his underwear? An image of him in nothing but boxers assaulted me, bringing heat to my skin. I thought back to the other morning. His bare chest. The indent of his hips. The ink on his thigh. I wished I could have gotten a closer look. I . . .

A knock on the door of the laundry room startled me right out of those dangerous, dangerous thoughts. When I turned, it was none other than the man I had just been picturing almost naked in my head.

Cameron stood tall under the doorframe, in workout clothes and with his hair a little wet. I wondered if it was raining or if practice had been that intense.

"Hi," I croaked.

"Hi," he said back.

We stared at each other, and there was something passing between us. I could tell. The last time we'd talked I'd said some things that should have probably remained thoughts. He was looking at me like that again. And it made my chest hurt with . . . something that felt a lot like longing.

"Darling?"

I cleared my throat. "How was practice?"

The corners of his lips twitched at my question. "The girls made you a get well soon card."

A spot in my chest warmed. "That's so nice of them," I admitted. Genuinely. But then . . . "I hope María didn't bully them into signing it."

"Believe me, they were all quite concerned. You did a number on all of us on Saturday. Even Diane asked if you were okay." Cameron took a small step forward. "I left the card on your bedside table." My bedside table. "You got everything washed?"

"Yes," I answered with a nod. "I . . . I hate to ask but did you happen to get me pajamas with everything else? Mine are nowhere to be found."

His expression turned rock solid. "No."

"Oh, okay. That's fine." I scratched the side of my head, feeling a little shifty under his gaze. "I sound like a jerk, don't I? Here you are doing all these things for me and I'm demanding more and more. I'm so sorry. I'll sleep in something else."

"You can borrow a shirt."

I opened the robe at the chest. "I already have this on."

The green in Cameron's eyes changed. "That's . . ." He trailed off with a strange breath. He frowned. "That's perfect. You're heading to bed?"

"Not yet?" I fumbled with the edges of the robe. "I'm actually a little hungry. And not sleepy at all after napping most of the day away."

Cameron stalked in my direction, and in two determined strides he was in front of me. The scent of him hit me right in the chest. Clean, woodsy, a hint of sweat. My stomach dropped with awareness. My heart sped up. "I'm damp and sweaty," he said, his words falling on my temple. "But I'd really like to carry you to the couch. Can I?"

I stared up at him, caught off guard by his question. The urge to lift my hand and reach for those dark locks of wet hair overwhelmed me.

"I know you hate it," he explained. "But if the sweat bothers you—"

"Please," I whispered. Just that. Because he couldn't have been any more wrong.

In a heartbeat, his arms were moving around me and he was picking me up. My cheek fell onto his chest. Cameron smelled like rain. Hard work. I closed my eyes. "I could get used to this."

I felt more than heard the sound that made his rib cage vibrate, and in what felt like not enough time, we were in the living room and he was depositing me onto the couch. His arms remained around my body for a moment longer than necessary, making me open my eyes.

I forced myself to speak, to drive my attention away from the face that was hovering too close. "Josie left mashed potatoes and a chicken casserole in the fridge," I said, my voice coming out all wrong. "I'll—"

His hand fell on my thigh, warm and heavy and solid. I looked down, wishing the thick fabric of the robe wasn't there. "Let me," Cameron said. And when I didn't complain, he stood up. His eyes went up and down my body. "I'm starving."

My stomach did a weird thing. "Me, too."

"Good. I'll put the food in the oven and jump into the shower while it heats up."

And with that, he disappeared behind the couch.

By the time we were done with dinner, my heart was doing funny things in my chest.

It was the domesticity of it all. The way he'd brought me a brimming plate of food. The fact that he'd set a glass of water and my painkillers on the coffee table, right in front of me. The way we were sitting on the couch, his thigh so close to my propped-up feet I could feel his body heat on my toes. Me, in a robe, and Cameron, in a sweatshirt I wanted to slip my hands under to see just how much it warmed his skin. Was he wearing a T-shirt underneath? I didn't think he was.

I didn't think I wanted to know the answer to the question bouncing off the walls of my mind either. Was this—this, right here—what the normalcy of being in a relationship looked like? Was this what a getaway in the mountains with your partner felt like? We'd even brought the cats.

The thought—the possibility—made me giddy, excited, curious. But it also made me incredibly sad. It made me grieve for what I never had. It made me long for more. And that was a dangerous thought. A scary one, too.

I sat up with a jolt, and Willow, who had been curled against my side, complained. "Sorry," I blurted out. "But I can't do this." I sprint-hopped away from the couch. "Where is it?"

Cameron was up on his feet immediately, but he must have seen the shift, the need for space, something to do, because he didn't come after me. He just watched. "Darling?"

Darling. It didn't bother me anymore, I decided. No. I loved hearing that. "My binder. The red one. Have you seen it?" I explained, reaching the kitchen. Making sure I stayed balanced on one leg, I started throwing drawers open. Utensils. Foil and wrapping papers. Candles. "You have candles. Tea lights. Also scented ones. Why?"

"Why wouldn't I?"

I shoved it closed. "Because I love scented candles and you're . . . I don't know. You're a man. English." One I wasn't supposed to find more attractive just by the simple fact that he had a drawer filled with candles.

"Is what bothers you the fact that I'm English or a man?"

I moved to the next one, finding only baking utensils. Did he bake, too? I threw it closed. "It makes it all worse."

"What does?"

God he was being so calm, so patient, as if I wasn't psycho-raiding his kitchen for a binder. I twisted my body, my gaze falling on a console by the entrance of the kitchen. "Ha," I said, limping my way over there. I snatched it, hopped back to the coach, and shoved it into his chest. "We've got work to do. I can't sit here and . . . vacation. This is not a weekend getaway."

Cameron held the binder to his chest and then, in some maneuver I didn't have time to anticipate or understand, his hand was wrapping around my wrist and we were plopping down on the couch.

"All right," he said. Calmly. His hip against mine and the binder balanced on his knee.

I gaped at him as he sat there, preoccupied with the one thing he'd despised so much in the past. He threw it open and started to browse through it, as if he was searching for something. He was doing all of that one handed while . . . His thumb slipped under the sleeve of my robe, making me notice his palm was wrapped around the wrist he'd pulled at. Still.

I cleared my throat. "There're three games ahead: Fairhill, Yellow

Springs, and New Mount. There's . . ." His thumb moved, swiping left and right. "The girls need the points. So far they've lost and tied. They need to win the next three games. If they don't . . ." Cameron shifted, leaning back and dragging me with him somehow. "If they don't, they won't even play for third or fourth place. I have—" I stopped myself. Before Saturday I'd been in conversation with a few local media outlets but hadn't closed on anything. And now . . . I wasn't sure I wanted to bring any press here. "I have a success story to sell to Miami. The Green Warriors need to win the Six Hills."

Cameron's tongue peeked out and wetted his lips. "Okay," he said, setting the binder in the small space between us. He released my wrist and planted his hand on my thigh. "Pick a kid." His fingers splayed. "Or a team we're up against."

My eyes widened with horror, or heat, I wasn't sure, when that simple touch zapped up my legs. "*Okay*?" I snatched the binder and busied myself with it. "No comment about the binder of hell? No peek at the very detailed section I have on you?" I stared, gawked really, at Cameron, as his expression turned pensive, but . . . relaxed. "Why are you not complaining and looking exasperated? Why are you not storming out of here because I'm difficult?"

"You're not difficult," he said slowly, and when his thumb latched on to my knee, he let out a strange sound. "You can be, though. When you want to. I couldn't figure out why. But I'm starting to understand. Either way, I'm done doing any of that."

"You're . . . done?" I asked, my voice barely there. Although what was wreaking havoc in my head was the *I'm starting to understand*. "What about the activity brochure? We're still signed up for every single thing in there. Have you forgotten that I dragged you down along with me? Because I haven't." I swallowed, hard. Hearing how little sense I was making. How . . . scared I was beginning to feel. "I'd really like for you to remember that."

"I do."

He does. He does what? And why is he still so calm? "So? Are you done with that, too? Because a sprained ankle is not going to stop me. It's not a war injury as much you're treating it like one."

Cameron released my knee, and just as I thought he was going to stand up or call me out on the attitude he didn't deserve, he set his palm on the side of my head.

"You want to play, love?" His voice had a dark edge to it. His fingers flexed. "You want a man that won't run away scared? A man that'll leave his bloody skin in the game?" My heart tripped. "I'll be your man, then."

CHAPTER TWENTY-FIVE

Adalyn

C ameron's words haunted me for a full week.

You want to play, love? I'll be your man, then.

That was what I got for getting . . . entangled with a high-performance athlete. Not entangled as in me and him but entangled as in me and him working together. And staying under the same roof. And eating together and . . .

Whatever. It didn't matter.

What was important here was that as of today, I was continuing business as usual. One week of house arrest had been more than I could afford. I'd already missed three practices and a game—the first the Green Warriors had won.

That was why I was here, walking—or lightly limping—onto the field with a heavy box in my arms. And it was fine. Perfect, really.

As if some kind of bell had gone off in his head, Cameron turned around. Swiftly. But slowly. As if he was some gruffly handsome model in an ad campaign for something like . . . shavers for men. Because had he trimmed his beard? And when? I'd seen him this morning and all that facial hair had been in its usual disarray.

He shot me an angry look across the grass.

Ah well. Back to business it was.

At least I knew what the scowling was for. Cameron didn't know I was coming to practice today. Technically, because I should—probably—be resting. That was why I'd called Josie, who had called Gabriel, who had asked his husband, Isaac, to pick me up from Lazy Elk and drive me to town. It was some complicated chain of favors I didn't understand, but like Isaac had said the moment I'd complained and profusely apologized for being an inconvenience, *This is how things work in a small town, honey.* He'd also told me to shush it before going into a ramble about how he'd been spending a lot of time in Charlotte for work—because of his *useless, turdy* boss—and complimented me for my look. Although his words had been *I can't believe you're making it work,* while glancing from my dress shirt to the hiking boots on my feet. I liked Isaac, and I got the impression he'd liked me, too.

Unlike someone currently in the middle of a practice field, surrounded by nine-year-olds and the one seven-year-old in a tutu, and sporting a newly trimmed beard that made him all the more handsome.

Cameron muttered something to Tony, the Green Warriors' new assistant coach, and stalked in my direction.

My stomach dropped. And it wasn't with dread. It was with something fuzzy and bubbly that made me feel light despite the fact he was looking at me with murder in his eyes.

"How's the new hire?" I asked when he came to a stop in front me.

Cameron snagged the box out of my grip with one quick, outraged motion. "Adalyn," he barked, sounding all angry and . . . soft. Ugh. I hated when he did that. "This weighs a ton."

I forced myself to roll my eyes, the bubbly riot in my stomach getting worse by the second. "I know," I admitted. "And before you ask, yes, I'm here. And yes, I'm fine and ready to work. And no, my ankle doesn't hurt. And yes, the boots you insist on me wearing all the time are actually, shockingly comfortable for something so ugly. And no, I'm not going to sit this one out or live like a recluse any longer after missing so much time with the team. And by the way? I might return to my cabin today."

Cameron stared back at me for a long moment, then he said all confident and smug, "No you won't."

I narrowed my eyes. "What did you do?"

Cameron shrugged.

"What did you do to the cottage, Cameron?"

"There's water damage in the bathroom."

I gave him a bland look. "Did you go in there with a bucket just to make sure of it?" Cameron smiled and yes, my heart toppled to my stomach at the sight. I sighed. The truth was that I was comfortable in Cameron's cabin. With him. I didn't want to leave, either. "Do you always get away with what you want?"

He took a step forward, getting so close I had to tip my head back to meet his gaze. "Hopefully."

My thoughts scattered. I had questions. I knew I had them. Important ones about the cottage. But his tongue peeked out and licked his bottom lip, dragging my attention there. "You trimmed your beard." His mouth twitched and my hand reached out. Unconsciously. Thoughtlessly. I stopped myself. "It looks good."

The fingers of his free hand wrapped around my wrist. "You can touch me." He brought my hand closer to his face, and my breath caught in my throat. But I closed the rest of the distance on my own, and when my palm reached his jaw, I cupped his face. My fingers grazed the surprisingly soft beard. The skin on his cheek and neck, too.

Cameron's eyes fluttered shut.

I moved my hand, my fingers brushing the side of his face with my nails.

"That feels so good," he hummed.

It did for me too. I—

A whistle was blown close behind.

I dropped my hand. "The uniforms have arrived." Green eyes reappeared. They were as dazed as I felt. "Finally," I croaked. "That's what, hmm, is in the box. I should stop petting your beard and . . . check them."

Cameron huffed out a laugh. "*Fecking* hell, darling." He shook his head. "You thought you were petting me?" Another chuckle. "Way to shoot a man down."

My cheeks warmed. But I refused to let this man sidetrack me again. "Did you just say 'fecking hell'?"

"I don't curse around the girls anymore. Manager said it was unprofessional."

Oh. "That's, um." All the air seemed to escape out of my lungs. "That is sweet. Thanks for going the extra mile, Coach."

Something flashed behind his eyes. Then Cameron shook his head, as if in . . . disbelief. "Ah Christ." Another one of those laughs toppled out. "I think you've broken me, love."

I frowned. I also blushed even further at that *love*.

Luckily, before I could say or do something strange like, let's say, drop to the grass in a tangle of emotions I didn't understand, I was being tackled from the side.

"Careful there," Cameron said in a gentle but firm voice, one of his hands falling on my shoulder. He stabilized me, and his fingers brushed the back of my neck. Tingles spread down my arm.

I looked down to find María hugging me.

"I'm just so happy you're okay," she mumbled against my side. She glanced up, a serious expression on her face. My chest tightened at the sight. "Did you get our card? Did you see that Brandy and Tilly also signed? I painted their paws and made them sign with them."

So the weird smudges of ink had been the goats.

"Yes," I admitted weakly. "I loved it. I . . ." I wasn't going to get emotional. I really wasn't. "It was beautiful. Thank you so much."

"We're just glad you're okay," Juniper said from the group, obtaining a wave of nods from the rest of the girls.

"I'm also glad, ma'am—Adalyn," Tony said from Cameron's side. Then added, "I told them they could take a five-minute break, Coach."

Cameron only lifted his eyes off me to give Tony a nod.

María released me, taking my hand before stepping away. "So what's in the box? Is it gifts?" She frowned. "You should have told us you were coming today. We could have thrown you a welcome party."

"That's really okay," I assured her, with a squeeze of her hand. The kid's smile turned wider. "And yes, I've come bearing gifts. It's a surprise. For everyone in the team. I just hope you like them."

"I looove surprises," María confessed. Followed by a long *ohhhhh* from the rest of the girls. She took a step forward and poked at the box in Cameron's arms. "Do you love surprises, too, Miss Adalyn?"

"Sure," I said, feeling the weight of Cameron's gaze on the side of my head.

"That's perfect," María answered. "That way we can exchange surprises today. It'll be like . . . Christmas. But in fall. Oh, by the way, are you coming to the fall fest? Will your foot be okay? We can go apple picking, or pumpkin bowling, or even sign up for the haunted corn maze race." María was beaming, vibrating with so much excitement that it was impossible for me to do anything but nod. "Awesome!" She returned her attention to the box. "Let's exchange surprises now then."

"María," Cameron warned. "What did we talk about earlier today?"

But María had never been intimidated by this stoic and secretly gentle man, so she went ahead and said, "I know you said it wasn't ready, but I think Miss Adalyn deserves her surprise now. She's been in pain, and surprises always cheer me up when I'm sick or sad. Plus, she brought gifts for the team, and we don't have a welcome party for her like you promised we would when she returned." The nine-year-old shot Cameron a hard look. "You're being a grumpy grump again, Coach Cam."

Cameron sighed.

I gaped at the kid. "Hey, you called him Coach Cam." María rolled her eyes. "Although you also called him a grumpy grump,"

I teased, looking at Cameron. He rolled his eyes. "Which I'm not against."

"Yeah, because Coach was being a total grump at practice all of last week, even on Saturday, when we won. And he worked so hard at the surprise, too. Even when Dad told him about a hundred times that he didn't need to help." She shook her head, and I shook mine in confusion, too. "Maybe it's the curmudgeons on his b—"

"María," Tony blurted out. "Not that again, Jesus. Just tell Miss Adalyn about the shed already."

Cameron grunted.

I frowned. "The shed?"

"Fiiiiiine," María stretched out the word. "Coach Cam had my dad and brother redo the shed into an office. For you. It's tiny but Coach helped and he was very proud before you got here. It will look super cute, I promise."

CHAPTER TWENTY-SIX

Adalyn

$\mathcal{T}$he Green Warriors won a second time.

Cameron said it was because of the new uniforms. The girls had absolutely loved them, because, as María had pointed out, they slayed. They really did slay. The shirts were charcoal black and mint green, with every player's name and number printed in pastel pink on the back, and the Miami Flames logo on the front. I'd ordered shorts and socks in green and black, so the girls could pick. And I'd gone as far as getting a skort that resembled a tutu for Chelsea. It hadn't been easy to find but she'd been so excited and shocked that I thought she'd stopped breathing for a second. Even Diane had been touched. But I wasn't responsible for the win. The girls were. They'd played a good game. And that wasn't on me.

It was all because of Cameron.

Cameron, who at yesterday's game had worn the matching tracksuit I'd ordered for him. And Cameron, who I was currently avoiding.

He'd built me an office. So I wouldn't need to sit on the bleachers. He'd paid for it out of his own pocket, and worked on it with Robbie, in secret. So while I was on his couch, plopped there like some kind of . . . wounded damsel, he'd been sweating building shelves. María had spat out all the details.

So, for the last few days, ever since the office reveal, I'd been a little angry. At myself, not him, because that had been the nicest, most thoughtful thing anyone had done for me. Ever. The reason I was avoiding Cameron was because I couldn't, for the life of me, think clearly when he came close. I melted away and all I could think of was that office. The scones he'd brought me this morning. The way his hand fell on my thigh. The beard he was so keen on keeping neat and trimmed. The urge to touch it, and him, again.

Ugh.

With a sigh, I scanned the stands before me, hoping—needing—to distract myself with the fall fest. There was an empty stage—which I hoped didn't imply another boogie night—a few food stands, a crafts and arts booth . . . Josie's Joint.

I walked up to Josie's coffee stand and blinked at the colorful display in front of me. There were pumpkins at the foot of the booth, red apples hanging from strings, tiny bales of hay decorating the bottom and the roof. There was even what looked like a . . . scarecrow. Female, judging by the braids, thick lashes, rosy cheeks, and the sign hanging from her neck: CARVE THE PATRIARCHY, ONE PUMPKIN AT A TIME.

Without warning, Josie's head popped up from underneath the kiosk, startling me.

"Oops," she said with that characteristically big smile. "Sorry, I didn't mean to . . . scarecrow you." A wink was thrown my way. "How do you like my booth? I've decided to lean more into my feminist strike this year. You know, with my who-needs-men policy and all."

"Men really are the last thing we need sometimes," I agreed. "And I love the booth. The town looks incredibly festive, but this is definitely my favorite spot."

She laughed, and it was bright and lighthearted and it made me wonder if I ever sounded that carefree. "As you can see," she said, spreading her arms, "no one does a fall festival like us. It's where the mountains meet southern charm." Her hands dropped. "Anyway, what can I get you?"

"What do you recommend?"

Her smile widened, those light blue eyes twinkling. She pulled out a board with the drink specials and set it in front of me. "Josie's Pumpkin Kick is my personal favorite. But if you're in the mood for something real strong, then I suggest you go for the Campfire Fizz. And last but most certainly not least, the Cocoa Apple Heart if you're not in the mood for caffeine."

I stared at the board and the woman by its side, suddenly . . . happy to be here. In Green Oak. "I'll have the Cocoa Apple Heart, it sounds amazing."

"Whoa," she said, her expression changing. "You're smiling really big right now, and for some reason I feel like I should give you a hug. Do you want one?"

"Okay," I heard myself whisper. Next thing I knew, Josie's body was sticking out of the booth and squeezing me. I squeezed back. "I'm sorry," I said when she released me. "I was feeling very grouchy today. And the idea of one of your drinks cheered me up. Even the scarecrow did, and I never liked them that much."

Josie chuckled. "You know what?" Her eyes trailed behind me for a moment, and then she said, "I think I'm going to prepare a complimentary Campfire Fizz. There might be someone you want to gift it to?" That gave away what she was looking at in the distance. Who. "In the meantime, you can tell me what he did for you to be grouchy."

I opened my mouth to shoot the conversation down, but— "He built me an office. Out of the shed by the practice field. He helped with, like, his hands and tools or whatever."

Josie nodded slowly. "And that is . . ." She trailed off, pulling out a box filled with syrup bottles from underneath the bar.

"Good," I answered. "It's thoughtful. And sweet." Her smile widened. "And it's also really bad," I added, to which she frowned. "I don't know. I can't decide. I'm not used to these things."

"To things like . . . someone going out of their way for you?

Slowly earning your trust? Taking care of you? Flirting? Wanting to bang the crap out of y—"

"Josie," I whispered.

She smirked. "Just saying it like I see it."

Was Cameron doing all those things? I thought he was, but then again, what did I even know?

"He really did a number on you, huh?" Josie said with a long exhale. "Cameron is not whoever hurt you so badly. He's not a bad guy. He's quite the opposite, in fact." Josie shook her head. "The man's like a nut. Tough to crack, but a softie at heart. Just like you. Maybe you should give him a chance." She lifted her eyes from her work, meeting mine. "You should give yourself a chance."

Give myself a chance.

I swallowed, trying to push down the sudden knot of emotion clogging my throat. I averted my eyes, feeling overwhelmed by Josie's words.

María materialized in the distance. She was with some of the girls from the team, all of them carrying caramel apples on long sticks. She spotted me and waved at me very enthusiastically.

I waved back.

"That kid adores you, you know?" Josie said, recapturing my attention.

When I looked back at her, she was opening a carton of milk. "The feeling is mutual."

Josie smiled. "That's good to hear." She grabbed one of those small metallic pitchers off a shelf. "I think she changed one of the baby goats' names to Adalina."

I huffed out a laugh. "I guess it could have been worse."

"Not everyone in town gets the privilege of having one of the Vasquezes' animals named after them." She chuckled but sobered up quickly. "Jokes aside, I think she looks up to you. You must remind her of her mom."

I didn't understand how such a warm and happy child could find anything remotely motherly about me, but I did care for the kid. I cared about María. And hearing that made me feel immensely honored. "How long ago did she pass?"

"When María was about six," Josie explained with a sad tilt to her lips. "The Vasquezes got here when Tony was little, bought a dying farmhouse and brought her back to life. They've done more for the community in a few years than most have in generations. And Robbie still offers to host every single activity or party in town. Most of them without any compensation in return. The landmark where we are right now, for example, belongs to the farm."

"It must be a lot of work for Robbie. Taking care of his family and the farm and everything else on his own can't be easy."

"It's not easy, that's for sure," Josie agreed, finishing up one of the drinks with whipped cream. "The farm struggled financially for a fair amount of time after losing María's mom." She lowered her voice. "And Robbie doesn't like to talk about it, but he was—and maybe still is—in a lot of debt." She sighed. "Luckily for all of us there's some kind of guardian angel looking over Green Oak. I like to think of her as a modern fairy godmother. And yes, it's a she, and she has Oprah's face." She grabbed a marker and began to write on a cup. "Nobody knows who it is, but when a local business struggles . . ." She waved the pen as if it was a wand. "Bibbidi-bobbidi-boo!"

I chuckled, caught off guard by the theatrics. "So, like, an angel investor?"

"Yes," she agreed. "But we choose to believe in the magic and not the fancy names." A shrug. "Anyways. The Vasquezes' farm is marching at full steam now. We just need a new happily ever after for Robbie. But I'm working on it. I'm an excellent matchmaker."

I looked over my shoulder, finding María in the crowd as she talked about something that required both her hands.

"She'll be fine," Josie said. "Both she and Tony. I was also raised by a single parent, and look at how well I turned out."

"You were?" I asked.

"Yes, ma'am. Never even met my dad." She placed a second cup in front of me. "I just know he chose not to be involved, and the money he sent every month was put into a savings account under my name by my mom."

A dozen questions rose to the tip of my tongue, but Josie sidetracked me with a laugh.

I frowned. "What?"

She pushed the two very elaborate and colorful drinks in my direction. "Girl, you better move and go rescue that very antsy-looking man before he murders someone. Namely, the president of the PTA."

I glanced back, finding a very tight-faced Cameron talking to Diane. Or rather, being talked at by Diane, if the supersonic speed at which her mouth was moving was anything to go by. Cameron's face scrunched up. I knew that look.

"Oh God," I mumbled, swiveling back to Josie. "I better go. How much do I owe you?"

"You can pay for these tomorrow, I have a serious favor to ask," Josie said, still looking behind me. Her brows rose on her forehead. "Oh. *Oh.* I think . . . Diane might be hitting on Cameron?"

I snatched the drinks up and turned around, walking away as fast as I could, and ignoring the laughter rolling out from Josie's booth. I knew why she laughed. She thought I was jealous. I wasn't. Cameron and I were . . . a team, of sorts, I guessed. We were partners. Coworkers. I owed him. Yes, that was what was making me speed up. Not Diane's flirting with him.

It took Cameron's eyes a few seconds to find me in the short distance. He widened them. *Hurry up*, he seemed to silently beg.

Diane seemed totally oblivious to his visible discomfort. And as I neared them, all that urgency faded and gave way to . . . amusement.

I rolled my eyes at him. *Grow up*, I sent him through the invisible line we were communicating through.

Understanding crossed his face. Then a corner of his lips tilted up, *Make me.*

Smug, competitive man, I thought. And he seemed to catch that, too, because he smiled at me. And I blushed.

When I reached them, I was so distracted, I could hardly take in

Diane's words. Something about her divorce or a hose that needed checking at her house.

"There's an emergency," I announced. Diane's voice came a stop. "And I need Cameron." Cameron's smile widened. "Most urgently." Most urgently? God, Adalyn.

Cameron cleared his throat, but I knew it was to cover a snort.

Diane laughed awkwardly. "Can't you grab someone else? I was about to explain to Cam how important it is for Chelsea to keep a balance between her ballet lessons and soccer practices."

I frowned. Was she? I swore she'd said something about a hose and her ex-husband. Cameron's eyes, still on me, widened in warning. "I'm afraid the emergency can't wait." I schooled my face into a stern expression. "There's been an accident. By the cheese stand." Diane's expression turned skeptical. "They need Cameron. Specifically. Because of his knowledge of . . . soft cheeses. Particularly."

"Soft cheeses?" Diane blinked.

"Mozzarella," I said. "And . . . Brie. Ricotta, also maybe feta. You know, cheeses that are soft and/or crumble when—"

"I think we better go," Cameron intervened. "To check on the, hmm, soft cheese emergency in person. It sounds important." I nodded my head. "And I would hate for the cheeses that crumble, in particular, to crumble too hard."

"But—" Diana started.

But Cameron's arm was snaking around my shoulders, his paw-like hand falling on my side, and turning us around and away. He lowered his voice, his head coming down, so close to my ear that I felt the words fall on my skin. "Christ, darling." He moved us along, away from Diane. "Soft cheeses? You couldn't think of anything better?"

"That woman makes me nervous." I shoved Josie's take-out cup into his hands. "A Campfire Fizz, for you."

He hummed deep in his throat, and I couldn't help but notice how we were walking with his arm around my shoulders.

I didn't complain. "It's one of Josie's seasonal drinks. I got a

Cocoa Apple Heart for myself." I lifted the whipped cream-topped cup and took a long swig. "Whoa."

"Good?" he asked.

"It's actually great," I answered, the swirl of flavors bringing me unexpected comfort. I eyed Cameron's drink and thought of Josie's words. "Try yours. It better be good because it cost me a *serious favor*, whatever that meant." I paused. "It's a little token of appreciation. A thank-you. For the office. And for everything else, really." I lifted my head, glancing at his profile. The corner of his lips was twitching. No. I couldn't survive another grin. Not at the speed we were walking. I returned my eyes to the unpaved way ahead of us. "Don't look so smug. You needed saving like a minute ago." I felt myself frown. "Was she . . . really flirting with you?"

Cameron picked up the pace, his arm now secured around me, and his hand resting on my waist. "Are you jealous?"

I didn't respond.

I could feel—sense, thanks to my Cameron Caldani sixth sense, which had now developed—that he was smiling. Big. Knowingly.

I was about to call him out on it when Diane called from behind us, "Hello? The cheese stand is right there! You've walked past it!"

"Oh God," I muttered, stealing a glance back. "She's chasing after us."

"Your ankle okay or should I throw you over my shoulder?"

"Huh?"

"Fuck it," he said. And in a quick maneuver I could have never anticipated, I was up in his arms. Drinks intact.

"Cameron—" I started, grabbing on to his jacket with one hand and holding my drink with the other. I spotted Diane over his shoulder. Her index finger was up in the air, her pace increasing. "Okay, I think it's time to run."

Cameron took off then, laughter rolling straight out of him, dark and rich and beautiful. Making his chest vibrate against my body with the sound. He made a sudden turn to the left, and honest to God, a giggle came out of me. The man who was now sprinting through the space between two stands rasped out something between a chuckle and a curse in response, and finally rounded a big truck that was parked a few yards away.

He came to a stop behind it, next to the truck's bed, which was filled with hay and provided a good cover. He peeked his head out, probably checking to see if we were still being chased.

When he faced me, my chest was heaving with my breath. My heart pounded with adrenaline that had little to do with the sprint and everything to do with the man who still had me in his arms.

Time seemed to slow, thicken, as he lowered me to my feet, a wave of very different emotions crashing into me when my boots touched the ground.

"Hey," Cameron said, his voice deep and as charged as I felt. "What's wrong?"

"Nothing." I thought I whispered. I looked into his eyes. Almost as green as the canopy of trees at his back. "I . . . I was a little jealous." My words fell in the small space between our bodies. So small it could be breached in a single breath. "I was jealous of Diane. I didn't like that she was flirting with you. But now I feel bad for running like that. Now—"

His free hand came to my jaw, his palm warm and fingers stretching to cup my face. "I know," he said, chin dipped down. His jaw was clenched with an emotion I couldn't read. "We'll apologize later, if it makes you feel better." A muscle jumped there. "I'll tell her I'm not interested. That I asked you to come up with something stupid to avoid an awkward conversation."

My throat dried at his words, the closeness, the awareness rushing up and down my body at the feel of his touch. "My excuse wasn't that stupid."

Cameron's mouth twitched, but he didn't smile. Instead, his lips parted and he expelled a soft gulp of air. The green in his eyes darkened and he moved closer, stepping into me until my back fell against the side of the truck.

My heart halted, and I was pretty sure a sound might have escaped at the sensation. The way his chest, hips, thighs, were now against mine. The way every point where our bodies touched tingled and burned. Every nerve ending turned into a live wire. I was ablaze.

Cameron hummed, that large hand that had been latched on to my face and neck climbing down my neck, shoulder, side, until reaching my waist. He squeezed. "It's been driving me so mad."

"What?" I whispered.

"Wondering if this was something you wanted," he answered with a frown. I opened my mouth, as if to tell him of course, how could I not want this, you, it's wanting it that makes me scared, but his hand moved. He clutched the fabric of my jacket. "That tiny whimper you've just made," Cameron said, voice rocky. "You made it that first night. When I put you to bed."

I closed my eyes. "I did?"

I felt him release my jacket. Then, his hand was at my back. His fingers splayed, climbing to my shoulder blades, reaching the nape of my neck. "You pulled me to bed, too, do you know that?"

I thought I managed a shake of my head. I couldn't know. I was too distracted, overpowered, by the sensation of his fingers grazing the bottom of my scalp, tangling in my hair, pulling me to him, my body into his.

"You let out that exact sound and pulled me by the shirt," he rasped out, the words right against my cheek. "And I had to settle with stroking your hair until you were asleep."

My free hand shot up on its own and latched on to his forearm. I didn't have words, I couldn't even think. So I let myself be. I gave myself a chance. Just like Josie had said.

I pulled at his sleeve, hard, like I imagined I'd done that night. Cameron's body came over me. Eyes still closed, I felt him, his weight, his warmth, the inside of his thighs coming over the sides of mine. I heard something drop to the ground. And then, both his hands on my face.

"Adalyn," I heard, the word falling right on my lips. "Open your eyes, love."

I opened them and for the first time I let myself really look at him. He was so devastatingly handsome, so fierce, so absolutely determined that I felt short of breath.

"I like your eyes on me," he said, his thumb trailing along my jaw, gently, softly, leaving a trail of tingles behind. He grazed the corner of my lips, and I watched his tongue come out and wet his. "What do you want from me?"

I tightened the grip on his arm. "A chance."

Cameron's nostrils flared, but he seemed to hesitate.

"You make me feel," I heard myself whisper. And I didn't know if something coherent could come out of me, but God, I wanted to try. "You make me feel like I've never felt with anyone before, Cameron. You make me want things I never wanted."

A groan left Cameron's mouth. His grasp of my face turned desperate, softer, if that could ever happen at the same time. Hips pressed against mine, and twin sighs escaped our lips. He felt so . . . big, hard, all over me. And he looked in pain. His eyes dipped to my mouth, frantically, his thumb traveling to my bottom lip.

God, I wanted to feel him. Against my lips. I turned my head. Kissed the pad of his thumb.

"Fuck," he grunted, something behind his eyes lighting up, breaking out, something powerful and dark.

I leaned forward, my patience done. Cameron did the same.

The sound of an engine coming to life sliced right through the moment.

We blinked at each other for an instant, chests heaving with heavy breaths, making sense of our surroundings.

"It's the truck," he finally whispered, his forehead falling against my shoulder. He groaned a curse.

Oh. Right. I'd forgotten all about that.

Cameron lifted his head and pulled me away from the side of the vehicle.

The sight of my hands in his made my heart skip a beat. It also reminded me of something. "I think we dropped both our drinks," I said, looking at the ground and finding them there. I glanced back at Cameron. I flushed. "I . . . You're smiling really big." Something took flight in my chest, and I made myself ask. "Why?"

"Because you've just given me a reason."

"A reason for what?"

"To play the longest game I ever have."

CHAPTER TWENTY-SEVEN

Cameron

$\mathcal{T}$he lasagna had five minutes left in the oven and Adalyn wasn't here.

I went to my phone and picked it up off the counter. I opened my contacts but . . . my finger halted in the air. I could already see her face. Her brown eyes rolling back and her mouth formulating some smart remark about how impatient I was. Maybe she'd call me a *nonna* again, just like she had the other day when I shoved more food on her plate without asking her first.

The corners of my lips tipped up and with a shake of my head I dropped the phone.

I really was an impatient bastard. But I didn't care. I was too old and too set in my ways to change that. I didn't think I could, either. Just like I couldn't help the need to . . . take care of her. Especially when she didn't herself. Or worse yet, when she didn't expect anybody else to.

Willow and Pierogi dashing in the direction of the front door was the only sign I needed to know that Adalyn was home. Home. Warmth spread in my chest.

I faced the entrance of the kitchen, much like my cats had just done, and waited silently for her to materialize. A trail of sweet mewing reached my ears, followed by the sound of Adalyn's soft voice. Her voice always did that when she talked to them, and it fascinated me. I loved how close she was with them, and Willow in particular. Every time I found them curled up on the couch, I had to stop myself from . . . jumping in and begging her to pet me instead.

I was fucking ridiculous.

Her form popped up at the end of the hall, cheeks pink from the increasingly cold air. I watched her unzip the jacket I'd gotten for her, probably unaware I was there, gawking, all my attention captured by those hands I wanted on me. The jacket opened, revealing one of those silky, thin button-downs she loved so much. She was wearing it with jeans and boots. I'd bought every item of clothing on her except for that shirt and her underwear. And a part of me rebelled at the fact. I wanted to pamper Adalyn. Bury her in nice things I knew she could probably afford herself. I didn't care.

"Hi," she said, finally noticing me. Her cheeks filled with a different shade of pink, and her eyes trailed down my body. She did that a lot lately. Openly checked me out. And I fucking loved it. "Cameron?"

I swallowed. "I love your hair today." I really did. It was down, wavy, free, not straightened or tight in some bun.

Adalyn's lips bobbed. "I . . . Oh. Thank you." She frowned. "You, um, looked . . . weird. As if you were about to sneeze. Or . . . hungry?" Her eyes widened. "Oh God, I'm super late, aren't I?" She pulled out her phone and checked the screen. "Please, tell me I'm not too late and ruined dinner."

The genuine worry in her face pushed me one step forward. I stilled myself. "You're just in time," I assured her, my voice sounding a little too rough still. "And I wasn't about to sneeze. Or hungry. That was just my face." Around you. Lately. Always. I'd need to work on it.

Her concern dissolved, giving way to that playfulness she had been showing me glimpses of these past days. "You still looked handsome," she said in a small voice. "It smells great, by the way. Very excited to see what you've cooked."

Enthralled, I watched her pad all the way to the kitchen island and take a seat. "How bad was it?"

A sigh came out of her lips. "Bad. It took Josie and I two rounds of milkshakes to cheer everyone up."

My hand closed around the bottle of red wine I'd gotten on my way home from the game. I'd already set two glasses on the island. "Red?" I asked, the intimacy of the scene catching me by total surprise. A new kind of warmth spread across my chest. I . . . liked this. How this felt. I cleared my throat. "I also have a bottle of white chilling in the fridge."

Her lips parted with a soft, "Oh." And my gaze fastened on her mouth. "What is this for? I would hardly celebrate the outcome of the game, even if we didn't lose."

"You also deserve to be comforted, darling. It wasn't just the girls not getting enough points to get to the final."

Adalyn sighed. "Red is perfect. Thank you, Coach."

I had to fight the urge to smile at her calling me that. Or growl, I wasn't sure. "Don't thank me just yet," I murmured, and served her a glass. "So two rounds of milkshakes?"

"Yes. The girls were so devastated I started getting everything Josie had behind the counter. Nothing was left, not even Josie's raisin cookies." Her hand came around the stem of the glass. "I mean, we all knew that if we didn't win this game against the New Mount Eagles we would only be able to fight for a third or fourth place. But I . . ." She averted her gaze, her lips closing around the brim and taking a long sip. "I don't know."

We had talked about this, long and hard. We'd established a strategy and the girls had entered that field today with a literal battle cry. Adalyn had gotten everything on camera. When we'd only managed another tie, I'd been ready to deal with the possible consequences that would have on Adalyn. I'd been prepared to weather a storm. Because I'd known just how badly Adalyn wanted—needed—the girls to get to that final that was no longer possible. But she'd been . . . okay. No. She'd been so concerned about the girls' reaction that she hadn't even shown disappointment herself. She'd put on a strong face.

It'd been impossibly hard not to kiss her in that moment.

It was impossible now. "Are you not a little devastated? You don't need to act strong around me, love."

Adalyn set the glass back on the island. "I'm disappointed. There was a lot at stake for me." She frowned. "But no, I'm not devastated. Somehow. It was me who got their hopes up. I wanted this for *them*."

There was a lot at stake for me.

I knew that she had messed up in some way or another and was trying to redeem herself. But I was starting to believe that there was more than just that.

"What exactly was at stake for you?" I asked.

Adalyn shook her head. "You know what the Miami Flames sent me here for," she said. And I knew. But I let her talk. Because now, I was certain I was missing something I'd overlooked. It was right there, in the way she wouldn't look at me. Her shoulders tensed. "I know that the condition had never been to win but . . . Well, I just hoped we would. A win is always a win. And you can better sell a win to the press. People love winners, we all know that. But I still have a lot of material to work with. And I'm planning something big for that last game. No matter where we end up. This is still a success story."

I frowned. *The condition*? Why would she say that instead of the goal or the milestone? But also . . . "There wasn't any press at today's game. Or the one before." I specifically remembered her mentioning talking to local outlets. "Why?"

She brought the glass to her lips again. But I could tell it was to give herself time.

I stared at her, in silence. Willing her to tell me the reason even though I knew. She must have done it for me. And that . . . made me want to scream for very different reasons. "Adalyn—"

"Enough about me, please." She tried to smile over her glass, but I didn't buy it. It was that plastic smile I didn't like. The one that wasn't hers. "What about you? What's Cameron Caldani's plan? How . . . long do you think you'll be in Green Oak?"

I remained quiet. Partly because of how she'd shot me down, and partly because of the reminder that none of us were here to stay. Or maybe I was. I didn't know.

Adalyn must have sensed some of my reluctance to talk about any of that, because she reached out and touched my arm. "We don't need to talk about it." She lowered her voice. "Can I ask you something else instead?"

I reached for my glass and brought it to my lips for one long swig. "You can ask me anything," I told her, returning the wine to the surface of the island. I just wish she'd extend the same offer to me.

"It's about your retirement."

I stiffened. So much that I had to focus on the touch of her fingers on my arm to simmer down enough to speak. "What about it?"

"I . . . I read about it," she admitted. "About you, too. A lot." Her cheeks were pink again, but not with embarrassment. With the opposite of that. And the fool in me thought, *That's my brave girl.* But she wasn't my girl. Not yet. "It was sudden. You had a few more years in you. Goalkeepers usually . . ." A shake of her head. "I don't need to explain this to you of all people. But your retirement came as a surprise. I was wondering if there was a reason."

I felt myself lean back, and Adalyn's hand fell off my arm with the distance.

I walked to the oven and took out the lasagna. Words were stuck in my throat, but this time it wasn't because of my reluctance to share, it was because I was readying myself to share this with her. It felt crucial that I did. But it wasn't easy.

Moments ago, when Adalyn had dodged my question, it had stung. But how could I expect her to completely open up when I wasn't doing that myself?

I leaned back on the counter, realizing I was somehow holding a spatula.

I dropped it next to the lasagna and braced my hands on the marble.

I closed my eyes, throwing myself back to that night.

"Someone broke in," I let out with a long, rough breath. "Into my house. In L.A."

I waited, heard my own words hanging in the air, feeling the usual pressure that came along with the memory. The horrible night. I opened my eyes and looked at her. All the blood had drained from her face.

"To this day, I don't even understand how it happened." I let my arms drop to my sides. "It had been the night after returning from a game in Austin. Usually, I left Willow and Pierogi with a neighbor, some old lady who claimed to be an old Hollywood star. I never recognized her from anything but she took good care of them, so I trusted her." I shook my head. "I'd been tempted to leave them with her an extra night and go straight to bed. I still have—or had—a few years left in me, you were right, but away games were starting to take their toll on me. Thing was, I missed the cats, and was worried about Willow being the pain in the ass she can be, so I just collected them, went home, and crashed."

Adalyn looked so distraught I had to look away.

"I . . ." The image of what happened next was as clear as the day in my head. "I think I slept at least five hours before hearing Willow's loud whining, so I . . . opened my eyes and saw him there."

A strange sound left her.

My eyelids shut. "For a second I thought I was dreaming. But then the guy moved, and I knew, someone had broken in. And was in my room. By my bed." My whole body started to shake. It wasn't as bad as it had been at first. But every once in a while, I still got the shakes. "I didn't even know how long the intruder had been in my room. Minutes, hours, the whole weekend I'd been away? I . . ." My words dried out. My vocal cords were not working anymore. "Fuck, I—"

I was tackled.

So hard I stumbled back into the counter. Arms came around my torso, meeting at my back, and I was squeezed. Hugged. As hard and tight as I'd ever been. A broken laugh left me as I threw my own arms around Adalyn's shoulders and brought her even further into my chest. As much as I could. I would have burrowed her inside me if I'd been able to. That was how good it felt to be hugged this fiercely by Adalyn Reyes.

"So this is what it takes, huh," I said, more to myself than her. I let my chin fall onto the top of her head and allowed myself to be comforted in a way I hadn't been since the events of that night.

Time ticked by, and with every passing second in our embrace, something heavy settled in my stomach. It should have made it better, having this woman I wanted, needed, craved, in my arms. But it didn't do just that. It also solidified one of my biggest fears after that night.

"What if I'd had a family in the house? A wife? Kids? What if . . ." What if you had been in my bed? "What if I'd had someone other than Willow and Pierogi in the house?" I was barely able to swallow the clog in my throat. "I wouldn't have been able to do anything, Adalyn. Not a single thing. And it would all have been because of me. Because of some career I chose when I was boy. Because of a life I chased because of my own pride. My family wouldn't want for anything, but what kind of life could I provide them with?" My breath turned ragged. "The guy, he was some crazed fan who was taken away and dealt with, but what if someone else comes along?"

Her arms squeezed harder around my waist. "It would have never been your fault. You aren't responsible for somebody else's actions. Not even when they claim they do it out of love or adoration or awe." Her voice cracked. "You're not responsible, Cameron. You hear me? You're not."

I let myself take a deep breath, probably the first one in a while. I filled my lungs with her scent, and fuck, it felt so good. So right.

Adalyn extricated her head from my chest and looked up. "You must know that I would have never said anything," she said, brown eyes shining with emotion. Guilt. "I swear to you Cameron, when I threatened to expose you to the whole town I—" Her voice broke off. "God, I am so sorry. I—"

"I know," I told her. And it dawned on me, just how certain I was. Had been. "I know now, okay?"

Her eyes kept twinkling with unshed tears, and I swore that if she cried right now it'd break me in half. "I must have made you feel so unsafe. And you must have really hated me. Why didn't you leave?"

"I'm one stubborn motherfucker," I said honestly. "I told you I was proud. And selfish." My throat worked, and I brought my hands up and down her back, comforting myself more than her. "And I didn't hate you. I could never hate you." Her face softened, even if only slightly. It brought me relief. "I was no angel, either, love. I treated you like shit. Said things I shouldn't have and never meant. I was mean to you." My hands closed around the fabric of her shirt. "And I hate that I was."

Adalyn released me then. She took a step back, and the absence of her felt like a punch to the gut.

"That's okay," she said, catching me by surprise. "You had good reasons to do all that."

My stomach dropped with some sense of relief, because she wasn't running away from me, but also with something I didn't like. Why wasn't she tucked in my arms? Why was she physically removing herself from me?

"I deserved it, honestly. What matters now is that you've forgiven me."

I felt myself pale. Deserved it? "Adalyn—"

"I'm going to run to the restroom, okay? I'll be right back so we can eat." She made herself smile. "I'm starving and I'm under the impression that lasagna might have come right out of *Nonna*'s recipe book."

It did. It was the ragù she prepared when I was a boy.

But before I could utter a word, she was walking away, and I was watching her leave. I started after her, then stopped myself. I'd give her the minute she so clearly needed.

On the island, my phone pinged with a notification.

An email from Liam.

I started putting down the device, but something caught my attention. Miami Flames.

I unlocked it and opened the email.

From: liam.acrey@zmail.com
To: c.caldani13@zmail.com
Subject: Miami Flames interest

C – Remember I put out some scouts to spread word around that there was MLS interest in you? Not a rumour anymore. The Flames seem to be looking for a big name for sporting director. Scouts claim it's to either fix media mess (link below) or cash in on attention. I think it's something else. Either way, big cash. Interested?

L.

PS: RBC is growing restless, you have until end of October to decide. Stop being a wanker and take it.

I immediately clicked on the link.

A video popped open, starting without me hitting play.

A woman entered what looked like the Flames' Stadium, stomping her way to one of those mascots shaped like a bird. Someone said, "Are you recording this?" And the camera moved closer, fully catching her face.

All the blood in my face dashed to my feet.

Adalyn.

Then it dashed right back to my head, making me see red.

"What the fuck."

CHAPTER TWENTY-EIGHT

Adalyn

$\mathcal{W}$hen I returned to the kitchen, I found a very different Cameron than the one I'd left there.

This one wasn't looking at me with all that softness and vulnerability that had made my chest hurt. This Cameron was mad. Upset.

Disconcerted.

"Adalyn," he said. That was all. Just my name.

I came to a stop. My gaze roamed all over his face, his stance, the kitchen, looking for an explanation. Had I done something to cause this? Minutes ago, I'd run into his arms because I hadn't been able to help myself. Because I'd felt so horrible at the idea of having used something so painful against him that I would have cracked in two if I didn't make sure he knew how sorry I was. Minutes ago, he was calling me love and telling me he'd hated being mean to me in the past. Cameron didn't know that I was used to not being wanted in places, I was used to imposing myself on people's lives and situations, with only a few exceptions like Matthew or my mother.

Cameron lifted his arm, making me notice the phone he was gripping in his fist. "What's this," he ground out, not even formulating the question.

A nanosecond was all it took me. Just a glimpse.

I had been mentally preparing myself for this, for him finding out, ever since that conversation with Diane and Gabriel. After I learned that Cameron hadn't known about it and apparently hadn't been curious enough to google me. But most of all, I'd been dreading this moment for the last few weeks. Days. It had been hanging over my head. I knew that Cameron was eventually going to see it.

But that didn't mean I'd been ready.

All the warmth in my body left me, and I was sure I wobbled a tiny step to the side, because the storm of emotion in Cameron's eyes wavered for an instant. He reached for me.

I widened my stance. I shook my head and told myself to stand straight. What was that thing Cameron told the girls? Soldier on.

"I think it's obvious from the clip," I told him. "Did you watch the whole thing?"

He let out a rough exhale. "I don't understand."

I didn't, either. I didn't understand why he was so upset, unless perhaps he hated being left in the dark or caught off guard. Perhaps he felt betrayed by me not telling him that he was walking around with a ticking PR bomb. After all, I was a meme, a viral thirty-second clip, a face used to sell energy drinks. Choose entertainment over dignity. I was every single thing he was running away from.

"There's nothing to understand," I said.

"Explain the video to me anyway," he pleaded, and now I could hear it in his voice. How hurt he was. How frustrated. "Please."

I averted my eyes. "What clip did you see? The techno remix? Or the one with classical music? Or perhaps you saw one of the choreographed dances or the theatrical reinterpretation of the audio. People are really talented nowadays." I shrugged. "Or maybe you saw the ad with my face. I'm sure it shows up under my hashtag by now."

"There is an ad," Cameron said very slowly. As if he couldn't even speak. "With your face?"

My stomach twisted. I was pretty sure I was going to be sick, but I managed a nod.

There was a long stretch of silence until Cameron spoke again. "What did he do?"

I felt my brows twisting, my eyes narrowing with doubt. That had been the same question my mother had asked. "He didn't do anything. It wasn't Sparkles's—or Paul's—fault. I did that."

Once more, Cameron didn't utter a single word for what seemed like an eternity. That was probably why my eyes found their way back to him. His face. He looked so utterly lost. Helpless. I hated putting that there. "I wasn't asking about the mascot. I was talking about your father. He's the owner of the club. What did he do about this?"

I blinked at him. He already knew that. "My father sent me here." Cameron's expression hardened. I fumbled with my hands. "The clip had gone viral in under a day." I pointed at the phone as it rested there, in his fist. "I was a PR problem for the club. Heck, I was a problem for him, and so I was sent here, on an assignment."

All that anger dissolved. "Don't say that."

"Say what?"

"That you're a problem." His voice cracked. "You're not a fucking problem, Adalyn."

Those guards I had been neglecting for the last days engaged, coming up at full force. "Don't pretend that you never saw me as a problem, Cameron." My words weren't harsh or accusing. I was simply stating a fact. And I wasn't mad or angry about that. I understood why he did. But that didn't mean I was able to stand here and listen to him taking my side when there was no such thing as sides in this. "What would you have done in his place, huh? Wouldn't you want to protect the team? The franchise? The empire he has built? His own name? Because I would. I was jeopardizing all of those things. I was a running joke—still am, for that matter. So, really, what would you have done instead?"

"Christ, Adalyn," he said. "I would have protected you. Not anything else. I would have done anything to protect you."

His words clashed against me with such force that I thought I might stumble backward. I braced a hand on the back of a stool.

"And how exactly would you have done that, Cameron? Going door-to-door telling every person watching to stop? Snatching their phones from their hands and smashing them against the floor? Or perhaps shouting at the press not to pay me any attention and focus on the un-shockingly lackluster season the team was having instead? Or—"

"Yes," he interjected. And the single word was suspended in the air for what seemed like an eternity. "I would have done all of those things." He crossed the distance separating us. "I would have done anything I could."

My next breath didn't make it in. Or out.

Cameron's hands came around my face, the contact of his skin against mine dizzying, overwhelming in a way I wasn't ready to process in that moment. But a way I didn't want to let go of. Not yet. I leaned into his touch.

"I would have done everything in my power to protect you." His thumbs brushed my cheeks, and as angry as he still looked, his voice was so soft, so gentle. "The internet was fucking bullying you, so I would have tried to fix this. And I would have never—fucking ever—treated you like a problem and shoved you aside to get you out of the way."

My chest was heaving at this point, and whatever I thought I'd felt disappeared, turning into hurt. A hurt I didn't want there but couldn't help. "But you wanted me out of here, too. And I don't blame you. I'm not mad or resentful." My throat tightened. "When I arrived in Green Oak, I was an inconvenience for you, and you wanted to shove me out. And I'm not blameless, but that's not that different from what my father did."

A strangled sound left him, his forehead falling on mine. My hands rose, and I wrapped my fingers around his wrists. Showing him that I wanted him right where he was. "I would have fucking cared, love. And I'm going to show you, okay?"

I couldn't imagine how, but I gave him a small nod.

Cameron seemed to breathe a little easier. "I'm not your father, and I don't really know him. But that's not . . ." His head shook against mine. "I hate what he did. His reaction." His hands moved down my cheeks, settling on the sides of my neck. "And if you think I'm not stubborn enough to go door-by-door, smashing phones against the ground, then you have me figured out all wrong."

A strange puff of air burst out, but I couldn't tell if it was a sob or a laugh. Probably neither. Because this was too much. It was too intense. And I didn't think I had the tools to process it. I wished I could keep my eyes closed until everything heavy and complicated inside my chest disappeared. I didn't want to turn back time and not have this conversation, because it had always been meant to take place, but I wished I could magically pop up in bed and will the rest of the night away. Wake up tomorrow, buried in the comforter of Cameron's guest room.

And, of course, this man who was still holding my face between his hands like his life depended on it seemed to somehow read my mind, because I was wordlessly being lifted off the ground and then, I was being deposited in the soft and plush cushions of the couch. I sighed, half happy to be granted the wish and half sad that this meant he was walking away. But then, a large body was curling along mine and what I knew was Cameron's arm was coming around my middle, curling over my waist, and dragging me to his chest.

"I know you hate being carried everywhere," he said into my hair. "But I've been stopping myself all night. Maybe all week."

An avalanche of contradicting feelings rioted and clashed inside me as I buried my hands between our bodies, letting my palms fall on his chest and my forehead rest against his chin. "I don't hate it."

I really didn't. I resisted it—him—because I liked being in Cameron's arms too much. Enough to remind myself that Green Oak was a bubble, and there was a life waiting for me back in Miami. One that I had fought hard to go back to but was starting to feel I didn't belong to anymore. Not like I thought I did.

And where did that leave me? Where did that leave us?

We spent the night on the couch.

Or so I thought. Now that I was blinking at the empty space beside me, I wasn't exactly sure if I'd slept alone.

Willow popped her head out from beneath the couch. The only warning she gave me was a mew before she curled in my lap. I petted her behind her ears, just like I'd learned she liked, wondering what time it was but not wanting to leave the safety of the couch or the blanket wrapped tightly around me.

Had I imagined everything? Had last night been a dream?

I dropped my hand to the side and felt the cushion still warm.

So I couldn't have imagined Cameron sleeping by my side.

I hadn't imagined the feel of my hands slipping under his shirt, or the feel of his smooth and warm skin under the pads of my fingers. I hadn't imagined his hands moving around me and finding a place on my back. Or how his thumbs had snuck under the waist of my jeans and how he had hummed deep in his throat. My eyelids fluttered shut, my breath coming out of me in a burst.

No wonder I'd woke up all aroused. No, that wasn't a word I would use for how I felt.

Horny. That's what I was. Hot. And bothered. And turned on. And he wasn't even here right now.

I reopened my eyes to Willow's bicolored gaze. She stared at me and then let out a sound that I interpreted as *Your thoughts are too loud, and I'm trying to sleep.*

"Sorry, girl," I told her, passing my fingers over her head one more time. I frowned, something occurring to me. "Hmm. I've never been this sexually frustrated before, so I'm trying to deal."

A deep chuckle came from the kitchen.

My upper body sprung up. My head swiveled in the direction of the sound.

Cameron was leaning on the island, petting Pierogi with one hand and holding a mug with the other. There was a huge grin on his face. "Morning to you, too, love."

Ugh.

I let myself fall on my back, disappearing from his sight behind the back of the couch. I brought my hands to my face and bit back a groan. That wasn't something Cameron needed to hear.

His head reappeared over the couch. He leaned on the edge with his elbows, still with the smuggest smile known to man.

"Don't let it get to your head," I said, busying my hands with Willow's fur. Trying to be casual. "Think of it as . . . morning wood. But for girls. Completely unrelated to you. It just happened." I shook my head. "Sexual frustration is common."

He let out a laugh this time. "Sure," he said. "Only we both know it was all me. In fact, it'd be easy to prove how much." And just as I was arching a brow, he was raising an arm and flexing his biceps. "See?"

I loved his arms. Specifically flexed like that. I let out a snort. "Really," I deadpanned. "What are you, ten?"

Cameron straightened up. And in a swift motion I would have never anticipated, he took off his shirt.

My mouth clamped shut. My whole face warmed. Heated. He didn't even need to flex. I swallowed. Hard. I was hornier than ever. "I keep forgetting how much you love to win," I said under my breath.

"Nah," he said, his lips inching higher. "You keep giving me reasons to play a harder and longer game, darling."

Remnants from last night came back to me, not of him and me on the couch, but our conversation. The way it had revealed so many crucial pieces to understanding each other. It had been intense, but it also had been needed. In this moment, I felt closer to Cameron than I did to anyone else. He'd bared himself to me, and I knew how hard it had been for him. It made me feel horrible for not doing the same. Not completely. But how could I have told him all the things that led me to my biggest mistake? I was still scared Cameron would look at me differently. Like my father or David had. I was terrified.

As if sensing my inner battle, Cameron's lightness vanished and he turned away from me.

My gaze followed him as he crossed the space to the far end of the living room, sculpted muscles dancing on his back and knocking every rational thought out of my head with each step he took. Cameron kneeled, disappearing from my sight for a second and popping up again holding a mat. It was The Mat. Which meant it was Yoga Time. I loved Yoga Time. It was the time of the day I could openly watch him.

"You're off the hook today," Cameron said, shooting me a knowing glance. "But you're joining me tomorrow." His expression turned serious. "I want you to try to meditate as well. I'm not in the best position to lecture anyone, God knows I have issues to sift through myself, but I think it will help you. With those bursts of anxiety you experience."

"My . . . panic attacks."

"Yes." He gave me a nod. "It won't fix them. I've learned that therapy is the key for that. But I'm not a therapist and I'm not your . . ." He trailed off, and my heart skipped a beat. "It's a start. Baby steps, yeah?" I gave him a nod, and he let out an exhale, as if relieved I was letting him try to help. God. This man. "Good. I'll guide you through the basics. Tomorrow. Worst case the workout will take your mind off things for a bit."

I watched him unroll the mat. There was a concerned look on his face. I didn't like it there. "I think you'll need to wear a shirt then," I told him. "I don't think my mind will be able to relax otherwise."

He gave me somewhat of a smile, as if he wanted to tell me that he appreciated me trying to lighten his mood. But the frown remained there.

"Cameron?" I said. He stopped what he was doing to look at me. "You shouldn't worry so much. I want to try the yoga and meditation. With you. But I . . . I'm okay. For the most part, I think. After last night, I don't want you to feel like you need to fix things for me. I've been doing fine on my own for a long time."

"I know," he answered simply. "I'm beginning to understand just how long." The emotion in his eyes seemed to brighten, making them look as green as ever. I couldn't look anywhere else. "I don't intend on slaying your dragons for you. Not because I don't want to, believe me, I do. But because you would hate it, and you don't need me to."

Pressure rushed to the backs of my eyes. And something strange happened. Something in the middle of my chest. A flutter I didn't understand. A longing for those things he'd just said I didn't need or want.

An emotion crossed Cameron's face, and I could tell from the way he widened his stance that he was stopping himself from coming my way. He cleared his throat. "Josie is picking you up in an hour, right?"

Right. "Girls' time, yes."

Cameron looked down at his feet for an instant. "I asked her to drop you back after lunch. And I made her promise to be on time, so I'd have you back soon. There's something I have planned for you. That okay?"

So I'd have you back soon. The strange flutter stirred. "Of course."

The relief in his face was so clear that it made me pause.

He'd thought I'd say no.

"I better go shower then," I said, turning away. I took two steps before turning. Cameron was still looking at me. He hadn't moved. "I wouldn't hate it, you know?" I told him, and he frowned. "I wouldn't hate it if you were the one slaying my dragons for me."

CHAPTER TWENTY-NINE

Adalyn

"Y ou sure you're doing okay?"

I nodded my head, not daring to lift my gaze off the path.

"We're almost there," Cameron added. I sensed him coming closer to me. He'd been walking behind me, touching my back or shoulder every once in a while, as if he'd known we were approaching a bigger rock or a patchier spot on the trail. He set his palm against the small of my back, his voice falling close to my ear. "You're doing great."

My breath swooshed out of me and my words came out garbled. "I'm just walking." His hand moved up, making its way around my waist, and he gave it a squeeze. I had to swallow before continuing, "This isn't even a hike or a trek. It's more like a str. . ." His jaw brushed my cheek, derailing my train of thought.

"You were saying?" he murmured. And when I didn't say anything, he chuckled. The dark and rich sound traveled straight to my gut. Maybe even lower than that. "Are you tired or hurting?"

"Huh, what?" I frowned, realizing I'd come to a stop. Oh. Right. I resumed walking. "I'm fine. And before you ask or offer, I don't need to be carried like a princess, either." Not that I would mind, honestly. I wasn't a huge fan of . . . this.

"A man can still hope," he said, letting his arm drop and waiting for me to take the lead again.

Before I took him up on the offer, I sped up, or rather, resumed the moderate pace I'd kept for the last twenty minutes. With Cameron's chuckle behind me, I tried my best to keep my focus on the path. On my legs. On the increasingly fast beating of my heart that had absolutely nothing to do with the exertion.

"So . . ." I started, glancing back at him over my shoulder. Mistake. That moss-green fleece he wore made his eyes pop like emeralds. I shook my head. I'd never compared anyone's eyes to gems before. "So I, hmm, I thought you weren't supposed to go on a hike when the sun is coming down soon?"

"Your foot was not up for a hike," Cameron said.

I frowned at the trail in front of me. "So what are we doing then?"

"The next best thing."

My lips pursed, ready to complain about him being so cryptic, but then, his arm snaked around my body again, and he guided me to the left.

Ugh, he smelled so good, so woodsy and fresh and just absolutely amazing, that I couldn't help but smell him. I sniffed him. Just like Willow or Pierogi did. And Cameron, who hadn't missed my reaction, let out a hum.

As if that deep, throaty sound wasn't enough, his head dipped and he said, "I'm finding it particularly hard to keep my hands off you." I came to a halt for an instant, unable to process the bubbling sensation building between my stomach and chest. He moved us forward. "It's seeing you in all these clothes I got for you."

A new wave of warmth climbed up my face. But it . . . it felt good. No. It felt great. Hearing his words, his confession, brought me a kind of pleasure I'd never felt before. Perhaps that was why I felt the urge to quiz him. To fully understand. I glimpsed down at myself. "But I'm all layered up," I croaked. This couldn't be all that attractive. Or appealing. "I'm the outdoors version of an onion. You insisted. How can you find this . . . attractive?"

Cameron let out a dark chuckle. "Would it be so terrible if having you warm and safe makes me hard?"

My blood swooshed down.

My legs failed. I swayed against him just as his other arm came around me, securing me to his side with a grunt.

Would it be so terrible if having you warm and safe makes me hard?

Something strange was happening to my body. It was shaking, trembling in response to his words. I started to turn, feeling the need to see his face after what he'd just said.

But something in front of us made me stop.

"Cameron?" I blinked, wondering how I'd missed what was before us. "What's this?"

It really was the stupidest question I could ask. But if the man currently supporting all my weight against his chest agreed, he didn't say so. "We're stargazing tonight." He walked ahead of me and pointed to his right. "The tent is a precaution. Just in case you get too cold and want to sneak in for a minute. I left a few blankets and a thermos inside it earlier today. But we're not camping out for the whole night." Cameron turned around to look at me, and he gave me a small smile. "We're parked only fifteen minutes away so we can go back whenever you want."

We're stargazing tonight.

My chest tightened, squishing my insides together. "You . . ." The word came out so rocky that I had to clear my throat. "You came by earlier to set this up? Is that why you weren't home when Josie dropped me off?"

Cameron's head tilted to the side, his jaw tightening. Something crossed his expression. Too quick for me to catch.

"What's wrong?" I whispered.

"Not a single thing is wrong right now." He stretched his hand, spreading those long five fingers I was growing obsessed with. "Come here."

Without hesitation, I crossed the short space that separated us. I looked at his hand as it hovered in the air, waiting for me. For us. And when I took it, I felt the touch of his skin deep in my gut. Something changed in that moment, I could feel it. Sense it shifting. Cameron guided me closer to the tent, releasing my hand to set down the backpack he was carrying. He produced and unrolled a thick blanket, setting it down on the ground, then pulled out of the tent an outdoorsy version of what I'd consider a picnic basket. Finally, he sat down on one side of the blanket, stretching his legs.

It was when he glanced up at me, a slow smile playing on his lips, that I realized I hadn't moved. He tugged down at the hem of my jacket, his mouth fully giving way to that grin I loved so much. But I still didn't move.

"Darling," he chastised, amusement dancing in his voice. "If you don't quit looking at me like that, I can't promise I'll let you see a single star tonight."

Promise me, I wanted to say. *Promise you won't. Promise you are all I'll see tonight.* But I didn't. I joined him on the blanket, my heart pounding with anticipation and . . . possibility. Yes, it had to be that making me breathless. A warm container was placed gently in my hands, and when I looked up, Cameron's eyes were on me. His expression was soft and hard, all at once.

"Thank you," I whispered.

Cameron's answer was a tilt of his head in the direction of my lap. The thermos. I lifted it up and took a tentative sip, tasting cocoa and milk. Warmth surged through me, partly because of the drink but mostly because of the man by my side. I set my eyes on the horizon before us, on the line the sloping terrain drew and how the sun had now almost disappeared behind it.

"I don't know what to say," I told him honestly, glancing sideways and discovering he hadn't stopped looking at me. "I'm not used to . . . this." I knew Cameron understood I wasn't talking about the outdoors, or the views, or warm beverages and thick blankets. That's probably why I turned back to look at the darkening sky. Soon, scattered points of light would spark to life above us. "The sun hasn't fully set yet and it's already so beautiful. I wasn't expecting that."

"It really is beautiful," he agreed, and dear God, I could feel his eyes on me. "You gave me the idea, you know."

I frowned. "How?"

"The night at the lake," he answered with a low chuckle. "You were lying on your back, covered in goat shit, and you were looking at the stars. You were not frowning, or wincing in pain, you were in blissful awe for a moment." I looked over at him, finding him shaking his head. "I'd never seen that look on your face. And the realization of how beautiful you looked and how outrageously I wanted you right then assaulted me. It caught me so off guard that I couldn't even speak." His jaw clenched. "And then you made it worse."

Words left me with a rocky exhale. "I did?"

"You had to go into the lake and pull that goddamn goat out of the water like your life depended on it," Cameron rasped out with a humorless laugh. "You, in heels and a fucking suit I . . ." A puff of air left him. "God, I'd never been more shocked and turned on in my whole life." His throat worked. "I think part of me decided that night that I would be taking you here."

I brought the thermos to my lips again, willing my heart to quiet, to stop drumming on my temples and let me enjoy the peace of this stunning place. But Cameron's words kept echoing in my head. The weight of them and what lay in between them. In between us.

My eyelids fluttered for an instant, and before I realized what I was saying, the words were leaving me. "What's next for you, Cam?"

It was the audible hitch in his throat that made me realize I'd called him Cam and not Cameron. "I don't know," he answered, and I could hear the honesty in his voice. I could also tell there was a hint of . . . fear, perhaps. Of uncertainty. "There's a pundit gig on the table, in London. I don't want it."

Why? I wanted to ask. *Are you not leaving the US then?* But I didn't know if I had the courage to ask him that. A part of me didn't want to hear the answer. I didn't want him to leave, but that was unfair. Because I wasn't staying in Green Oak, either. I was leaving soon.

Cameron's body shifted on the blanket, coming closer to me. I was shaking again but it wasn't because I was cold, and I think Cameron knew that. "Looking forward to returning home?" he asked.

"I don't know." I looked down at my feet. *Home.* "I thought I'd be glad when this whole thing came to an end, and I could go back to my life. But I . . . It's strange. I've never felt like I wasn't part of the Miami Flames, but the more time I spend here, the more detached I become. Like I was never part of them. Not really."

Cameron's palm settled on my thigh, the weight and warmth seeping through the thick fabric of the pants he'd insisted I wore. He squeezed, those long fingers tightening against my skin in a way that made me think—wish—he was doing more than just that.

"I always dreamed of being in charge of the club one day," I heard myself confess. "You know, take over from my father. Maybe that's why I didn't hesitate to come here. It was a way to redeem myself and earn back his respect after I embarrassed him." The words I'd heard David say that day returned. "Although, I don't think my father ever fully believed in me. And I guess I proved him right."

"Stop that," Cameron said from my side. "Stop justifying every single person who treats you like rubbish." His brows furrowed, and when his lips parted I knew the question that was coming out of them. "What happened, love?" he asked me, voice soft. "What was done to you for you to break like that?"

Break.

I had broken, hadn't I?

Yes. There was no question.

Blood rushed to my head at the scattered memories of that day, the clip, but most of all, of Cameron's reaction to seeing it. His words.

I would have done everything in my power to protect you.

"Nothing was done to me." I stumbled over my words, feeling my hands shake and setting the thermos beside my hip. "I am the only one responsible for my actions, and believing otherwise would be stupid. And immature." I shook my head. "What happened is not worth wasting this beautiful night with you."

Cameron's palm lifted off my thigh and landed on the back of my head. His fingers slipped into my hair. He tilted my head so I would look at him. "Let me be the judge of what's worth my time," he told me, all that softness melting away.

And I could see it in his eyes, clear as the day. *I would have fucking cared. Tell me. Trust me.*

So the words rolled off my tongue. "My ex, David, had been lying. Using me. And my father had been part of it."

Cameron's eyes darkened with an anger that reminded me of last night, of his reaction to seeing the stupid clip. For a second, I'd thought he'd release me, that he'd move away, but instead, his touch turned more possessive, more intent, against the side of my head. As if he was scared I'd go somewhere. Or perhaps he thought I'd break again.

"Turns out, I'd been nothing but collateral in a business transaction," I told him. And God, I felt sick to my stomach hearing the words. Allowing myself to think of it for the first time. I pushed through. "David had never wanted to date plain ol' Adalyn. He'd only wanted the daughter of Andrew Underwood. And my dad had encouraged it because we just . . . made sense. David was the son of a business partner and I was his daughter. Same circles, same age. He . . ." Cameron's expression tightened, and I let out a humorless laugh. "He promised David a high management position in the club if he married me. Like I'm some . . . stock or possession you exchange. Or worse yet, like he didn't believe David—or anyone— would do that without some kind of motivation or compensation. I don't know."

No words came out of the man in front of me. His only response was a brush of his thumb against my jaw. Soothing. Encouraging. All while a storm brewed behind the green of his eyes.

"My father wasn't wrong," I continued. "David had never intended to marry me. Probably not even date me, seeing as I am 'frigid, boring, and forgettable in bed.'" I gestured in air quotes. Those were his exact words. And I shouldn't care but . . . I did. A part of me did. "That's why the moment he'd locked in the position, and it was announced, he dropped me like the dead weight I was. 'Dodged a bullet,' he said." A humorless chuckle left me. "I can't even imagine how mad my father must have been when his plan not only backfired, but he ended up being extorted by David."

I could almost picture my father's face. The way it contorted when something didn't go his way. And what was stranger, how could someone who had played so many people be played like that? I couldn't understand.

"Extorted how?" Cameron asked, making me realize I was lost in thought.

"David threatened to come clean if my father fired him or demoted him." The day of the incident with Sparkles had been the anniversary party and there had been pre-celebration drinks. I knew what alcohol did to David. It made him cocky. Braggy. "I overheard David. He was so happy, telling all of this to . . . Paul. Sparkles. He was blabbing all his secrets to the mascot of the team. A giant bird made of polyester. Right there, in the stairwell, where anyone could have heard. As if this was some locker story you shared with your teammates instead of . . . my life."

I stopped talking, needed a second to myself. Focusing on Cameron's touch.

"I felt so incredibly small," I continued, voice breaking. "Deemed unsuitable by David. Incapable of handling one of the most natural things in life by my father. Not enough. And what was worse, I felt betrayed by the club I'd given so much to. Sparkles being the one listening to all of this made it so much worse in some bizarre way." My voice wavered again. "So, when I saw the silly bird shaking his ass in the middle of everything and everyone that represented the Miami Flames, not even ten minutes later, as if nothing had happened, as if my whole world hadn't been turned on its axis, I did break."

Cameron's eyes roamed all over my face, my body, in a desperate, aimless way. And when they finally returned to mine, I recognized the question in them. So I nodded—how could I not—and before I could so much as blink, he was settling me on his lap and bringing me to his chest.

"The last thing I remember is walking toward Paul," I whispered, and Cameron's arms came around my shoulders and waist. Tighter. As tightly as I'd ever been held. "Then, Sparkles's head was at my feet."

Cameron hummed deep in his throat, the sound reverberating against my body.

"I wouldn't blame you if you thought I was crazy," I heard myself say. "Seeing as even that way, even after everything I heard, I'm here, proving myself to them. To him. Instead of confronting them." My voice turned into a murmur. "But I guess I'm not that brave. And I still messed up. I hate messes. I'm usually the one who cleans them up."

That club was everything I knew. My life was the Miami Flames and, therefore, my father. So what else could I have done but try to win them back?

"Do you want to hear what I think?" Cameron asked.

I closed my eyes, burying my head beneath his chin, sticking my nose right into his chest. God, I loved it here. I loved how solid he felt against my skin. How safe. I didn't want to lose that. "No, I really don't want to. But I also know you're going to tell me anyway."

A short puff of breath fell against my temple, and for an instant panic settled in my gut at his silence. I cared what Cameron thought of me. I cared how he felt and how he saw me. I cared too much, and I realized now that it wasn't something new. A part of me had always cared.

"I think," he finally said, his hand suddenly cupping my face and tipping my chin up. "That for someone who's always justifying everybody else's shit behavior, you're extremely hard on yourself." The green of his eyes darkened, and his tongue flicked over his bottom lip, as if preparing himself for what was coming next. "I think that you've worked so hard at keeping yourself contained, so in control and safe behind that hard shell you put around yourself, that it was all bound to collapse." His gaze dropped down to my lips, and his thumb caressed the line of my mouth. "I also know that I'll need to stop myself from catching a flight to Miami the moment we get up from this blanket." His frown turned serious. Focused. Distracting.

"And last but certainly not least . . ." he trailed off, his voice changing, morphing into a rasp.

I could do nothing but watch as the man holding me inhaled deep and slow through his nose, as if needing a pause. A moment. A curse left him under his breath, and before I could prepare, his hands were moving, reaching around my waist and guiding me around his lap until we were fully facing each other.

My body lit up, and I rested my palms on his chest. My heart pounded, mirroring the way his chest seemed to thrum against my hands.

"Last but not least," he resumed, voice so low I wouldn't have heard it if I wasn't so close. "I know, with terrifying certainty, that once the shock and anger at the world for being so fucking ugly had passed, I've never been more in awe, more stunned silly, more turned on, by such a display of viciousness." He pushed me up with his legs, leveling my gaze with his, and making my knees fall onto the blanket on each side of his hips. "So much that ever since seeing that video, I've been physically restraining myself from kissing you. From taking your mouth and feeling all that fire burning inside you against my tongue."

All that fire.

Fire. Cameron saw fire in me.

And it did feel like flames were suddenly licking at my skin from the inside, making me so suddenly hot that I was finding it hard to pull in a breath. All I could think was *Kiss me. Please. Take my mouth.* "That's ridiculous," I whispered.

"Maybe," he said, his expression tightening, the tilt of his mouth severe. "But it doesn't make it any less true."

My hands closed around the fabric of his jacket. I'd never experienced this kind of need in my life. This dizzying attraction that went beyond looks and ink and muscles. It was him. Cameron, who caused this craving to pierce right though me.

Cameron's chin dipped down. "Don't you see? You are anything but dispassionate, Adalyn. You're relentless, determined, fiery, and have made every moment I've happened to be next to you as alive as the fucking sun lighting everything up at dawn. Anybody who fails to see that is either blind or some worthless piece of sh—"

"Cameron," I whispered, bringing his words to a stop.

Something passed between us.

His jaw clenched. "Tell me," he said. My heart sped up, wanting out of my chest. His hands moved around my waist, his fingers pressing into my skin with barely restrained pressure. "Give me permission to—"

I closed the distance between our mouths.

Cameron was stunned for a fraction of a second, as if he had expected me to deny him, and then he melted against me, making a deep, throaty sound. His mouth moved on mine, lips parted, and one of his hands moved up, finding the back of my head, bringing me closer to him.

Every cell, every ounce of who I was, came alive against his lips. Cameron deepened the kiss, and when a whimper climbed out of my chest, his fingers curled around my hair. My arms flew to his neck in response, snaking around it and clutching him to me with a desperation I'd never felt before him.

Another groan vibrated against my chest, mouth, body, and I felt his other hand move to my back, stopping at the base of my spine. He pulled me deeper into his lap. Hips clashed, and God, I could feel him so hard and hot beneath me, so unbelievably solid against my body, that all sense escaped me.

I came up for air with a breathless gasp. And Cameron's mouth dropped to my jaw, traveled along my skin, down my neck and up to my ear. He nipped at a sensitive spot there, and when my eyelids fluttered shut, a loud moan I wasn't sure was mine echoed in the night.

"Fuck," he rasped against my skin.

Waves of tingles—sparks, electricity—spread throughout me as my blood pulsed, swirling with need and traveling right where the junction of my thighs met his. I opened my eyes again, finding his gaze on me, attentive, determined, letting me know that there was no turning back. This was a kiss that changed something, and

I should know that. Cameron was telling me. And I wasn't fighting that notion, or him, any longer.

I was giving myself a chance.

Fingers that were now shaking moved to the back of his neck, and this time I savored the taste of his lips, memorized the feel of this tongue against mine and let my whole body shake with the sensation of kissing and being kissed like this.

We came up for air at the same time, breathless, drunk, and Cameron whispered, "Tell me you feel this, too."

I gave him a single nod, telling him silently that I wanted to feel even more. Everything. Cameron thrusted his hips up. A moan fell off my lips at the friction, the sensation it created against a growingly sensitive spot between my legs. God, I was pulsing. Pounding with need.

"More?" Cameron asked against my lips. And when I didn't answer, he tightened his grip on me, pulling gently just as he jerked my body closer to him with a new motion of his hips. Another brisk thrust. My lips parted with an abandoned sound, and he said, "That's what I thought."

I closed my eyes again, trying to get a hold of every single sensation wreaking havoc inside of me, pushing me further and further into the night. Into him. Cameron.

He moved then, widening his legs and positioning me in a way that heightened that swirling need coursing through me. Now, I could feel him grow impossibly hard under me, I could feel his heat. Instinctively, I swayed my hips.

Oh God.

"Again," he demanded, bringing both of his hands behind my head. When I didn't move, still too stunned by how good that had felt, he took my mouth, begging and commanding me to move. My hips swayed again. Then again, and again. And when Cameron broke the kiss, he moved his mouth to my ear. "Good girl."

A reckless sound left me in response, something inside of me overpowering all sense, making me sink and push and stroke myself against his length with utmost desperate need.

"Let's see how sweet you come," he rasped in my ear, accompanying my motions with his hips. My whole body was trembling now, pulsing with every rough drive of our hips. My hands started moving, desperately seeking ways to get rid of whatever was between us. I tugged at his jacket, at mine, wanting to tear them apart. Make them disappear. One of Cameron's hands snatched my wrists. "Ride me like this," he ordered, voice impossibly dark.

He released my hands for an instant, but only to bring them behind my back. My body arched with the change, my hips shifted, and his length rubbed right against my clit. "I need to feel you," I mumbled. I wasn't even talking about the grip he had on my hands. I wanted *him*. "I need to feel your skin."

"I'm not taking a single thing off you or me," he whispered against my mouth. "What did I tell you, huh, love?" He thrust his hips, pushing me further and further into him. "I'm a little mean when I have to be. Now, lift your hips and make yourself come against me."

I thought a noise—a sound I should have recognized—came from somewhere around us. But I didn't care. I couldn't when a stream of moans was leaving my throat. When I was too lost to this, to us, to care. So I swayed against Cameron, obeying his demand and getting lost in every inch of him that was now roughly rubbing against my clit. Oh God. "Cameron?" I whimpered.

"Let go, love," he said with such desperation, such need, that it tipped me closer to the edge. His free hand trailed down my back, reaching my ass, his palm pressing, pushing my hips to ride him faster. Harder. "I want you to let go and show me how fucking bright you burn."

An explosion took place behind my eyelids, my whole body turning into nothing but a bundle of nerves, vibrating, pulsing with release so intense that I thought it would never come to an end.

"Fuck," Cameron whispered, letting go of my wrists and ass to bring his hands to my face. He pulled me in, placing a hard kiss on my mouth. "So goddamn beautiful," he murmured, letting his forehead rest on mine.

I hummed, feeling depleted and numb, letting all my weight fall on him. I reopened my eyes, realizing only then that I'd closed them at some point. Cameron's nostrils flared. His mouth parted with a rough exhale. I moved my hands over his chest, feeling how hard he was breathing.

I met his gaze, that deep shade of green swirling with need. I wanted to see him. I wanted to—

Cameron kissed me again. Hard and soft, all at once. I melted against him, my hands seeking, going down his chest, and reaching the edge of his coat. I slipped my fingers underneath, just like I couldn't before, and hooked my thumbs on the loops of his pants. "Ah, love," he breathed out, followed by a humorless laugh. "I'm not fucking you in the middle of the woods."

I tugged at his pants, releasing a breath. "But only I finished. I owe you an orgasm."

"You don't owe me a single thing." He kissed the tip of my nose, then lowered his voice to a dark rasp, "I promise to come as hard as I've ever done when I'm finally inside you. But not here."

My throat worked, the sweet taste of happiness and possibility making my lips turn up. I bit back on the smile. "Presumptuous of you to think that that's in the cards for you."

That lopsided grin took shape. "Foolish of you to think that I'm not still playing the long game here."

My face fell, my heart jumping to my throat. I stared back at him, trying to squash the hope in my gut, the need to demand that he really mean those words. "Cam—"

My phone rang. And I . . . Had it done that before? I was vaguely aware.

With a grunt, Cameron stretched his arm and pulled the device out of the front pocket of the backpack.

He handed it to me, and I picked up the call without breaking eye contact with him.

Foolish of you to think that I'm not still playing the long game here.
How long? I wanted to ask. How—

Josie's voice came through the line, but I was so focused on

Cameron's eyes, on the eruption of hope and fear in my chest, that I wasn't making out any of her words. Not until a certain phrase slipped through.

"What?" I blurted out, snapping right back into the real world. "What do you mean my mother is here?"

CHAPTER THIRTY

Adalyn

Cameron pulled up a few feet before Josie's Joint.

He killed the engine, and the silence that filled the car made it easier for me to hear my heart beating in my chest. "I'm so sorry," I whispered.

His palm fell on my thigh again, heavy and warm, and my whole body awoke at the touch. Goodness me, is this what adolescence should have felt like? This restlessness, this sultry warmth climbing up and down my bloodstream, this . . . horniness.

"What are you sorry about, love?" the man beside me asked, like I didn't have about a hundred reasons to apologize.

"Because you organized a beautiful night, and instead of gazing at the stars, I somehow managed to babble at you, leave you sexually frustrated, and get you to pick up my mother."

He shook off a laugh that made me glance at him. Ugh, he was really so handsome when he smiled like that. "I thought I'd made myself clear . . ." he said, throwing his door open.

I started frowning, but then my gaze was glued to him, his ass, his shoulders, all of him, as he walked around the car with confident long strides. This was possibly worse than being sixteen.

Cameron pulled open the door and leaned inside. "The stars in the sky are not going anywhere," he said, his voice nothing but a low rumble. "You don't babble, ever. You shared something with me after I asked." His head dipped, his expression turning severe. "I'm the furthest thing from sexually frustrated," he added, his eyes sweeping down my neck, and all the way to my chest before returning to my mouth. "If anything, I'm starved." He cleared his throat. "And I'm curious and a little excited to meet your mother."

"Of course you are," I murmured. "Everyone is curious, and a little excited, where Maricela Reyes is concerned."

"Let it go," he said, before kissing me hard and fast on the lips. "Whatever is making you worried, make it disappear. There's no use for it now." He touched his forehead with mine for an instant. Just a touch. "I'm here."

My throat contracted as I looked up at him. But that part of me that had been always willing to fight him, to contradict him, was down for the night, and probably would be from now on, seeing as I was incapable of resisting Cameron Caldani anymore. The truth was that I loved when he did that, when he stated things so certainly. It made me feel lighter, less burdened. It made me want to release the control to him, just so he'd prove to me that I could.

I sighed, then I told him, "Lead the way."

He snatched my hand in his and pulled me up and out of the car. He didn't let go. Not even when he pushed the door open for me and waited for me to go in first, and not when I scanned the shockingly crowded café and found my mother surrounded by a group of laughing locals.

"Mom?" I asked, and whatever Cameron had heard in my voice made him squeeze my hand.

My mother's head turned, her whole face brightening when she saw me. "Adalyn, *mi amor*." She scrambled out of the chair she'd been elegantly sprawled on. "Excuse me," she told the people around her as she moved toward us. "My daughter is here!"

Maricela Reyes launched herself at me with an "*Ay, hija*." And when her voice wavered, my chest did, too. Ugh. This was what I'd been trying to avoid all along. "I was so worried about you." She released me from the hug but planted her hands on my shoulders. Her eyes narrowed. "Have you been sick? Your cheeks are red, and your lips look swollen."

My hand flew to my mouth. Or it would have, if it hadn't been held by Cameron.

Maricela tsked, looking me up and down. "Your father wouldn't tell me where you are, can you believe that?" A shake of her head. "Always with his little secrets, but that's not new. But to do this to my own daughter, as if you were one of his chess pieces. *Ay, no.*" She looked back over her shoulder. "Josie, sweetheart? Can you bring some water for my daughter? She looks about to faint." Her gaze shifted to my right. Her eyes narrowed. "Maybe two glasses instead of one?"

"I'm—" Cameron started, making me notice I hadn't introduced him.

"Cam," my mother finished for him. "Coach Cam. I've heard about you. Just now. You took my daughter into the woods. At night."

Cameron didn't wince. Instead, I felt his thumb swiping over the back of my hand. "That's the one, yes."

"Well, Cam," my mother said, arching her brows. "I hope you were up to no good. Because my daughter needs a little—"

"Mami," I warned.

Maricela Reyes rolled her eyes just as Josie popped over her shoulder with the two glasses of water. "Thank you, Josie. You were right, I like them together. They're even wearing matching outfits and I've never seen my daughter in mountain boots, let me tell you that much."

Cameron's head came down, and he whispered, "I like her."

"Of course you do," I muttered.

Cameron was obviously happy about her praise for the stupid boots but also, who wouldn't like beautiful and fun Maricela Reyes?

"What are you two whispering about?" my mother said, holding the two glasses and shoving them into our chests. "Drink," she ordered. "Then, you can tell me what your intentions are with my Adalyn."

I spat out the water. "Mom."

"*Siempre* mom this, mother that." She waved her hand in front of her. "*Soy tu madre*, I say it like it is. I didn't go through a ten-hour birth to bat the bush around."

"Beat around the bush," I corrected her.

"I like batting better," she answered, nonchalantly. "It comes from hunting times, you know. I read it in a magazine," she explained, looking over at Josie like she was her new best friend. She pulled up her arms. "They used to hit at bushes and trees, and you know what they used? Sticks. Now what's just like a stick to hit on things? A bat. No offense, but some of these things you say don't make sense."

Josie clicked her tongue. "Oh my God, she might be right."

"I . . ." I released a deep breath, readying myself to ask her what in the world was she doing in Green Oak, but a couple I recognized as parents of one of the kids on the team came into the café, a very enthusiastic nine-year-old dashing right behind.

For the first time, I took in the inside of the café, noticing how crowded it was for this time in the evening, how loud and excited the chatter was.

I shot Josie a questioning glance. "What's happening here?"

She blinked. "I told you on the phone," she said, but I must have been frowning at her because she immediately elaborated. "One of the teams leading the Six Hills was disqualified." She clapped her hands, and my frown deepened even more. "A whistleblower called the *County Gazette*, they apparently had thirteen-year-olds in their roster. Every team in the standings is climbing up a spot. So that means that—"

"The Green Warriors are in the final," I finished for her.

Josie gave a delighted jump, and I could only blink at her.

The Green Warriors are in the final.

For an instant, I was too stunned to speak. Or move.

And then, I was moving. Just like that day all those weeks ago, when I'd turned my life upside down. Only this time, the dam had broken for a completely different reason.

I launched myself at Josie. With a shocked laugh, she wrapped her arms around me. We squeezed each other, and when I released her, I turned on my heels.

Cameron's eyes were on me, just like I'd known they would be, wrinkling at the corners with a smile. I threw myself at him, too. And when I landed against his chest, his arms were already open. Laughter rolled off him, and it was deep and rich and it traveled right into my heart.

I was happy. Ecstatic.

"We made it, Coach," I said into his neck. And I didn't care that my mother was there, or Josie, or the whole team and half the town. I didn't even care that this was just some recreational team with a roster of kids. I didn't even care that we hadn't won anything yet, or that I was celebrating some other team being disqualified. I could only think of how happy my kids would be. How big María's smile would be. How good this would be for the town. "We freaking made it!"

Cameron's mouth came to my ear, and he said low, so low only I could hear, "I could fucking eat you right now." Which only made me giggle.

"*Mira, mira.* Look," I heard my mother say with a laugh. "They totally banged. Do you think they're past the *situationship* stage?"

Josie's laughter reached my ears. "I sure hope so, Maricela."

Cameron let out a grunt that I interpreted as a promise.

I extracted my head off his neck, but he didn't release me. I guessed that that was okay, social cues had never been his thing. "Where in the world did you learn that, Mom?"

"I have a TickTack now."

"TikTok?"

She rolled her eyes. "A clock always made *ticktack-ticktack*, so if anything, that name is wrong."

Oh God.

She was actually right.

Cameron pressed his lips to the top of my head before lifting my mother's giant suitcase and walking out.

My mother stared at him as he left, just like I had been doing, and then turned to give me a look.

"What?" I whispered.

"No, *nada*," she said, lifting her hands in the air. But I could see her smirk. She took one of the stools from Cameron's island out and plopped herself down. "Sit down with me."

"Mami," I warned with a sigh. "Cameron will be back in a few minutes, and he's taking the couch tonight. We should probably call it a night and have whatever conversation you want to have tomorrow morning when we are all rested."

"Okay, one?" She lifted her hands in the air. "There's no need to be coy around me. You two can share a bed." Flashes from earlier tonight came back, making me feel breathless. My mother clicked her tongue. "And two? That man will not be back until you go looking for him. He said he would get the rooms ready for us but he's giving us space to talk. So sit."

I crossed my arms over my chest. "But—"

"*Ahora*, Adalyn."

I took out the stool with a roll of my eyes. "Happy?"

"Not really," she said, her expression serious. "Why did you not come back home immediately? Why would you take part in your father's games? And more importantly, why did I have to buy Matthew off to know where you were?"

"What could you possibly offer him to rat me out like this?"

My mother shrugged. "I'll never say. A mother doesn't betray her children. And that man is like the son I never had."

I opened my mouth to complain but my mother arched her brows, reminding me I had questions to answer. "This is not a game. I really messed up, Mom. There's a conduct clause in my contract—"

"You are his daughter," she interjected. "He shouldn't care about clauses."

"I'm also his employee," I countered, feeling that chest tightness that stopped air getting to my lungs. "And hopefully, because I'm both, one day I'll be the one he picks to take over for him." These were words I'd said more than once, words I'd worked for, dedicated myself to fulfill, but somehow . . . Someway, they now tasted bitter in my mouth. I ignored it. "I needed to fix it. To show him he could trust me. I also wanted to help the team after my . . . slip."

Maricela Reyes shook her head, making those beautiful dark waves move around her face. "There's something you're not telling me. I know."

I willed my face to remain still, my expression blank. I couldn't tell my mother about David, or what Dad had done out of some . . . sense of responsibility that only made me feel small and inadequate. If my mother heard about any of that, what had happened to Sparkles wouldn't be anything in comparison to what she would do. She would catch a flight to Miami right now and—

That was exactly how Cameron had reacted to the story. Tonight. It had been so clear from his words, his face, the way he'd held me, everything. He . . . cared about me. That much.

"You know how much I love my job," I continued, a little breathless. "The club. How much respect I have for what Dad does."

"You're getting it all wrong, *mi amor*." A long sigh left through her nose. "I loved your father. I still do. I don't think you can ever stop loving your first great love, and he was that for me. But ever since you were little, you've had him on this pedestal nobody else can reach. Not even you."

"Is that so wrong?" I asked her, honestly. "Is it so bad to aspire to be like him? To want to impress him?"

"I don't know." She shook her head, and I believed she genuinely didn't. "But while you're on your way there, you're climbing, getting higher and higher, and I'm scared you'll fall. I'm scared he'll do something to shatter all that faith you have in him."

I felt the ball in my stomach shift. He'd tested that faith, hadn't he? But then, he'd also succumbed to David's demands to protect our relationship. To spare me the heartbreak after learning he'd asked David to marry me. And that meant something. It had to.

"Your father is a good man," she continued. "Or maybe he was, once upon a time. Now he's too wrapped up in his own greatness. He believes that everyone around him is at his disposal, for his own plots and schemes." Her hands went up in the air, and she spread and wiggled her fingers. "He believes he's the puppet master."

"One doesn't get where he is without that kind of scheming."

"I wouldn't know." She averted her gaze for an instant, and when eyes as brown as mine returned to my face, I knew my mother was about to tell me something she never had before. "I don't like that you've kept things from me. Not when your father has, too. Secrets."

"I'm sorry, Mami." For better or worse, I had kept things from her. "Deep down I kept this from you not to upset you. Do you think Dad meant to do that, too? With his secrets?"

"I don't think so. Otherwise I'd know where he came from," she offered. "There's a black smudge covering a big part of his past. He lets people believe he's from Miami, but he's not." A shake of her head. "I found out from the letters."

"The letters?"

"Right before I discovered I was pregnant with you, I found a stack of letters in his desk. And I wasn't snooping." She rolled her eyes at me before I made the remark. "They were all from a woman, addressed to him personally, and when I asked him about them, he went pale as a ghost and mumbled something about his childhood. That's how I knew. You know your father doesn't shake up easily."

"Was he—"

"Cheating?" she finished for me. "No. He swore it wasn't that, and I believed him." A finger tapped the side of her head. "You know I can tell when someone's lying." She really could. "But he never told me what it was really about." Her hand reached out across the tabletop, and when she wrapped her fingers around mine, I squeezed. "That's why I never married him. I am sorry for not giving you a normal family, but I couldn't. It wasn't the letters, it was him not trusting me enough to tell me the truth. I was an open book, I gave him my all. And him keeping from me the things that made him the man he was . . . It showed me that I was never an equal to him."

"You've never told me any of this," I said, barely managing to suppress the emotion in my voice. "And you're my family, okay?" Did my mother really believe I blamed her for not marrying my dad? That our family wasn't normal? "You were all the family I needed growing up." I cleared my throat. "And let's face it, you make any room, any house, feel like it's full of people."

That had been meant to be a joke, but God, it was nothing but the truth.

My mother smiled, and her eyes began to water. "Love is a funny game, *mi amor*. There are no rules, and no matter how hard you try to win, one way or another, your heart is always on the line." A shaky breath left her. "I'm sorry I never told you this. I never wanted to change the way you looked at him."

I clasped her hands in mine. And thought of her words, of how true they rang in my head. How heartbreaking it must have been for her to know she was pregnant and had to share a life with a man she loved but who didn't love her back enough to trust her.

She shook her head. "So, speaking of love, are you going to finally explain to me why you're living with a man?" A wink was thrown my way, and luckily, I wasn't given an opportunity to speak. "I won't complain, though. This Cameron is so handsome. And tall. Oh, how tall he is." She arched her brows. "I would also bet he could pick both of us up and not break a sweat. And those tattoos I've just seen on his arm?" Her lips pursed with mischief. "Does he have mo—"

"Mami, no." I was not going to discuss Cameron's possibly hidden tattoos with my mother.

"You're no fun," she said with a shrug. "Then tell me if he's the reason you didn't go back to Miami. Does he treat you like you deserve?"

My whole face flushed all shades of red. "He . . ." I trailed off, suddenly lost for words. Does he treat me like I deserve? My heart pounded in my chest with the answer. "Yes. He treats me like no one ever has."

My mother blinked once, twice, three times. And to my utter shock, she broke into laughter. *"Dios mío, hija."*

I felt the tips of my ears burn.

"I've never seen you like this." She patted her chest, one last chuckle rolling off her before she sobered up. She pinned me with a serious look. "You have it just as bad."

"Just as bad?"

"As him, *mi amor.*" She jumped off the stool and came to stand in front of me. She cupped my cheeks. "I've been in town for two hours, and every single second of the time he's been in front of me, he's been looking at you like you're *un pastelito* he wants to eat." She lowered her voice to a whisper. "I was joking about the banging earlier. I wanted to see if he'd react in a way I didn't like." My eyes widened with horror. "Don't worry, he passed my test. Now, really, have you kissed him yet?" My jaw fell to the floor. "Yeah. That's what I thought."

Cameron's words echoed in my head, *I could fucking eat you right now.* Then the memory of his lips against mine. His hands, all over me. The way I'd— No. I couldn't think of that with my mother, apparently a witch, here.

"I like you like this," she said, so softly I barely heard her. "You're shining."

Show me how fucking bright you burn.

My heart leaped in my rib cage, and a chuckle left my mother's lips before she wrapped her arms around me, enveloping me in Maricela Reyes's tightest hug. "This is all I wanted. Making sure that you were okay. Now that I know that, I will be here for just the night." She sighed, but it wasn't sad. "I know that man is not going to touch you as long as I'm here and, *hija,* you need to get—"

"Mom. Jesus, please stop," I begged. But this time, it was with a laugh.

And to her credit, she did stop. Although not without telling me,

"I don't think we want to bring Jesus into this particular conversation, *mi reina*."

I couldn't sleep.

There was too much noise in my head. My conversation with my mother had left me . . . unsettled in both negative and positive ways. For one, I felt like I understood her, now more than ever. And I wished we'd talked about this before. That I wouldn't have shut her down so many times in the past and had given her the chance to tell me these things. I also felt bad for not taking her side more. Horrible. Guilty, for allowing my father to claim he cared about her when he could never back up those words with actions.

It wasn't the only reason I felt restless. There was this constant hum at the back of my head. One that had been there ever since I'd met Cameron. Growing louder with every day that passed. With every second spent in this roller coaster our relationship had been. A hum that had shifted tonight. A hum that batted its wings when I thought of every day preceding this night. Or the way I felt with him. Or how I'd never been looked at like he looked at me. Even at the beginning, when we'd clashed, disagreed, and bickered, I'd never felt invisible when it had been him in front of me. He'd always, always given me his full attention. For better or worse.

And now . . . now I wanted more. I wanted more than just his attention. I wanted to feel like I'd felt tonight. Seen. Connected. Not to someone, but to him. Cameron.

Without really knowing how, I rolled off Cameron's large bed, and my bare feet padded over the hardwood. I made it to the living room and immediately zeroed in on his shape.

He occupied most of the couch, and the blanket that had once covered him was bunched up at his waist. The urge to go to him doubled. The need to wrap myself around him and cover us both. It wasn't a sexual thing, even though I knew the moment I touched him, my blood would once again swirl with need. No, this was something else.

I walked to the couch. There was barely any space by his side, but I didn't care. I felt vulnerable, as if I'd been torn inside out, my rawest parts on display. I set a knee by his hip, and slowly curled beside him.

A grunt left his throat, and in a swift, smooth motion, his arms were around me and he was on his side. He looked down, eyes half-open, and pulled me into his chest.

"Hi," I whispered.

He hummed, and I felt the sound against my belly and breasts. "Can't sleep?"

I gave him a small shake of the head. Without a word, I moved my hands, reaching the hem of his sleeping shirt. Not breaking eye contact, I slipped my fingers under it. I set my palms against his smooth and hard skin, letting the warmth travel up my arms and down my spine.

Cameron let out a shaky exhale. "Love," he said, and I knew it was a warning.

"I just need to touch you," I confessed, moving my hands up, pressing the tips of my fingers into his skin. "I need to feel you close." His eyes darkened, and his mouth pressed into a line. He was looking at me so seriously. So stern. As if my plea was a life-changing event. "I want you as close as anyone has ever been."

His arms tightened around me, and he pulled me close, much closer, lodging me into his body and trapping me there. I could feel his heart, pounding in his chest. "Better?"

I nodded and closed my eyes, reveling in the feeling. "Can you touch me, too?"

A growl fell out of his lips, and I knew it was costing him part of his restraint, but he complied. Of course he did. Cameron pulled the blanket over us, and only then, moved his hands beneath the only thing I wore over my underwear—one of his shirts—and he wrinkled it up with his wrist as his palms traveled up my back.

I shifted against him, feeling him growing hard against my belly. A shallow breath left my parted lips. And before I could move again, Cameron stilled my body against his.

"Cameron?" I whispered. "Can I ask you something?"

"Don't ask me to fuck you, love," he said, his voice nothing more than a rasp. "Because I will."

A breathy laugh fell off my lips. "I would love nothing more," I told him, meaning every word. And he must have been shocked by my admission because his body froze beneath mine. Just for a second. Then, it resumed with a shake, and I could feel his blood pulsing under my touch, his need growing with mine. "But I know it wouldn't be fair with my mother across that wall. I know . . ."

My throat worked with the unfinished thought.

But I knew—felt, deep inside of me, based on tonight, and based on an instinctive and intrinsic part of myself that only answered to him—that sex with Cameron wouldn't be just a quick and silent affair. It wouldn't be something I'd like to do with my mother on the other side of the wall.

"Hmm," I murmured. "On a second thought, maybe we should put my mother in Sweet Heaven Cottage."

"It's not a cottage," he grunted quickly. I frowned but he re-arranged me, thrusting one of his knees between mine and distracting me. "And that *we* you said like nothing?" A pause. "It all but killed me. So ask me your question."

"Do you think I'm a little like her?" A shallow breath left my lips, and Cameron waited, as if he knew that wasn't what I actually wanted to ask. "Or do I fade away beside her? Am I not a little black-and-white and cold and dull?"

We'd always been so different, she and I, and sometimes . . . Sometimes I'd wondered if I couldn't be a little more like her. Now, I also wondered if my father had seen me before that video at all. If the world had. If Cameron really did.

He nudged his forehead against mine until I looked at him. His eyes were so bright, so open and full of raw honesty, that it made my pulse waver. "You are all I can see," he told me, his words falling right on my lips. "Even when I close my eyes, you're all I see."

It was my turn to hum against his skin, just so I would tame the uproar in my rib cage. He always did that. Always gave me these perfect answers I almost couldn't believe. "Cameron?"

"Yes, love?"

My question was nothing but a whisper. "Tell me a secret. Something no one knows."

If he was surprised by my words, he didn't say or do anything to show me. All he did was bring one of his hands higher, until it rested against the back of my neck. "I was so scared," he said, and I knew what he was talking about. He gently brought my head against his chest, offering himself as a pillow. Asking me for a comfort I'd never deny. "I'm still terrified." I counted his heartbeats—one, two, three, five, ten—under my cheek, wishing I could stay there forever. Every night. Until the end of time. "I never dated Jasmine Hill. That was all Liam, my agent. He set me up, and I sat through dinner not to be rude. The media blew it out of proportion, but I haven't been with anyone since coming to the US."

We remained in silence for another moment, and I was so busy restraining myself after his last confession that I almost missed his next words.

"The lodge is mine now," he said, and I stilled. "It wasn't easy, but I closed on the purchase of Lazy Elk this morning."

My heart tripped. Then started pounding at double, triple, quadruple pace.

"What?" I whispered. But what I wanted to ask was *why*?

Cameron seemed to understand. "I'm not shy when I want something. And I'm not shy with my money, either. I worked hard for it." His voice turned lighter. Confident. Cocky in a way only Cameron made work. "That cottage is coming down. I'll build you something else."

I . . . wanted to let him. I wanted the implications of all of that, too. They made me happy. The happiest I'd been in a long time. And a handful of other emotions I didn't think I'd be able to handle if I wasn't in his arms. "That's more than one secret," I told him. "And I only asked for one."

Time ticked by without a word being said, and I was so warm, so comfortable, so safe, tucked against Cameron's body, that I started tipping into darkness. Half here and half not. So, when he spoke again, I brought his words with me. Into my dreams. "I'll always give you more than what you ask for, love. Even when you don't know what you want."

CHAPTER THIRTY-ONE

Cameron

$\mathcal{I}$ looked at Tony from the sidelines.

He stood on the midfield line, surrounded by an enthralled group of nine-year-olds blinking at him like he'd hung both the moon and the stars in the sky.

I smirked. He was a good young man, and you could tell he'd loved the game for a long time. It had taken him some time to get used to the looks the kids gave him—starry except for Juniper, who was stern and cautious—but he'd managed to channel that attention into work.

The first half of today's practice had been intense. We'd moved past simple exercises like "protect the cone" to more elaborate drills that require things like quality passes. It hadn't been easy, but the girls' enthusiasm had been unmatched. Even Juniper, who I'd taken aside and personally worked with on her keeper's skills, had been happy to move from basic footwork and diving to a little fun sliding. We'd both gotten dirty but it'd been worth it. She'd been fantastic at it.

I could think of a certain manager who'd been very happy about the girls' evolution. I eyed what had been nothing but a shed weeks ago, wondering what the woman inside was doing. Was she warm enough in there? October was growing chillier by the day, and even though I'd gotten one of those electric heaters from Moe's, it still was cold as hell outside. Or like Moe had said, *Asscrack cold.*

Pulling my phone out of the pocket of the hoodie I'd grabbed today, I checked the screen. I might still catch Liam if I rang him now. After that, I'd go check on Adalyn.

I tapped on his name and brought the device to my ear.

"Hell must have broken loose if Cameron Caldani himself is calling me."

I sighed. "And look what I get for it." I didn't wait for his retort. "I have questions. About your email."

"Wowzers. Straight to the point, are you?" He let out a chuckle. "Okay, shoot."

"You said the Miami Flames were searching for a new sporting director," I said, making sure my tone was as neutral as possible. "To possibly make up for a media situation."

"Yeah," Liam confirmed. He chuckled, and I knew exactly what he was going to say. "Did you see the video? That woman was w—"

"Yes." The word was hissed between my teeth. I closed my eyes, trying to keep a hold of the ball of dread taking shape in my gut. "I saw it. Of course I did. You said you suspected the reason was something else. Unrelated to that."

A sigh came through the line. "I did. My contacts are mostly in the west, but I have a few ears and eyes on Miami. But they . . ." He hesitated. "Nothing is confirmed. It's just talk for now. The situation is unclear. It all might be related to the media fiasco, I'm afraid."

A pair of big, rounded brown eyes popped up in my mind. A set of beautiful lips. The warmth and softness of her hands on my skin. "Tell me what you know."

A moment of silence. "Are you okay, man?" When I didn't answer, Liam clicked his tongue. "All right. I hear the team might change hands. Soon. That could explain why someone'd be poking around. My guess, of course."

Fuck. I brought a hand to my face, trying to rub some of the growing clamminess away. An acquisition? A handover? Worst thing was, Adalyn must be in the dark about that, otherwise she would have told me. She'd be on the next flight out. "How sure are you about this?"

"For now, it's nothing but whispers."

"Are you certain?"

"Yeah, man." A pause. "But what is this about?"

"Can you find out for certain? And keep me in the loop if you find anything? Even if you think it's probably not important. I want to know." I didn't wait for his answer, fully knowing that if I asked, he would. "Thanks for helping with the other thing, by the way. The lodge. I didn't properly say thanks."

Liam laughed. "Now you're thanking me? Christ, Cameron." I heard him exhale through the line. "Listen, whatever is going on with you, you need to sort it out. Sort yourself out and decide whether you want to finally shoot your career dead. Just . . . try to be done with this live, laugh, love phase of yours ASAP, yeah? I won't be playing housies with you anymore. I'm not your PA or your agent—any longer—and I have shit to do. So make up your mind about what your priorities are."

"I know what my priority is," I said, no hesitation. "Say no to all offers on the table." And then, I hung up.

A throat was cleared by my side.

I turned, and that beautiful half smile I was quickly becoming addicted to welcomed me. Something right between my chest and gut tightened with a clarity I hadn't felt for a long time.

"Taking a little break, Coach?"

My lips twitched at her tone, and I tried my hardest to push aside the information I'd just learnt. But I wouldn't worry Adalyn over something I wasn't sure of. That would sidetrack her and quash the hope and excitement about the Green Warriors I could see bubbling in her with my own two eyes. I wanted nothing but to protect this woman from any possible heartbreak or hit. So I'd have Liam find out about every possible angle, and only then, only when I knew for sure, I'd take her myself to Miami and demand an explanation from her father. We'd get through it together. Until then, she deserved to enjoy today, tonight's pregame dinner, and tomorrow's game. Win or lose, I'd do anything to give her a taste of the happiness I could provide for her.

"Are you okay?" she asked, frowning.

I squared my shoulders. I pushed all of that aside and refocused on what was in front of me. On today. "I don't know, boss." I gave her a very obvious once-over. "You tell me. Am I in trouble?"

Her lips pursed, and the flush in her cheeks told me everything I needed to know. "You might be." Her voice wavered with barely contained desire. "Now that I caught you delegating your responsibilities to Tony, and there're only a few minutes left of practice, there's something I need to discuss with you." Her throat worked. "Can I see you in my office?" She lifted her chin. "Now."

I wasn't going to lie, I grew harder in my joggers at the bossy tone. I crossed the distance that separated us and towered over her until she had to lean her head back. My gaze dipped to her mouth. "Lead the way." I licked my lips. "Miss Reyes."

I waited until she moved first. Selfish bastard that I was, I did it so I could watch her ass in that pair of jeans as she walked. The way her hair moved over her shoulders and her hips swayed with every determined step. Boy. I really was starved for her.

Once we were inside the clean but cramped space, I closed the door behind me and watched her turn around to face me. Her cheeks flushed, and she leaned on the edge of her desk.

"Can you, um, close the door?" A pause. "Coach?"

I tilted my head, biting back a smile. The door was already closed but I didn't say anything and gave her nod. I loved that she was this discombobulated. I loved that I made her like that. It was how I felt most of the time. My gaze dipped to her chest, waist, legs, then up again, to that beautiful face that was telling me she was trying to work through something in her head. Something that was sending her tongue out to lick her lips.

Practice would be wrapping up any minute now, and I'd never

been more glad to have Tony out on the grass. I moved my hand behind my back and shifted the lock into place.

"I . . ." Adalyn whispered. "You . . ." She wetted her lips again, fumbling with her hands. "You're not in trouble, actually. Or maybe, you are. I guess that depends."

I frowned at her nervousness, and I had to stop myself from blurting out some bullshit like *you look beautiful when your brows furrow in thought*. I walked up to her. My hands flexed with the urge to touch her, but I stilled them against my sides and waited. Encouraging her to say whatever she wanted to say with a nod of my head.

"I . . ." she started again, her voice soft. "I wanted to officially thank you." She spread her arms briefly before letting them fall. "For this. For last night. For every single thing you've done for me. I'm . . ." Her tongue came out, wetting her lips. "I don't know what I've done to deserve it, but I'm very grateful for your thoughtfulness." Her hand lifted, and I watched it cross the small space between us and land softly on my chest. My gaze returned to hers. "And I want to show you how much."

That palm pressed onto me, guiding me back and around the desk.

I offered no resistance. I went.

When the back of my legs hit her office chair, her other hand joined my chest. She trailed them up, all the way to my shoulders. She pushed me down. "Sit," she said, softly. So softly that I wanted to go toward her instead. But I flopped my body onto the chair, fascinated, enthralled, by the determination in her eyes. The anticipation parting her lips. What a beautiful, brave woman she was. My chest hurt just by looking at her.

Adalyn stood right in front of me, one single step away. Her hands went to the zipper of her jacket. She shrugged it off. Her chest heaved with a rough breath, making the fabric of her blouse press against her skin. The line of tiny buttons keeping it together tensed. And I could only think, *That goddamn blouse. I want to rip it open with my teeth.*

My hands flew to the arms of the chair, fingers latching on tight just so I wouldn't reach for her.

Adalyn walked into my open legs, her gaze roaming all over my face. Until her eyes tipped down. Low. All my blood swirled in that direction. If she did what I thought—hoped, craved—she would, all my restraint would leave me. Gone in an instant. I knew. "Adalyn." Her name dropped off my lips. "Darling, I—"

She braced both hands on my thighs and kneeled.

My eyes closed, a curse leaving my parted lips.

I felt her hands trail up my legs, her touch gentle but determined, sending more blood straight to my dick. Making me pulse with anticipation.

"Adalyn," I repeated, as a prayer more than a warning this time. I opened my eyes to her, staring at the growing bulge tenting my track pants. Fuck. I was so hard, and she hadn't even . . . "Are you going to touch me, love?" I asked her, hearing my voice crack.

Adalyn bit her bottom lip. In thought. Lust. She gave me a quick nod, but took her time to move her hands. I groaned, impatient, the sound making her smile. Her palms finally moved, and she slipped her fingers under the bottom hem of my hoodie. She latched on to the waistband of my pants.

She tugged.

"Tell me," I told her, hearing my voice crack with need. God, I wanted her. Now. I've wanted her for days now. Weeks. "Tell me what you'll do to me and I'll lift my hips."

"I . . ." She looked up, meeting my gaze. Good grief. Stunning, incredible woman, kneeling between my legs. "I want to be sexy. To be seen like this, by you. I've been planning this moment all day in my head. I want to pull these down and . . ." Her eyelids fluttered closed for a brief second. "Take you in my mouth. I want to make you feel like you made me feel that night. But I—" She shook her head. "I'm losing my nerve. I don't know how to be in charge in this scenario. I'd much rather you . . ."

She didn't need to finish that statement.

I looked into her eyes one more second, baring all my need,

letting it out to play on my face. "Take me out," I told her, my words nothing but a snarl. "You're safe to show me what you want to do, but I'll help." Her gaze dipped down, and I lifted my hips. The large outline of my dick pressed against the fabric. "Fuck," I rasped at the sight. Adalyn's grasp on the waistband tightened but she didn't move her hands. "I've never been this hard in my life, love. Will you do something about it?"

Breath caught in Adalyn's throat and her hands moved, hovering in the air for a second. Hesitant. Telling me she wanted me to guide her through this. To encourage her. To—her fingers grazed me through the fabric of the joggers. I groaned. Deep and guttural and full of need.

She finally pulled the pants down, freeing me of one of the two layers separating her from me.

I knew exactly how long I'd last on this chair.

"You have two minutes to play with me," I told her, unable to stop my hips from thrusting up into her grip. Her hand grasped my cock in response, giving me one slow stroke through the fabric. It wasn't enough. "Boxers," I growled. "Now, please."

In one motion, my underwear was down and my dick was springing free before resting against my stomach.

"I've been thinking of this," Adalyn said, her soft confession bringing me back to earth for an instant. Something inside of me yielded at her words. Her gaze met mine. "I think I've wanted you for a long time now, Cameron."

The arms of the chair creaked under the tightening grip of my hands. "Stroke me, then." I expelled all the air in my lungs through my nose. "Suck me or lick me or torture me any way you want. Do it now, before I break."

Curiosity mixed in with need in the brown of her eyes, spurring my own desire on. And before I knew what was hitting me, her palms were around my cock, skin against skin, and she was giving me one hard stroke.

My eyes fell shut, my whole body jumping on the chair. "Harder," I told her. Demanded. Begged. Adalyn complied, both hands engulfing me again. Moving head to root. "Just like that," I encouraged her. She stroked me again. "Make me beg, darling. Make me hurt for more."

I sensed her move between my legs, coming closer, leaning further into me, and when her strokes ceased, I knew what was going to come. My eyes opened, zeroing in on that beautiful mouth of hers as it closed around my cock.

Fuck. Jesus Christ. God. I'd never prayed this hard in my life but Christ. I'd venerate her mouth. This woman. Her heart. My hips thrust upward, pushing further into her mouth. Adalyn moaned around me and I—I couldn't be gentle, I was on my breaking point. I was going to burst. "Three sucks," I gritted between my teeth. "That's all you get."

Adalyn moved her head up and down a second time, and when a moan climbed up her throat and fell against my dick something in me snapped.

"I lied," I said, my hands moved to her head, and I gently but firmly lifted her off me. Her lips were cherry red and her cheeks blushed with the most beautiful pink to date. "Stunning, beautiful, gorgeous woman," I murmured, making her look at me in a way she never had before. My heart raced in my chest, drumming along the pulse making my blood thrum. "You win, love. You do. You have."

Before she could say a word, I snatched her wrists, and pulled us both up. Then, I swirled her around.

"Hands on the desk," I told her, my voice barely a growl. She complied, and when her palms hit the wooden surface, I moved over her. "That's a good girl," I said against her ear. "This is going to be fast."

"I don't want fast," she all but whimpered. My hands moved to her front, my fingers closing around the fabric of her blouse. "I want . . . I want . . ."

"This fucking thing has been driving me insane," I confessed, pulling at the fists of silky material. "It has snuck into my dreams," I whispered against the skin of the back of her neck. "That's how much I've wanted to rip all these buttons off. How much I've thought of what you hide underneath."

Those beautiful breasts. That smooth skin. That precious heart.

Her body shook under mine, and her hips pushed back, her ass pressing against my hard length. "Yes. To all of that."

I pulled her blouse apart, making those tiny buttons burst and fly. "Fuck. *Fuck.*" Without losing a single second, I brought her body to mine, arching her back, just so I could have a goddamn look at her. Glorious, beautiful lace covered her breasts. Lavender. "My fantasies didn't live up to this. To what a stunning woman you are."

"Cameron?" My name toppled off her lips in a whine. But my hands were busy moving up, my palms trailing over her skin, fingers reaching her breasts and closing possessively around them. Her eyes fluttered closed. "Make us feel good."

Us.

I was tipped over the edge.

An incomprehensible sound left my mouth, and I returned her hands to the desk, curving my body over hers. I unzipped her jeans, pushed my hand in, and encountered more of that lace. Making sure I'd touched her only over her panties—or I'd really fucking lose my mind—I trailed my fingers over her folds. "My Adalyn, so wet and perfect."

Adalyn spasmed beneath me, and my hips thrusted against her ass.

I moved my fingers, exerting pressure when I reached the top, then drawing circles over her clit.

"Out there," I told her, bringing my other hand to my cock and stroking myself as I stroked her. "You can boss me around. Say the word and I'll obey. You have me wrapped right around your finger." I felt her grow restless under my rough touch, the fabric of her panties now drenched. I tunneled into my fist, helplessly pressing my hips into her. "But behind closed doors?" I released us both, turned her around and all but shoved her onto the desk. I moved into her, fitting myself between her open legs. "In here," I told her, meeting her gaze. I pumped myself into my fist, my knuckles pressing against her folds. We both bit back a groan when my cock grazed her drenched panties. "In here, it's me who's in charge."

Her lips parted with a whimper that I knew was a yes. A please. A confirmation. A green light. And when I resumed moving, jerking into her as I stroked us both, her arms moved around my neck.

"Cameron," she said, voice beautifully broken.

I pressed my forehead to hers, bucking into her. "Come, love." I moved, making sure my tip was hitting the right spot with every thrust. "Come and I swear, I'll fuck you so good and long tonight."

Adalyn's whole body spasmed, and I went right behind, spilling all over her belly. She looked down, and her gaze turned as hazy and blissed out as I'd ever seen, making me want to rip her panties off and slip right into her. I'd be hard again in a minute. I'd been permanently hard for days.

But I didn't. I rested my forehead to hers, and then, I wrapped my arms around her body, bringing her to me. I couldn't stop myself, I couldn't help it. I wanted her right there. Beneath me, against me, in my arms. I wanted to be inside this woman, in any way I could.

Her lips touched the corner of my mouth, as if she'd known exactly what I was thinking, and I moved, taking them with a hard and desperate kiss. It wasn't enough. I wanted more. But I stepped back. Without a word, I gently pulled her arms out of her now ruined blouse and cleaned her belly off with it.

With a press of my lips to her temple, I brought her down off the desk and buttoned her jeans. In an ideal world we weren't in a makeshift office with barely any heating. In that world, practice hadn't wrapped up and we weren't supposed to go help set up tonight's pregame dinner. Instead, I could peel every item of clothing off her body and lick every inch of her. But this wasn't an ideal world, so I tucked myself into my pants and made myself ignore the way I was already hardening again.

I shrugged my hoodie off. "Arms up," I told her, and when she lifted them in the air, I slipped it over her head.

"What about you?" I heard muffled against the fabric as I tugged it into place.

I pulled her arms into the sleeves. "I have enough memories of you coming against me to keep me hot for a lifetime."

Adalyn let out a soft sound I tried my best to ignore. She looked so . . . mine right this moment. It took my breath away.

"Tonight," I promised, nostrils flaring.

Adalyn smiled, and it was shy and beautiful and it made me want to beat on my chest. "Tonight."

CHAPTER THIRTY-TWO

Adalyn

$\mathcal{T}$onight.

Tonight was the night. And I'd never felt more unprepared.

Could someone lose their virginity a second time? It wasn't even like it had been that long since I'd had sex. Or perhaps it was. It all blurred together somehow. Every past experience faded to gray now that I knew what Cameron's touch felt like.

Tonight was different.

It felt like more.

More than just sex. More than just wanting someone. More than physical attraction.

There was a raw need inside of me that wouldn't stop making demands. I wanted to be close to Cameron. Closer. I wanted to be kissed and taken and thrown around. I wanted him to look at me like he had earlier today, when his face had gone all soft. But also like he couldn't wait to eat me whole. I wanted him to give me his slow smile and his frown and his head tilt when he was trying to sneak inside my head. I wanted to make him laugh and for him to call me love not because it was sweet or sexy in that English gruffness, but because no one had ever called me that, and it felt right that only he did. But above all else, I wanted to be wanted by him. Craved. Like someone craved that feeling in your chest that lit everything else up. Like I craved him.

The touch of his palm on my thigh brought me right back, and when I looked at him, the green of his eyes gave him away.

He couldn't wait to bolt. He—we—were only here because I'd asked him to stay a little longer. Josie had thrown a good luck dinner for everyone on the team who wanted to join, and most of the parents had turned up.

"Why so serious, Coach?" I asked, the corners of my lips bending upward. "This is for good luck. I didn't peg you for someone who would disrespect a nice rite like this."

The smirk that he gave me sent the blood rushing to my head. He leaned forward and spoke right against the shell of my ear. "I can think of a couple of things we could implement for good luck." His lips brushed my skin, sending a wave of shivers down my spine. "If we leave right now."

My heart throttled in my chest. "I think . . ." I swallowed, wondering how strange it would be for me to jump into his lap right now with half the town sitting at the table. "I think that's something we can discuss. But we're not leaving just yet. Boss's orders."

He hummed against my skin, and when he withdrew his mouth, his head didn't go too far.

God. Maybe I wasn't doing myself any favors. How long were good luck dinners supposed to last?

My phone pinged from the table, so I picked it up and checked the notifications. My mother.

"Did she make it all right?" the man beside me asked with what I knew was genuine concern.

" 'Drive was okay,' " I read out loud for him.

He sighed. "I could have driven her myself. Asheville is only a couple of hours away."

I melted against his side at the reminder of him offering, I wasn't going to lie. " 'I gave Vincent my handle,' " I continued reading. " 'He's young but I could teach him a few things.' " A pause. "Oh boy."

"Who was Vincent again?"

I looked up at him. "Josie's friend's cousin, I think? He had come to town to talk some business with Josie and was returning to Asheville today." Cameron muttered something, and I placed my hand against his cheek. "Stop being so sweet. I . . . I'm struggling to keep my hands off you as it is, Cam."

He leaned against my touch with a sigh. "Call me Cam again."

I lowered my voice. "Cam."

Cameron let out a little grumble. "Okay, now tell me, how am I being sweet and why should I stop?"

"Worrying over my mother," I answered, barely able to ignore the roaring in my chest. "It's making it really hard for me to resist you."

His head turned, lips grazing the skin of my palm, then trailed down to my wrist. "Why would you ever want to resist me?" He nipped at my skin, wickedly fast. "It's frowned upon. Experts recommend not resisting things that are good for you."

I giggled. Giggled.

Cameron's eyes shifted to mine, and when he said against my skin, "I could spend a lifetime hearing that sound." I didn't even question his words. I knew they were true.

My chest expanded. "I—"

Someone cleared a throat next to me, and we both turned.

"Hi," Mr. Vasquez—Robbie—said, a careful expression on his face. María was by his side, and she nudged his leg before smiling at me. He rushed out, "I'm sorry to interrupt."

"That's okay," I assured him. And I meant it. "You're not interrupting anything."

The man by my side grunted a soft complaint.

Robbie's eyes shot to Cameron before returning to my face. "I just wanted to say thank you. For what you've done for Tony and María, and for . . . everything. Ever since Tony started spending time with the team, he . . . he sounds and looks more like himself. It has made me realize that he was spending too much time on the farm. Working too much when he's just a kid. I—" His throat worked.

"Thanks for giving him a job doing something he loves." Robbie looked down at his daughter with a smile. "Happy?"

She lowered her voice to a loud whisper. "Ask her for the tickets."

The man cursed under his breath. "María—"

"Do it," she repeated. "You told me you were a j-word to her, so apologize. You make me apologize all the time when I'm rude, then it'll be okay to ask. Tony will love it. You know he wants to try out for that team in Charlotte. He'll lose his mind."

The man pressed his lips into a tight line and sent me an apologetic look. "Please, ignore—"

"Consider it done," I told him. "We can talk about dates tomorrow after the girls' game. There was something else I wanted to ask you anyway. But it can wait. We'll talk tomorrow." Robbie still looked unsure, so I felt the need to slip into my old self. "The Miami Flames will be happy to have you for a visit, I promise."

Cameron's body tensed against mine. It was only an instant, but all the hard muscles I was leaning against flexed and tightened with his breath.

María clapped her hands, recalling my attention. "Yay!" she exclaimed, throwing herself at me without warning. "Celebration hug," she said against my cheek, and I couldn't help it. I squeezed her in my arms. Then, as if she wasn't thinking about it, she let out a soft, "Ah. This feels so good. We should do it more often."

I hugged her even tighter.

When she released me, she was smiling, and I didn't know what my face was doing but my chest felt like mush. "I'll see you tomorrow, Miss Adalyn." She looked at the man sitting by my side. "I'll see you tomorrow, too, Coach Campanile."

Robbie muttered something under his breath.

Cameron let out a chuckle, bringing his arms around my shoulders and pulling me back to him again.

"Oh!" María said, already walking away as she pulled at her dad's hand. "Don't forget to give Coach his shirt!" Then, she disappeared around the far end of the long table, dragging Robbie along with her.

"What shirt?" Cameron asked.

I sighed. "That was supposed to be a surprise." I shook my head. "It's back ho—" I stopped myself. I didn't know why, but I did. I cleared my throat. "Back at the Lazy Elk."

Cameron hummed. "Close," he murmured, his arm snaking around my waist. "It's okay, love. I'm not one to give up at halftime."

Cameron unlocked the front door of the cabin and stepped to the side.

I looked inside, toward the hallway that turned to the right, leading to Cameron's room. Right across from what had been mine. My eyelids fluttered shut for just an instant.

I turned around. Faced him. Blocked his way into the cabin. Deep green eyes met mine, and I said, "Hi."

"Hi," he said back. His lips twitched, and I thought he'd give me a slow smile, which would dazzle me and perhaps distract me from my thoughts. But instead, he clenched his jaw. I watched his eyes as they roamed all over my face, settling on my lips for what felt like a long time, but was just a second or two, and that giddiness, that anticipation, before Cameron had been so uncharacteristically mine, bubbled up inside.

"What's on your mind?" I asked him.

He brought his hand to my face, brushing my cheek with the back of his hand. "Several things," he confessed in that calm, stern tone, as if he didn't mind I was keeping us from crossing the threshold of the door. "I'm thinking, thank God, that dinner is finally over." I smiled at that, and the pad of his thumb grazed my bottom lip. "I'm also thinking, Christ, she's so beautiful in this light. With the full moon shining so brightly over us. Would it be too corny to point it out? Would she laugh? I love her laugh."

My smile fell, my heart doing this weird thing against the walls of my chest. "That would be one of the most beautiful things I've ever been told." I wrapped my fingers around his wrist, felt his pulse under my thumb. It was a quick, hurried beat. Was he nervous, too? "I wouldn't laugh. I would probably stall for a longer time."

"Stall," he repeated slowly. "Tell me why."

I opened my mouth to say something I suspected sounded a lot like: Because it's you, and it's me. And I've never felt like this. But the answer that left me was, "It's hard to explain."

If today—the last days—had proved anything, it was that I wasn't a seductress. And with Cameron I didn't mind. *It's me who's in charge.* He said that earlier today. I wanted him to offer again. To take charge. I'd never felt safer, freer, than when he took over for me. And yet . . . this nervousness made me wonder and doubt myself. What could I possibly have done to deserve this, to earn him wanting me this much. I—

"Try me," Cameron said.

"I . . ." I tried, knowing I probably would voice it in a way it didn't make sense. "I've always felt like I never really clicked anywhere. Like, I always needed to make a bigger effort to show everyone that I deserved to be there. And here you are." I shook my head. "Making me feel like you'd close the gap to get to me. Like, I don't need to convince you. You—"

"Fuck him," Cameron said, bringing my gaze to him. "Fuck them. Fuck everyone who has made you feel like you're not worth everything you deserve."

Something locked inside of my chest. Loudly. So very close to my heart. "You don't have to—"

I was lifted up and dropped on a wide shoulder.

"No more overthinking," he said, walking us both inside. "No more questioning how I feel toward you. I didn't sit through a full hour of campfire songs so you could find a reason to boot me when I finally get you home." His other hand fell over the backs of my knees, securing me against him, as if he feared I'd try to jump out of his arms. "This," he said, stomping into the living room. "I had to restrain myself from taking you and throwing you over my shoulder like this. Josie is a horrible singer."

I blinked down at his back, his ass, his long legs, and I . . . I burst out laughing.

He came to a stop immediately, loosening the vise of his arm, removing me from his shoulder, and placing me in front of him. I steadied myself against his chest.

"I'm already tempted to do that again," he said, his eyes dancing between my mouth and eyes. The beating of his heart drumming against my palms, quicker than a few moments before. "I could do it every day. With every door."

"It can be discussed." I was still half laughing, but when Cameron's jaw clenched again, all of that lightness dissolved. "Okay, I should give you your spoiled surprise."

He opened his mouth, but I was already stepping away from him and whirling on my heels. I walked to the guest room and fished the gift out of the wardrobe I'd hid it in.

When I turned around, Cameron was leaning against the frame of his bedroom door, right across from mine. I swallowed. Padded closer to him with the pink bag in my hands.

I offered it to him.

Cameron opened it and extracted what was inside. The bag dropped to our feet. His hands held the shirt in the air.

" 'This coach kicks monkey bum,' " he read out loud. He swallowed. " 'Coach Chamomile, Green Warriors of Green Oak. Six Hills Little League, NC.' "

My heart raced. "It's so silly," I said, hearing my voice sound low and guarded. "I had it made so the girls could sign it tomorrow." A shaky breath left me. "María helped come up with the first part."

Cameron's arms dropped. He looked at me with an emotion I didn't recognize. One that wasn't any of the ones I'd expected the shirt to cause.

"It was supposed to be a joke," I explained. "I . . . I thought you'd find it funny."

A muscle in his jaw jumped. "There's no press attending tomorrow's game, is there?"

My stomach dropped at my feet. "Of course not."

"There hasn't been any press at any game."

My throat tightened, clogged, and I had to make myself swallow. "I would never put your anonymity or privacy at risk. Not after what you told me."

"But you only found out about that recently," he countered, taking a step closer to me. "You changed your mind before that. Why?"

I felt myself shaking. Trembling. "I could still make it work."

Another step. "At the cost of your ticket back to Miami?"

My mouth clamped shut. My heart raced. My eyes fluttered shut. Cameron's fingers brushed my cheek. "Yes or no, love?"

I met his gaze, and there was so much in there, so much that mirrored exactly how I felt. Desperate. Needy. Falling so fast and hard I could barely breathe. "Yes," I said. "At any cost. I was and will protect you at whatever the cost."

He cupped my face. "I see you, Adalyn." His other hand joined, and the shirt he'd been holding fell to our feet. "I goddamn see you, love. But you finally opening up like that for me? It makes it impossible for me not to crack open in return."

I grasped his wrists. "And how would you do that?"

"Treating that side you hide," he said against my mouth. "I want to spoil it rotten, just because I can. I want to bury you in pillows when you're cold and carry you to my bed in my arms every night. Kissing you hard when we bicker and reminding you just how crazy you make me."

A kind of pressure I wasn't familiar with rose in my chest. It reached my eyes, making them sting. And I wanted to burst. Really burst. I felt so happy, so ecstatic, so . . . full of that something I didn't think I could say out loud, or even think, that I wanted to burst open at the seams and let him see.

A broken laugh fell off my lips, and I didn't even recognize myself when I said, "You've just made my surprise look really bad."

"I loved the surprise," he said softly, so softly it felt like a caress. He pulled me into his body and started walking backward, pulling us into his room. "I'll blame the surprise when I lose control tonight."

I shook my head, a single tear helplessly creeping down my cheek. "Why?"

"Because now I know you're happy, really happy. And this tear?" he added, pressing his mouth against my skin and tracing the wet trail with his lips. "It's proof of how much." He tilted my head back, kissing the brow of the culprit eye. His gaze dipped down to my lips. "Now, I can take your mouth and know that you know how I feel. That this doesn't need to be earned. You already own the right."

This time, it wasn't Cameron waiting for me to cross the distance and kiss him. He did.

Cameron took my mouth, parting my lips with such hunger I had to link my arms behind his neck for support. Our tongues brushed and I pulled him to me, briskly, need pulsing in my belly, ears, limbs, chest, everywhere. And with a growl, he moved forward, dragging his hands down my throat, shoulders, waist, coming around my hips and landing on my ass. He lifted me up.

As if I'd done this a hundred times, I closed my legs around his waist. I braced my arms on his shoulders, pushing my body upward, searching for the right spot, until the junction of my thighs rubbed right against the hard ridge in his pants. His chest vibrated with a growl, and when he came up for air, the green of his eyes shone as bright as I'd ever seen a color shine. His mouth came down again, not wasting more than a second, and he grazed the side of my neck with his teeth.

I threw my head back, whimpered, and then, I was being dropped on something soft. His bed.

A cloud of his scent enveloped me. The sensation made my chest so full, so packed to the brim with bliss, that I swore I could fly.

"That smile" was all but growled from the foot of the bed. I looked over at Cameron. My lips didn't waver. "Come here," he said, tugging at my foot. "I need that smile against my mouth."

His hands wrapped around my ankles and I let him drag me all the way to where he was. I went up on my knees and met his gaze, still smiling, still feeling so full I might burst. I crossed the distance, pressing my mouth to his, doing as he asked.

A groan left him and then he was grazing his lips all over my face. Sweet but firm caresses that went up and down and left and right, making shivers spread and twinkle down my arms.

"I've never wanted anyone like this," I whispered against his mouth, placing my palms on his shoulders. One short breath left me. And I let my fingers fall down his torso, until I reached the hem of one of his fleeces that I now loved so much. I closed my fists around the fabric. "I've never felt this safe, this cherished, this wanted, this . . ." Loved. "I want you so bad."

Cameron's body shook. With restraint, with need, with that emotion I was so scared to voice? I couldn't know. I didn't think I cared. Not right in that moment as I felt his hands come around mine and tug up. "Undress me," he said in barely a rasp.

I pulled it up, his hands leaving mine to help when I couldn't reach all the way up his arms. A beautiful collage of ink and skin was revealed before me. A new kind of need reeled in. The need to touch, memorize, brand, and make him mine.

"Show me," he told me, pushing his body against my hands. "Show me how bad you want me."

Deliberately slowly, I pressed my lips to his chest, right above his heart, marked with the design of a rose. I could feel his muscles flexing in response. His skin was so smooth, so solid and hard, and his heart drummed briskly, almost too fast. I grazed my teeth over all that ink, and his hand landed on the back of my neck.

I moved upward, leaving a trail of open-mouthed kisses all the way to the bottom of his throat, feeling his fingers slip into my hair. I nipped at the skin, a little harder this time, and a groan came from his lips. It felt amazing to have such an imposing man crumbling down under my touch like that.

My eyelids fluttered closed at the thought, and before I could anticipate his next move, he was bringing us both down on the bed.

His scent blanketed me, filling my lungs again, feeling like more. His weight pressed so sweetly against me that I circled my arms around his neck and pushed him down. Cameron resisted, his hand right by my head.

"I'm going to knock down every wall left standing," he said against my ear, his other hand moving, climbing up my side, and taking the fabric of my sweater and shirt with it. "And once I'm inside," he rasped, the pads of his thumbs reaching the underside of my breast. He moved his fingers over my bra, roughly, desperately. "I'm going to bury myself so deep into you"—he brought the lace down, making my breast topple out—"that you won't be able to tell where you end and where I start."

"Yes," I whispered. "To all of that. Yes. A hundred times."

A dark chuckle left him in response. Then, he was lifting my arms over my head and securing them against the comforter. His mouth came down on my breast, and my breath caught. A hum vibrated against my skin then, he was grazing my nipple with his teeth. Pulling. Tugging. Making my back arch off the bed.

He did the same to the other one, and I complained, feeling restrained, wanting to touch him. Wanting my mouth on him, too.

With a brisk motion, the clothes that had been bunched at the top of my chest were off, together with my bra. Cool air teased my skin, and I felt my eyelids flutter closed, overwhelmed by the sensation of being bared to him. It hadn't been a long time since someone had seen me like this, but this felt like so much more than naked skin.

There was a growl. Followed by a curse.

I opened eyes I hadn't known were closed, finding Cameron straddling my hips, wide chest heaving, lines upon lines of ink swaying with every muscle that flexed in tension.

"I could look at you all night," he said, his hands engulfing my sides. "You drive me mad with need." He dragged his fingers down, reaching the hem of my jeans. "In the best of possible ways." His fingers worked the button undone. "Lift up."

I did, no hesitation. And Cameron didn't waste a single second in pulling my jeans down and off my legs, throwing them on the floor.

He bent down again, slowly this time, placing one open-mouthed kiss against my pulse.

"Cameron," I said, begged. My hands flying to the waist of his pants, hooking around the belt loops as he left more kisses down my chest, reaching the swell of my breasts. Continuing to my navel. My hip bone. I lost my grasp of the waistband of his jeans. "I need you inside of me. Now."

A dark chuckle left him. "But I haven't even tasted you on my tongue."

And just like that, he was spreading my legs, first with his hands, then with his shoulders, and at last, his head was between my thighs. My breathing had lost all sense of control, anticipation and need so thick in my blood that I swore I could feel it swirling with every violent beat of my heart.

He pressed his mouth against that pulsing bundle of nerves covered by the fabric of my panties. Urgency, clear and loud, shot up my body, driving a curse to fall off my lips.

He trailed his teeth up and down my folds, and I could feel his lips through the fabric, that trimmed beard I loved stirring awake dozens of nerve endings. I'd thought it was too much, too quick, too good, but then, he shoved my underwear aside with his teeth, and repeated the motion with his lips. He sucked, his tongue thrusting inside, and that's when I saw real, twinkling stars behind my eyes. Felt them under my skin.

A groan fell against my clit, and that thumb he'd teased my nipples with joined his mouth, drawing circles over that throbbing spot that demanded release. My head spun. My pulse raced. My whole body shook.

Without stopping those wicked motions of his hand, Cameron moved up my body, taking back my mouth and swallowing all the moans toppling right out of me.

"Open your eyes," he demanded. And I did. "Look at me," he said, as if I could look anywhere else when all that fierceness and need was twisting his handsome face.

Gazes locked, he went up on his knees and undid his pants, drawing my eyes down just in time to watch him pull himself out. He closed his fist around his hard cock and gave himself one rough stroke.

"Fuck," he said before releasing his dick and closing those strong fingers around the fabric of my panties. He ripped them off me, threw them aside and teased my folds and clit again.

I moaned louder, impossibly so, and then, when he brought that exact hand around his cock and stroked himself again, I thought I'd come. I didn't need more than seeing him coating himself in me. I reached down with my hand, all sense of control lost, and touched myself.

"Mine," he warned, snagging my hand and coming down on me. His hard and sticky length fell right against my clit. "Condom," he exhaled the word with a gulp of air. "I need—"

"Pill," I whispered. "I'm on the pill. I want you. Just you. I'm clean. Are you—"

"Yes." His fingers tightened around my wrists, and he brought them over my head again. Cameron's weight shifted, his hips wedging into mine, opening me right up. "Now," he said, positioning the head of his cock at my entrance. "Now, you move with me." He pushed, and my back arched with a loud whimper. He thrusted again. Harder that time. And again. "Now you come for me."

At his command, I did. Stars flashed behind my eyelids, pleasure rippled inside of me, shoving me into darkness for one blissful moment. And God. I'd never orgasmed so fast in my life.

"You come so sweet," he said against my ear, riding me through the wave of pleasure until my body was nothing but a spent tangle of limbs. "You come so bright."

I moved my mouth, but no words came out, I was too lost to the sensations, too lost to the feel of him still moving inside of me, filling me up.

A rough press of his lips against mine, and then, I was being flipped onto my belly.

His hands moved to my sides, and when he lifted my body up, I felt him hot and hard and wet against my back. Rough palms dragged up and down my ribs, stomach, thighs, then climbed to my breasts. He tugged at one of my nipples, bringing that need back alive. His thighs shifted underneath me, the shaft of his cock nudging at my entrance from behind, and a new rush of urgency made my head spin. I pressed myself onto him.

"Tell me," Cameron said, grazing his teeth over the side of my neck. "Tell me you want me like this," he demanded, moving his hips and bringing his shaft to tease my clit. "Tell me you're mine to take if that's what you want."

"Cameron," I whimpered, and he rewarded that with a kiss on my shoulder. "I have only wanted you," I all but expelled the words. The sound rough and drenched in need but oh so right. "I want you any way possible."

He moved his cock, the head gliding in. "Then, tell me to fuck you."

"Fuck me," I whispered. "Please."

He thrusted all the way in, the position, the size of him, the way we fit together just now pulling twin groans from both our mouths.

"Ah fuck, love," he growled, plunging into me. "How goddamn soft and perfect you are." His arms came around my waist, his thrusts increasing in pace, losing all sense of rhythm. "I'm buried so deep inside you." His hand moved to where we were joined, and he pressed his palm there. "We might be at odds sometimes. Drive each other crazy. But this is how we fuck." His fingers circled my clit. "This is how I'll always fuck you, no matter what. This is us."

"Yes," I whimpered, getting lost in the tsunami of sensation barreling into me again. "This is us. Just with you. Only us." He groaned behind me, shifting the angle and hitting a different spot. More stars. More waves of pure and raw sensation. Too much and not enough. "Make me come. Come inside of me."

His free hand moved to my jaw, gently, firmly, his hips pushing up and up. "I promised you that much, didn't I?" He moved my head, making me meet his eyes. "Look at me, see what you do to me." The rhythm of his thrusts broke. "Come with me, love." His voice cracked. "Let me see you shine."

Release grabbed me, snatching me and spinning me, making my whole body throb as I screamed Cameron's name.

As if in sync, his large and solid body spasmed beneath me, his limbs and cock jerking with his release, my own name leaving his mouth in a growl as he held on to me tighter than I'd ever been held by anyone in my life.

Chests heaving, we remained in that high, his hips still rocking, his hand still moving over my clit, and his cock still hard inside of me. Cameron's mouth pressed on the side of my jaw, and my head fell back on his chest.

I didn't know how long we stayed in that position, I only knew that at some point, he slipped out of me and rearranged me in his arms. He returned me back to the living world with a kiss and asked me to go pee because he'd come inside me and it was important that I did. Then we slipped into the shower he turned on and he brought me to his chest. We let the hot stream of water fall over us, turning our skin sleek under each other's fingertips.

"Adalyn, love," he whispered in my ear, his hands trailing up and down my back. "This is no longer a game." My heart swelled in my chest at his words. At the possibility they painted. The truth that I hid. "Tell me you understand."

I extricated my head from his chest, making sure I met his gaze. I understood. So much that I was beginning to see how I'd never stood a chance. The moment I'd set foot in Green Oak, I'd already lost. But now, my heart was on the line, too. Now, what was at stake was greater than redemption. Larger than fixing a PR mess or earning back someone's trust.

But this was Cameron. And I trusted him like I'd never trusted anyone. I saw that. So I kissed him in the center of his chest, and when I said, "I know," I meant every word.

CHAPTER THIRTY-THREE

Adalyn

I woke up to a nudge on my face and the characteristic buzzing of a phone.

My eyes blinked open to a set of eyes I hadn't been expecting.

"Willow?" I mumbled.

Her paw came down again, pressing on my cheek as she sat beside my pillow.

I looked behind her, finding empty the side of the bed where Cameron had been.

After what had been the best night of sleep in weeks—months, maybe even years—I hadn't even noticed him getting up. I was renewed and sore in the best possible way. Yes. What we'd done last night had been the best sex of my life—ground-shaking, multiple orgasms kind of best.

And Cameron? He was a snuggler. A cuddler. And as much as I'd never been one myself, snuggles with Cameron, I had learned, led to the best in-the-middle-of-the-night sex. Lazy and sultry and—

The phone I'd ignored buzzed again, making me roll in the direction of the sound.

I sat up, resting my back against the headboard Cameron had used as leverage in some of that middle of the night—

Willow mewed over the buzzing.

"Yeah, yeah. I know," I told her, setting her on my lap while I reached for the phone. "I'm obsessed with your daddy."

"You're what?" A male voice came from the speaker of the phone.

I looked up, seeing Matthew's face on the screen. Oops. I must have accepted the call. "I'm . . ." I started, but then I took in the dark bags under his eyes. The way his hair stuck in all directions. "What's wrong with you?"

"Is that a cat?" he asked, ignoring my question. Willow mewed and lifted her head to check the screen. "Why do you have a cat?"

"Matthew," I said, now seriously. "What's going on? You're calling me very early in the morning." A pang of guilt cut through me. I'd been so wrapped up in my own life that I hadn't checked on him in a while. "What's going on?"

His jaw clenched, and he didn't need to say a word for me to know that there was something wrong. Probably more than one thing.

"Matthew—"

"Oh my God," he suddenly groaned. He shut his eyes in a dramatic way. "Are you naked under that cat? Wait. Don't tell me."

"There's a comforter between the cat and me."

A female voice sounded in the background.

Matthew sighed before turning his head around and yelling, "MA! I TOLD YOU I WAS GOING TO MAKE A CALL."

I blinked in surprise. "You're back home? In Massachusetts?"

"Is that Adalyn?" was said in the back. "Tell her to come visit. God knows you need—"

"NOT THAT AGAIN, MA." He faced me. "It's a long story." A shake of his head. "Anyway. I guess that explains why you look . . ." He trailed off, looking all but miserable. "Like that."

"How do I look?" I huffed.

"Beautiful," Cameron answered. "Stunning, really."

My head swiveled in the direction of that deep, sultry, accented voice that was whispering all kinds of things in my ear last night. He was shirtless, and he looked so handsome and inviting from his spot at the door that I could only gape.

"And thoroughly fucked," he added, making my jaw drop to the floor.

Matthew let out a strange sound from the phone.

Cameron ignored all of that. He crossed the distance to me with long, determined strides, green eyes boring into mine. He reached the side of the bed and leaned forward. "You're naked, in my bed, with my cat on your lap, speaking to some other man. Should I be concerned, love?"

"Cameron," I mumbled like an idiot, instead of a simple no. Or a *Don't be ridiculous, isn't it obvious that I'm crazy about you?* Or a *Your biggest concern should be me, helplessly falling for you, if you don't stop saying things like that.* But my brain wasn't working.

"*CAMERON?*" My best friend spit from my phone. "As in Cameron Caldani, as in *the* CAMERON CALDANI?" A panicked pause. "Is that Cameron Caldani's cat? You're in Cameron Caldani's BED." His voice went high. "Is Cameron Caldani the one who thoroughly f—"

"Matthew," I stopped him. "Can you please stop saying his name like that? Actually, it would be nice if you would also stop emphasizing all that stuff."

Cameron placed a mug in my hand and kissed me. Hard. Briefly but intently enough for his mouth to part mine.

Matthew gasped.

And I . . . I was too dazzled by that kiss. Distracted. I wanted more kisses like that. More growly noises from his chest, I—

"You're with Cameron Caldani," my best friend murmured, as if the knowledge was sinking in just now. "I have questions. First one is where is my shirt? Second is how serious are you? How did any of this happen? Are we becoming brothers-in-law?"

Cameron sat on the edge of the bed, placing an arm around my shoulders and muttering, "This should be fun."

I sighed. "Cameron, this is my best friend, Matthew Flanagan. And, Matty, this is—"

"Cameron Caldani," he finished for me, eyes growing three sizes. But at least he wasn't gasping. "Big fan, Mr. Caldani. I've followed your career for years. I—" He stopped himself. "Hold on, before I go on, I feel like, as Adalyn's best friend, I should extend a warning."

"Matthew, no," I whispered loudly. "And stop calling him by his full name, please. You're making this very weird."

Cameron pulled me closer with the arm that was snaked around my shoulders, and only when I was tucked against his side did he sneak his hand below the comforter and place it on my naked thigh. "Let the man talk." He squeezed my leg, and my blood rushed to that exact point. "I don't scare easily."

My best friend looked so starstruck I doubted he'd be able to scare a fly right now, but he cleared his throat. "Adalyn's last boyfriend was a complete tool."

"I already like where this is heading," Cameron muttered, and his hand moved to my belly, pushing me closer still.

Matthew continued, "I knew the moment I met him that I'd eventually want to break his face." I tensed. Matthew didn't know what Cameron did. "I waited for him to give me a reason, a good solid one I could use in case I needed to defend myself in court, but he never did." A moment of silence followed that. "I don't really know you, Cameron. But I like you. A lot. If you knew how much you'd probably be weirded out but—"

"Jesus, Matthew," I hissed. "Get to the threatening because we have a game to attend."

Matthew rolled his eyes before his expression turned stern. "But as much as I love the man on the field, I will break your face if you hurt her." I sighed, not because I doubted him but the opposite. And I feared this would actually scare Cameron away. "I'd love nothing more than for you to be with her, give her a family of cute cats, babies, or whatever makes us best friends for life, but don't break her heart. Because if you do, I swear I will—"

"I won't," Cameron stated. Firmly. No hesitation. "And she's the one with the power and choice to do all those things. Not me. I'm just waiting for her to let me."

My heart tripped. My soul might have left my body for all I knew.

I was going to faint. Or throw up. I really was.

What in the world was going on? Why were they talking about families of cats and babies and why was Cameron talking like . . . Like I just needed to sign on the dotted line to get it? I—we hadn't even talked about what this meant. The future. I was leaving Green Oak. Soon after this game, if I had to guess. And he . . . He'd just bought this lodge.

I'm just waiting for her to let me.

Now my heart doing pirouettes. We needed to talk. Not about cats or babies, because that was ridiculous, but about whatever came after this. After now.

"All right," Matthew said, clapping his hands and bringing me back. "Now that that's out of the way. Can I ask you a few questions, Mr. Caldani?"

The man beside me flinched. And yet, he said, "Sure."

"No," I interjected with a firm tone, finally returning to myself. "No questions. No journalist shenanigans. Turn it off."

My best friend's mouth hung open for a moment, his brows in a frown. "But—"

"I said no," I repeated, hearing one too many emotions in my voice. "Cameron only said yes because you're my friend. But the truth is that his personal life is none of your or anybody's business. He'll talk when he decides to talk, and if that never happens, then that's okay."

Matthew recovered quickly, just like he always did. God, I felt like a jerk, but I'd already hurt Cameron by threatening to expose him. And even if that felt like an eternity ago, I shook with guilt even thinking of putting him in that situation again.

"I'm sorry," Matthew said, and I knew he meant it. His eyes turned in Cameron's direction. "I think she might keep you, man.

Adalyn never goes all Rottweiler on me. Except for that time I dragged her to Saint Patrick's—"

"Matthew, please." I groaned. "You promised me not to ever talk about that again."

"All right," my best friend said. "I really need to go, now." His tone turned somber. "Addy?" he said, and I realized I wasn't bothered by that anymore. "There's something you need to see. That was why I was calling you. It's in your email." He looked over at the man beside me again. "Take care of her, will you? I . . . She'll push through anything but sometimes it's good not to do it alone."

Something sounded in the background, behind Matthew's chair, but before I could discern any of it, or even process the meaning of what he'd just said, the call was over.

Cameron took the mug from my hand.

"Hey, I'm not done with—" I started.

But Cameron's mouth was on mine, his hands on my waist, and my back was hitting the bed. He came over me, and an immediate sense of rightness, of safety and excitement and warmth, fell over me, enveloping me and making my mind stop.

Willow mewed somewhere far away, as if she'd run from the room, and Cameron bit my lip again, demanding all my attention back.

"You beautiful, fierce girl," he said against my lips. His hips settling between mine. "Protecting me like that." That mouth trailed down my neck. "It's gotten me rock-hard."

My hands moved to his head, my fingers slipping into his hair, hardly resisting the feel of his mouth as it continued down. "I thought you—" Cameron nipped at my nipple and I arched my back. "I think . . ." His tongue trailed down to my belly. "I think—" He placed a hard kiss on my hip. "I think we—"

His head lifted, his gaze meeting mine. "What do you think we should do, love?"

My chest heaved up and down, need surging through me and making it difficult to think. "Talk. I think we should talk."

I waited for his reaction, almost afraid of him possibly brushing it off or walking away.

But Cameron's lips twitched, bending upward and giving shape to that blinding smile. "We'll talk, then." He placed one more kiss on my belly, then climbed up and pushed his lips to my jaw. My eyelids fluttered closed and when they reopened, he was standing at the side of the bed, looking down at me as I laid sprawled in the comforter. Still. "We have a few hours until the game. I left breakfast in the kitchen for you. Fresh coffee, too. I'll jump in the shower to take care of this." He gripped himself through his sleeping pants. I swallowed. "It's an open invitation for you to join. Either way, we'll talk before leaving the house."

In awe, I watched him pull something out of the pocket of his sweatpants. Then he leaned forward and slipped it over my head. I looked down, finding his signet ring hanging on a chain.

"For good luck," he said. "So you don't forget just how superstitious I am." And with that, he turned around and left me right where I was.

Jesus. Was this my life now? Being invited by beautiful gruff men to have shower sex and wearing their family heirlooms around my neck?

It's an open invitation for you to join.

I sprung up. The heels of my feet hit the floor so hard, I probably left a mark. We were going to talk either way. He'd said so himself. So we could have a few orgasms first, couldn't we? Cameron was giving me the choice. Just like he always did. He'd known there was something on my mind and offered me an in and an out. He'd made sure either way, I knew he'd be there.

Stroking himself.

I started for the bathroom, but then, my phone pinged again.

Almost instinctively, I had a glimpse at the notification. It was Matthew's email.

There had been something about him, something about what he'd said that had left me unsettled. There was something up with Matthew and the answer might be in that email.

I picked up the phone. Unlocked it. Opened my inbox and tapped on the mail.

CHAPTER THIRTY-FOUR

Adalyn

*I*t was Cameron's voice that returned me back to earth.

"Adalyn?"

I blinked, the screen of my phone now black.

How long had I been staring into blank space?

Everything was a blur. I didn't even remember putting on one of Cameron's shirts or coming to the kitchen. I just remembered opening Matthew's email and needing to move. Feeling cold. Needing a glass of water. Needing to breathe.

"Adalyn?" Cameron's voice came again, a panicked edge in it this time. I heard his steps, then his hands were around my face. "You need to breathe, love."

Was I not breathing?

Air got stuck in my throat, making me gasp and giving me an answer.

Cameron's eyebrows knotted, concern twisting his expression. He was right. Cameron had been right all this time. This had to be a panic attack. And it was something I shouldn't brush off. I should see someone about it. I probably had triggers I should know about. I—

"I need to leave," I croaked. "It's my father. Matthew's email. I need to catch a flight back to Miami."

His hands fell around my face. He tilted my face back. Met my gaze. "Breathe."

He was right, I needed to do that.

"That's it," he said, as I limited myself to inhaling and exhaling big pulls of air. "Good job, darling."

The noise in my head started to quiet down. The thumping in my chest gradually came down. But then, new emotions seeped in. Guilt. Sorrow. Shock. Cameron must have been so scared when found me like this. So concerned, so blindsided by . . . me. I shook my head.

"My father is selling the club." The words left me in a gurgle. The pressure in my chest rose. I focused on Cameron's face. On letting the green of his eyes ground me. "To David, according to what Matthew has been told by one of the journalists in his network. And it has to be because of me. It has to be because Dad has no other choice after I messed everything up. David's probably blackmailing him in some way, using me as collateral again. He must be exploiting the situation I put the Flames in with the video. Otherwise, Dad would never do that. He . . ." Something crossed Cameron's expression. "My father would never sell."

"None of this is your fault," he said with confidence. Determination. That urge to make it better, to take the concern away from me. "You hear me? Nothing. You're not responsible."

Those words brought relief, but he . . . Why wasn't he more shocked? What had that emotion flashing through his face been?

"Adalyn," he said. Slowly, carefully. "Yesterday—"

It hit me then. "You knew."

There was silence. A silence I didn't want to understand.

I leaned back. I looked at his face. At that handsome face I loved so much. Yes, I did love many things about Cameron. But I—I made myself speak through the thick lump lodged in my throat. Even if it was just to repeat the same two words. "You knew."

Cameron's expression wavered but I knew he wasn't going to

deny it. He wasn't going to try and play it down, either. Cameron wasn't that kind of man. "I didn't know for sure."

I felt like my legs might double under my weight.

My mouth opened and closed wordlessly, until I managed to summon my voice. "How long have you known?"

"A day," he said. "But I didn't really know. Not for sure." He retrieved his hands, reluctantly, as if he knew I needed the space but was unsure about letting go. "Liam, my former agent. He's the one who heard the rumors. He only mentioned it because the Flames asked about me."

The Flames. They'd asked about Cameron? What else had I missed? Clearly, too much. "I didn't know," I murmured. "But I should have known. All of this."

"I don't think your father wanted you to know," Cameron answered so simply, so easily, that a part of me wished to be mad. But I wasn't. I was confused. And hurt. His arm reached out, but he stopped himself. His hand made a fist by his side. "It wasn't really an offer, and had it come to that, you would have been the first person to hear before I considered it. But that's not what's upsetting you." He paused, and I— God, why was I feeling so . . . lost right now? Why did I feel like everyone was keeping me in the dark about my own life? "I was going to tell you about the rumors, love. But I'm not going to lie to you, I was going to wait until later today."

And that's what I couldn't understand.

I should be packing my bags right now. I should be on a flight, going back to Miami to fix this. To stop this. To tell my father not to let David manipulate him, that I knew about the bribing. That he shouldn't sell. But instead I was here, trying to figure out why I felt so . . . heartbroken. Betrayed.

Needing to think, to order my emotions and the whirling thoughts in my head, I pushed away. I put distance between us and stopped at the counter at the opposite side of the kitchen.

A strangled sound left Cameron.

I shoved away how horrible that made me feel, how much I

hated being the one responsible for such a loud sign of distress, but I couldn't articulate a thought when he touched me. All I felt was him.

"You knew what David was doing," I told him, trying to understand. "You know how I feel about the club, too." I shook my head. "And you were letting me stay here in this . . . fantasy world. Playing games." I ignored the hurt in my chest at hearing my own words. "God knows what David must have done to make my father consider a transfer. This is all my fault."

Cameron stepped in my direction. His mouth opened.

I held up a hand. "Don't make excuses for me or what I've done. Not now, please." I brought my hands to my temples. Closed my eyes for an instant. God. What was I doing? "I should be packing, not playing house with you."

His jaw clenched so tight, I could barely see his lips. "This was never a game." He took one step forward. And I moved back, the bottom of my spine hitting the counter behind. "I was not goddamn playing, Adalyn. And you told me yourself you understood that. Last night."

"But you kept me in the dark," I told him, in a low, quiet voice I didn't like. Cameron's mouth parted but no words came out. "Just like them. Even if it was only for a day." I shook my head. "You know? All I've ever wanted was to be . . . seen. To leave a mark. To earn his approval and prove to everyone that I could be just like my father." My own words echoed in my ears, as if I was hearing them out loud from my own mouth for the first time. "And now, it's possible that I'm too late and I can't do anything to fix any of this." My voice broke, and I had to clear my throat before continuing. "I really wish you were right. I really wish this whole thing wasn't a game, but life is one. And no matter how much I try, I seem to always, always lose." I closed my eyes, my head too fuzzy. My thoughts meshing and mixing about. "My being here was always meant to be temporary, anyway."

"Don't," Cameron said.

My throat felt tight, a spot between my chest and stomach turning too tender, too weak. "I need to go. I should have been on a flight by now. I need to fix this before it's too late."

Cameron stepped in my direction, so carefully, so slowly, that I wasn't even sure he'd moved. "Adalyn—"

"No." My head gave one brisk shake. I didn't want to hear him excusing me. Or taking my side. I didn't want to hear him saying that this wasn't a game again. "You should have told me the moment you heard. Even if it was just rumors."

"Maybe I should have." His whole face tightened up, as if he wanted to shut down but couldn't. Every emotion started bubbling up to the surface. His nostrils flared. "But that's not what I did, so no."

I blinked, taken aback by the blunt admission.

"*No*," he repeated, firmly. "I did what I did, and as much as I hate that you found out like this, I don't regret taking the decision not to tell you until I was sure of that really happening. You know why? Because I goddamn refuse to let them take something else away from you."

That tender spot in my chest spread, growing larger, making me so vulnerable I was now terrified of his next words.

His barely controlled demeanor broke. "I meant it when I said that I see you." He dropped his arm. "I fucking see you, and I see what your father has done to you. And what David has done, too." The green in his eyes swirled with frustration, his mouth pursed, so close to a snarl. "For all I know, this could be that fucking crook spreading word to purposely hurt you. I needed to be sure that wasn't the case."

My eyes widened at the possibility of David being behind this. Behind the information that had been in Matthew's email.

Cameron continued, voice softening, "I am a selfish man, Adalyn. And I wanted you to have this. I didn't want him—them—to ruin today for you. This one thing you worked so fucking hard for. I couldn't care less about the little league, but I was bloody winning this for you. I wanted you to go to the game and be fucking ecstatic. Not a worry in your mind. Smile and laugh the way you so rarely do. Have a good time with me and the girls and collect the joy you deserve. The goddamn love you don't need to earn. That's what my selfishness makes me do."

The tips of my fingers started to feel funny. Numb. And tingly. All at once. "Don't tell me to smile more. Or worry less." I clasped my hands together, scared they'd start shaking. And the odd sensation spread out and up my arms. "I am who I am."

"I know, love." His voice wavered. "I don't want to change you. I wouldn't change a single thing about you, as much as sometimes you drive me absolutely insane." He shook his head, as if lost for an instant. "You are who you are. And I love that. Let those goddamn smiles be rare as long as they're mine."

You are who you are.

And I love that.

Let those goddamn smiles be rare as long as they're mine.

Mine.

My heart dropped to my feet, and God, that stupid hole that had opened in the middle of me pulsed, pounded with need, demanding to be filled.

The words barely made it out of me when I spoke, "That's beside the point."

I regretted my words. Almost immediately. It wasn't beside the point. What he'd said . . . it had been everything. Every single thing.

Cameron's gaze didn't falter. "That's all right." He took a step forward. "I'll be your punching bag." Another step. "I'll be whatever you need me to be. I'll jump on a flight and hold your hand. I'll help you break something with your bare hands. Fuck, I'll just stand there and watch." He reached me, and my whole body reacted to him. To his closeness. To his words. "Anything you need. You want to go now. We'll go."

You are who you are.

And I love that.

"I don't need you to protect me," I told him, and I wished I believed my own words. I wished I wasn't feeling like all I wanted was to jump into his arms. But that only made me the same woman who'd lost control of her life that day. The same woman who couldn't keep a hold of her emotions. "This. This is why you didn't tell me. You don't trust that I can handle things. On my own. And I might deserve that after what happened with Sparkles and every time you've seen me lose control, but I've been handling things on my own my whole life, Cameron. And I've been fine."

"Don't you think I know?" He huffed, and that's when I knew he was breaking. Cameron was breaking down. "I know you don't need me, or anyone else. I know you're more than okay on your own. Jesus, Adalyn, that's what pushes me to want to guard you like a goddamn dog."

His hand cupped my face then, and God. It felt so right. His touch so comforting, so warm in that way that made me feel so alive. I closed my eyes.

His voice softened. "You're so strong, so fiercely independent, that I want to keep you happy and safe before you have to." He caressed my jaw. And only then I realized my teeth were clattering with restraint. "I trust you. Not even once have I doubted you're capable of withstanding a single thing that life throws at you. But that doesn't mean I don't want to stop anything from ever hurting you again."

My heart pounded recklessly in my chest, reverberating in my temples and head. I closed my eyes, making the effort to pull oxygen into my lungs. In through my mouth. Out through my nose.

That's what pushes me to want to guard you like a goddamn dog.

In through my mouth. Out through my nose.

I trust you.

But did I trust myself?

I opened my eyes. "You should take the job with the RBC. It's the opportunity of a lifetime."

Another of those strangled sounds left him. And my heart thrummed in my temples now. *Take back the words*, a voice in my head begged. *Take them back. Ask him to go to Miami with you today. Don't do this alone when you don't have to.*

"No," Cameron said. Stated. Firmly. Not even a trace of doubt in his voice. Stubborn, hardheaded man. His perseverance only made me want to scream. Cry. Be in his arms. "It was never up for consideration, but now it's not even an option that would ever cross my mind. I'm not leaving."

My heart pounded so hard, so loud, that when I said, "Why?" I didn't think I heard the word. "Why wouldn't you take it? England is your home."

Cameron's jaw tightened. His hand dropped. "Don't." He shook his head. "Don't make me say the words out loud. Not now. Not right before you try to push me away."

The words.

What words?

The ones that were trying to barge right out of me?

I guessed it didn't matter. It didn't matter whatever he thought was being left unsaid. Because as much as I understood why he'd kept this from me, we no longer belonged to the world where nine-year-olds played soccer, where we attended fall fests and shared a cabin.

It was time for me to go back to where I did belong.

At my silence, Cameron's eyes closed. He only stood there, like that, for an instant. Then, he walked away.

There was a long moment in which the only sound was my shallow breathing and his steps as he moved toward the door. And I kept thinking how much of a mess I'd made for someone who had kept it together for such a long time. For someone who'd been accused of not showing enough emotion so many times.

Let those goddamn smiles be rare as long as they're mine.

I brought my hand to my chest, failing to soothe the tightening vise squeezing my heart.

"Did you really mean it, love?" he asked, and only then, I realized he was looking at me from the door. He hadn't left. "When you told me you wouldn't mind if I was the one to slay your dragons." Something in me broke. "Did you mean that?"

I had meant it. With every ounce of who I was.

But everything had changed now. This wasn't about taking his guest room or working with him on the team. It wasn't about accepting needing his touch. The bubble had burst, the fairytale had torn, and I'd dropped to the floor with a thump. Just like my mother had predicted. This was real life. And my father was selling the club I'd considered home my whole life to the man who'd used me to manipulate him.

CHAPTER THIRTY-FIVE

Cameron

$\mathcal{I}$'d fucked up.

Royally.

I never acted without a reason, without a well thought out plan. But this time I'd made a mistake. Adalyn was right, I shouldn't have decided what was best for her without letting her have a say in it. Even though all I'd wanted was for her to have this one goddamn thing. Even though I knew her, and I knew she'd sacrifice her own happiness. Go to Miami and fix a situation she wasn't responsible for.

Those goddamn fuckers were using her like a chess piece in their sick power game. And it made my blood boil.

But as much as I wanted to protect her, I had miscalculated. I'd fucked up. And now, I also knew that I shouldn't have left the cabin. I shouldn't have convinced myself that Adalyn needed space. I shouldn't have left her and hoped for the best. I should have stayed.

Because now Adalyn wasn't here. She wasn't coming to the game, and I didn't know if she was ever coming back.

I looked at my feet, the sound of the gathering crowd and the girls nothing but a low buzz.

I don't need you to protect me . . . You don't trust that I can handle things on my own.

Christ. I'd been such a moron. She believed that now. I'd led her to believe that. Even when all I think is how strong and brave she is. And how I worry about how little she actually needs me.

And now she was on her way to the airport, and I was here, my hands tied behind my back by my own actions. My stomach twisted at the thought of her sitting alone on that plane. Not having anyone to squeeze her hand in case she needed reassurance. I whipped out my phone and opened the flights app, but the reminder of her words brought my fingers to a halt.

You don't trust that I can handle things.

I'd trust her with anything I had. But would she believe that if I planted myself in Miami? Would she think I was doing exactly what she'd accused me of? Would she tell me I was trying to fight her battles?

I expelled a forceful gulp of air. Shook my head. Locked my phone. I went to put it away but then pulled it back out and unlocked it. "Fuck," I muttered. "Bloody fucking hell," I continued, and her face popped behind my eyes. *Language, Coach*, she'd say with that tilt of her lips. It felt like a blow to my face. "You absolute toad." I closed my eyes. "How could you lie to her, you—"

"Coach Cam?"

"María," I said with a shake of my head, steeling myself before turning. "Hey, you called me Cam."

María shrugged a shoulder. "You're wearing your special shirt," she told me, as if that explained why. Fuck, now my chest hurt again. "That's good. But who is a toad? And who did he lie to?"

I sighed, incapable of mustering the strength to come up with an answer for her.

She narrowed her eyes, but rather than suspicion, she did it with understanding. "Is that why Miss Adalyn is running late? I thought she'd braid my hair again. Like last time." She pointed at the side of the field where the team was gathering up. "Chelsea brought face paint, so she doesn't need to use her fancy lipstick to draw lines on our cheeks again."

"I . . ." Fuck me. I couldn't do this. Air was getting stuck in my throat. "I don't think Miss Adalyn is coming to the game, María."

"Why?"

"There was an emergency back in Miami, and she had to go."

María tilted her head. "Why aren't you with her, then?" she asked. And God. It was such a simple question, formulated with such genuine shock, as if there was no other possibility than me being by her side, that it almost brought to my knees.

I . . . blurted out nothing but the truth. "I messed up. I made her believe I didn't trust her to handle things on her own. I . . ." Treated her like the one man I'd tried to protect her from had. "But she'll be back," I heard myself say. "She'll come back. You guys are still very important to her."

María stared back at me, while I braced myself. If there was a kid on the team who wouldn't hesitate to wipe this field with my ass, it was her. And I'd deserve it. I had already deserved every scowl and skeptical look she'd thrown my way for how I'd treated Adalyn at the beginning. And I'd take this, too.

She made a face. Then, tilted her head. "Would braiding my hair make you feel any better?"

I opened my mouth to decline but found myself giving her a nod instead.

"Okay," she said with a sigh before taking my hand and dragging me all the way to the bench. "Sit here," she ordered. And down I went. She stood in front of me. "I hope you're better at it than Tony. His braids really suck."

I looked at the back of her messy head of hair, welcoming the sense of purpose, even if for a few minutes, and got to work.

"Have you had many girlfriends, Coach Cam?"

I frowned, caught off guard by her question. "No. I haven't had a girlfriend for a while, no."

She sighed, and that sigh should have told me enough. "Do you love Miss Adalyn?"

My hands froze in the air, and I swore my heart came to a halt. "Yes," I rasped out, resuming the random twirling and weaving of hair.

"Have you told her?"

I cleared my throat to speak. "No."

María huffed. "Then, how is she supposed to come back?" Now my goddamn heart was breaking all over again. "How will she know where to follow her heart?"

My eyes closed. "That's part of the problem, I'm afraid."

"Love is never part of the problem," María answered. And Christ, why did words spoken by a nine-year-old hit me so hard?

"It's a little more complex than that, sweetheart."

"But I've seen the face she makes at you when you touch her."

My fingers faltered for an instant. "And what face is that?"

"The same face Brandy makes when she realizes I'm the one petting her," she said, and I bit back a chuckle. But then, the kid continued, "Like she can finally be at ease. Like she was scared but now she's okay. Because with me, she's always, always safe."

You make me feel like I've never felt with anyone before, Cameron. You make me want things I never wanted. Adalyn's voice seemed to take shape in my head, eclipsing the pounding in my chest.

Oblivious to how much of an effect her words were having on me, María continued, "You told us that life is hard. You said that a loss is only the end of one game. That we should stand up and chase the prize. Losing a game is just tripping, it makes you tough as long as you stand up."

"I . . . did." I had told the kids that. And I'd been sure my words had crushed them. And now they were being thrown back at my face, crushing me.

María handed me an elastic over her shoulder. "Is Miss Adalyn your prize?"

"No." My throat worked. "She's not a prize to be won." I took the elastic from her. "She's . . . not a game. She's more than something you win. She's more than a loss. She's everything that's worth playing for. She's everything in between."

"See?" she said with that nonchalance only kids had. "Love is never the problem. Love is easy, like in the movies. We're the ones who make it complicated. That's why I'll forgive her for missing the game." I finished tightening the elastic. "But if she really is your everything, and she's dealing with something important, then shouldn't you be with her? Even if you messed up. What if she needs a sub to play in her place? She might not like you right now, but that doesn't mean she doesn't want you there."

Before I could even utter a word, she turned around.

Her brown eyes inspected me, and I just blinked at her in disbelief. Thinking about what she'd said. Thinking how much sense she made. How easy it seemed when she put it like that.

"Can I have your phone?" María asked.

I handed it to her, my head still whirling.

María looked at herself in what I assumed was the camera of the device. She sighed.

"Coach Cam?" she called, and my gaze refocused on her. "Your braids suck." She handed back my phone and I blinked at the kid. "Will you ask her to teach you?"

Like the hopeless and foolish man I was, I whispered, "When?"

And María pursed her lips, as if the answer was the most obvious thing in the world. "When you get her back."

CHAPTER THIRTY-SIX

Adalyn

$\mathcal{I}$ hated myself for the words that were about to come out of my mouth, I really did.

"Do you want to keep your job?" I squeaked, feeling even worse than I thought. "Do you even know who I am?"

"Yes." The guy blinked. "And your access has been revoked, Miss Reyes. I can't let you through."

So he knew. This bastard.

This bastard. That was exactly what Cameron would have said. I'd even heard the words uttered by his voice in my head. If he was here he would—

No.

I let out a bitter laugh that soon morphed into something that sounded a lot like the start of a sob. I'd been doing that a lot today. Almost sobbing. Almost breaking. Almost calling Cameron. Almost texting Josie to beg her to apologize to the girls for me. Almost letting myself feel like I was making a mistake.

The stoic man in front of me frowned.

"Listen," I said slowly, squaring my shoulders, lifting my chin. "I know it's late, and it's clear you're just doing your job here. I applaud and thank you for that. But this is an emergency, and I know my father is here. He's always here and his driver is right outside." I looked at him, straight in the eye. Begging, pleading. "You need to let me through."

He hesitated. Looked around. But then he shook his head. "I'm not going to be able to do that, Miss Reyes."

I closed my eyes, refusing to break in front of this man.

I couldn't believe I wasn't being let into the place I'd worked my entire adult life. I couldn't believe I couldn't go into the place I had hoped for so long to own one day. I couldn't believe my father hadn't answered his phone any of the times I'd called. Not even once. I—

"Boss?"

My eyelids lifted, seeing a face I wasn't expecting to be here at this time.

"I can't believe it's you," Kelly continued, her heels clicking in my direction. "Whoa, what's with the glow-up? You're slaying the runway, boss. And the hair. Oh my God, your hair is all wild and . . . beautiful."

For an instant, I looked down, taking in my jeans, boots, and overall practical wear. Then I shook my head. "Kelly," I said, my eyes finding hers with enough gravity to make her blink. "Can you please let . . ."

"Billie," the man said when I looked at him. "Ellis."

Kelly looked over at him. "Really?"

Billie sighed. "I'm fifteen years her senior, ma'am. And the resemblance to her name is purely coincidental."

"That is hilarious," Kelly murmured, inspecting him and not even cracking a smile. "Are you new here?" Billie's mouth bobbed, clearly surprised. "You're cute. What's your handle, not-really-billie-ellis or something like that?" She whipped out her phone. "I would—"

"Kelly," I called, my voice desperate and tired and . . . hopeless, if I had to pick. "Can you explain to Mr. Ellis that I need to get through so I can deal with that emergency we talked about on the phone?" She blinked at me. "He seems to believe that my access has been revoked, but I very clearly remember being asked by my father to come here. Today." I made a face at her. "You remember, right?"

My former assistant started nodding slowly. "Ohhhhhhh. Right. Yes." Her head turned around, searching the empty hall, before returning her attention to us. "The emergency," she said more confidently. "Billie, do you want to be the guy who didn't let the big boss's daughter in during the"—she lifted her hands, slicing the air—"major-est crisis of the year?"

Billie frowned, but some pink spread across his cheeks.

"Exactly," Kelly agreed. "That's not a great look, is it?" Billie shook his head. "Great. Now, open the barrier so she can save the day." She placed a hand on her hip. "Unless you think a woman can't be the hero. Is that what we're dealing with here?"

"Wh—What?" His eyes widened. "No. I am a feminist."

She gave him a grin. "Barrier, please?"

It took him a few seconds and a curse but the glass gate that granted access to the office area opened up.

I sprinted through the hallway in the direction of my father's office, hearing Kelly's heels following behind.

"Boss?" She called, and when I didn't turn or stop, she sped up. "Whoa. You run fast in those things." I did. I might be starting to love my boots. "I'm so sorry I kinda cold-shouldered you, but I really had no choice—"

"That's okay, Kelly," I assured her, turning a corner.

"Okay, phew," she answered, now a little breathlessly. "Now that that's out of the way, there's something you should know before—"

"I know," I interjected, speeding up. "And I'm going to stop this some way or another."

"But, Boss, they're . . ."

I reached the door, vaguely aware of Kelly setting a hand on my shoulder and saying something, but I was not wasting a second more. I'd let this go on long enough. I was taking back control and putting a stop to David's manipulation. I was telling my father I knew everything and stopping the transaction. I threw open the door.

Two heads turned in my direction.

"Adalyn," my father said in a shockingly calm and cold voice that made me pause.

I opened my mouth to say something, any of the things that I'd rehearsed in my head, but all I could think of was *What's David holding in his hands?* Because that couldn't be—

"Hey, sweet-tea," David said with a smile I couldn't believe I'd ever found anything but a sneer. "Oh wait, do they drink sweet tea over there?" His eyes trailed up and down my body, a shiver crawling down my arms. "Well, that's definitely a surprise. Why are you dressed like some . . . lumberjack bimbo?"

I heard Kelly scoff behind me.

My father rolled his eyes and said, "David." As if this man hadn't just disrespected me and that single warning was enough.

Why did that suddenly irk me so much? That disregard for what was said to me in front of him. That lazy way in which he trusted that I could handle myself. I could, but shouldn't he be doing more than that?

David shrugged. "My apologies. Hey, I have a surprise for you." He lifted what he'd been holding. "Cool, huh?"

My throat dried. It was one of the Miami Flames jerseys. I recognized it. Except for the sponsor printed at the front it. That was new. It was the logo of the energy drink. The one with my face.

My jaw fell to the floor. I— Focus, Adalyn. I turned my attention to my father. "I know." Something faltered in his expression. My heart thrummed in my ears. "I know everything, Dad. So you can stop this."

"David," he immediately said. "Give us a minute." He started to complain but my father held up a hand. "Alone. This is not your office yet."

Yet.

David's eyes found mine as he walked toward me, and when he passed me, he winked. It made my skin crawl.

The door closed behind me, and only then did I allow myself to move forward, closing the distance to the now vacant chair across from my father's desk. I'd sat there not that long ago. Only now it seemed like it had been a lifetime ago.

Cameron's green eyes popped in my head, and I felt my knees falter, an overwhelming sensation filling up my chest. *I wish he was here*, my head seemed to chant. Not holding my hand, but ready, close enough to hold it if I needed it to be held. As if trying to appease the hollowness, I patted my chest, finding something under my shirt.

Cameron's ring. It was still there, hanging from the chain he'd fastened around my neck this morning.

"I hid all of this to protect you," my father said, bringing me back.

I swallowed hard. Thinking of the last man who'd told me something similar. But it . . . It somehow felt different. It had a different effect. A part of me seemed hesitant to believe Dad. "I don't need you to protect me. I'm not a child. I could have taken the truth."

My father sighed, and it was a curt, quick sound that managed to carry so much. "That's exactly what your mother told me." He shook his head. "You look a lot like her today."

"I do?"

He gave me a nod. "I never wanted it to happen this way," my father continued, looking down at the desk. "All this time, it's always been my one regret. What kept me from your mother and you." He shook his head. "Looks like I seem to repeat my mistakes. Do you resent me, Adalyn? Does she resent me as well?"

I opened my mouth, but something stopped me from speaking. She? "Mom? Why would she resent you for this?"

My father's brows met in question. He wasn't talking about Mom.

"Who are you referring to?" I asked. And because there was something at the back of my head, something that started to buzz, I added, "Who should resent you, Dad?"

Andrew Underwood seemed so openly confused for a second that when he answered, it was nothing but a rasp. "Josephine."

My heart stopped for an instant. Josephine? But it couldn't—

"What has Josie to do with selling the club?"

He paled.

My knees faltered then. I leaned my hand on the chair, gaping at him. Taking in his expression. He looked like a ghost. And that reminded me of what my mother had said. The letters.

Your father has secrets.

Then more started toppling in, flooding me with memories. Facts that hadn't been pieced together.

You'll leave tomorrow. On an assignment . . . It's something I've actually been thinking about for a while.

There's some kind of a guardian looking over Green Oak.

Robbie doesn't like to talk about it, but he was—and maybe still is—in a lot of debt.

"You're Green Oak's angel investor." My throat worked but the lump remained lodged there, making it hard for me to speak. I clutched Cameron's ring. Then, something else Josie had said that day barreled right into me. Something that couldn't mean what I thought it did. But it had to. "What are you trying to tell me? Why did you bring up Josie? I need to hear it. Out loud."

He stared at me, and then he said, "Josephine is your half sister." And the confirmation felt like a bucket of water had been thrown in my face. "She's my daughter," he added, and there wasn't a trace of guilt in his voice or his face. There wasn't shame. Or remorse. Longing. There was nothing.

Nothing at all.

"I thought you'd realized," he said. "I thought that was why you were here and what had prompted that dramatic entrance. You said you knew everything."

I . . . didn't think I could breathe. I had a sister. A half sister. Dad had another daughter. "You thought I knew about Josie? But— You . . ." My gaze roamed around his face. It was impassive. "You're not surprised or angry. You're fine. I . . ." My head was whirling, shooting thoughts left and right. Piecing things together and tearing others apart. I gasped for air. "Were you hoping I'd find out about

Josie?" But it couldn't be, could it? "Was that why you shipped me off there?"

"Yes and no," he admitted quickly. Far too quick for me to process. "I sent you there because Green Oak seemed like an experience you could benefit from. But I'd be lying if I said I didn't assume you'd put it together." He shrugged. "I guess I was wrong."

His words reverberated in my head as I stared into my father's eyes. They were Josie's light blue eyes. Only they lacked everything hers had. A powerful emotion rippled through me at the realization, at how obvious it had been, at how he'd just put me down for not piecing it together.

He always did that. Put me down. Hid things.

"You guess you were wrong?" I repeated, something rioting in my chest. Something that had nothing to do with how I'd just been heaving for a breath. "You sent me out there knowing I might find out about a half sister you've been hiding from me, knowing I'd interact with her, possibly befriend her, and you shrug it off like that?"

"Once more, I thought that was why you were here," he said. And God, there was so much noise in my ears. My head. I couldn't think. I missed Cameron's hands, anchoring me to the world. "I've been expecting this for a while now."

I briefly closed my eyes, gave myself a few seconds to sieve through the surge of ugly and overpowering emotions climbing up and down. "I was here because I heard rumors of you selling the Flames. To David. Because I know about him using you. Using me. Because I thought I was somehow responsible for him forcing your hand."

He sighed. "It's late. Let's go home and continue this some other time. There's no stopping the sale of the club anyway, but I'm sure you'll have questions about that. I'll ask my driver to drop you off at your apartment."

The rush of blood in my rib cage, my head, at his words had been so loud that for a second I'd thought I hadn't heard him right. It was impossible, after all, that someone broke this kind of life-changing news to his own daughter and then followed it up with that. My head lifted, and what had been a scattered mind focused.

"No," I all but spat, taking in the blank expression on his face. "You're not dismissing me like this. I've given up a lot to be here right now." I'd let the girls down. Left a heartbroken Cameron behind.

He checked his watch again. "It's late, Adalyn," he said slowly. "And you're clearly rattled and in no shape to have a discussion. I'm doing this for your own good. Just like everything else."

"You mean hiding I have a sibling or asking David to marry me in exchange for a job, as if I was nothing but cattle being traded?"

His jaw clenched. "That's an exaggeration."

A clarity that hadn't been there all these years crystallized. "What else then? Maybe it was the way you overlooked my efforts to impress you. To earn your approval and respect. Was that for my own good?"

"I never overlooked you, Adalyn."

"Then why?" I asked him, my voice terrifyingly calm. "Why would you offer your daughter to a horrible man? Why would you let him play us both by not telling me when you should have? I had to find out from his own lips during the anniversary of the club. How is any of that protecting me? How is sending me off, banishing me, doing that? You never checked on me, not once." I brought my hand to the middle of my chest. "You're my father."

My father nodded his head slowly, then let out a chuckle I didn't understand. "So that's what made you get like that and attack Sparkles? Good God, Adalyn. It almost cost me the club."

All semblance of hope still in me vanished.

"That's all you have to say," I said, not asked. Because I didn't need an answer. He'd given me one. I shook my head. "It wasn't about me, was it? Nothing was."

"Everything I do is for us," he said, something getting through to him. "David threatened going to some gossip site with the story of our arrangement if I took the VP position from him. The sponsors too. But that's water under the bridge. Honestly, I thought you had a little more self-respect than letting this bother you."

So Dad had never been protecting our relationship. Or me. He'd only protected himself. His name. And that broke my heart. It had been tearing all throughout this conversation, I realized. But it completely shattered now.

Silence fell in the office for a long moment. I couldn't believe I'd come here, broken the girls' trust. Missed out on today. I'd taken a hundred steps back, and it made my chest hurt like it never had. I clutched Cameron's ring in my fist.

"How much in debt is the Vasquez farm in?" I didn't need to say more. I knew my father understood.

"Big debt."

I nodded my head. "Josie. How did it even happen?"

My father's eyes narrowed, and any other time, that look would have been enough to silence me. But I suddenly didn't care. I didn't want his respect. I only wanted answers. "I always made sure Josephine was taken care of growing up. I provided for her. I invested in the town so she didn't have to grow up in the same sad place where I was born."

He lets people believe he's from Miami, but he's not. Those had been Mom's words.

And that's how the next and last piece of the puzzle fell into place. Dad was from Green Oak.

"That was never my place," he stated, as if it was some card he could play. As if that was meant to justify everything he'd said or done. "I was always meant for greater things. That's why I packed my bags the moment I could, leaving nothing and no one behind. I only returned once. Shortly before meeting your mother." He sighed. "But it never meant anything, it was just a careless night that I've been paying for all my life." Eyes that were nothing like Josie's looked at me. "I'm not proud of it, but I don't regret my decisions."

"You're not proud of it," I repeated his words. A sad, hopeless huff left me. "You talk about a smart, beautiful, hardworking woman like she's some bad investment you don't want to think about." I shook my head. Suddenly needing to move. I braced both hands on the back of the chair in front of me. Looked down before meeting his gaze. "Did you ever intend for me to take over?"

His shoulders sunk with what I knew was rebuff. "You could have any role within our portfolio. Real estate, infrastructure companies, even one of the resorts we own. Have your pick. But not the club. I'm selling the Miami Flames to David and his father." He walked around his desk. "It's decided."

I remained quiet. He was not getting it. Dad wasn't getting any of this.

"You'll move past your infatuation with the club." His hands smoothed out the lapels of his jacket. "It was dying a slow death anyway, it has been for a decade now, so be happy we'll make a profit thanks to your little impromptu breakdown and that sponsor deal David has in line."

Thanks to me, or at my expense? I wanted to ask.

But it didn't matter. It didn't matter that my father was allowing that energy drink to sponsor the team or taking their money. Nothing really mattered.

This had never been about legacy or infatuation, not even money.

"Sell the goddamn club," I heard myself say. My father winced back. "This was never about me. Or the Flames. It was about you." My hand flew to my chest again, clutching Cameron's ring. I knew what being shielded, cared for, protected was. Cameron had claimed to be selfish, but I saw now how wrong he'd been. He'd done all of that selflessly. For me. With my best interest at heart. Even if he'd made a mistake. "It's on you if you don't want to understand."

I turned around, making my way to the exit.

"Adalyn," my father warned.

I didn't stop. "You have twenty-four hours to tell Mom and Josie," I said, not looking back. "I'm giving you the chance not to make the same mistake you did with me. But if you don't tell them, I will." I came to a stop in front of the door. "You're also relieving all of the current Vasquez debt. I guess it won't hurt with all that profit my breakdown made you."

I opened the door, no hesitation, only one goal in mind.

And when I spoke next, it was with one thought, one man, one plan in mind, and one foot on the other side. At the beginning of the rest of my life. "Oh, and in case it wasn't clear? I resign."

CHAPTER THIRTY-SEVEN

Cameron

$\mathcal{I}$ pressed the phone to my ear, feeling my knuckles crack.

"Pick up, pick up," I begged. Prayed. "Come on, love. Pick up the phone."

When the voice I was dying to hear never came, I cursed under my breath. I hung up, stopping myself from throwing the damn thing out of the cab window.

Christ, where was she? Had something happened? Why wasn't she picking up her phone? It was so goddamn late and I—

My phone rang.

I picked up immediately.

"Cameron," Adalyn said. My name off her lips flew straight to my gut. Chest. Heart. "Cam?"

"Where are you." I heard myself bark. I closed my eyes. This wasn't the way to win her back. To grovel like I was determined to. To show her I trusted her. "I— Where are you, love? I need an address."

Voices in the background got through. A female one and a male one. Was she listening to me?

"Adalyn?"

"Oh God, you're not going to believe this," she said. And why was her voice breaking? "My father—I— Oh God. I've been so stupid. I wish you were here. I—"

"I'm in Miami, I'm coming to you right now, but I need you to tell me where you are."

Something that sounded a lot like a sob left her, and Christ, my fingers tightened around the phone in my hand. Adalyn spoke. "I'm on my way out of the Miami Flames grounds. I was going home when I saw all your missed calls."

"Can you wait there for me?" For the first time in hours, I breathed a little easier. "Don't go home yet. I'm coming to you. Just . . . wait for me. Please."

"But—" she started.

But I was already barking at the driver, "Can you drive faster?" The guy shot me a glance. "I'll pay you double." He throttled the engine. "I'm almost there, love." My hand tightened around the phone. "I know you didn't need me today, but fuck, Adalyn. I hated how you left, I hated not knowing if you'd come back. I think I need to hold your hand. Make sure you're okay. Just— Do this for me? Please? Don't go to your apartment yet. I have a hundred apologies I need to say."

"Cameron," she said again, and my heart seemed to skip one, two, five beats. "I didn't mean my apartment. I meant Green Oak." A strangled sound came from the beautiful and smart woman on the other side. And I thought I stopped breathing. "I meant you."

I spotted what without a doubt were the facilities. And when we entered the parking lot I told him, "Stop the car." I pulled more money than I'd promised him out of my wallet and clasped it to his shoulder.

"Sir, you can't—"

Oh, but I could. I flung open the car door and ran the few yards to the entrance of what had to be the offices. I dashed through the glass doors, and there she was. Adalyn, my Adalyn. She was right there, like I'd asked, with her phone at her ear and an expression of concern. I realized I hadn't hung up.

Our eyes met across the big hall.

Her lips wobbled for an instant. And then, she was on the move.

Fuck. Not once in my life had I felt an urgency this powerful, this strong, to wrap my arms around someone gunning in my direction at that speed.

Adalyn landed against my chest, and I brought her to me, into me, everything finally quieting down. The riot clattering in my head, the storm of emotion that had been gathering in my chest. The world. Nothing around me mattered except her.

"This is where I meant," she said against my neck. "It's you, Cameron. I was coming back to you."

My hand closed around the back of her head, my fingers slipping into her hair. I tugged so she would look at me. "I'm so goddamn sorry. Tell me you forgive me, please." I needed to hear it. I needed to make sure. "Tell me you'll give me the chance to show you that I trust you and only want what's best for you. Don't let this go before I've gotten the chance to show you how good we can be together."

She smiled, and it was the most beautiful thing I'd ever seen. "Only if you tell me the words. The ones you didn't want to say."

I swallowed. Then, slowly, almost as if I was scared she would disappear, I closed the distance between our mouths, taking her lips with every single ounce of who I was. I told her with everything I had.

And only when I knew she'd felt them, I said, "Because I fucking love you." I pressed my forehead to hers. "Because I'm crazy about you and I—fuck, Adalyn. I'll buy the Flames for you if that's what you want. I'll sit back and watch you conquer the world. I don't know how to express how much I care and want you. I've given myself to you, but if that's not enough then I'll do anything—"

"I fucking love you, too, Cameron Caldani," she whispered against my lips. "And I only need you."

Before I was ready, she pulled away, taking something out of her shirt. My ring dangled off the chain around her neck, and I knew then that I'd marry this woman one day. I'd give her the cats, the babies, a farm of terrifying baby goats if she wanted one. I'd do anything in my power to get that chance. I knew with every ounce of who I was.

"There's so much I need to tell you," she said, a shadow crossing her expression. "Starting with how wrong I was about pushing you away and thinking you didn't have my best interest at heart but—" She swallowed. "Wait. Oh my God. Did we win? Will the girls forgive me?"

We. That *we* did me in.

I took her mouth again, tasted her on my tongue. I knew she wanted the answer, but I wanted her. And I was selfish enough to take it when I could. We came up for air, her lips swollen, and her eyes glazed. "The girls will come around, and the Green Warriors are the winners of the Six Hills Little League. The story will be all over the local press tomorrow. County and state." Her eyes widened. "I called them myself. When they heard who I was—"

Adalyn mouth parted. "You did what?"

A throat was cleared, making us turn.

A woman was looking at us with a huge smile. Fuck. How long had she been there? "Sorry to interrupt, that was fire and I will surely be fantasizing about it more than I should probably admit, but . . ." Her eyes pointed to her right.

A blond man was walking—sauntering, really—through a barrier, smirking at a wide-eyed security guy who was avoiding my gaze. Fuck, how many people had just watched me eat my woman's face? I guessed I didn't care.

The man spotted us, and I felt Adalyn tense.

That was the only indication I needed to know who that was.

I released the woman tucked into my chest and strode in his direction, ignoring the twin gasps of surprise behind me. "David?" I asked when I reached him.

The wanker smiled. He smiled. "Hi—"

I grabbed him by the collar. Gave him a little tug. The guy went white as a sheet. I was being a Neanderthal. I knew that. This wasn't right. But I couldn't help myself. "Thank you," I told him. Or gritted between my lips. "Somehow, I have your stupidity to thank for changing my life."

The man frowned, his lips bopping like some fish I suddenly wanted to throw around. I felt a hand on my shoulder. The simple touch immediately settling me down. "I'm sorry, love," I told Adalyn, who was now by my side. I turned my gaze on David and added, "You know how I have a mean streak."

David blinked. "You're . . . You're Cameron Caldani." He seemed to think about something, then his eyes darted to one side. "Kelly? If you don't put that phone down, you're losing your job."

"Oh," Kelly, as I'd just learned, answered. "I quit. I overheard everything that went on in that office tonight and you're a piece of shit."

"What the fuck—" David started.

I tightened my grip. "Language." David's lips thinned, and I smiled. I wasn't going to hit him. I wanted to, but I didn't think Adalyn would see that as a gesture. Plus, I—

The fingers on my shoulder squeezed. "Hey, love?" Adalyn said.

My eyes were on her in a heartbeat. "You calling me love?" I whispered. "Now, that's playing dirty." Almost as dirty as the things I was visualizing doing to her while she repeated that word over and over.

"Oh, I know," she admitted with a flush. "But I don't want you getting into trouble for me." I hesitated and her fingers trailed up, all the way to my neck. She flicked her fingers along my skin there, and fuck, this woman had me eating out of her palm. "Please?"

I released David with a jerk of my arms.

He stumbled backward, sputtering, "What is wrong with you?" He fumbled with his shirt, sending us a glance. "And since when are you two a thing?"

"That's none of your business," Adalyn told him. "And also? You're a dragon I can slay myself."

Before I could even blink, Adalyn threw her free arm out and landed a punch on David's jaw.

He doubled over with a groan.

"Okay." I grabbed Adalyn by the waist, pulling her back just in case there was any more slaying planned. "Unexpected but deserved."

David recovered, glancing back at us. "You're not getting away with this. You—"

"She is," Kelly said from her spot. "You think this is the only thing I have on video? Bitch, please. I recorded Adalyn's conversation with her father, among many other things." She turned toward us. "Shall we go now?"

Adalyn nodded and turned around. I brought her to my side and walked off with her. "My fucking warrior." I pressed a kiss to the top of her head. "That was extremely arousing, but it's going to hurt tomorrow."

Her lips pinched in pain. "It already does," she murmured. I grabbed her hands in mine and inspected the one she'd thrown the hook with. "Next time I'll let you do the punching."

I was pretty sure my whole body smiled. "Next time?"

She shrugged. "You know, if my experience with the Green Warriors is anything to go by . . . the youth club I'm starting could get me into some trouble I might need assistance getting out of." I came to a momentary halt. "I was thinking rural North Carolina. Coaching director position is open if you're interested. I think the manager will try her best to make it worth your time." She let out a puff of air through her nose. "What do you think? Interested?"

Before I knew what I was doing, her hand was to my mouth. "Interested?" I pressed my lips to the back of her fingers. "I'm ravenous, love."

Those beautiful brown eyes sparked with happiness and a world of possibility, making my heart want to pound out of my chest and into her hands. In that moment, I was hopelessly, thoroughly hers.

"Tell me the words," I pleaded, needing to hear them again. Every day that was to come. Every night I wanted her tucked against me.

"I fucking love you, Cameron Caldani," Adalyn said.

I fucking loved her, too.

With everything I had.

And when she gave me the most breathtaking smile, I knew, with a conviction I'd never felt before, that with this woman by my side I'd be in for the fiercest, most beautiful game of my life. One where losing wasn't in the odds, and one that kicked off today. With this woman's smile and her in my arms.

EPILOGUE

A little over a year later . . .

Adalyn

*G*o on, love.

He didn't need to say the words. I could see them written in his face. It was one of the things I loved about him, about us, the way we didn't need to utter a word to know what the other one was thinking. A touch was enough. A brush of hands. A glance. A tilt of the head. A twitch at the corner of his lips. A subtle change to the green of his eyes.

Or in this case, as Cameron stood in front of the goal during the one-year anniversary of the Warriors Soccer Youth Club, the start of a lopsided smile.

We were on the grass, kicking off the celebration with a one-on-one, as per popular demand. Cameron's gloves were still very much hung up—literally, as we had them on the wall in our office—but in the last year, he had found his place on the sidelines, coaching our youngest female division and directing the coaches we'd recruited for the older ones. He was still attending therapy sessions on the regular to help him deal with the repercussions of the break-in, but Cameron was no longer so reticent about standing tall in the middle of crowds or attracting attention. I'd also done my fair share of therapy, and I'd quickly realized that it was something I should have done much, much earlier. Not just to have someone showing me how I'd been bottling up every worry in my head in an attempt at controlling my life, or that the relationship with my father had been an unhealthy one, but to learn the tools to process the chaos in my head and not let it turn into panic.

Either way, I was happy. We were happy. I didn't regret cutting ties with the Miami Flames—not even when David seemed to be earning a reputation for making bad choices and the club might be paying the consequences. There was a piece of my heart that would always belong to the Flames but I wasn't looking back. The MLS was behind me, and Cameron and I were developing talent. It was the most gratifying thing either of us had ever done. We were based somewhere between Green Oak and Charlotte, and we had kids coming from all over the area, rural and urban. It hadn't been easy to build something from scratch, but we were both as hardheaded as we were driven. With that and the contacts Cameron and I had in the industry, the club had taken off relatively quickly. Now the goal was growing enough to cater to professional leagues.

There was a long road ahead, and starting over was terrifying, but my life had never been fuller, richer, or simply better, than right now. It was because of this venture and the community that claimed me as theirs, but it was also because of the man I had by my side. Providing a kind of safety I hadn't known before him, and making every step of the way a little less scary and a lot less lonely.

Because with Cameron, I didn't know loneliness. With him, my sharp edges didn't matter, I was loved and appreciated and cherished not in spite of them but because of them. And I couldn't have been happier. Luckier. Loved him any more. I reminded him every day. Every night. Every chance I got.

Cameron lifted his hands in front of him, pinned me a challenging look, and made a come-at-me gesture.

Cocky, competitive man. I loved that he was mine.

I smiled my biggest smile, my Cameron smile, and continued my trajectory, juggling the ball in my feet as I ran. In sneakers, by the way. Cameron widened his stance, his eyes zeroing in on me as I entered the penalty area.

Someone from the stands screamed, "GO, LITTLE SIS! KICK HIS ASS!"

Josie. My chest warmed. She'd become such an important part of my life. My confidant. The person I didn't know I needed until she all but appeared out of thin air. Dad had tried to make amends with both of us throughout the last few months. And while we were still reluctantly processing everything, especially Josie, we'd found some peace in the knowledge that he was at least trying.

Cameron stepped forward, his body locking into a position I knew was all technique and prowess. It said, showtime. I narrowed my eyes at him, focusing on my aim as I whirled for the left—his weakest angle. He smirked at that. So I threw my leg back, my own smirk shaping up. And kicked, shooting for the top corner of the net.

He jumped, lunging his body into the air with his arms up, just like I'd seen him instruct the kids so many times in the last months. The display was unnecessary, considering the speed the ball carried, but it was beautiful. Powerful. Hot. Extremely so. Because it was him, sure. But because he was not letting me win. Cameron never let me win. And I loved that about him.

His palms blocked the ball. And when he landed on the ground with the sphere clutched against his chest, he did so smiling. Grinning. He looked up, sending me an impressed glance from the grass and winked.

Oh boy.

The crowd, which consisted of the club's kids and their families, cheered from the stands.

Tony, who juggled college and a job as assistant coach with us, clapped from the sidelines before jogging in our direction to retrieve the ball and get it signed by everyone on the staff.

"Good save, Coach Chamomile!" María, who had come down from Green Oak with Robbie, hooted. I turned, immediately spotting her. She'd grown since last month, when she'd come over for a girls-only sleepover with me, Josie, Willow, and Pierogi. She waved at me. "I was just being nice!" she shouted before turning around and pointing at the back of her shirt. It read TEAM ADA and it had a selfie of me and Brandy stamped on it. "I'll always root for the girls' team."

Laughter rolled off me, remembering the day of the picture. We'd been saddled with babysitting Brandy for a weekend. If there was one goat Cameron was reluctantly tolerating, it was Brandy.

As if summoned by my mind, Cameron's arms snaked around my waist. I immediately relaxed against him, and he nudged the side of my neck with his nose.

"That was an excellent shot, love," he said against my skin.

"Oh, I know," I admitted. "I've been practicing with Tony. Watching tape of some of your old games to learn how you react. Just for this."

Cameron's head snapped up. He met my gaze, the green in his eyes darkening. "That's incredibly arousing."

My stomach fluttered. But I shook my head. "How's that even possible?"

"Anything that involves you turns me on," he countered. It wasn't a lie. I knew that. And he wasn't the only one feeling that way. Him touching me right now, with his arms around me, his scent deliciously floating into my lungs, the feel of his body standing so close, it was all making my blood swirl. His tongue peeked out, and he wetted his lips. "Do you think we could sneak out without being noticed? Let's say . . . right now?"

I'd love nothing more. "We're in the middle of a party," I said, a little too breathlessly. "We literally kicked it off just now, and we're supposed to make speeches."

Cameron hummed deep in his throat. "How about in ten minutes?"

I let out a laugh.

"Fifteen? Your office or mine?"

"You're impossible."

The corners of his lips kicked up. "Impossibly in love with you."

Dammit. I kissed him. I couldn't not kiss him when he said those things. Cameron immediately rearranged me in his arms and took over with a throaty groan. He parted my mouth with his, making my back arch and me climb on my tiptoes. God, I loved when he did that. It quieted everything, made the world around us disappear.

"So?" he whispered against my lips when we came up for air. "Five minutes? One? Right now? It'll be fast." His mouth came to my ear. "Fast and hard."

My eyes fluttered closed, but I shook my head. I cupped his face with both hands and made him look straight at me just so he'd stop whispering dirty words in my ear with a crowd swirling around. "I fucking love you, Cameron Caldani," I told him, and his face immediately softened. "And I'd love nothing more than office sex right now." He perked up. "But we're not going anywhere until I either see or hear that speech you've written. Before everybody else does. I don't want figures of speech or sports metaphors that make children cry. It has happened one too many times."

A small frown shaped his brow. "Last time it wasn't my fault. Tony encouraged me to phrase it like that."

"Well, Coach. Maybe you shouldn't rely on a nineteen-year-old, then. Rely on your boss instead. I'll never steer you wrong and always tell you when your wording sucks."

His jaw clenched. "That's not helping with the hard-on, love."

That brought heat to my cheeks, but I rolled my eyes. "We're surrounded by people, stop talking about your hard—"

A throat was cleared behind me.

Josie was there, a cringey expression on her face. "Why do I always walk in on you while you're either about to have sex or talking about having sex?"

Cameron laughed. Openly and freely, like he couldn't care less about scandalizing Josie. Truth was, I knew he didn't.

I opened my mouth, but a groan came from the phone I hadn't seen Josie holding up. My phone. I'd given her my things before jumping on the grass for the kickoff. A voice spoke, "Not exactly excited to hear how one of my idols riles my best friend."

"Matthew?" I asked.

Josie made a face and turned over the phone. Matthew's face filled the screen. "He kept calling you, so I picked up," she explained. "Does he always talk this much? No wonder you've never invited him for a visit."

A huff came from the phone. "I talk too much? You just gave me a ten-point list of reasons why you're Adalyn's new best friend."

"Because I am," Josie pointed out with a smile. "I'm also more than just that. I'm her sister, so game over for you, I guess." She glanced up at me and mouthed, *He's cute. But annoying.*

Matthew exhaled loudly. "I can read lips and I just saw you doing that. The back camera was on since you switched it around to show me the facilities I hadn't seen in person."

Josie shrugged. "I thought you wanted to be shown around. Considering you were never invited and all."

"Sure thing, sweetheart," Matthew drawled. "You think I'm cute."

"And annoying."

Matthew grinned. "Sticking with cute. I have excellent selective hearing."

Josie snorted and launched herself into a speech that included a list of celebrities she thought were cuter than him. Matthew listened carefully, as if taking mental notes to refute her.

Cameron's hand shifted to my waist. "That's . . . a shocking turn of events. I think we should intervene." A pause. "Should I do it or will you?"

"I'll take this one for the team," I said, reaching out and grabbing the phone from a surprisingly reluctant Josie. She flushed, whirled around, and ran away with a quick "See ya!" Literally. I filed that for later and refocused on Matthew. "Okay, what's up? Why were you calling? Something happened?"

"I . . ." Matthew trailed off. His expression fell. "Is the lodge you own in Green Oak free?"

I frowned.

"Yeah," Cameron said, and I could hear the same hint of concern I was feeling in his voice. "We're living closer to the club now."

Matthew nodded. "Then, I have a favor to ask."

ACKNOWLEDGMENTS

Hi, you. I can't believe you're still sticking with me. And for that, not only do you deserve all the cake (served by a grumpy but secretly soft man—shirtless, too, because why not?), but you've also earned being at the top of my acknowledgments. Always. Because without you, the reader, the blogger, the romance lover, I wouldn't be here. So thank you for showing up, putting up with my endless shenanigans, and making this dream still possible. It makes me so incredibly happy and honored that I get to make you smile and fall in love with love a little bit more with my words. I owe you everything.

Jess, Andrea, Jenn, and everyone at Sandra Dijkstra, thank you for being the best dream team an author could ever ask for. And Jess? Thank you for (still) keeping me together when I want to burst at the seams with all kinds of fears that are very reasonable sounding in my head. You're my superstar agent slash therapist slash godmother. Never leave me, pls.

Kaitlin, Megan, Morgan, and the beautiful team at Atria: Thank you for all the incredible work you do to put my books out there in the world. I cannot wait to see you again, hug you, fangirl over Cameron, *and* go to goat yoga. Yes. Sorry, but you promised. I don't care if it's New York. Make it happen. Do it for us.

Molly, Sarah, Harriett and the rest of my fantastic UK team: By the time this book comes out, I'll be just about to finally meet you. I hope you're prepared to be squeezed, because you'll soon learn that I *am* a hugger. Thank you so much for your continual efforts and for always being the kindest to me. I appreciate you more than I can say.

Hannah, hi :) You've been a very important part of these past few months, and I'm so happy I get to call you a friend. I'm also happy I get to text-scream at you and be that annoying girlie who insists on seeing the glass half-full. Can't wait for those pictures of husbandbyhan posing with *The Long Game*.

Mr. B., where are my flowers? I love you, but jeez, man.

Mamá y Papá, gracias por ser mis mayores cheerleaders—and Mamá? Stop taking selfies with my readers at events, you're stealing my thunder.

María, gracias por estar ahí (y sobre todo por aguantarme). I promise you, I'll introduce you to one of the firefighters that work next door. I just need to figure out a creative way to get stuck somewhere.

Erin, thank you for being the best beta reader one could ask for. I can't believe it's been almost three years since I asked you to read *TSLD*. I'm so very grateful for you (and your knowledge of poultry).

And before I go, I want to squeeze a few words in to say that I hope you love Cameron and Adalyn's journey as much as I do. This wasn't an easy book to write for a long (and frankly boring) list of reasons. We all struggle in one way or another. That's why both Adalyn and Cameron (but especially Adalyn) were handed more than a few messy pieces of myself. I can only hope you see the magic in their imperfections and vulnerabilities and are able to relate to them. Hopefully, you get to find some happiness in them, too—and come scream at me in my DMs. Because writing slow-burn romance about imperfect, stubborn idiots and not being yelled at is, as Joey would say, "like Friday with no two pizzas."

ABOUT THE AUTHOR

ELENA ARMAS is a Spanish writer, self-confessed hopeless romantic, and proud book hoarder. Now, she's also the author of international and New York Times bestsellers *The Spanish Love Deception* and *The American Roommate Experiment*. Her books are being translated into more than thirty languages—which is bananas, if you ask her.